IT'S A
PICTURE OF
DEATH.

STILL LIFE WITH CROWS

READERS RAVE ABOUT
STILL LIFE WITH CROWS

"A dazzlingly frightening read!"
—Rick Dempster Sr. (Queensbury, NY)

"Best thing since *Relic*. Absolutely wonderful—kept me up at night and I loved every minute of it."
—Sandie Morris (St. Joseph, MO)

"It hooks you from the opening. I will never look at cornfields and caves the same way ever again. Absolutely a wonderful read, and another notch in your list of winners."
—Doug Arbuckle (Lewisburg, WV)

"This book had all of your usual Preston-Child trademarks, plus much more. The story dripped with suspense and the plot caught you with hooks, reeling you in fast. Special Agent Pendergast was in top form, as always."
—Rob McCoy (Napa, CA)

"With each turning page I was captivated by the suspense. A true masterpiece."
—Kelley Vickers (Seguin, TX)

"I couldn't put it down. I am an avid reader who can rarely find novels that are so well written and at the same time evoke so many emotions."
—Gail Milgroom (Las Vegas, NV)

"You've done it again. A superb book, greatly enjoyed by us, screamed over, laughed over, cursed at—all in all a marvelous experience."
—Jim and Dorris Reader (Pflugerville, TX)

more . . .

"I have to tell you I stayed up till 2:30 last night finishing STILL LIFE WITH CROWS. What an on-the-edge-of-your-seat and scary book!!!! It was excellent! I had just read *The Cabinet of Curiosities* and can't say which one is better. They are both terrifying and extremely gripping."
　　　　—Lorine Allan (Camino, CA)

"It was everything I've come to expect from a Preston-Child novel—tons of fascinating bits of history and science and trivia, suspense, interesting characters, the ending with the surprise twist."
　　　　—Allison Lane (Birmingham, AL)

"It was worth the wait!"
　　　　—Jim and Julie Russell (Wilmington, DE)

"I cannot think of a book that I have enjoyed more."
　　　　—Charles and Judy McFarland (San Angelo, TX)

"You take me on a casual stroll, that turns into a trot, that turns into a run, that turns into an all-out race for my life. I love that about you. I've never had more fun reading books."
　　　　—Ramona Curbeam (Riva, MD)

"Agent Pendergast is a brilliant protagonist who seems to have unbelievable canny when it comes to anything and everything."
　　　　—Leigh Hembd (Wonewoc, WI)

"I didn't want the book to end, but at the same time couldn't stop myself from finishing the book. I haven't been this scared by a book in a long time. It was horror and mystery well served on a silver platter."
　　　　—Ronda Thrweatt (Columbus, OH)

CRITICAL ACCLAIM FOR THE THRILLERS OF DOUGLAS PRESTON AND LINCOLN CHILD

THE CABINET OF CURIOSITIES

"A great novel . . . Preston-Child are at the top of their game. . . . It all comes together with a zing."
  —*Publishers Weekly* (starred review)

"Intelligent, witty, fast-moving, and fun."
  —*San Jose Mercury News*

"An absolutely terrific thriller . . . wonderfully spooky. . . . This adventure has all the elements of the perfect summer read. . . . Another big winner."
  —*Library Journal* (starred review)

•

"Fascinating and creepy . . . a gripping story of suspense that is a thrill-a-page."
  —*Brunswick Times Record News* (ME)

"A marvelous work . . . compelling . . . rich in detail . . . the scientific thriller at its very best."
  —*Tacoma Reporter* (WA)

"Great fun . . . as always, they keep the action moving and their characters simple yet dynamic. . . . Perfect summer beach reading."
  —*Portsmouth Herald* (NH)

"This is one of their best . . . sharply drawn characters, snappy dialogue, and plenty of action."
  —*Booklist*

more . . .

THE ICE LIMIT

"Compelling . . . riddled with subplots, treachery, and betrayal . . . packs a series of surprise wallops."
—*Toronto Star*

"Their most expertly executed entertainment yet . . . a big-boned thriller, one that will make a terrific summer movie as well as a memorable hot-day read."
—*Publishers Weekly*

"Opens with a bang. . . . With increasing momentum, budding romances, raging storms, and sinister mysteries clash, collide, and hurtle toward an explosive climax."
—*Portsmouth Herald* (**NH**)

"An ultra action-packed adventure that will thrill with its nonstop action. Preston and Child put the pedal to the metal. . . . A real kicker."
—*Midwest Book Review*

"Chock-full of cliff-hanging surprises and unexpected twists. . . . If nonstop thrills and genuinely satisfying adventure are what you're after, then look no further."
—*Providence Sunday Journal*

THUNDERHEAD

"Chilling . . . redefines 'page-turner.' "
—*Denver Rocky Mountain News*

DOUGLAS PRESTON
AND
LINCOLN CHILD

STILL LIFE
WITH
CROWS

GRAND CENTRAL
PUBLISHING

NEW YORK BOSTON

Copyright © 2003 by Lincoln Child and Splendide Mendax, Inc.
Excerpt from *Brimstone* copyright © 2003 by Lincoln Child and Splendide Mendax, Inc. All rights reserved. Except as permitted under the U.S. Copyright Act of 1976, no part of this publication may be reproduced, distributed, or transmitted in any form or by any means, or stored in a database or retrieval system, without the prior written permission of the publisher.

Cover design by Diane Luger
Cover illustration by Stanislaw Fernandes

Grand Central Publishing
Hachette Book Group USA
237 Park Avenue
New York, NY 10017
Visit our Web site at www.HachetteBookGroupUSA.com

Grand Central Publishing is a division of Hachette Book Group USA, Inc. The Grand Central Publishing name and logo is a trademark of Hachette Book Group USA, Inc.

Printed in the United States of America

Originally published in hardcover by Hachette Book Group USA
First Paperback Printing: July 2004

16 15 14 13 12 11 10 9 8

Lincoln Child dedicates this book to his daughter, Veronica.

Douglas Preston dedicates this book to Mario Spezi.

Acknowledgments

Lincoln Child would like to thank Special Agent Douglas Margini for his ongoing advice on both law enforcement matters and electric guitars. I would also like to thank my cousin, Greg Tear, and my friends Bob Wincott and Pat Allocco, for particularly sage advice on the manuscript. Victor S. was very helpful in providing certain necessary details. I'd like to thank the following people for helping make sure that the life of a writer need not be that of a monk: Chris and Susan Yango, Tony Trischka, Irene Soderlund, Roger Lasley, Patrick Dowd, Gerard and Terry Hyland, Denis Kelly, Bruce Swanson, Jim Jenkins, Mark Mendel, Ray Spencer, and Malou and Sonny Baula. Thanks to Lee Suckno for various and sundry ministrations. Most importantly, I want to thank my parents, Nancy and Bill Child, my brother, Doug, and my sister, Cynthia, my daughter, Veronica, and especially my wife, Luchie, for their love and support. I would also like to gratefully acknowledge my adoptive hometown of Northfield, Minnesota, which—in the nostalgic spyglass of memory—retains all the charms and graces of small-town America while somehow managing to avoid its limitations.

Douglas Preston would like to express his very great appreciation to Bobby Rotenberg for reading the manuscript and offering excellent suggestions. I thank my daughter Selene for her invaluable advice, especially with the character of Corrie. I am deeply indebted to Karen Copeland for her tremendous help and support. And I thank Niccolò Capponi for innumerable fascinating literary conversations and excellent ideas. My thanks goes to Barry Turkus for dragging me up and down the Tuscan hills *in bici,* and to his wife, Jody. I also wish to thank some of my Florentine friends for providing a counterbalance to many solitary hours spent in front of the computer. They are Myriam Slabbinck, Ross Capponi, Lucia Boldrini and Riccardo Zucconi, Vassiliki Lambrou and Paolo Busoni, Edward Tosques, Phyllis and Ted Swindells, Peter and Marguerite Casparian, Andrea and Vahe Keushguerian, and Catia Ballerini. I am also most indebted to our Italian translator, Andrea Carlo Cappi, for his friendship and advocacy of our books and for giving us a piece of excellent advice on this novel in particular. And how can I help but acknowledge the incomparable Andrea Pinketts? Finally, I want to express my greatest appreciation to my wife, Christine, and my two other children, Aletheia and Isaac, for their constant love and support.

And, as always, we want to thank in particular those people without whom the novels of Preston and Child would not exist: Jaime Levine, Jamie Raab, Eric Simonoff, Eadie Klemm, and Matthew Snyder.

•　　　•　　　•

Although we have used southwestern Kansas as the location for this novel, the town of Medicine Creek, as well as Cry County and many of the other towns and cities mentioned in the novel, are either fictitious or are used fictitiously, as are the characters that populate them. We have not hesitated to alter the geography of southwestern Kansas to suit our fictional purposes. Readers with a farming background will note that we have also taken some liberties with our agricultural facts. For example, southwestern Kansas is mostly wheat-growing country, not corn, and some details about the maturation and harvesting of corn have been altered for the purposes of the story.

STILL LIFE
WITH
CROWS

One

Medicine Creek, Kansas. Early August. Sunset.

The great sea of yellow corn stretches from horizon to horizon under an angry sky. When the wind rises the corn stirs and rustles as if alive, and when the wind dies down again the corn falls silent. The heat wave is now in its third week, and dead air hovers over the corn in shimmering curtains.

One road cuts through the corn from north to south; another from east to west. Where the two roads cross lies the town. Sad gray buildings huddle together at the intersection, gradually thinning along both roads into separate houses, then scattered farms, and then nothing. A creek, edged by scraggly trees, wanders in from the northwest, loops lazily around the town, and disappears in the southeast. It is the only curved thing in this landscape of straight lines. To the northeast rises a cluster of mounds surrounded by trees.

A giant slaughterhouse stands south of the town, lost in the corn, its metal sides scoured by years of dust storms. The faint odor of blood and disinfectant drifts in a plume southward from the plant, riding the fitful currents of air. Beyond, just over the horizon, stand three gigantic grain silos, like a tall-masted ship lost at sea.

The temperature is exactly one hundred degrees. Heat lightning flickers silently along the distant northern horizon. The corn is seven feet high, the fat cobs clustered on the stalks. Harvest is two weeks away.

Twilight is falling over the landscape. The orange sky bleeds away into red. A handful of streetlights blink on in the town.

A black-and-white police cruiser passes along the main street, heading east into the great nothingness of corn, its headlights stabbing into the rising darkness. Some three miles ahead of the cruiser, a column of slow-circling turkey vultures rides a thermal above the corn. They wheel down, then rise up again, circling endlessly, uneasily, rising and falling in a regular cadence.

Sheriff Dent Hazen fiddled with the dashboard knobs and cursed at the tepid air that streamed from the vents. He felt the vent with the back of his hand but it wasn't getting any cooler: the AC had finally bit the dust. He muttered another imprecation and cranked down the window, tossing out his cigarette butt. Furnacelike air boiled in, and the cruiser filled with the smell of late-summer Kansas: earth, cornstalks. He could see the circling turkey buzzards rise and dip, rise and dip above the dying smear of sunset along the horizon. *One ugly motherfucker of a bird,* thought Hazen, and he glanced over at the long-barreled Winchester Defender lying on the seat beside him. With any luck, he'd get close enough to assist two or three of them into the next world.

He slowed and glanced once again at the dark birds silhouetted against the sky. *Why the hell aren't any of them landing?* Turning off the main road, he eased the cruiser onto one of the many rutted dirt lanes that cut their way through the thousand square miles of corn surrounding Medicine Creek. He moved forward, keeping a watch on the sky, until the birds were almost directly overhead. This was as close as he was going to get by car. From here, he'd have to walk.

He threw the cruiser into park and, more out of habit than necessity, snapped on the lightbar flashers. He eased his frame out of the cruiser and stood for a moment facing the wall of corn, drawing a rough hand across his stubbled chin. The rows went in the wrong direction and it was going to be a bitch getting through them. Just the thought of shouldering through all those rows made him weary, and for a moment he thought about putting the cruiser in reverse and getting the hell back to town. But it was too late for that now: the neighbor's call had already been logged. Old Wilma Lowry had nothing better to do but look out her window and report the location of dead animals. But this was his last call of the day, and a few extra hours on Friday evening at least guaranteed him a long, lazy, boozy Sunday fishing at Hamilton Lake State Park.

Hazen lit another cigarette, coughed, and scratched himself, looking at the dry ranks of corn. He wondered if it was somebody's cow who'd wandered into the corn and was now dead of bloat and greed. Since when was it a sheriff's responsibility to check on dead livestock? But he already knew the answer: ever since the livestock inspector retired. There was nobody to take his place and no longer a need for one. Every year there were fewer family farms, fewer livestock, fewer people. Most people only kept cows and horses for nostalgic reasons. The whole county was going to hell.

Realizing he'd put off the task long enough, Hazen sighed, hiked up his jangling service belt, slipped his flashlight out of its scabbard, shouldered the shotgun, and pushed his way into the corn.

Despite the lateness of the hour, the sultry air refused to lift. The beam of his light flashed through the cornstalks stretching before him like endless rows of prison bars. His nose filled with the smell of dry stalks, that peculiar rusty smell so familiar it was part of his very being. His feet crunched dry clods of earth, kicking up dust. It had been a wet spring, and until the heat wave kicked in a few weeks back the summer sun had been benevolent. The stalks were as high as Hazen could ever remember, at least a foot or more over his head. Amazing how fast the black earth could turn to dust without rain. Once, as a kid, he'd run into a cornfield to escape his older brother and gotten lost. For two hours. The disorientation he'd felt then came back to him now. Inside the corn rows, the air felt trapped: hot, fetid, itchy.

Hazen took a deep drag on the cigarette and continued forward, knocking the fat cobs aside with irritation. The field belonged to Buswell Agricon of Atlanta, and Sheriff Hazen could not have cared less if they lost a few ears because of his rough passage. Within two weeks Agricon's huge combine harvesters would appear on the horizon, mowing down the corn, each feeding half a dozen streams of kernels into their hoppers. The corn would be trucked to the cluster of huge grain silos just over the northern horizon and from there railed to feed lots from Nebraska to Missouri, to disappear down the throats of mindless castrated cattle, which would in turn be transformed into big fat marbled sirloins for rich assholes in New York and Tokyo. Or maybe this was one of those gasohol fields, where the corn wasn't eaten by man or even beast but burned up in the engines of cars instead. What a world.

Hazen bullied his way through row after row. Already his nose was running. He tossed his cigarette away, then realized he should probably have pinched it off first. Hell with it. A thousand acres of the damn corn could burn and Buswell Agricon wouldn't even notice. They should take care of their own fields, pick up their own dead animals. Of course, the executives had probably never set foot in a real cornfield in their lives.

Like almost everyone else in Medicine Creek, Hazen came from a farming family that no longer farmed. They had sold their land to companies like Buswell Agricon. The population of Medicine Creek had been dropping for more than half a century and the great industrial cornfields were now dotted with abandoned houses, their empty window frames staring like dead eyes over the billowy main of crops. But Hazen had stayed. Not that he liked Medicine Creek particularly; what he liked was wearing a uniform and being respected. He liked the town because he knew the town, every last person, every dark corner, every nasty secret. Truth was, he simply couldn't imagine himself anywhere else. He was as much a part of Medicine Creek as Medicine Creek was a part of him.

Hazen stopped suddenly. He swept his beam through the stalks ahead. The air, full of dust, now carried another smell: the perfume of decay. He glanced up. The buzzards were far above now, directly over his head. Another fifty yards and he would be there. The air was still, the silence complete. He unshouldered his shotgun and moved forward more cautiously.

The smell of decay drifted through the rows, sweeter by the moment. Now Hazen could make out a gap in the corn, a clearing directly ahead of him. Odd. The sky had flamed its red farewell and was now dark.

The sheriff raised his gun, eased off the safety with his thumb, and broke through the last corn row into the clearing. For a moment he looked around in wild incomprehension. And then, rather suddenly, he realized what he was looking at.

The gun went off when it hit the ground and the load of double-ought buckshot blew by Hazen's ear. But the sheriff barely noticed.

Two

Two hours later, Sheriff Dent Hazen stood in approximately the same spot. But now, the cornfield had been transformed into a gigantic crime scene. The clearing was ringed with portable sodium vapor lights that bathed the scene in a harsh white glow, and a generator growled somewhere out in the corn. The Staties had bulldozed an access road into the site, and now almost a dozen state cruisers, SOC trucks, ambulances, and other vehicles sat in an instant parking lot carved out of the corn. Two photographers were taking pictures, their flashes punctuating the night, while a lone evidence gatherer crouched nearby, picking at the ground with a pair of tweezers.

Hazen stared at the victim, sickness rising in his gut. This was the first homicide in Medicine Creek in his lifetime. The last killing had been during Prohibition, when Rocker Manning had been shot at by the creek while buying a load of moonshine . . . that was back in, when, '31? His granddaddy had handled the case, made the arrest. But that was nothing like this. This was something else entirely. This was fucking madness.

Hazen turned from the corpse and stared at the makeshift road through the corn, cut to save the troopers a quarter-mile hike. There was a good possibility the road had destroyed evidence. He wondered if it was standard Statie procedure, or if they even had a procedure for this kind of situation. All the activity had an ad hoc air about it, as if the troopers were so shocked by the crime that they were just making it up as they went along.

Sheriff Hazen didn't hold Staties in particularly high regard. When you got down to it they were basically a bunch of tight-jawed assholes in shiny boots. But he could sympathize. This was something beyond anyone's experience. He lit a fresh Camel off the stub of his last one and reminded himself that it wasn't really his first homicide. It wasn't his case at all. He may have found the body, but it was outside the township and therefore outside his jurisdiction. This was a Statie job, and thank the risen Lord for that.

"Sheriff Hazen?" The towering Kansas state trooper captain came crunching over the corn stubble, his black boots shining, his hand outstretched, mouth tensed in what was supposed to pass for a smile. Hazen took the hand and shook it, annoyed by the man's height. It was the third time the captain had offered him his hand. Hazen wondered if the man had a bad memory or if he was just so agitated that the handshaking was a nervous reaction. Probably the latter.

"The M.E.'s coming down from Garden City," the captain said. "Should be here in ten minutes."

Sheriff Hazen wished to hell he'd sent Tad out on this one. He would've gladly given up his weekend fishing—Christ, he would've even stayed sober—to miss this. On the other hand, he thought, perhaps this would have been too much for Tad. In so many ways he was still only a kid.

"We've got ourselves an artist here," said the trooper, shaking his head. "A real artist. You think this'll make the *Kansas City Star?*"

Hazen didn't reply. This was a new thought to him. He thought of his picture in the paper and found the idea displeasing. Someone walking past with a fluoroscope bumped into him. Christ, the crime scene was getting to be more crowded than a Baptist wedding.

He filled his lungs with tobacco, then forced himself to look out over the scene yet again. It seemed important that he should see it one more time, before it was all disassembled and put into bags and taken away. His eyes played over it, automatically committing every hideous little detail to memory.

It had been set up almost like a scene in a play. A circular clearing had been made in the heart of the cornfield, the broken stalks carefully stacked to one side, leaving an area of dirt clods and stubble perhaps forty feet in diameter. Even in the terrible unreality of the moment, Hazen found himself marveling at the geometrical precision with which the circle had been formed. At one end of the clearing stood a miniature forest of sharpened sticks, two to three feet high, pushed into the earth, their cruel-looking ends pointing upward. At the precise middle of the clearing stood a circle of dead crows spitted on stakes. Only they weren't stakes but Indian arrows, each topped by a flaked point. There were at least a couple dozen of the birds, maybe more, their vacant eyes staring, black beaks pointing inward.

And in the center of this circle of crows lay the corpse of a woman.

At least Sheriff Hazen thought it was a woman: her lips, nose, and ears were missing.

The corpse lay on its back, its mouth wide open, looking like the entrance to a pink cave. It had bleached-blond hair, a clump of it ripped away and missing; the clothes had been shredded in countless small, neat, parallel lines. There was no sense of disorder. The relationship between the head and the shoulders looked wrong: Hazen thought her neck was probably broken. But there was no bruising on the neck indicating strangulation. If it had been broken, the act had been done by a single hard twist.

The killing, Hazen concluded, had taken place elsewhere. He could see marks in the earth going back not quite to the edge of the clearing, indicating the body had been dragged; extrapolating the line, he saw a gap in the corn rows where a stalk had been broken off. The troopers hadn't seen it. In fact, some of the marks were being obscured by the comings and goings of the Staties themselves. He turned toward the captain to point this out. Then he stopped himself. What was wrong with him? This was not his case. Not his responsibility. When the shit hit, the fan would be blowing in someone else's direction. The minute he opened his mouth the wind would shift his way. If he said, "Captain, you've destroyed evidence," on the witness stand two months from now he'd be forced to repeat it to some asshole of a defense lawyer. Because whatever he said now would come up at the trial of the maniac who did this. And there would be a trial. A guy this crazy couldn't get away with it for long.

He inhaled a lungful of acrid smoke. *Keep it zipped. Let them make the mistakes. It's not your case.*

He dropped the butt, ground it beneath one foot. Yet another car was now bumping carefully along the access road, its headlights stabbing up and down through the corn. It came to a stop in the makeshift lot and a man in white got out, carrying a black bag. McHyde, the M.E.

Sheriff Hazen watched as the man gingerly picked his way among the dry clods, not wanting to soil his wingtips. He spoke to the captain and then went over to the body. He stared at it for a moment from this angle and that, then knelt and carefully tied plastic bags around the hands and feet of the victim. Then he drew some kind of device out of his black bag—it was called an anal probe, Sheriff Hazen remembered abruptly. And now the M.E. was doing something intimate to the corpse. Measuring its temperature. Jesus. Now there was a job for you.

Sheriff Hazen glanced up into the dark sky, but the turkey vultures were long gone. They, at least, knew when to leave well enough alone.

The M.E. and the paramedics now began packing up the corpse for removal. A Statie was pulling up the arrows with the crows, labeling them, and packing them into refrigerated evidence lockers. And Sheriff Hazen realized he had to take a leak. All that damn coffee. But it wasn't just that; acid was starting to boil up from his stomach. He hoped to hell his ulcer wasn't coming back. He sure didn't want to toss his cookies in front of these characters.

He glanced around, made sure he was not being noticed, and slipped into the dark corn. He walked down a row, inhaling deeply, trying to get far enough away that his own piss wouldn't be found and marked as evidence. He wouldn't have to go far; these Staties were not showing much curiosity about anything beyond the immediate crime scene.

He stopped just outside the circle of lights. Here, buried in the sea of corn, the murmur of the voices, the faint hum of the generator, and the bizarre violence of the crime scene seemed far away. A breeze came drifting past, only a slight movement of the muggy air, but it set the corn around him swaying and rustling. Hazen paused a minute, filling his nostrils. Then he unzipped, grunted, and urinated loudly on the dry ground. Finally, with a big noisy shake that set his gun, cuffs, club, and keys rattling, he put everything back in and patted it into place.

As he turned, he saw something in the reflected glow of the lights. He stopped, shining his flashlight across the corn rows. There it was, in the next row over. He looked more closely. A piece of cloth, caught high up on one of the dry husks. It appeared to be the same as the material the victim was wearing. He shone his light up and down the row, but he saw nothing else.

He straightened up. He was doing it again. This wasn't his case. Maybe he'd mention it; maybe he'd let the Staties find it on their own. If it really meant anything, anyway.

When he pushed his way back into the clearing, the trooper captain came forward at once. "Sheriff Hazen, I was just looking for you," he said. He was carrying a handheld GPS unit in one hand and a USGS topographical map in the other, and his face was wearing a very different expression than it had just moments before. "Congratulations."

"What's that?" asked Hazen.

The captain pointed to the GPS device. "According to this reading, we're inside the boundary of the township of Medicine Creek. Twelve feet inside the boundary, to be exact. Which means it's your case, Sheriff. We're here to help, of course, but it's your case. So let me be the first to offer my congratulations."

He beamed and held out his hand.

Sheriff Dent Hazen ignored the hand. Instead he plucked the pack of cigarettes from his breast pocket, shook one out, pushed it between his lips, and lit it. He inhaled and then spoke, the smoke puffing out with his words. "Twelve feet?" he repeated. "Jesus Christ."

The captain let his hand fall to his side.

Hazen began to talk. "The victim was murdered somewhere else and carried here. The murderer came through the corn over there, dragged her the last twenty feet or so. If you follow the row backward from that broken stalk, you'll come to a piece of caught fabric. The fabric matches that of the victim, but it's caught too high on the stalk for her to have been walking, so he must've been lugging her on his back. You may see my footprints and the place where I took a piss in the adjoining row; don't bother with that. And for God's sake, Captain, do we really need all these people? This is a crime scene, not a Wal-Mart parking lot. I want only the M.E., the photographer, and the evidence gatherer on site. Tell the rest to back off."

"Sheriff, we do have our procedures to follow—"

"My procedures are now your procedures."

The captain swallowed.

"I want a pair of certified, trained AKC police bloodhounds here ASAP to get on the trail. And I want you to get the forensic evidence team down from Dodge."

"Right."

"And one other thing."

"What's that?"

"I want your boys to pull over any arriving press. Especially television trucks. Tie them up while we complete work here."

"Pull them over for what?"

"Give 'em all speeding tickets. That's what you boys are good at, right?"

The captain's tight jaw grew even tighter. "And if they're not speeding?"

Sheriff Hazen grinned. "Oh, they'll be speeding, all right. You can bet your ass on it."

Three

Deputy Sheriff Tad Franklin sat hunched over his desk, filling out reams of unfamiliar paperwork and trying to pretend that the unruly knot of television and newspaper reporters just outside the plate glass window of the Medicine Creek Sheriff's Department didn't exist. Tad had always liked the fact that the sheriff's HQ was located in a former five-and-ten-cent storefront, where he could wave to passersby, chat with friends, keep tabs on who was coming or going. But now the disadvantages of the office had suddenly become obvious.

The fiery light of yet another hot August sunrise had begun spilling down the street, stretching long shadows from the news trucks and gilding the unhappy faces of the reporters. They had been up all night and things were beginning to look ugly. A steady stream came and went from Maisie's Diner across the street, but the plain food only seemed to make them grumpier.

Tad Franklin tried to concentrate on the paperwork, but he found himself unable to ignore the tapping on the window, the questions, the occasional shouted vulgarity. This was getting intolerable. If they woke Sheriff Hazen, who was grabbing a few winks in the back cell, things might get even uglier. Tad rose, tried to put on as stern a look as possible, and cracked open a window.

"I'll ask you once again to step back from the glass," he said.

This was greeted with a muffled chorus of disrespectful comments, shouted questions, a general undercurrent of irritation. Tad knew from the call letters on the vans that the reporters weren't local; they were from Topeka, Kansas City, Tulsa, Amarillo, and Denver. Well, they could just ride on back home and—

Behind him, Tad heard a door thump, a cough. He turned to see Sheriff Hazen, yawning and rubbing his stubbly chin, the hair on one side of his head sticking out horizontally. The sheriff smoothed it down, then fitted on his hat with both hands.

Tad closed the window. "Sorry, Sheriff, but these people just won't go away—"

The sheriff yawned, waved his hand casually, turned his back on the crowd. A particularly angry reporter in the rear of the crowd shouted out a stream of invective, in which the words "redneck in miniature" could be heard. Hazen went to the coffee pot, poured a cup. He sipped it, made a face, spat the coffee back into the cup, hawked up a loogie, deposited it in the cup as well, and then poured everything back into the pot.

"Want me to get a fresh pot?" asked Tad.

"No thanks, Tad," the sheriff replied, giving his deputy's shoulder a gruff pat. Then he turned back to face the group through the glass once more. "These folks need something for the six o'clock news, don't you think?" he said. "Time for a press conference."

"A press conference?" Tad had never attended a press conference in his life, let alone been part of one. "How do you do that?"

Sheriff Hazen barked a laugh, briefly displaying a rack of yellow teeth. "We go outside and answer questions." He went to the old glass door, unlocked it, and stuck his head out.

"How you folks all doing?"

This was greeted by a surge and an incomprehensible welter of shouted questions.

Sheriff Hazen held up an arm, palm toward the crowd. He was still wearing his short-sleeved uniform from the night before, and the gesture exposed a half-moon of sweat that reached halfway to his waist. He was short, but short like a bulldog, and there was something about him that commanded respect. Tad had seen the sheriff loosen the teeth of a suspect almost twice his size. *Never get in a fight with anyone under five foot six,* he told himself. The crowd fell silent.

The sheriff dropped his arm. "My deputy, Tad Franklin, and myself will give a statement and answer questions. Let's all behave like civilized people. What say?"

The crowd shuffled in place. Lights went on, mikes were boomed forward; there was the clicking of cassette recorders, the fluttering of camera shutters.

"Tad, let's give these good folks some fresh coffee."

Tad looked at Hazen. Hazen winked.

Tad grabbed the pot, peered in, gave it a quick shake. Then he reached for a stack of Styrofoam cups, stepped out the door, and began doling out the coffee. There were some sips, a few furtive sniffs.

"Drink up!" Hazen cried good-naturedly. "Never let it be said we're not hospitable folks here in Medicine Creek!"

There was a general shuffling, more sipping, a few covert glances into the cups. The coffee seemed to have subdued, if not broken, the spirit of the group. Though it was barely dawn, the heat was already oppressive. There was no place to put down the cups, no trash can to drop them in. And a sign outside the door to the sheriff's office read NO LITTERING: $100 FINE.

Hazen adjusted his hat, then stepped out onto the sidewalk. He looked around, his shoulders squared to the crowd as the cameras rolled. He then addressed the group. He told in dry police language of finding the body; he described the clearing, the body, and the spitted birds. It was pretty vivid stuff, but the sheriff managed to handle it matter-of-factly, throwing in a folksy comment here and there, in a way that neutralized most of the gruesome aspects. It amazed Tad how easygoing, even charming, his boss could be when he wanted to.

In the space of two minutes he was finished. A flurry of shouted questions followed Hazen's speech.

"One at a time; raise your hands," the sheriff said. "It's just like in school. Anyone who shouts goes last. You begin." And he pointed to a reporter in shirtsleeves who was enormously, spectacularly fat.

"Are there any leads or suspects?"

"We've got some very interesting things we're following up. I can't say any more than that."

Tad looked at him with surprise. What things? So far, they had nothing.

"You," said Hazen, pointing to another.

"Was the murder victim local?"

"No. We're working on identification, but she wasn't a local. I know everyone around these parts, I can vouch for that myself."

"Do you know how the woman was killed?"

"Hopefully, the medical examiner will tell us that. The body was sent up to Garden City. When we get the autopsy results, you'll be the first to know."

The early morning Greyhound, northbound from Amarillo, came rumbling up the main street, stopping in front of Maisie's Diner with a chuff of brakes. Tad was surprised: the bus almost never stopped. Whoever came or went from Medicine Creek, Kansas, anymore? Maybe it was more reporters, too cheap to provide their own transportation.

"The lady, you, there. Your question, ma'am?"

A tough-looking redhead poked a shotgun mike at Hazen. "What law enforcement agencies are involved?"

"The state police have been a big help, but since the body was found in Medicine Creek township, it's our case."

"FBI?"

"The FBI doesn't get involved in local murder cases and we don't expect them to take an interest in this one. We've put some pretty heavy-duty police resources on the case, including the special crime lab and homicide squad up in Dodge City, who spent the whole night at the site. Don't you all worry that just Tad and me are going to try to solve this on our own. We're good at hollering, and we're going to holler loud enough to get what we need to solve this case, and quick, too." He smiled and winked.

There was a roar as the bus pulled away in a cloud of dust and diesel fumes. The sound temporarily drowned out the press conference. As the fumes cleared, they revealed a lone figure standing on the sidewalk, small leather valise sitting on the ground next to him. He was tall and thin, dressed in dead black, and in the early morning light he cast a shadow that stretched halfway across downtown Medicine Creek.

Tad glanced at the sheriff and noticed that he'd seen the man, too.

The man was staring across the street at them.

Hazen roused himself. "Next question," he said briskly. "Smitty?" He pointed to the well-lined face of Smit Ludwig, the owner-reporter of the *Cry County Courier,* the local paper.

"Any explanation for the, ah, the strange tableau? You got any theory on the arrangement of the body and the various appurtenances?"

"Appurtenances?"

"Yeah. You know, the stuff around it."

"Not yet."

"Could this be some kind of satanic cult?"

Tad glanced involuntarily across the street. The black-clad figure had lifted his bag but was still standing there, motionless.

"That's a possibility we'll be looking into, for sure," said Hazen. "We're obviously dealing with a very sick individual."

Now Tad noticed the man in black taking a step into the street, strolling nonchalantly toward them. Who could he be? He certainly didn't look like a reporter, policeman, or traveling salesman. In fact, what he most looked like to Tad Franklin was a murderer. Maybe *the* murderer.

He noticed that the sheriff was also staring, and even some members of the press had turned around.

Hazen fished a pack of cigarettes out of his shirt pocket. He resumed talking. "Whether it's a cult, or a lunatic, or whatever, I just want to emphasize—and Smitty, this will be important for your readers—that we're dealing with out-of-town, perhaps out-of-state, elements."

Hazen's voice faltered as the figure in black stopped at

the edge of the crowd. It was already well into the nineties but the man was dressed in black worsted wool, with a starched white shirt and a silk tie knotted tightly at his neck. Yet he looked as cool and crisp as a cucumber. The gaze from his silvery eyes was directed piercingly at Hazen.

A hush fell.

The black-clad figure now spoke. The voice wasn't loud, but somehow it seemed to dominate the crowd. "An unwarranted assumption," the figure said.

There was a silence.

Hazen took his time to open the pack, shake out a butt, and slide it into his mouth. He said nothing.

Tad stared at the man. He seemed so thin—his skin almost transparent, his blue-gray eyes so light they looked luminous—that he could have been a reanimated corpse, a vampire fresh from the grave. If he wasn't the walking dead he could just as easily have passed for an undertaker: either way, there was definitely the look of death about the man. Tad felt uneasy.

His cigarette lit, Hazen finally spoke. "I don't recall asking your opinion, mister."

The man strolled into the crowd, which parted silently, and halted ten feet from the sheriff. The man spoke again, in the mellifluous accent of the deepest South. "The killer works in the blackest night with no moon. He appears and disappears without a trace. Are you really so sure, Sheriff Hazen, that he is not from Medicine Creek?"

Hazen took a long drag, blew a stream of blue smoke in the general direction of the man, and said, "And what makes you such an expert?"

"That is a question best answered in your office, Sheriff."

The man held out his hand, indicating that the sheriff and Tad should precede him into the little headquarters.

"Who the hell are you, inviting me into my own damn office?" Hazen said, beginning to lose his temper.

The man looked mildly at him and answered in the same low, honeyed voice. "May I suggest, Sheriff Hazen, that that equally excellent question is also best answered in private? I mean, for *your* sake."

Before Sheriff Hazen could respond, the man turned to the reporters. "I regret to inform you this press conference is now over."

To Tad's absolute amazement, they turned and began shuffling away.

Four

The sheriff took up position behind his battered Formica desk. Tad sat down in his usual chair with a tingling sense of anticipation. The stranger in black placed his bag by the door and the sheriff offered him the hard wooden visitor's chair that he claimed would break any suspect in five minutes. The man settled into it with one smooth elegant motion, flung one leg over the other, leaned back, and looked at the sheriff.

"Get our guest a cup of coffee," said Hazen, with a faint smile.

There was enough left in the pot for half a cup, which was quickly passed.

The man accepted it, glanced at it, set it down on the table, and smiled. "You are most kind, but I am a tea drinker myself. Green tea."

Tad wondered if the man was weird, or possibly a faggot.

Hazen cleared his throat, frowned, shifted his squat body. "Okay, mister, this better be good."

Almost languidly, the man removed a leather wallet from his jacket pocket, let it fall open. Hazen leaned forward, scrutinized it, sat back with a sigh.

"FBI. Shit-fire. Might have known." He glanced over at Tad. "We're running with the big boys now."

"Yes, sir," said Tad. Although he'd never actually met an FBI agent before, this guy looked exactly the opposite of what he thought an FBI agent should look like.

"All right, Mr., ah—"

"Special Agent Pendergast."

"Pendergast. Pendergast. I'm bad with names." Hazen lit another cigarette, sucked on it hard. "You here on the crows murder?" The words came out with a cloud of smoke.

"Yes."

"And is this official?"

"No."

"So it's just you."

"So far."

"What office are you out of?"

"Technically, I'm with the New Orleans office. But I operate under, shall we say, a special arrangement." He smiled pleasantly.

Hazen grunted. "How long will you be staying?"

"For the duration."

Tad wondered, *For the duration of what?*

Pendergast turned his pale eyes on Tad and smiled. "Of my vacation."

Tad was speechless. Did the guy read his mind?

"Your *vacation?*" Hazen shifted again. "Pendergast, this is irregular. I'm going to need some kind of official authorization from the local field office. We're not running a Club Med for Quantico here."

There was a silence. Then the man named Pendergast said, "Surely you don't want me here *officially*, Sheriff Hazen?"

When this was greeted with silence, Pendergast continued pleasantly. "I will not interfere with your investigation. I will operate independently. I will consult with you regularly and share information with you when appropriate. Any, ah, 'collars' will be yours. I neither seek nor will I accept credit. All I ask are the usual law enforcement courtesies."

Sheriff Hazen frowned, scratched, frowned again. "As for the collar, frankly I don't give a damn who gets the credit. I just want to catch the son of a bitch."

Pendergast nodded approvingly.

Hazen took a drag, exhaled, took another. He was thinking. "All right, then, Pendergast, take your busman's holiday here. Just keep a low profile and don't talk to the press."

"Naturally not."

"Where are you staying?"

"I was hoping to receive the benefit of your advice."

The sheriff barked a laugh. "There's only one place in town, and that's the Kraus place. Kraus's Kaverns. You passed it on the way in, big old house set out in the corn about a mile west of town. Old Winifred Kraus rents out rooms on the top floor. Not that she has many takers these days. And she'll talk you into a tour of her cave. You'll probably be the first visitor she's had in a year."

"Thank you," said Pendergast, rising and picking up his bag.

Hazen's eyes followed the movement. "Got a car?"

"No."

The sheriff's lip curled slightly. "I'll give you a lift."

"I enjoy walking."

"You sure? It's almost a hundred degrees out there. And I wouldn't exactly call that suit of yours appropriate dress for these parts." Hazen was grinning now.

"Is it indeed that hot?" The FBI agent turned and reached for the door, but Hazen had one more question.

"How did you learn about the murder so quick?"

Pendergast paused. "By arrangement, I have someone at the Bureau watching the cable and e-mail traffic of local law enforcement agencies. Whenever a crime within a certain category occurs, I'm notified of it immediately. But as I said, I'm here for personal reasons, having recently concluded a rather strenuous investigation back east. It's simply that I'm intrigued by the rather, ah, interesting nature of this particular case."

Something in the way the man said "interesting" raised the hairs on the back of Tad's neck.

"And just what 'certain category' are we talking about here?" The sarcasm was creeping back into the sheriff's voice.

"Serial homicide."

"Funny, I've only seen one murder so far."

The figure gradually turned back. His cool gray eyes settled on Sheriff Hazen. In a very low voice he said, "So far."

Five

Winifred Kraus paused in her cross-stitch to gaze at the very strange sight out her parlor window. She felt vaguely frightened. A tall man in black was walking down the middle of the road, carrying a leather valise. He was several hundred yards away, but Winifred Kraus had sharp eyes and she could see that he was ghostly-looking, thin and insubstantial in the bright summer light. She was frightened because she remembered, as a child many years ago, her father telling her that this was the way death would arrive; that it would happen when she least expected it: just a man strolling down the road, coming up the steps and knocking on the door. A man dressed in black. And when you looked down at his feet, instead of shoes you'd see cloven hooves, and then you'd smell the brimstone and fire and that would be it and you'd be dragged screaming into hell.

The man was approaching with long, cool strides, his shadow eating up the road before him. Winifred Kraus told herself she was being silly, that it was just a story, and that death didn't carry a valise anyway. But why would anyone be dressed in black at this time of year? Not even Pastor

Wilbur wore black in this heat. And this man wasn't just wearing black, but a black suit, jacket and all. Was he selling something? But then where was his car? Nobody walked on the Cry County Road—no one. At least not since she was a little girl, before the war, when the drifters used to come through in the early spring, heading for the fields of California.

The man had paused at the spot where her rutted and dusty drive met the macadam of the road. He looked up at the house, right at the parlor it seemed, and Winifred automatically laid aside her cross-stitch. Now he was stepping into her lane. He was coming to the house. He was actually coming to the house. And his hair was so white, his skin so pale, his suit so black . . .

There was the low rap of the doorknocker. Winifred's hand flew to her mouth. Should she answer it? Should she wait for him to go away? *Would* he go away?

She waited.

The knock came again, more insistent.

Winifred frowned. She was being an old silly. Taking a deep breath, she rose from the chair, walked across the parlor into the foyer, unlocked the door, and opened it a crack.

"Miss Kraus?"

"Yes?"

The man actually bowed. "You aren't by chance the Miss Winifred Kraus who offers lodging to travelers? And, I'm given to understand, some of the most excellent home cooking in Cry County, Kansas?"

"Why, yes." Winifred Kraus opened the door a little wider, delighted to find a polite gentleman instead of Death.

"My name is Pendergast." He offered his hand, and after a moment Winifred took it. It was surprisingly cool and dry.

"You gave me quite a start, walking up the road like that. Nobody walks anymore."

"I came by bus."

Abruptly remembering her manners, Winifred opened the door wider and stepped aside. "I'm sorry, do come in. Would you like some iced tea? You must be dreadfully hot in that suit. Oh, forgive me, there hasn't been a death in your family—?"

"Iced tea would be lovely, thank you."

Winifred, feeling a strangely pleasant confusion, bustled back into the pantry, poured a glass over ice, added a fresh sprig of mint from the planter in her windowsill, placed the glass on a silver tray, and returned.

"There you are, Mr. Pendergast."

"You are too kind."

"Won't you sit down?"

They sat in the parlor. The polite man crossed his legs and sipped his tea. Close up, Winifred could see he was younger than she'd first thought: what she had taken to be white hair was instead remarkably blond. He was quite handsome and elegant, too, if one didn't mind such pale eyes and skin.

"I rent three rooms upstairs," she explained. "You have to share the bath, I'm afraid, but there's nobody presently—"

"I'll take the entire floor. Would five hundred dollars a week be acceptable?"

"Oh, my."

"I will pay extra, naturally, for my board. I'll only be requiring a light breakfast and the occasional afternoon tea and dinner."

"That's rather more money than I usually ask. I wouldn't feel right—"

The man smiled. "I fear you may find me a difficult boarder."

"Well, then—"

He sipped his tea, placed it on the coaster, and leaned forward. "I don't want to shock you, Miss Kraus, but I do need to tell you who I am and why I'm here. You asked me if there has been a death. In fact, as you probably know, there has. I am a special agent for the FBI investigating the murder in Medicine Creek." He flashed his badge, as a courtesy.

"A murder!"

"You haven't heard? On the far side of town, discovered last night. You will no doubt read all about it in tomorrow morning's paper."

"Oh, dear me." Winifred Kraus felt dazed. "A murder? In Medicine Creek?"

"I'm sorry. Does that change your mind about taking me in as a lodger? I'll understand if it does."

"Oh no, Mr. Pendergast. Not at all. I'd feel much safer, really, having you here. A murder, how very dreadful . . ." She shuddered. "Who on earth—?"

"I'm afraid I'll have to disappoint you as a source of information on the case. And now, may I examine my rooms? There's no need to show me upstairs."

"Of course." Winifred Kraus smiled a little breathlessly as she watched the man climb the stairs. Such a polite young gentleman, and so . . . Then she remembered the murder. She rose and went to the telephone. Perhaps Jenny Parker would know more. She picked up and dialed the number, shaking her head.

After a swift inspection, Pendergast chose the smallest room—the one in the rear—and laid his valise on its princess bed. On the bureau stood a swivel mirror, in front of which was set a china washbasin and pitcher. He pulled open the top drawer, releasing the faint scent of rosewater and oak. The drawer was lined with shellacked newspapers from the early 1900s, advertising farming equipment. In a corner stood a chamber pot, the lid placed upside down in the old-fashioned way. The walls were papered in a Victorian flowered print, much faded; the moldings were painted green and the ceiling was beadboard. The curtains were hand-embroidered lace.

He returned to the bed, laid one hand lightly upon the bedspread. It had been needlepointed in a pattern of roses and peonies. He examined the stitching closely. Hand done. It had taken someone—no doubt Miss Kraus herself—at least a year.

Pendergast remained motionless, staring at the needlepoint, breathing the antique air of the bedroom. Then, straightening, he walked across the creaking floorboards to the old rippled window and looked out.

To his right and down, set back from the house, Pendergast could see the shabby low metal roof of the gift shop. Behind, a cracked cement walkway ran down to a depression leading to a rupture in the earth, where it disappeared into darkness. Beside the gift shop, a peeling sign read:

KRAUS'S KAVERNS
THE BIGGEST CAVE IN CRY COUNTY, KANSAS

MAKE A WISH IN THE INFINITY POOL
PLAY THE KRYSTAL CHIMES
SEE THE BOTTOMLESS PIT
TOURS AT 10:00 AND 2:00 DAILY
TOUR GROUPS, BUSES WELCOME

He tried the window, found it opened with surprising ease. A muggy flow of air came into the room, carrying with it the smell of dust and crops. The lace curtains bellied. Outside, the great sea of yellow corn stretched to the horizon, broken only by distant lines of trees along the bottomlands of Medicine Creek. A flock of crows rose out of the endless corn and fell back in, feasting on the ripe ears. Thunderheads piled up to the west. The silence was as unending as the landscape.

In the hallway at the bottom of the stairs, Winifred Kraus replaced the telephone in its cradle. Jenny Parker wasn't in. Perhaps she was in town, getting news. She'd try calling again after lunch.

She wondered if she should bring the nice man, Mr. Pendergast, a second glass of tea. Southerners were so well-bred; she believed they drank a lot of iced tea on big shady verandas and such. It was such a hot day and he'd walked from town. She went into the kitchen, poured a fresh glass, began mounting the stairs. But no—she should let him unpack, have his privacy. What was she thinking? News of the murder had her all in a tizzy.

She turned to descend the staircase. But then she stopped again. A voice had sounded from upstairs: Pendergast had said something. Was he speaking to her?

Winifred cocked her head, listening. For a moment, the house was still. Then Pendergast spoke again, and this time, she made out what he was saying.

"Excellent," came the dulcet voice. "Most excellent."

Six

The road was as straight as the nineteenth-century surveyor's original line of sight, and it was flanked by two unmoving walls of corn. Special Agent Pendergast walked down the shimmering road, his polished black oxfords—handmade by John Lobb of St. James's Street, London—leaving a row of faint impressions in the sticky asphalt.

Ahead, he could see where heavy vehicles had come in and out of the cornfield, leaving brown tracks and clots of dirt on the road. Approaching, he turned to make his way along the crude access road that had been bulldozed into the cornfield to the murder site. His feet sank into the powdery earth.

Where the access widened into a makeshift parking lot a state trooper cruiser sat, motor running, water dripping into the dirt from the AC. Yellow crime-scene tape blocked off the site, wound around tall stakes hammered into the earth. Inside the cruiser a trooper sat, reading a paperback.

Pendergast approached and rapped on the window. The man gave a start, then quickly recovered. Hastily putting the paperback aside, he got out and faced Pendergast, squinting in the hot sun, hooking his arms into his belt loops. A river of cool air flowed out.

"Who the hell are you?" he demanded. The trooper's arms were covered with fine red hair and the leather of his boots creaked as he moved.

Pendergast displayed his shield.

"Oh. FBI. Sorry." The trooper looked around. "Where's your car?"

"I'd like to take a look at the scene," Pendergast replied.

"Be my guest. There's nothing left, though. It's all been carted away."

"No matter. Please don't allow me to disturb you further."

"Quite all right, sir." The trooper, with no little relief, climbed back into his cruiser and closed the door.

Pendergast moved past the car and gingerly ducked beneath the yellow tape. He advanced the last twenty yards to the original clearing. Here he paused, surveying the site. As the trooper had said, it was empty: nothing but dirt, crushed corn stubble, and thousands of footprints. There was a stain in the very center of the clearing, not particularly large.

For several minutes, Pendergast remained motionless beneath the merciless sun. Only his eyes moved as they took in the clearing. Then he reached into his suit jacket and removed a photograph of the body in situ, from close up. Another photograph showed the overall site, the spitted birds and the forest of sticks. Pendergast rapidly reconstructed the original scene in his mind and held it there, examining it.

He remained motionless for a quarter of an hour. Then at last he returned the photographs to his jacket and took a step forward, examining the stub of a cornstalk that lay at his feet. It had been broken, not cut. Moving forward, he picked up a second stub, then a third and a fourth. All broken. Pendergast returned to the edge of the clearing, selected a cornstalk that still stood. He knelt down and grasped it at the bottom, but no matter how hard he tried, he could not break it.

He ventured farther into the clearing itself. It hardly mattered where he put his feet—it could not be more disturbed. He moved slowly, crouching now and then to examine something in the riot of corn and dust. Once in a while he would pick up something with a pair of tweezers he'd removed from a suit pocket, look at it, and release it. For almost an hour he moved across the clearing in this fashion, bent over in the baking sun.

He kept nothing.

At last, he reached the far end of the clearing and moved into the dense corn rows themselves. There had been a few pieces of torn fabric found clinging to some of the cornstalks, and it wasn't difficult to find the tags marking their locations.

Pendergast moved down the row, but there were so many footprints and dog prints that it was hopeless to try to follow anything. The report said that two different sets of bloodhounds had been put on the track but had refused to follow it.

He paused in the forest of corn to slip a tube of glossy paper from his pocket and unroll it. It was a photograph, taken at some unidentified point before the crime, showing the field from the air. The corn rows did not go in straight lines, as it seemed at ground level, but rather curved to follow the topography of the landscape, creating elliptical, mazelike paths. He located the row in which he stood and carefully traced its curve. Then, with difficulty, he forced his way into the next corn row, then the next. Once again he examined the aerial photograph, tracing the path of the current row. Much better: it went for a long distance across flat ground and then dropped down toward the bottomland near Medicine Creek, at a point where the creek looped back toward the town.

It was, in fact, the only row that actually opened onto the creek.

Pendergast walked down the row, heading away from the murder site. The heat had settled into the corn and, in the absence of wind, was baking everything into place. As the land gradually declined toward the creek, a monotonous landscape of corn revealed itself, stretching to an ever more remote horizon, oppressive in its landlocked vastness. The distant creek, with its clumps of scraggly, half-dead cottonwoods, only added to the sense of desolation. As Pendergast walked he would stop occasionally to examine a cornstalk or a piece of ground. Once in a while his tweezers would pluck something up, only to drop it again.

At long last, the corn row opened onto the bottomland along the creek. Where the cornstalks and field dirt gave way to sandy embankments, Pendergast stopped and glanced downward.

There were footprints, here in the firm sand: they were bare, and deeply impressed. Pendergast knelt, touched one print. It was from a size eleven foot. The killer had been carrying a heavy body.

Pendergast rose and followed the tracks to where they entered the creek. There were no corresponding tracks exiting on the far side. He walked up and down the creek, looking for a point of emergence, and found nothing.

The killer had walked for a long distance in the creek bed itself.

Pendergast returned to the corn row and began making his way back to the clearing. The town of Medicine Creek was like an island in a sea: it would be difficult to come or go without being seen. Everyone knew everybody and a hundred pairs of keen old eyes, staring from porches and windows, watched the comings and goings of cars. The only way an outsider could arrive at the town unseen was through this sea of corn—twenty miles from the next town.

His first instincts had been confirmed: the killer was probably among them, here, in Medicine Creek.

Seven

Harry Hoch, the second-best-performing farm equipment salesman in Cry County, rarely picked up hitchhikers anymore, but in this case he thought he'd make an exception. After all, the gentleman dressed in mourning was standing so sadly by the side of the road. Hoch's own mother had been taken just the year before and he knew what it was like.

He pulled his Ford Taurus into the gravel just beyond the man and gave a little toot. He lowered his window as the man strolled up.

"Where you headed, friend?" Hoch asked.

"To the hospital in Garden City, if it isn't too much trouble."

Harry winced. The poor guy. The county morgue was in the basement. Must've just happened. "No trouble at all. Get on in."

He cast a furtive glance as his passenger stepped into the car. With that pale skin, he was going to catch a wicked sunburn if he wasn't careful. And he sure wasn't from around these parts; not with that accent, he wasn't.

"My name's Hoch. Harry Hoch." He held out his hand.

A cool, dry hand slipped into his. "Delighted to make your acquaintance. My name is Pendergast."

Hoch waited for the first name, but it never came. He released the hand and reached over to crank up the AC. A frigid blast came from the vents. It was like hell out there. He put his car into gear and pressed the accelerator, shooting back onto the road and picking up speed.

"Hot enough for you, Pendergast?" said Hoch after a moment.

"To tell you the truth, Mr. Hoch, I find the heat agrees with me."

"Yeah, okay, but a hundred degrees with one hundred percent humidity?" Hoch laughed. "You could fry an egg right there on the hood of my car."

"I have no doubt of it."

There was a silence. *Strange fellow,* Hoch thought.

His passenger didn't seem inclined toward small talk, so Hoch just shut up and drove. The silver Taurus flew along the arrow-straight road at ninety, leaving a wake of swaying, trembling corn behind. One mile looked pretty much like the next and there were never any cops in this area. Harry liked to move fast on these lonely secondary roads. Besides, he felt good: he had just sold a Case 2388 Combine with a six-row corn head and chaff-spreader bin extension for $120,000. That was his third for the season and it had earned him a trip to San Diego for a weekend of booze and bumping uglies at the Del Mar Blu. Hot damn.

At one point the road widened briefly, and the car shot past a group of shabby ruined houses; a row of two-story brick buildings, gaunt and roofless; and a grain silo, its upper half listing over a weed-choked railroad siding.

"What is this?" Pendergast asked.

"Crater, Kansas. Or I should say, *was* Crater, Kansas. Used to be a regular town thirty years back. But it just dried up, like so many others. Always happens the same way, too. First, the school goes. Then the grocer's. Then you lose the farmers' supply. Last thing you lose is your zip code. No, that's not quite right: last to go is the saloon. It's happening all over Cry County. Yesterday, Crater. Tomorrow, DePew. The day after that, who knows? Maybe Medicine Creek."

"The sociology of a dying town must be rather complex," said Pendergast.

Hoch wasn't sure what Pendergast was getting at and didn't risk a reply.

In less than an hour, the grain elevators of Garden City began rising over the horizon like bulbous skyscrapers, the town itself low and flat and invisible.

"I'll drop you right off at the hospital, Mr. Pendergast," said Hoch. "And hey, I'm sorry about whoever it was that passed. I hope it wasn't an untimely death."

As the orange-brick hospital appeared, surrounded by a sea of shimmering cars, Pendergast replied, "Time is a storm in which we are all lost, Mr. Hoch."

It took Hoch another half an hour of fast driving, with the windows down, to get the creeps out of his system.

Sheriff Hazen, wearing a surgical smock that was two sizes too big and a paper hat that made him feel ridiculous, stood and looked down at the gurney. A toe tag was dangling from the right foot, but he didn't need to read it. Mrs. Sheila Swegg, twice divorced, no children, thirty-two years of age, of number 40A Whispering Meadows Trailer Estate, Bromide, Oklahoma.

White fucking trash.

There she was lying on the steel table, butterflied like a pork chop, organs neatly stacked beside her. The top of her head was off and her brain sat in a nearby pan. The smell of putrefaction was overwhelming: she'd been lying in that hot cornfield for a good twenty-four hours before he'd gotten there. The M.E., a bright, bushy-tailed young fellow named McHyde, was bent over her, cheerfully slicing and dicing away and talking up a storm of medical jargon into an over-hanging mike. Give him five more years, thought Hazen, and the biting acids of reality will strip off some of that cheerful polish.

McHyde had moved from her torso up to her throat and was cutting away with little zipping motions of his right hand. Some of the cuts made a crackling sound that Hazen did not like at all. He fished in his pocket for a cigarette, remembered the no smoking sign, grabbed a nearby jar of Mentholatum instead and dabbed some beneath each nostril, and focused his mind elsewhere: Jayne Mansfield in *The Girl Can't Help It,* polka night at the Deeper Elks Lodge, Sundays with a six-pack fishing at Hamilton Lake State Park. Anything but the remains of Sheila Swegg.

"Hmm," said the M.E. "Will you look at that."

As quickly as they had come, the pleasant thoughts went away. "What?" Hazen asked.

"As I suspected. Broken hyoid bone. Make that *shattered* hyoid bone. There were very faint bruises on her neck and this confirms it."

"Strangled?"

"Not exactly. Neck grasped and broken with a single twist. She died of a severed spinal column before she could strangle."

Cut, cut, cut.

"The force was tremendous. Look at this. The cricoid cartilage is completely separated from both the thyroid cartilage and the lamina. I've never seen anything like it. The tracheal rings are crushed. The cervical vertebrae are broken in, let me see, four places. *Five* places."

"I believe you, Doc," Hazen said, his eyes averted.

The doctor looked up, smiled. "First autopsy, eh?"

Hazen felt a swell of irritation. "Of course not," he lied.

"Hard to get used to, I know. Especially when they start to get a little ripe. Summertime's not good. Not good at all."

As the doctor returned to his work, Hazen became aware of a presence behind him. He turned and jumped: there was Pendergast, materialized out of nowhere.

The doctor looked up, surprised. "Sir? Excuse me, we're—"

"He's okay," said Hazen. "He's FBI, working on the case under me. Special Agent Pendergast."

"Special Agent Pendergast," the M.E. said, with a new edge to his voice, "would you mind identifying yourself for the tape recorder? And throw on some scrubs and a mask, if you don't mind. You can find them over there."

"Of course."

Hazen wondered how the hell Pendergast had managed it, without a car and all. But he wasn't sorry to see him. It occurred to Sheriff Hazen, not for the first time, that having Pendergast on the case could be useful. As long as the man kept with the program.

Pendergast returned a moment later, having expertly slid into the scrubs. The doctor was now working on the victim's face, peeling it away in thick rubbery flaps and clamping them back. It had been bad enough before, when just the nose, lips, and ears had been missing. Hazen stared at the bands of muscle, the white of the ligaments, the slender yellow lines of fat. God, it was gruesome.

"May I?" Pendergast asked.

The doctor stepped back and Pendergast leaned over, not three inches from the stinking, swollen, featureless face. He stared at the places, torn and bloody, where the nose and lips had once been. The scalp had been peeled back but Hazen could still see the bleached-blond hair with its black roots. Then Pendergast stepped back. "The amputations appear to have been performed with a crude implement."

The doctor raised his eyebrows. "A crude implement?"

"I would suggest a superficial microscopic examination with a comprehensive series of photos. And part of the scalp has been ripped off, as you no doubt have noted."

"Right. Good." The doctor sounded irritated at the advice.

Hazen had to smile. The Agent was showing up the Doc. But if Pendergast were right about this . . . He stopped himself from asking just what kind of "crude implement" Pendergast had in mind. He felt his gorge rising and immediately turned his mind back to Jayne Mansfield.

"Any sign of the lips, ears, and nose?" Pendergast asked.

"The police couldn't find them," said the M.E.

Hazen felt a surge of annoyance at this implied criticism. The M.E. had been at it all afternoon, making one snide comment after another about the shortcomings of Hazen's report and, by extension, his police work. Fact was, by the time he stepped in, the state police had already royally fucked it up.

The doctor resumed cutting away at the earthly remains of Sheila Swegg. Pendergast began to circle the table, looking first at one organ and then at another, hands behind his back, like he was viewing sculpture in a museum. He got to the toe tag.

"I see you have an ID."

"Yeah," said Hazen with a cough. "Some cracker from the Oklahoma panhandle. We found her car, one of those Korean rice-burners, hidden in the corn five miles the other side of Medicine Creek."

"Any idea what she was doing there?"

"We found a bunch of shovels and picks in the trunk. A relic hunter—they're always sneaking around the Mounds, digging for old Indian artifacts."

"This is a common occurrence, then?"

"Not around here so much, but yeah, some people make a living at it, driving from state to state looting old sites for stuff to sell at flea markets. Every mound, battleground, and boot hill from Dodge City to California's been hit by them. They got no shame."

"Does she have a record?"

"Petty shit. Credit card fraud, selling phony crap on eBay, nickel-and-dime insurance scams."

"You've made excellent progress, Sheriff."

Hazen nodded curtly.

"Well," said the doctor. "We're just about done here. Do either of you have any questions or special requests?"

"Yes," said Pendergast. "The birds and the arrows."

"In the fridge. You want to see them?"

"If you please."

The doctor disappeared and came back a moment later wheeling another gurney, on which the crows had been neatly laid out in rows, each with its own toe tag. *Or claw tag, maybe,* Hazen thought. Next to them was a pile of arrows on which the birds had been skewered.

Pendergast bent over them, reached out, paused. "May I?"

"Be my guest."

He picked up an arrow in a latex-gloved hand, turning it around slowly.

"You can pick those replicas up at almost any gas station between here and Denver," said McHyde.

Pendergast continued turning it in the light. Then he said, "This is no replica, Doctor. This is a genuine Southern Cheyenne cane arrow, feathered with a bald eagle primary and tipped with a type II Plains Cimarron point in Alibates chert. I'd date it between 1850 and 1870."

Hazen stared at Pendergast as he placed the arrow back down. "All of them?" he said.

"All of them. It was evidently a matched set. A collection of original arrows like this, in this superb condition, would fetch at least ten thousand dollars at Sotheby's."

In the ensuing silence, Pendergast picked up a bird and turned it gently around, palpating it. "Completely crushed, it seems."

"That right?" The doctor's voice had grown wary, irritated.

"Yes. Every bone broken. It's a sack of mush." He glanced up. "You are planning to necropsy the birds, are you not, Doctor?"

The doctor gave a snort. "All two dozen of them? We'll do one or two."

"I would strongly recommend doing them all."

The doctor stepped back from the gurney. "Agent Pendergast, I fail to see what purpose that would serve, except to waste my time and the taxpayers' money. As I said, we will do one or two."

Pendergast laid the bird back on the tray and picked up another, palpated it, and then another, before finally selecting one. Then, before the doctor could object, Pendergast plucked a scalpel from the surgical tray and made a long, deliberate stroke across the bird's underside.

The doctor found his voice. "Just a minute! You're not authorized—"

Hazen watched as Pendergast exposed the crow's stomach. The agent paused briefly, scalpel poised.

"Put that bird down this instant," said the doctor angrily.

With one swift stroke, Pendergast opened the bird's stomach. There, pushing out from among rotting kernels of corn, was a misshapen, pinkish thing that Hazen abruptly realized was a human nose. His stomach lurched again.

Pendergast laid the crow back down on the tray. "I will leave the finding of the lips and ears in your capable hands, Doctor," he said, pulling off the gloves, mask, and scrubs. "Please send a copy of your final report to me, care of Sheriff Hazen."

And he walked out of the room without a backward glance.

Eight

Smit Ludwig sat at the counter of Maisie's Diner, plate of cold meatloaf sitting barely touched in front of him, stirring his cup of coffee. It was six o'clock and he had a story due and he wasn't getting anywhere with it. Maybe, he thought, the story was too big. Maybe he wasn't up to it. Maybe, in all the years of writing about 4-H fairs and the occasional car accident, he'd lost the edge. Maybe he never had the edge to begin with.

He stirred and stirred.

Through the plate glass front of Maisie's, Ludwig could see the closed door of the sheriff's office across the street. God, how that pugnacious, butt-ignorant sheriff got under his skin. Ludwig hadn't been able to pry any information from him. And the state police had told him nothing either. He couldn't even get the M.E. on the phone. How the hell did they do it at the *New York Times?* No doubt because they were big and powerful, and not to talk to them was worse than talking to them.

He looked back down at his coffee. Problem was, nobody was scared of the *Cry County Courier.* It was more like a local joke. How could they respect him as a reporter when he came by the next day selling ad space, and came by again the day after at the wheel of the delivery truck because his driver, Pol Ketchum, had to take his wife to Dodge City for chemotherapy?

Here was the biggest story of his career and he had nothing for tomorrow's paper. Nothing. Course, he could always recycle what he had reported yesterday, work a new angle, hint about leads, play up the "no comments," and produce passable copy. But the savagery and strangeness of the crime had aroused sleepy Medicine Creek, and people wanted more. And a part of him wanted to rise to the occasion, to do well by the story. A part of him wanted—now that he finally had the chance—to be a real journalist.

He smiled at himself and shook his head. Here he was, wife passed away, daughter long gone to greener pastures on the West Coast, paper losing money, and him nearing sixty-five. *A real journalist.* It was a little late for that. What was he thinking?

Ludwig noticed that the low susurrus of conversation in the diner had suddenly faltered. Out of the corner of his eye he saw a black form hovering outside Maisie's. It was that FBI agent, examining the menu taped to the glass. Then the figure moved to the door and pushed it open. The little bell tinkled.

Smit Ludwig rotated slightly on his stool. Maybe all was not lost. Maybe he could get something out of the agent. It seemed unlikely, but it was worth a try. Even the tiniest crumb would do. Smit Ludwig could do wonders with a crumb.

The FBI man—what was his name?—slid into one of the banquettes and Maisie shoved off to get his order. There was no problem hearing Maisie—her booming voice carried into every corner of the diner—but he had to strain to hear the agent's soft replies.

"The blue plate special today," Maisie boomed out, "is meatloaf."

"Of course," the FBI man said. "Meatloaf."

"Yup. Meatloaf and white gravy, mashed garlic potatoes—homemade, not out of the box—and green beans on the side. Green beans have iron, and you could certainly use some iron." Ludwig had to suppress a smile. Maisie was already starting in on the poor stranger. If he didn't gain ten pounds by the time he left, it wouldn't be for lack of browbeating.

"I see you have pork and beans," the man said. "What type of legumes, precisely, do you employ?"

"Legumes? No legumes in *our* pork and beans! Only fresh ingredients. I start with the best red beans, toss in some fatback, molasses, spices, then I cook 'em overnight, with the heat on low as a whisper. The beans just melt in your mouth. One of our most popular dishes. Pork and beans, then?"

This was starting to become entertaining. Ludwig swiveled a bit farther to get a better view of the action.

"Fatback, my goodness, yes, how nice . . ." the agent repeated vaguely. "And the fried chicken?"

"Double-dipped in Maisie's special corn batter, deep fried to a golden crisp, smothered in white gravy. Goes great with our special sweet-potato fries."

The man looked from the menu to Maisie and back again, a strangely blank expression on his face. Then he spoke. "You must have access to high-quality Angus beef in these parts."

"We certainly do. I can cook a steak ten ways from

Sunday. Fried, chicken-fried, grilled, broiled or pot-roasted or broasted. With Velveeta steak fries and green goddess salad. Rare, medium, or well done. You tell me how you want it and if I can't do it, it don't exist."

"Would you happen to have a sirloin cut?" he inquired. The man had a silken, almost buttery voice that, Ludwig noticed, had at least half the diner listening raptly.

"You bet. Top sirloin, filet, New York strip, you name it, we got it."

There was a long silence. "You say you're willing to prepare steak in any fashion?"

"That's right. We take care of our customers." Maisie glanced over at Smit Ludwig. He smiled quickly. "Right, Smitty?"

"That's right, Maisie," he replied. "The meatloaf is heaven."

"Then you better get to work and finish it!"

Ludwig nodded, still grinning.

Maisie turned back at the FBI man. "You tell me how you like it, and I'll be glad to oblige."

"I wonder if you would be so kind as to bring me out a well-trimmed top sirloin of about six ounces for my inspection."

Maisie didn't bat an eye at this request. If the man wanted to see the steak before she cooked it, the man would see the steak before she cooked it. Ludwig watched her go in the back and return with a nice filet. The best, Ludwig knew, she would save for Tad Franklin, who she had a soft spot for.

She angled the plate under the man's nose. "There you are. And you won't find its equal until you get to Denver, I promise you that."

The man looked at the steak, then picked up his knife and fork and trimmed off the fat along one side. Then he handed the plate back to her. "I'd be grateful if you would run it through a meat grinder, set on medium."

Ludwig paused. Run a filet mignon through a meat grinder? How was Maisie going to react now? He practically held his breath.

Maisie was staring at the FBI agent. The diner had gone very still. "And how would you like your, er, hamburger cooked?"

"Raw."

"You mean very rare?"

"I mean raw, if you please. Please bring it back to me with an uncooked egg, in the shell, along with some finely chopped garlic and parsley."

Maisie swallowed visibly. "Sesame or plain bun?"

"No bun, thank you."

Maisie nodded, turned, and then—with a single backward glance—took the plate and disappeared into the kitchen. Ludwig watched her depart, waited a beat, and then made his move. Taking a deep breath, he picked up his coffee and strolled over, pausing in front of the FBI agent. The man looked up and fixed Ludwig with a long, cool gaze from a pair of extremely pale eyes.

Ludwig stuck out his hand. "Smit Ludwig. Editor of the *Cry County Courier.*"

"Mr. Ludwig," said the man, shaking the proffered hand. "My name is Pendergast. Do sit down. You were at the press conference early this morning. I must say you asked some rather insightful questions."

Ludwig flushed at the unexpected praise and eased his creaky and not exactly youthful frame into the banquette opposite.

Maisie reappeared in the swinging kitchen door. In one

hand, she carried a plate mounded with freshly ground sirloin, in the other, a second plate with the rest of the ingredients, and an egg in an egg cup. She set both plates before Pendergast.

"Anything else?" she asked. She looked stricken—and who wouldn't be, Ludwig thought, running a decent sirloin like that through a meat grinder?

"That will be all, thank you very much."

"We aim to please." Maisie attempted a smile, but Ludwig could see she was thoroughly defeated. This was something utterly foreign to her experience.

Ludwig—and the entire diner—watched as Pendergast sprinkled the garlic over the raw meat, added salt and pepper, cracked the raw egg on top, and carefully folded the ingredients together. Then he molded it with his fork into a pleasing mound, sprinkled parsley on top, and sat back to contemplate his work.

Suddenly, Ludwig understood. "Steak tartare?" he asked, nodding toward the plate.

"Yes, it is."

"I saw somebody make that on the Food Network. How is it?"

Pendergast delicately lifted a portion to his mouth, chewed with half-closed eyes. "All that is lacking is a '97 Léoville Poyferré."

"You really should try the meatloaf," Ludwig replied, lowering his voice. "Maisie has her strengths and weaknesses: the meatloaf is one of her strengths. It's damn good, in fact."

"I shall take it under consideration."

"Where are you from, Mr. Pendergast? Can't quite place the accent."

"New Orleans."

"What a coincidence! I went there for Mardi Gras once."

"How nice for you. I myself have never attended."

Ludwig paused, the smile frozen on his face, wondering how to steer the conversation onto a more pertinent topic. Around him, the low murmur of conversation had picked up once again.

"This killing's really shaken us up," he said, lowering his voice still further. "Nothing like this has ever happened in sleepy little Medicine Creek before."

"The case has its atypical aspects."

It appeared Pendergast wasn't biting. Ludwig knocked back his coffee cup, then raised it above his head. "Maisie! Another!"

Maisie came over with the pot and an extra cup. "You need to learn some manners, Smit Ludwig," she said, refilling his cup and pouring one for Pendergast as well. "You wouldn't yell for your mother that way."

Ludwig grinned. "Maisie's been teaching me manners these past twenty years."

"It's a lost cause," said Maisie, turning away.

Small talk had failed. Ludwig decided to try the direct approach. He removed a steno notebook from his pocket and placed it on the table. "Got time for a few questions?"

Pendergast paused, a forkful of raw meat halfway to his mouth. "Sheriff Hazen would prefer that I not speak to the press."

Ludwig lowered his voice. "I *need* something for tomorrow's paper. The townspeople are hurting. They're frightened. They've got a right to know. *Please.*"

He stopped, surprising even himself at the depth of feeling in his comments. The FBI agent's eyes held his own in a gaze that seemed to last for minutes. At last, Pendergast lowered his fork and spoke, in a voice even lower than Ludwig's own.

"In my opinion, the killer is local."

"What do you mean, local? From southwestern Kansas?"

"No. From Medicine Creek."

Ludwig felt the blood drain out of his face. It was impossible. He knew everyone in town. The FBI agent was dead wrong.

"What makes you say that?" he asked weakly.

Pendergast finished his meal and leaned back. He pushed his coffee away and picked up a menu. "How is the ice cream?" he asked, with a faint but distinct tone of hope in his voice.

Ludwig lowered his voice. "Niltona Brand Xtra-Creamy."

Pendergast shuddered. "The peach cobbler?"

"Out of a can."

"The shoo-fly pie?"

"Don't go there."

Pendergast laid down the menu.

Ludwig leaned forward. "Desserts are not Maisie's strong point. She's a meat and potatoes kind of gal."

"I see." Pendergast regarded him once again with his pale eyes. Then he spoke. "Medicine Creek is as isolated as an island in the wide Pacific. Nobody can come or go on the roads without being noticed, and it's a twenty-mile hike through the cornfields from Deeper, the nearest town with a motel." He paused, smiled faintly, then glanced at the steno book. "I see you're not taking notes."

Ludwig laughed nervously. "Give me something I can print. There's one unshakable article of faith in this town:

the killer and the victim are both 'from away.' We have our share of troublemakers, but believe me, no killers."

Pendergast looked at him with mild curiosity. "What, exactly, constitutes 'trouble' in Medicine Creek?"

Ludwig realized that if he wanted information, he was going to have to give some in return. Only there wasn't much to give. "Domestic violence, sometimes. Come Saturday night we get our share of drunken hooliganism, drag racing out on the Cry Road. Last year, a B-and-E down at the Gro-Bain plant, that sort of thing."

He paused. Pendergast seemed to be waiting for more.

"Kids sniffing aerosols, the occasional drug overdose. Plus, unwanted pregnancies have always been a problem."

Pendergast arched an eyebrow.

"Most of the time they settle it by getting married. In the old days the girl was sometimes sent away to have her baby and it was put up for adoption. You know how it is in a small town like this, not a lot for a young person to do except—" Ludwig smiled, remembering back to the days when he and his wife were in high school, Saturday night parking down by the creek, the windows all steamed up . . . It seemed so long ago, a world utterly gone. He shook off the memory. "Well," he said, "that's about all the trouble we ever get around here. Until now."

The FBI agent smiled and leaned forward, speaking so softly Ludwig could barely hear him. "The victim has been identified as Sheila Swegg, of Oklahoma. A petty criminal and con artist. They found her car hidden in the corn five miles out on the Cry Road. It seems she'd been digging up at some Indian mounds in the area."

Smit Ludwig looked at Pendergast. "Thank you," he said.

Now, this was much better. This was more than a crumb. It was practically a whole cake. He felt a surge of gratitude.

"And another thing. Arranged with the body they found a number of antique Southern Cheyenne arrows in almost perfect condition."

It seemed to Ludwig as though Pendergast was looking at him intently. "That's extraordinary," he replied.

"Yes."

They were interrupted by a sudden commotion outside, punctuated by a voice raised in shrill protest. Ludwig glanced across the street and saw Sheriff Hazen marching a teenage girl down the sidewalk, toward his office. The girl was protesting gamely, digging in her heels, lunging against her handcuffs, her black fingernails cutting the air. He knew immediately who she was; it was all too obvious from the black leather miniskirt, pale skin, spiked collar, Day-Glo purple hair, and the glint of body piercings. A shrieked phrase managed to penetrate the plate glass of Maisie's Diner—"eclair-eating, fart-biting, cancer-stick–smoking"—before the sheriff manhandled her through the door of the office and slammed it behind him.

Ludwig shook his head in amused disbelief.

"Who is she?" Pendergast asked.

"Corrie Swanson, our resident troublemaker. I believe she's what kids call a 'Goth' or something like that. She and Sheriff Hazen have a tiff going. Looks like he's finally got something on her, judging from the cuffs."

Pendergast laid a large bill on the table and rose, nodding to Maisie. "I trust we shall see each other again, Mr. Ludwig."

"Sure thing. And thanks for the tips."

The door jingled shut. Ludwig watched the dark form of Special Agent Pendergast as he passed by outside the window and moved down the dusky street until he merged with the falling darkness.

Ludwig slowly sipped his coffee, mulling over what Pendergast had said. And as he did so, the front-page story he'd been assembling in his head changed; he broke down the type, rewrote the opening paragraph. It was dynamite, especially the stuff about the arrows. As if the murder wasn't bad enough, those arrows would strike a particularly unpleasant note to anyone familiar with the history of Medicine Creek. As soon as he'd gotten the paragraph right, he rose from the table. He was over sixty and his joints ached from the humidity. But even if he wasn't the man he used to be, he could still stay up half the night, write a snappy lead with two scotches under his belt, slap together an impeccable set of mechanicals, and make deadline. And tonight, he had one hell of a story to write.

Nine

Winifred Kraus bustled about the old-fashioned kitchen, making toast, setting out a pitcher of orange juice, boiling her guest's egg, and making his pot of green tea. Her busyness was an effort to keep her mind off the horrible news she had read that morning in the *Cry County Courier*. Who could have done such a terrible thing? And the arrows they'd found with the body, surely that couldn't mean that . . . She shook the thoughts from her head with a little shiver. Despite the strange hours Special Agent Pendergast kept, she was very glad to have him under her roof.

The man was quite particular about his food and his tea, and Winifred had taken pains to make sure everything was perfect. She had even gotten out her mother's old lace tablecloth and had laid it, freshly ironed, on the breakfast table, along with a small vase of freshly cut marigolds to make everything as cheery as possible. Partly it was to cheer her own distressed state.

As she moved about the kitchen, Winifred felt her dread over the murder slowly supplanted by a sense of anticipation. Pendergast had asked to take the morning tour of the

Kaverns. Well, he hadn't asked exactly, but he'd seemed quite interested when she suggested it the night before. The last visitors tó the Kaverns had been over a month ago, two nice young Jehovah's Witnesses who took the tour and then had the kindness to spend most of the day chatting with her.

Precisely at eight she heard a light tread on the stair and Mr. Pendergast came gliding into view, dressed in the usual black suit.

"Good morning, Miss Kraus," he said.

As Winifred ushered him into the dining room and began serving breakfast, she felt quite breathless. Even as a girl, she'd loved the family business: the different people from all over the country, the parking lot full of big cars, the murmurs of awe and amazement during the tours. Helping out in the cave, doing tours, had been one way she'd tried to earn the approval of her father. And although things had changed completely with the building of the interstate up north, she'd never lost that feeling of excitement before a tour—even if it was a tour of one.

Breakfast finished, she left Pendergast with that morning's *Cry County Courier* and went on ahead to the Kaverns. She visited the Kaverns at least once a day even when there were no visitors, just to sweep up leaves and replace bulbs. She now did a swift check and found that all was in tip-top order. Then she went behind the counter of the gift shop and waited. At a few minutes to ten, Pendergast appeared. He purchased a ticket—two dollars—and she led him along the cement walkway, down into the cut in the earth, to the padlocked iron door. It was another scorcher of a day, and the cool air that flowed from the cave entrance was pleasantly enticing. She unlocked and removed the padlock, then turned and launched into her opening speech, which hadn't varied since her pa had taught it to her with a switch and ruler half a century before.

"Kraus's Kaverns," she began, "was discovered by my grandfather, Hiram Kraus, who came to Kansas from upstate New York in 1888 looking to start a new life. He was one of the original pioneers of Cry County, and homesteaded a hundred and sixty acres right here along Medicine Creek."

She paused and flushed pleasurably at the careful attentiveness of her audience.

"On June 5, 1901, while searching for a lost heifer, he came across the opening to a cave, almost completely hidden by scrub and brush. He came back with a lantern and axe, cut his way down the slope into the cave, and began exploring."

"Did he find the heifer?" Pendergast asked.

The question threw Winifred off. Nobody asked about the heifer.

"Why, yes, he did. The heifer had gotten into the cave and fallen into the Bottomless Pit. Unfortunately, she was dead."

"Thank you."

"Let's see." Winifred stood at the cave entrance, trying to pick up the thread once again. "Oh, yes. Right about this time the motorcar was making its debut on the American scene. The Cry Road started to see some motorcar traffic, mostly families on their way to California. It took Hiram Kraus a year to build the wooden walkways—the same ones we will walk on—and then he opened the cave to the public. Back then, admission was a nickel." She paused for the obligatory chuckle, grew a little flustered when none was forthcoming. "It was an immediate success. The gift shop soon followed, where visitors can buy rocks, minerals, and fossils, as well as handcrafts and needlepoint to benefit the church, all at a ten percent discount for those who have taken the Kaverns Tour. And now, if you will kindly step this way, we will enter the cave."

She pulled the iron door wide and motioned Pendergast to follow her. They descended a set of broad, worn stairs that had been built over a declivity leading into the bowels of the earth. Walls of limestone rose on both sides, arching over into a tunnel. Bare bulbs hung from the rocky ceiling. After a descent of about two hundred feet, the steps gave onto a wooden walkway, which angled around a sharp turn and entered the cavern proper.

Here, deep beneath the earth, the air smelled of water and wet stone. It was a smell that Winifred loved. There was no unpleasant undercurrent of mold or guano: no bats lived in Kraus's Kaverns. Ahead, the boardwalk snaked its way through a forest of stalagmites. More bulbs, placed between the stalagmites, threw grotesque shadows against the cavern walls. The roof of the cave rose into darkness. She proceeded to the center of the cavern, paused, and turned with her hands unfolded, just as her pa had taught her.

"We are now in the Krystal Kathedral, the first of the three great caverns in the cave system. These stalagmites are twenty feet high on average. The ceiling is almost ninety feet above our heads, and the cavern measures one hundred and twenty feet from side to side."

"Magnificent," said Pendergast.

Winifred beamed and went on to talk about the geology of the chalk beds of southwestern Kansas, and how the cave had formed from the slow percolation of water over millions of years. She ended with a recitation of the names Grandfather Hiram had given to the various stalagmites: "The

Seven Dwarves," "White Unicorn," "Santa's Beard," "Needle and Thread." Then she paused for questions.

"Has everyone in town been here?" Pendergast asked.

Again, the question brought Winifred up short. "Why, yes, I believe so. We don't charge the locals, of course. It would hardly do to profit from one's neighbors."

When no more questions were forthcoming, she turned and led the way through the forest of stalagmites and into a low, narrow passageway leading to the next cavern.

"Don't bump your head!" she warned Pendergast over her shoulder. She entered the second cavern, strode to the center, and turned with a sweep of her dress.

"We are now in the Giant's Library. My grandfather named it that because, if you look to your right, you will see how layers of travertine have built up over millions of years to form what looks like stacked books. And over on that side, the vertical pillars of limestone on the walls appear to be shelved books. And now—"

She stepped forward again. They were about to come to her favorite part, the Krystal Chimes. And then suddenly she realized: she had forgotten her little rubber hammer. She felt in the pocket where she kept it hidden, ready to bring it out to the surprise of the guests. It wasn't there. She must have left it back in the gift shop. And she'd forgotten the flashlight, as well, always brought along in case the electricity failed. Winifred felt mortified. Fifty years of giving tours and she had never once forgotten her little rubber hammer.

Pendergast was observing her intently. "Are you all right, Miss Kraus?"

"I forgot my rubber hammer to play the Krystal Chimes." She almost felt like crying.

Pendergast glanced around at the forest of stalactites. "I see. I imagine those resonate when tapped."

She nodded. "You can play Beethoven's 'Ode to Joy' on those stalactites. It's the highlight of the tour."

"How very intriguing. I shall have to return, then."

Winifred searched her mind for the continuation of the talk, but could find nothing. She began to feel a rising panic.

"There must be a great deal of history in this town," Pendergast said as he casually examined some gypsum feathers glinting in a pool of reflected light.

Winifred felt a glow of gratitude for this little rescue. "Oh yes, there is."

"And you must know most of it."

"I suppose I do know most everything," she said. She felt a little better. Now she had a second tour to look forward to, and she would never forget her rubber hammer again. That dreadful murder had upset her a great deal. More than she'd realized, perhaps.

Pendergast bent to examine another cluster of crystals. "There was a curious incident at Maisie's Diner last evening. The sheriff arrested a girl named Corrie Swanson."

"Oh, yes. She's a troublemaker from way back. Her father ran off, and the mother is the cocktail waitress at the Candlepin Castle." She leaned forward and spoke in a whisper. "I think she drinks. And . . . sees *men*."

"Ah!" said Pendergast.

Winifred was encouraged. "Yes. They say Corrie takes drugs. She'll leave Medicine Creek, like so many others, and good riddance. That's how it is nowadays, Mr. Pendergast: they grow up and leave, never to come back. Though there are some I could name that stick around who *ought* to leave. That Brushy Jim, for instance."

The FBI agent seemed to be intently examining a dripstone mound. It was nice to see someone so interested. "The sheriff seemed to be rather enthusiastic in making Miss Swanson's arrest."

"I shouldn't wonder. And yet that sheriff's a bully. That's what I think. And I'll say it to anyone. Just about the only person he's nice to is Tad Franklin, his deputy." She stopped, wondering if she had gone too far, but Mr. Pendergast was looking at her now, nodding sympathetically.

"And that son of his is also a bully. He thinks having a sheriff for a father gives him the right to do whatever he pleases. Terrorizes the high school, I hear."

"I see. And this Brushy Jim you mentioned?"

Winifred shook her head. "The most disreputable fellow you ever saw." She clucked disapprovingly. "Lives in a junkyard out on the Deeper Road. Claims to be descended from the lone survivor of the Medicine Creek Massacre. He was in Vietnam, you know, and it did something to the man. Turned his brain. You just won't see a lower specimen of humanity, Mr. Pendergast. Uses the Lord's name in vain. Drinks. Never sets foot in church."

"I saw a large banner being erected on the front lawn of the church last evening."

"That's for the fellow from Kansas State."

Pendergast looked at her. "I'm sorry?"

"He wants to plant a new cornfield here. Some kind of experiment. They've narrowed it down to two towns, us and Deeper. The decision's to be announced next Monday. The man from Kansas State's due to arrive today and the town is laying out the red carpet for him. Not that everybody's happy about it, of course."

"And why is that?"

"Something about the corn they want to test. It's been fiddled with somehow. I don't really understand it, to tell you the truth."

"Well, well," Pendergast said, and then held out his hand. "But here I am, interrupting the tour with questions."

Winifred remembered the thread. She bustled forward happily, leading Pendergast to the edge of a wide, dark hole from which even cooler air was rising. "And here is the Bottomless Pit. When Grandfather first arrived, he tossed a stone down and *he did not hear it land.*" She paused dramatically.

"How did he know the heifer was down there?" Pendergast asked.

She was thrown into a sudden panic. Once again, nobody had asked the question before.

"Why, I don't know," she said.

Pendergast smiled, waved his hand. "Do continue."

They passed on to the Infinity Pool, where Winifred was disappointed that he did not make a wish—the collecting of tossed coins had once been a profitable sideline. From the Pool, the walkway looped back to the Krystal Kathedral where they had begun. She finished her lecture, shook Pendergast's hand, and was surprised but pleased to find herself generously tipped. Then, slowly, she led the way back up the wooden stairs to the surface world. At the top, the heat struck her like a hammer. She paused again.

"As I mentioned, all tour members are allowed a ten percent discount from the gift shop on the day of their tour." She hustled back into the shop and was not disappointed when Pendergast followed.

"I should like to see the needlepoint," he said.

"Of course." She directed him to the display case, where

he spent a great deal of time poring over the work before choosing a beautiful cross-stitched pillowcase. Winifred was especially pleased because it was one she had done herself.

"My dear great-aunt Cornelia will adore this," Pendergast said as he paid for the pillowcase. "She's an invalid, you see, and can only take pleasure in small things."

Winifred smiled as she gift-wrapped the parcel. It was so nice having a gentleman like Mr. Pendergast around. And how thoughtful to think of his elderly relation. Winifred was sure Pendergast's great-aunt would love the pillowcase.

Ten

Corrie Swanson sat on the little folding bunk in the lone holding cell of the Medicine Creek jail, staring at the graffiti that covered the peeling walls. There was quite a lot of it, and despite the variety of inks and handwritings it was remarkably consistent in subject matter. She could hear the television set blaring in the sheriff's office up front. It was one of those sick soap operas for housewives with empty lives, complete with quavering organ music and hysterical female sobbing. And she could hear the sheriff moving noisily around the office in his clown shoes, restlessly, like a ferret in a cage, rustling paper and making phone calls. How could such a short man have such big feet? And smoking, too—the place stank. Four more hours and her mom would be sober enough to come down and get her. So here she was, being "taught a lesson"—her mother's words—listening to the comings and goings of the world's most ratlike human being. Some lesson. Well, it wasn't any worse than sitting at home, listening to her mother's nagging or drunken snoring. And the folding bunk was at least as comfortable as the broken-down mattress in her own bedroom.

She heard a door slam in the outer office, footsteps, muffled greetings. Corrie recognized one of the voices. It was Brad Hazen, the sheriff's son and her classmate, with his jock friends. They said something about going into the back to check out the TV.

Quickly, she lay down on the bunk and turned her face to the wall.

She heard them moving around the inner office. One of them started changing the television channels, finger held to the button as it clicked through one raspy channel after another: game shows, soaps, cartoons, all divided by loud blasts of white noise.

Search unsuccessful, the shuffling of footsteps and grunted comments began again. Corrie heard them pass the open doorway to the back room, where her cell was located. There was a sudden pause and then Brad spoke in a low undertone. "Hey guys, check out who's here. Well, well, well."

She heard them shuffling through the doorway, snickering and whispering. There were at least two of them, maybe three. No doubt Chad was one of them, and probably Biff, too. Brad, Chad, and Biff. The fucking Hardy Boys.

Someone made a low farting sound with his lips. There was suppressed laughter.

"What's that smell?" It was Brad again. "Somebody step in it?"

More low laughter. "What'd you do this time?"

Corrie spoke without turning around. "Your Deputy Dawg John Q. Ratface left his car running, keys in the ignition, windows down, for half an hour in front of the Wagon Wheel while he refueled on eclairs. How could I resist?"

"My what?"

"Your Ripley's Believe It or Not amazing chain-smoking eclair-to-shit converting dad."

"What the hell are you talking about?" The voice was rising.

"Your *father*, dork."

Muffled laughter from his two friends.

"What a twat," Brad said. "At least I've *got* a father. Which is more than I can say for you. And you don't exactly have much of a mother, either." He cackled and someone— Chad, probably—made another disgusting sound with his mouth.

"The town slut. She was in this cell just last month, wasn't she, on a drunk and disorderly. Like mother, like daughter. Guess the apple never falls far from the tree. Or in your case, the shit never falls far from the asshole."

There was another burst of smothered laughter. Corrie lay still, facing the wall.

Brad resumed his whisper. "Hey, did you read the paper today? Says the murderer might be local. Maybe a devil worshiper. You fit the bill, with that fucked-up purple hair and black eye makeup. Is that what you do at night? Go out and do mumbo-jumbo?"

"That's right, Brad," said Corrie, still not turning around. "At the dark of each moon, I bathe in the blood of a new-born lamb and recite the Curse of the Nine Gates, and then I summon Lucifer to wither your dick. If you have one."

This brought forth another muffled snicker from Brad's friends, but Brad didn't join in.

"Bitch," Brad muttered. He advanced a step and lowered his voice still further. "Look at you. You think you're so cool, all dressed in black. Well, you're *not* cool. You're a loser. And I'll bet for once you're not lying. I'll bet you *do*

go out at night for a little animal killing. Or better yet, animal fucking." He gave a low chuckle. "Because no *man* would ever want to screw you, you freak."

"If I see any *men* around here I'll let you know," Corrie replied.

She heard the door into the back room open and a sudden silence fell. The sheriff spoke, his voice low, calm, and full of menace.

"Brad? Just what do you think you're doing?"

"Oh, hi, Dad. We were just talking to Corrie here, that's all."

"Is that so?"

"Right."

"Don't bullshit me. I know exactly what you were doing."

There was a tense silence.

"You harass a prisoner of mine again and I'll book you and lock you up myself. You hear me?"

"Yes, Dad."

"Now get the hell out, you and your friends. You're late for scrimmage."

There was the sound of guilty shuffling as Brad and his friends left the cellblock. "You all right, Swanson?" the sheriff asked gruffly.

Corrie ignored the question. Soon the door closed and she lay there, alone once again, listening to the sounds of the television and the voices in the outer office. She tried to keep her breathing normal, tried to forget what Brad had said. One more year and she was out of this loser town, this butt-crack capital of Kansas. One more year. Then it was goodbye, Medicine Shit Creek. It occurred to her, for the millionth time, that if she hadn't blown it in tenth grade she'd already be out of here. And now she had done it to herself again. Well, no use thinking about that.

The door to the outer office tinkled again. Someone new had come in. A conversation began in the outer office. Was it Tad, the deputy? Or her mother, sober for once? But no—the new arrival, whoever it was, spoke so softly that Corrie couldn't tell if it was a man or a woman. The sheriff's voice, on the other hand, took on a hard edge, but Corrie couldn't make out the words over the blaring of the television set.

Eventually, she heard footsteps enter the back room.

"Swanson?"

It was the sheriff. She heard him draw heavily on his cigarette and smelled the fresh smoke. There was a rattle of keys, a click as her cell was unlocked. The rusty iron door creaked as it opened.

"You're out of here."

She didn't move. Hazen's voice sounded particularly thick. Something had made him mad.

"Someone just made your bail."

Still she didn't move. And the other voice spoke. It was low and soft, with an unfamiliar accent.

"Miss Swanson? You are free to leave."

"Who are you?" she asked without turning around. "Did Mom send you?"

"No. I am Special Agent Pendergast of the FBI."

God. It was that creepy-looking man in the undertaker's getup she'd seen walking around town.

"I don't need your help," she said.

His voice still heavy with annoyance, Hazen said to Pendergast, "Maybe you should've saved your money and stayed out of local law enforcement business."

But Corrie had grown curious despite herself. After a moment, she asked, "What's the catch?"

"We'll speak about it outside," said Pendergast.

"So there *is* a catch. I can just imagine what it is, you pervert."

Sheriff Hazen issued a burst of laughter that degenerated into a smoker's hack. "Pendergast, what'd I tell you?"

Corrie remained curled on the folding bed. She wondered why this Pendergast was offering to bail her out. It was clear that Hazen didn't particularly like Pendergast. She remembered a phrase: the enemy of your enemy is your friend. She sat up and looked around. There he was, the undertaker, arms folded, looking at her pensively. The little bulldog Hazen stood next to him, arms squared, scalp glistening under the thinning crew cut, razor rash on his face.

"So I can just get up and walk out of here?" she asked.

"If that's what you want," Pendergast replied.

She got up, brushed past the FBI agent, past the sheriff, and headed toward the door.

"Don't forget your car keys," called Hazen.

She paused in the door, turned, held out her hand. The sheriff was standing there, dangling them in his hand. He made no move to give them to her. She took a step forward and snatched them.

"Your car's out back in the lot," he said. "You can settle up the seventy-five-dollar towing fee later."

Corrie opened the door and went outside. After the air-conditioned jail it felt like walking into hot soup. Blinking against the glare, she made her way around the corner and down the alley to the little parking lot behind the sheriff's office. There was her Gremlin, and there, leaning against it, was the pervert in the black suit. As she approached, he stepped forward and opened the door for her. She got in without a word and slammed the door behind her. Slipping the key into the ignition, she cranked the engine, and after turning over a few times it coughed into life, laying down a huge cloud of oily smoke. The man in black stepped away. She waited a moment, then leaned out the window.

"Thanks," she said grudgingly.

"It was my pleasure."

She pressed the accelerator and the car stalled. *Shit.*

She restarted it, revved a few times. More smoke poured out. The FBI man was still there. What the hell did he want? She had to admit, he didn't really look like a pervert. Curiosity finally got the better of her and she leaned out the window once again.

"All right, Mr. Special Agent. What's the catch?"

"I'll tell you while you give me a lift back to Winifred Kraus's place. That's where I'm staying."

Corrie Swanson hesitated, then opened the door. "Get in." She swept a heap of McDonald's trash off the passenger seat onto the floor. "I hope you're not going to do something stupid."

The FBI agent smiled and slid in beside her as smoothly as a cat. "You can trust me, Miss Swanson. Can I trust you?"

She looked at him. "No."

She popped the clutch and peeled out of the parking lot, leaving behind a pall of oilsmoke and a nice ten-inch pair of tire marks on the sheriff's asphalt. As she careened out of the alley and slewed onto the street, she was gratified to see the stumpy little sheriff tumble angrily out the door and start to shout something just as her black contrail obliterated him from view.

Eleven

The commercial district of Medicine Creek, Kansas, consisted of three dun-colored blocks of brick and wooden shopfronts. It took Corrie three, perhaps four heartbeats to reach its edge. As she jammed on the accelerator, the rusted frame of the Gremlin began to shake. There was a pile of some three dozen tapes littering the space between the front seats: her favorite death metal, dark ambient, industrial, and grindcore music. She riffled through them with one hand, passing over Discharge, Shinjuku Thief, and Fleshcrawl before finally selecting Lustmord. The dislocated, eldritch sounds of "Heresy, Part I" began to fill the small car. Her mother refused to let her play her music out loud in the house, so she'd retrofitted a tape player to the old Gremlin.

Speaking of her dear, nurturing parent, it was going to be a bitch going home. By now, her mother would be half drunk, half hungover—the worst combination. She decided she'd drop this Pendergast guy off at the old Kraus place, then go park under the powerlines and kill a few hours with a book.

She glanced over at the FBI man. "So, what's with the black suit? Somebody die?"

"Like you, I'm rather partial to the color."

She snorted. "What's this catch you were talking about?"

"I need a car and driver."

Corrie had to laugh. "What, me and my stretch AMC Gremlin?"

"I came by bus and I'm finding it rather inconvenient to be on foot."

"You've got to be kidding. The muffler is shot, the thing goes through a quart of oil a week, there's no AC, and the interior is so full of fumes I've got to keep the windows open, even in winter."

"I propose compensation of a hundred dollars a day for the car and driver, plus a standard rate of thirty-one cents per mile for fuel and depreciation."

A hundred bucks was more money than Corrie had ever seen at one time. This couldn't be happening, it had to be some kind of bullshit. "If you're a hotshot FBI special agent, where's your own car and driver?"

"Since I'm technically on vacation, I haven't been issued a car."

"Yeah, but why me?"

"Quite simple. I need someone who knows Medicine Creek, who has a car, and has nothing better to do. You fit the bill. You're no longer a minor, correct?"

"Just turned eighteen. But I've got another year of high school. And then I'm out of this Kansas shithole."

"I hope to have concluded my work here long before school begins next month. The important thing is, you *do* know Medicine Creek—don't you?"

She laughed. "If hating is knowing. Have you thought about what the sheriff's going to think about this arrangement?"

"I expect he'll be glad you found gainful employment."

Corrie shook her head. "You don't know much, do you?"

"That lack of knowledge is what I hope to rectify. Leave me to deal with the sheriff. Now, do we have a deal, Miss Swanson?"

"A hundred bucks a day? Of course we have a deal. And please, do I look like a 'Miss Swanson' to you? Call me Corrie."

"I shall call you Miss Swanson and you shall call me Special Agent Pendergast."

She rolled her eyes and swept purple hair out of her face. "Okay, *Special Agent* Pendergast."

"Thank you, Miss Swanson."

The man slid a wallet out of his suit coat and removed 5 hundred-dollar bills. She could hardly take her eyes off the money as he casually unwired her broken glove compartment, placed the bills inside, and wired it back up. "Keep a written record of your mileage. Any overtime beyond eight hours daily will be paid at twenty dollars an hour. The five hundred dollars is your first week's pay in advance."

He pulled something else out of his suit coat. "And here is your cell phone. Keep it turned on at all times, even when charging at night. Do not make or receive personal calls."

"Who am I gonna call in Shit Creek?"

"I haven't the faintest idea. And now, if you'd be so kind as to turn the car around and give me a tour of the town?"

"Here goes." Corrie glanced in her rearview mirror to make sure the coast was clear. Then she swung the wheel around violently, braking and accelerating at the same time. The Gremlin slewed around in a one-eighty, tires squealing, and ended up pointed back in the direction of town. She turned to Pendergast and grinned. "I learned *that* playing *Grand Theft Auto* on the computers at school."

"Very impressive. However, I must insist on one thing, Miss Swanson."

"What's that?" she said, accelerating back toward town.

"You must not break the law in my employ. All traffic rules must be strictly obeyed."

"Okay, *okay.*"

"The speed limit on this road is forty-five, I believe. And you have not buckled your seatbelt."

Corrie glanced down and saw she was going fifty. She eased down to the correct speed, then slowed even further as they entered the outskirts of town. She tried to fish the seatbelt out from behind the seat, the car swerving back and forth as she drove with her knee.

"Perhaps it would be more convenient if you pulled off to the side of the road to do that?"

Corrie gave an irritated sigh and pulled off, retrieved the belt, and buckled herself in. She started up again with another screech of rubber.

Pendergast settled back. The passenger seat was broken, and he reclined into a semi-supine position, his head just barely at the level of the window. "The tour, Miss Swanson?" he murmured, eyes half closed.

"Tour? I thought you were kidding."

"I am anxious to see the sights."

"You must be on drugs. The only sights around here are fat people, ugly buildings, and corn."

"Tell me about them."

Corrie grinned. "Okay, sure. We're now approaching the lovely hamlet of Medicine Creek, Kansas, population three hundred and twenty-five and dropping like a stone."

"Why is that?"

"Are you kidding? Only a dipshit would stay in a town like this."

There was a pause.

"Miss Swanson?"

"What?"

"I can see that an insufficient, or perhaps even defective, socialization process has led you to believe that four-letter words add power to language."

It took Corrie a moment to parse what Pendergast had said. " 'Dipshit' isn't a four-letter word."

"That depends on whether you hyphenate it or not."

"Shakespeare, Chaucer, and Joyce all used four-letter words."

"I see I am dealing with a quasi-literate. It is also true that Shakespeare wrote:

> *In such a night as this,*
> *When the sweet wind did gently kiss the trees*
> *And they did make no noise, in such a night*
> *Troilus methinks mounted the Troyan walls,*
> *And sighed his soul toward the Grecian tents,*
> *Where Cressid lay."*

Corrie looked at the man reclining in the seat beside her, his eyes still half closed. He was seriously weird.

"Now, may we continue with the tour?"

Corrie glanced around. The cornfields were reappearing on both sides of the road. "Tour's over. We've already passed through town."

There was no immediate response from Pendergast, and

for a moment Corrie worried that his offer would be rescinded and all that money in the glove compartment would vanish back into the black suit. "I could always show you the Mounds," she added.

"The Mounds?"

"The Indian Mounds down by the creek. They're the only thing of interest in the whole county. Somebody must've told you about them, the 'curse of the Forty-Fives' and all that bullshit."

Pendergast seemed to think about this for a moment. "Perhaps later we will see the Mounds. For the present, please turn around and pass through town once again, as slowly as possible. I wouldn't want to miss a thing."

"I don't think I'd better do that."

"Why not?"

"The sheriff won't like it. He doesn't like cruising."

Pendergast closed his eyes completely. "Didn't I say I would concern myself with the sheriff?"

"Okay, you're the boss."

She pulled to the side of the road, made a nice three-point turn, and headed back through town at a crawl. "On your left," she said, "is the Wagon Wheel Tavern, run by Swede Cahill. He's a decent guy, not too smart. His daughter is in my class, a real Barbie. It's mostly a drinking establishment, not much food to speak of except Slim Jims, peanuts, the Giant Pickle Barrel—and, oh, yeah, chocolate eclairs. Believe it or not, they're famous for their chocolate eclairs."

Pendergast lay motionless.

"See that lady, walking down the sidewalk with the Bride of Frankenstein hairdo? That's Klick Rasmussen, wife of Melton Rasmussen, who owns our local dry goods store. She's coming back from lunch at the Castle Club, and in that bag are the remains of a roast beef sandwich for her dog, Peach. She won't eat at Maisie's on account of Maisie being her husband's girlfriend before they got married about three hundred years ago. If only she knew what Melton gets up to with the gym teacher's wife."

Pendergast said nothing.

"And that dried-up old bag coming out of the Coast to Coast with a rolling pin is Mrs. Bender Lang, whose father died when their house was burned down by an arsonist thirty years ago. They never found out who did it, or why." Corrie shook her head. "Some think old Gregory Flatt did it. He was the town drunk and kind of nuts, and one day he just sort of wandered off into the corn and disappeared. Never found his body. He used to talk about UFOs all the time. Personally, I think he finally got his wish and was abducted. The night he disappeared there were some strange lights in the north." She laughed derisively. "Medicine Creek is an all-American town, and everybody's got a skeleton in his closet. Or *her* closet."

This, at least, roused Pendergast, who half opened his eyes to look at her.

"Oh, yes. Even that dippy old lady whose house you're staying in, Winifred Kraus. She may act pious, but it's all a crock. Her father was a rum-runner and moonshiner. Bible-thumper, too, on top of that. But that isn't all. I heard that when old Winifred was a teenager, she was known as the town vamp."

Pendergast blinked.

Corrie snickered, rolled her eyes. "Yeah, there's a lot of that going on in Medicine Creek. Like Vera Estrem, who's doing the wild thing with the Deeper butcher. If her husband ever finds out, there's going to be blood. Dale Estrem's the head of the Farmer's Co-op and he's the meanest man in Medicine Creek. His grandfather was a German immigrant and during World War II he went back to fight for the Nazis. You can imagine what the town thought of that. The grandfather never returned. Screwed the whole family, basically."

"Indeed."

"We've got our share of nutcases, too. Like that tinker who comes through here once a year and camps out in the corn somewhere. Or Brushy Jim, who did one tour too many in Vietnam. They say he fragged his lieutenant. Everybody's just waiting for him to 'go postal' one of these days."

Pendergast had lain back in the seat again. He looked asleep.

"Anyway. There's the Rexall Drug. That empty building is where the Music Shop used to be. There's Calvary Lutheran Church. It's Missouri Synod. The pastor is John Wilbur. A fossilized specimen if ever there was one."

There was no response from Pendergast.

"We are now passing Ernie's Exxon. Don't get your car fixed there. That's Ernie himself at the pump. His son's the biggest pothead in Cry County and old Ernie doesn't have a clue. And that old wooden building is Rasmussen's, the dry goods store I told you about. Their motto is, 'If you can't find it here, you don't need it there.' I've always wondered where 'there' was. There's the sheriff's office on the left, but I hardly need to point *that* place out. And there's Maisie's on the right. Her meatloaf is just edible. Her desserts would give a hyena the runs. Uh-oh, I knew it. Here he comes."

Corrie watched in the rearview mirror as the sheriff's cruiser pulled out of the alleyway, lights flashing.

"Hey," she said to the motionless Pendergast. "Wake up. I'm getting pulled over."

But Pendergast seemed sound asleep.

The sheriff came right up behind her and gave his siren a crank. "Please pull off to the side of the road," his voice rasped through the loudspeaker atop the car. "Remain inside your vehicle."

It was the same thing that had happened to her at least ten times before, only this time Corrie had Pendergast in the car. She realized the sheriff probably hadn't seen him, he was sunk so low in the seat. His eyes remained closed even through the siren and the noise. Maybe, she thought, he was dead. He certainly looked dead.

The door of the cruiser flung open and the sheriff came sauntering up, billy club flapping at his side. He placed his meaty palms on the open passenger window and leaned in. When he saw Pendergast, he jerked back abruptly. "Jesus!" he said.

Pendergast opened one eye. "Problem, Sheriff?"

Corrie enjoyed the look that came over the sheriff's face. His entire face flamed red, from the fuzz-covered folds of skin piled up against his collar to the tops of his hair-clogged ears. She hoped Brad would age just like his father.

"Well, Agent Pendergast," Hazen said, "it's just that we don't allow cruising back and forth through town. This is the third time she's been through."

The sheriff paused, obviously awaiting some kind of explanation, but after a long silence it became clear he wasn't going to get any.

At length, Hazen pushed himself away from the car. "You may go on your way," he said.

"Since you've taken an interest in our movements," said

Pendergast in his lazy drawl, "I should inform you that we'll be driving through town again, and perhaps even a fifth time, while Miss Swanson shows me the sights. After all, I *am* on vacation."

As Corrie looked at the darkening expression on Sheriff Hazen's face, she wondered if this so-called Special Agent Pendergast really knew what he was doing. It was no joke making an enemy like Hazen in a town like Medicine Creek. She'd been stupid enough to do it herself.

"Thank you for your concern, Sheriff." Pendergast turned to her. "Shall we go, Miss Swanson?"

She hesitated a moment, looking at Sheriff Hazen. Then she shrugged. *What the hell,* she thought as she accelerated from the curb with a little screech and a fresh cloud of black smoke.

Twelve

The sun was settling into a bloody patch of cloud along the horizon as Special Agent Pendergast exited Maisie's Diner, accompanied by a slender man in a Federal Express uniform.

"They told me I'd find you in there," the man said. "Didn't mean to interrupt your dinner."

"Quite all right," Pendergast replied. "I wasn't especially hungry."

"If you'll sign for it now, I'll leave everything by the back door."

Pendergast signed the proffered form. "Miss Kraus will show you where to put it all. Would you mind if I take a look?"

"Help yourself. Takes up half the truck."

The shiny FedEx truck was parked outside the diner, looking out of place on the dusty, monochromatic street. Pendergast peered into its interior. Along one wall were perhaps a dozen large boxes. Some had labels reading PERISHABLE—CONTENTS PACKED IN ICE.

"They're all from New York," the driver said. "Starting a restaurant or something?"

"It's my deliverance from Maisie."

"I'm sorry?"

"Everything seems to be in order, thank you."

Pendergast stepped back and watched the truck glide off into the soupy evening. Then he began strolling east, away from the dying glow of the horizon. Within five minutes, he had left the town of Medicine Creek behind. The road stretched ahead like a dark faultline in the corn.

He quickened his pace. His errand was a vague one, an intuition more than a certainty. Intuition, Pendergast knew, was the end result of the most sophisticated kind of reasoning.

Twilight and crows rose from the fields, and the smell of cornstalks and earth drifted on the air. Headlights appeared, grew larger, and then a huge semi-trailer came shuddering past, leaving dust and diesel in its wake.

Two miles out of town, Pendergast stopped. A dirt track ran away from the road here, angling off to the left between walls of corn. Pendergast followed it, moving with long silent strides. The track began to rise more sharply, heading for a dark cluster of trees on the horizon, surrounding three dark low outlines framed against the dusky sky: the Mounds. Leaving the corn behind, the track turned into a trail. Ahead were the trees, giant cottonwoods with massive trunks, bark as rough as fractured stone. Broken limbs lay scattered on the ground, clawlike branches upturned.

As he entered the shadowy confines of the grove, Pendergast paused to look back. The land fell away in a long, gentle declivity toward the town. The distant streetlights formed a glowing cross in the sea of dark corn. The Gro-Bain plant lay south of town, a low cluster of lights all by itself. The creek lay between them, a meandering line of cottonwoods that snaked through the landscape of corn. As flat as the land looked at first sight, it had its gentle undulations, its rises and its bottomlands. The point on which he stood was the highest for many miles.

The summer darkness had fallen heavily on the land. If anything, the air had grown muggier. A few bright planets glowed in the dying sky.

Pendergast turned and walked deeper into the darkness of the grove, becoming virtually invisible in his black suit. He followed a trail that wandered uncertainly through rabbit-brush and oak scrub. After another quarter mile, Pendergast stopped again.

The Mounds were just ahead.

There were three of them, low and broad, arranged in a triangle, rising twenty feet above the surrounding land. The flanks of two of the mounds had worn away, exposing lime-stone ledges and heavy boulders underneath. The cotton-wood trees were thicker here and the shadows were very deep.

Pendergast listened to the sounds of the August night. A chorus of insects trilled furiously. Blinking fireflies drifted among the silent trunks, their streaked lights mingling with the distant heat lightning that flickered to the north. A cres-cent moon hung just above the horizon, both horns pointed upward.

Pendergast remained motionless. The night sky was now blossoming with stars. He began to hear other sounds: the rustlings and scratchings of small animals, the flutterings of birds. A pair of close-set eyes glowed briefly in the dark. Down by the creek a coyote howled, and at the very edge of hearing, from the direction of the town, a dog barked a reply. The sliver of moon cast just enough light to see by.

Night crickets began to chirrup, first one, then others, the sounds rising from the tall grass.

At last, Pendergast moved forward, toward the three dark mounds. He walked slowly and silently, his foot crackling a single leaf. The crickets fell silent. Pendergast waited until, one by one, they resumed their calls. Then he moved on until he reached the base of the first mound. Here he knelt silently, brushed aside the dead leaves, and dug his hand into the soil. He removed a fistful, rolled it between his hands, and inhaled.

Different soils had distinctive smells. This, he confirmed, was the same soil as that found on the tools in the back of Swegg's car. The sheriff had been right: she had been digging for relics in the Mounds. He pinched some earth into a small glass test tube, stoppered it, and slid it into the pocket of his suit jacket.

Pendergast rose again. The moon had disappeared below the horizon. The fireflies had stopped blinking; the heat lightning grew less frequent, then ceased altogether. A profound darkness slowly enveloped the Mounds.

Pendergast moved past the first mound, then the second, until he stood at their center, three dark swellings growing gradually indistinguishable. Now the darkness was complete.

Still, Pendergast waited. A half hour passed. An hour.

And then, suddenly, the crickets fell silent.

Pendergast waited for them to start their chorus again. His muscles gathered, tensing. He could feel a presence in the dark to his right: a presence of great stealth. It was moving very silently—too silently even for his highly sensitive ears. But the crickets could feel vibrations in the ground that humans could not. The crickets knew.

He waited, tensed, until the presence was no more than five feet away. It had stopped. It, too, was waiting.

One by one the crickets resumed their chirruping. But Pendergast wasn't fooled. The presence was still there. Waiting.

And now, the presence moved again. Ever so slowly, it was coming closer. One step, two steps, until it was close enough to touch.

In a single movement, Pendergast dropped to one side while pulling his flashlight and gun and aiming both toward the figure. The beam of the light illuminated a wild-looking man crouching in the dirt, a double-barreled shotgun pointing to the spot where Pendergast had been standing a moment before. The gun went off with a great roar and the man staggered back, shrieking unintelligibly, and in that instant Pendergast was on top of him. Another moment and the shotgun was on the ground and the man was doubled over, held in a hammerlock, Pendergast's gun pressed against his temple. He struggled a moment, then went limp.

Pendergast loosened his grip and the man fell to the ground. He lay there, an extraordinary figure dressed in buckskin rags, a string of bloody squirrels slung around his shoulder. A giant handmade knife was tucked into his belt. His feet were bare, the soles broad and dirty. Two very small eyes were pushed like raisins into a face so wrinkled it seemed to belong to a man beyond time itself. And yet his physique, his glossy and extraordinarily long black hair and beard, told of a robust individual no more than fifty years of age.

"It is inadvisable to fire a gun in haste," said Pendergast, standing over the man. "You could have hurt someone."

"Who the hell are you?" the man shrilled from the ground.

"The very question I was going to ask you."

The man swallowed, recovering slightly, and sat up. "Get your goddamned light out of my face."

Pendergast lowered the light.

"Now who the deuce do you think you are, scaring decent people half to death?"

"We have yet to establish decency," said Pendergast. "Pray rise and identify yourself."

"Mister, you can pray all you like and it don't mean shit." He rose to his feet anyway, brushing the leaves and twigs out of his beard and hair. Then he hawked up an enormous gob of phlegm and shot it into the darkness. He wiped his beard and mouth with a filthy hand, front and back, and spat again.

Pendergast removed his shield and passed it before the man's face.

The man's eyes widened, then narrowed again. He laughed. "FBI? Never would've guessed it."

"Special Agent Pendergast." He closed the leather case with a snap and it disappeared into his jacket.

"I don't talk to FBI."

"Before you make any more rash declarations which will cause you to lose face later, you should know you have a choice. You can have an informal chat with me here . . ." He paused.

"Or?"

Pendergast smiled suddenly, his thin lips stretching to expose a row of perfect white teeth. But the effect, in the glow of the flashlight, was anything but friendly.

The man removed a twisted chaw from his pocket,

screwed a piece off, and packed it into his cheek. "Shit," he said, and spat.

"May I ask your name?" Pendergast asked.

The silence stretched on for a minute, then two.

"Hell," the man said at last. "I guess having a name's no crime, is it? Gasparilla. Lonny Gasparilla. Can I have my gun back now?"

"We shall see." Pendergast bobbed the beam of his light toward the bloody squirrels. "Is that what you were doing up here? Hunting?"

"I ain't hanging around the Mounds for the view."

"Do you have a residence nearby, Mr. Gasparilla?"

The man barked a laugh. "That's a funny one." Again, when there was no reply from Pendergast, he jerked his head to one side. "I'm camped over yonder."

Pendergast picked up the shotgun, broke it open, ejected the spent shells, and handed it empty to Gasparilla. "Show me, if you please."

Five minutes of walking brought them to the edge of the trees and into the sea of corn. Gasparilla ducked into a row and they followed it down a dusty, beaten path. A few more minutes brought them to a cottonwood grove that lined the banks of Medicine Creek. The air here smelled of moisture, and there was the faint sound of water purling over a bed of sand. Ahead was the reddish glow of a campfire, built against a clay bank. A big iron pot sat atop the fire, bubbling, smelling of onions, potatoes, and peppers.

Gasparilla picked some pieces of wood off a pile and banked them beside the coals. Flames rose, illuminating the little campsite. There was a greasy-looking tent, a log for a seat, an abandoned wooden door set on more logs to make a table.

Gasparilla plucked the bundle of squirrels off his shoulder and dropped them on the makeshift table. Then he took out his knife and went to work, slicing one open, pulling out the guts and tossing them aside. And then, with one sharp tug, he tore off the skin. A series of swift chops took off the head, paws, and tail; a few more hacks quartered the animal, and it went into the simmering pot. The process for each squirrel took less than twenty seconds.

"What are you doing here?" Pendergast asked.

"On tour," said the man.

"Tour?"

"Tool sharpening. Make two rounds of my territory in the warm months. Go south to Brownsville for the winter. You got it, I sharpen it, from chainsaws to combine rotors."

"How do you get around?"

"Pickup."

"Where's it parked?"

Gasparilla gave a final savage chop, tossed the last squirrel into the pot. Then he jerked his head toward the road. "Over there, if you want to check it out."

"I plan to."

"They know me in town. I ain't never been on the wrong side of the law, you can ask the sheriff. I work for a living, same as you. Only I don't go sneaking around in the dark, shining lights in people's faces and scaring them half to death." He threw some parched lima beans into the pot.

"If, as you say, they know you in town, why do you camp out here?"

"I like a little elbow room."

"And the bare feet?"

"Huh?"

Pendergast shone his light at the man's filthy toes.

"Shoes are expensive." He rummaged in a pocket, pulled out the chaw of tobacco, screwed off another piece, and shoved it in his cheek. "What's an FBI man doing out here?" he asked, poking his cheek with a finger, adjusting the chaw to his satisfaction.

"I imagine you could guess the answer to that question, Mr. Gasparilla."

The man gave him a sidelong glance but did not reply.

"She was digging up in the Mounds, wasn't she?" Pendergast asked at last.

Gasparilla spat. "Yeah."

"How long?"

"Don't know."

"Did she find anything?"

He shrugged. "It ain't the first time there's been digging in the Mounds. I don't pay much attention to it. When I'm here I only go up there to hunt. I don't mess around with the dead."

"Are there burials in the Mounds?"

"So they say. There was also a massacre up there once. That's all I know and all I want to know. The place gives me the creeps. I wouldn't go up there except that's where all the squirrels are."

"I've heard talk of some legend associated with the place. The 'curse of the Forty-Fives,' I believe."

Gasparilla said nothing, and for a long time the camp was quiet. He stirred the pot with a stick, occasionally darting glances at Pendergast.

"The murder occurred three nights ago, during the new moon. Did you see or hear anything?"

Gasparilla spat again. "Nothing."

"What were your movements that evening, Mr. Gasparilla?"

Gasparilla kept stirring. "If you're hinting that I killed that woman, then I just about figure this conversation's over, mister."

"I'd say it's just begun."

"Don't get snippy with me. I never killed nobody in my life."

"Then you should have no objection to detailing your movements that day."

"That was my second day here at Medicine Creek. I hunted up at the Mounds late that afternoon. She was there, digging. I came back here at sunset, spent the night in camp."

"Did she see you?"

"Did *you* see me?"

"Where was she digging, exactly?"

"All over. I gave her a wide berth. I know trouble when I see it." Gasparilla gave the stewpot a brisk stir, brought out an enameled tin bowl and a battered spoon, ladled some stew into it. He scooped up a spoonful, blew on it, took a bite, dug the spoon in again. Then he stopped.

"I suppose you'll be wanting a bowl."

"I would not object."

Wordlessly, he brought out a second bowl, held it up before Pendergast.

"Thank you." Pendergast helped himself to the pot, took a taste of the stew. "Burgoo, I believe?"

Gasparilla nodded and stuffed a goodly amount in his mouth, juice dribbling down into his tangled black beard. He chewed loudly, spat out a few bones, swallowed. He wiped his mouth with his hand, then wiped his hand on his beard.

They finished their stew in silence. Gasparilla stacked the

bowls, leaned back, took out the plug of tobacco. "And now, mister, if you got what you're looking for, I hope you'll be about your business. I like a quiet evening."

Pendergast rose. "Mr. Gasparilla, I will leave you in peace. But first, if there's anything you'd care to add, I would advise you to tell it to me now, rather than waiting for me to discover it myself."

Gasparilla spat a brown rope of saliva in the direction of the creek. "I don't particularly care to get involved."

"You're already involved. Either you are the murderer, Mr. Gasparilla, or your continued presence here puts you in grave danger. One or the other."

Gasparilla grunted, bit off another plug, spat again. Then he asked, "Do you believe in the devil?"

Pendergast regarded the man, his pale eyes glinting in the firelight. "Why do you ask, Mr. Gasparilla?"

"Because I don't. As far as I'm concerned, the devil's a lot of preacher bullshit. But there *is* evil on this earth, Mr. FBI Agent. You asked about the curse of the Forty-Fives. Well, you might as well get on home right now, because you ain't never going to get to the bottom of *that*. The evil I'm talking about, most of the time it's got an explanation. But some of the time"—Gasparilla spat more tobacco juice, then leaned forward as if to impart a secret—"some of the time, it *just don't*."

Thirteen

Smit Ludwig pulled his AMC Pacer into the parking lot of Calvary Lutheran, which was wall to wall with hot cars glittering in the August sun. A big placard, already curling in the intense heat, was affixed to the front of the neat, redbrick church. It announced, 33RD ANNUAL BAKED TURKEY SUPPER SOCIABLE. Another, even bigger placard beside it burbled, MEDICINE CREEK WELCOMES PROFESSOR STANTON CHAUNCY!!! There was a touch of desperation, Ludwig thought, to the three exclamation marks. He parked his car at the far end of the lot, got out, dabbed the back of his neck with a handkerchief, and walked up to the entrance.

Then he paused, hand on the door. Over the years, the town had gotten used to his nice human interest stories; to his uncontroversial coverage of church and school, 4-H and Boy Scouts and Future Farmers of America. They had gotten used to the *Courier* glossing over and even ignoring the petty crimes of their children—the occasional joyrides, the drunken parties. They had taken for granted his downplaying of the inspection problems at Gro-Bain, the rising injury rate at the plant, the union troubles. They had forgotten that the *Courier* was a newspaper, not the town PR organ. Yesterday, all that had changed. The *Courier* had become a real paper, reporting real news.

Smit Ludwig wondered just what the reaction would be.

With his free hand, he nervously fingered his bow tie. He'd covered the Baked Turkey Sociable for every one of its thirty-three years, but never had he approached it with such trepidation. It was times like this that he most missed his wife, Sarah. It would have been easier with her on his arm.

Buck up, Smitty, he told himself, pushing open the doors.

The Fellowship Hall of the church was jammed. Practically the entire town was there. Some were already seated, eating, while others had formed long lines to load up on mashed potatoes, gravy, and green beans. Some were even eating the turkey, although Smitty noticed, as usual, that the Gro-Bain plant workers were nowhere to be seen in the turkey lines. It was one of those things that nobody ever mentioned: how little turkey was actually consumed at the Turkey Sociable.

A huge plastic banner on one wall thanked Gro-Bain and its general manager, Art Ridder, for their generosity in providing the turkeys. Another banner on the opposite wall thanked Buswell Agricon for their ongoing donations for the upkeep of the church. And yet another banner, the biggest of all, trumpeted the arrival of Stanton Chauncy, the year's guest of honor. Ludwig looked around. Familiar faces all. One of the joys of living in small-town America.

From across the room, Art Ridder caught his eye. Ridder was wearing a maroon-and-white polyester suit, and the usual smile was plastered on his unnaturally smooth face. His body was as solid as a chunk of suet, and he moved through the crowd slowly, without deviating from his path.

People moved for Art Ridder, thought Ludwig, not the other way around. Maybe it was the faint smell of slaughtered turkey that seemed to hang around him, despite heavy doses of Old Spice; or maybe it was that he was the town's richest man. Ridder had sold the turkey plant to Gro-Bain Agricultural Products and had stayed on as its manager, though they'd written him a nice fat check. He said he "liked the work." Ludwig thought it was more probable Ridder liked the Town Father status that being plant boss conveyed.

Ridder was still approaching, eye on the reporter, the smile stamped on his face. Of all people, he was probably the least likely to appreciate yesterday's article on the murder. Ludwig braced himself.

Out of nowhere, salvation—Mrs. Bender Lang darted up, whispered something in Ridder's ear. Abruptly, the two veered off. *This fellow Chauncy must be about to arrive,* Ludwig thought. Nothing else would have made Ridder move that fast.

In all thirty-three years of the Sociable's history, this was the first year that the guest of honor had not been selected from among the town's own. That in itself demonstrated the importance that Medicine Creek placed in impressing Dr. Stanton Chauncy of Kansas State University. It was Chauncy who'd decide, by next Monday, whether or not Medicine Creek would become the test site for several acres of genetically modified corn, or . . .

A high, shrill voice intruded on his thoughts. "Smit Ludwig, how dare you!" He turned to find Klick Rasmussen at his elbow, her beehive hairdo bobbing at about the level of his shoulder. "How *could* it be one of us?"

He turned to face her. "Now, Klick, I didn't say I believed—"

"If you didn't believe it," cried Klick Rasmussen, "then why did you *print* it?"

"Because it's my duty to report all the theories—"

"What happened to all the *nice* articles you used to print? The *Courier* used to be such a *lovely* paper."

"Not all news is nice, Klick—"

But Klick wouldn't let him finish. "If you want to write trash, why don't you write about that FBI agent wandering about town, asking questions, poking his nose where it doesn't belong, filling your head with darn-fool ideas? Let's see how *he* likes it. And on top of that, raising the whole business of the Ghost Warriors, the curse of the Forty-Fives—"

"There wasn't anything in the paper about that."

"Not exactly in so many *words,* but with that business about the old Indian arrows, what *else* are people going to think? That's all we need, a resurrection of that old story."

"Please, let's be reasonable—" Ludwig took a step back. In the distance, he could see Swede Cahill's wife, Gladys, approaching them, preparing to wade in. This was worse than he'd imagined.

Suddenly Maisie appeared from nowhere, her bulk covered by a white apron. "Klick, leave Smitty alone," she said. "We're lucky to have him. Most counties our size don't even have a newspaper, let alone a daily."

Klick took a step backward. Ludwig felt doubly grateful to Maisie, because of the awkwardness he knew existed between the two women. Maisie was perhaps the only person in the room who could have called Klick Rasmussen off so quickly. Klick shot one dark glance at Ludwig, then turned toward the approaching Gladys Cahill, and the two drifted off toward the turkey tables, talking in low voices.

Ludwig turned to Maisie. "Thanks a lot. You saved me."

"I always take care of you, Smit." She winked and went back toward the carving station.

As Ludwig turned to follow, he noticed that a hush was falling over the room. All eyes had swiveled in the direction of the door. Instinctively, Ludwig followed suit. There, framed against the golden sky, was a figure in black.

Pendergast.

There was something distinctly creepy in the way the FBI agent paused in the doorway, the bright sunlight silhouetting his severe form, like some gunslinger entering a saloon. Then he strode coolly forward, eyes roving the crowd before locking on Ludwig himself. Pendergast changed course immediately, gliding through the crowd toward him.

"I'm relieved to see you, Mr. Ludwig," he said. "I know no one here but you and the sheriff, and I can't very well expect the busy sheriff to take time for introductions. Come, lead the way, if you please."

"Lead the way?" Ludwig echoed.

"I need introductions, Mr. Ludwig. Where I come from, it's a social error to introduce oneself rather than have a proper introduction from a third party. And as publisher, editor, and chief reporter for the *Cry County Courier,* you know everyone in town."

"I suppose I do."

"Excellent. Shall we begin with Mrs. Melton Rasmussen? I understand she is one of the leading ladies."

Ludwig paused in mid-breath. Klick Rasmussen, of all people, who he'd just gotten free of. A profound sinking feeling settled on Ludwig as he looked around the room. There was Klick at one of the turkey tables, holding forth with Gladys Cahill and the rest of the usual gang.

"Over there," he said, leading the way with a heavy tread.

As they approached, the gaggle of ladies fell silent. Ludwig saw Klick glance at Pendergast, her features pinching with displeasure.

"I'd like to introduce—" began Ludwig.

"I know *very well* who this man is. I have only one thing to say—"

She stopped abruptly as Pendergast bowed, took her hand, and lifted it to within an inch of his lips, in the French manner. "A great pleasure, Mrs. Rasmussen. My name is Pendergast."

"My," said Klick. Her hand went limp within his.

"I understand, Mrs. Rasmussen, that you are responsible for the decorations."

Ludwig wondered where Pendergast had learned this little tidbit. The man's southern accent seemed to have deepened to the consistency of molasses as he gazed at Klick intently with his strange eyes. To Ludwig's private amusement, Klick Rasmussen blushed. "Yes, I am," she said.

"They are enchanting."

"Thank you, Mr. Pendergast."

Pendergast bowed again, still holding her hand. "I've heard a great deal about you, and now I'm delighted to make your acquaintance."

Klick blushed again, even more deeply. As she did so, Melton Rasmussen, having seen the exchange from afar, abruptly arrived. "Well, well," he said heartily, sticking his hand out and interposing himself between his plump, blushing wife and Pendergast, "welcome to Medicine Creek. I'm Mel. Melton Rasmussen. I realize the circumstances could be a little happier, but I think you'll find the Kansas hospitality of Medicine Creek to be just as warm as it always was."

"I have already found it so, Mr. Rasmussen," said Pendergast, shaking his hand.

"Where're you from, Pendergast? Can't quite place the accent."

"New Orleans."

"Ah, the great city of New Orleans. Is it true they eat alligator? I hear it tastes like chicken."

"In my view the taste is more like iguana or snake than chicken."

"Right. Well, I'll stick to turkey," said Rasmussen with a laugh. "You come by my store sometime and have a look-see. You're welcome anytime."

"You're very kind."

"So," said Rasmussen, moving a little closer, "what's the news? Any more leads?"

"Justice never sleeps, Mr. Rasmussen."

"Well, I've got a theory of my own. Would you like to hear it?"

"I'd be delighted."

"It's that fellow camped down by the creek. Gasparilla. He's worth looking into. He's a strange one, always has been."

"Now, Mel," scolded Klick. "You know he's been coming around for years and he's never been in any kind of trouble."

"You never know when somebody's gonna go queer on you. Why does he camp way out there on the creek? Isn't the town good enough for him?"

The question hung in the air, unanswered. Klick was staring past her husband, her mouth forming a small, perfect O. Ludwig heard a hushed murmur ripple through the assembly. There was a brief clapping of hands. He turned to see

Art Ridder and the sheriff escorting a man he didn't recognize through the crowd. The man was small and thin, with a closely trimmed beard, and he wore a light blue seersucker suit. In his wake came Mrs. Bender Lang and a few of the town's other leading ladies.

"Ladies and gentlemen, friends and neighbors of Medicine Creek!" Art Ridder boomed to the assembly. "It is my great privilege to introduce this year's guest of honor, Dr. Stanton Chauncy of Kansas State University!"

This was followed by thunderous applause and a few piercing whistles. The man named Chauncy stood, nodded once at the crowd, then turned his back on them and began to converse with Ridder. Slowly, the applause faltered into silence.

"Mr. Ludwig," Pendergast said. "There's a group of gentlemen in the far corner—?"

Ludwig looked in the indicated direction. Four or five men in bib overalls were drinking lemonade and talking amongst themselves in low voices. Rather than joining in the applause, they were looking in the direction of Chauncy with narrowed eyes.

"Oh, that's Dale Estrem and the rest of the Farmer's Co-operative," Ludwig replied. "The last of the die-hard hold-outs. They're the only ones who haven't sold out to the big farming conglomerates. Still own their own farms around Medicine Creek."

"And why don't they share in the town's good feeling?"

"The Farmer's Co-op holds no truck with genetically modified corn. They fear it'll cross-pollinate and ruin their own crops."

Ridder was now introducing the man from Kansas State to select knots of people.

"There are several other introductions I'd like you to make, if you would," Pendergast said. "The minister, for example."

"Of course." Ludwig scanned the crowd for Pastor Wilbur, finally spotting him standing alone, in line for turkey. "This way."

"Tell me about him first, if you please."

Ludwig hesitated, not wishing to speak ill of anybody. "Pastor Wilbur's been here for forty years, at least. He means well. It's just that . . ." He faltered.

"Yes?" said Pendergast. Ludwig found the man's gray eyes focused on him in a most unsettling way.

"I guess you'd have to say he's a little set in his ways. He's not really in touch with what's happening, or *not* happening, in Medicine Creek these days." He struggled a moment. "There are some who feel a younger, more vibrant ministry would help revive the town, keep the youngsters from leaving. Fill the spiritual void that's opened up here."

"I see."

The minister raised his head as they approached. As usual, a pair of reading glasses was perched on the end of his nose, whether or not he was reading anything. Ludwig figured he did it to look scholarly. "Pastor Wilbur?" Ludwig said. "I'd like to introduce Special Agent Pendergast of the FBI."

Wilbur took the proffered hand.

"I envy you, Pastor," Pendergast said. "Ministering to the souls of a community such as Medicine Creek."

Wilbur gazed benevolently at Pendergast. "It is at times a fearsome responsibility, being entrusted with so many hundreds, Mr. Pendergast. But I flatter myself that I've shepherded them well."

"It seems a good life here," Pendergast went on. "For a man of God such as yourself, I mean."

"God has seen fit to both bless me and bring me trials. We all share equally in the curse of Adam, but perhaps a man of the cloth shares more than most." Wilbur's face had assumed a saintly, almost martyred demeanor.

Ludwig recognized that look: Wilbur was about to spout one of his prized little scraps of poetry.

"Alas," Wilbur began, *"what boots it with uncessant care, to tend the homely, slighted shepherd's trade?"* He looked through his reading glasses at Pendergast with evident satisfaction. "Milton. Naturally."

"Naturally. *Lycidas.*"

Wilbur was slightly taken aback. "Ah, I believe that's correct, yes."

"Another line from that elegy comes to mind: *The hungry sheep look up and are not fed.*"

There was a brief silence. Ludwig looked back and forth between the two men, uncertain what, if anything, had just passed between them.

Wilbur blinked. "I—"

"I look forward to greeting you again in church on Sunday," Pendergast interjected smoothly, grasping Wilbur's hand once more.

"Ah, yes, yes, so do I," Wilbur said, the note of surprise still detectable in his voice.

"Excuse me!" The booming voice of Art Ridder, amplified, again cut through the babble of overlapping conversations. "Ladies and gentlemen, if you would all be so kind, our guest of honor would like to say a few words. Dr. Stanton Chauncy!"

All around the Fellowship Hall, people put down their

forks and turned their attention to the little man in the seer-sucker suit.

"Thank you," the man said. He stood erect, hands folded in front of him like he was at a wake. "My name is Stanton Chauncy. Dr. Stanton Chauncy. I represent the Agricultural Extension of Kansas State University. But of course you know that." His voice was high, and his man-ner of speaking was so crisp and precise that his words were almost overarticulated.

"The genetic enhancement of corn is a complicated sub-ject, and not one that I can readily elucidate in a venue such as this," he began. "It requires knowledge of certain disci-plines such as organic chemistry and plant biology that one could not expect a lay audience to possess." He sniffed. "However, I will attempt to impart the most rudimentary of overviews to you this afternoon."

As if of one mind, those who had gathered in the Fel-lowship Hall appeared to slump. There was a collective ex-halation of breath. If they had hoped to hear praise heaped on their town or their Sociable, or even—dared one hope?—word of Chauncy's impending decision, they were sadly disappointed. Instead, the man launched into an ex-planation of corn varietals so detailed that the eyes of even the most enthusiastic corn farmer glazed over. It almost seemed to Ludwig as if Chauncy was *trying* to be as boring as possible. Whispered conversations resumed; forkfuls of mashed potato and turkey gravy were slipped into furtive mouths; small streams of people began moving back and forth along the far walls of the hall. Dale Estrem and the Farmer's Co-op crowd stood at the back, arms folded, faces set hard.

Smit Ludwig tuned out the droning voice as he looked

around the hall. Despite everything, he appreciated the small-town atmosphere of the Sociable: its homespun provinciality, and the fact that it brought the community together, even forcing people who didn't like each other to acknowledge the other and be civil. It was one of the many reasons why he never wanted to leave—even after his wife had passed away. A person could not get lost in Medicine Creek. People were taken care of, nobody was forgotten, and everyone had a place. It wasn't like that in L.A., where old people died unloved and alone every day. His daughter had been calling a lot lately, urging him to relocate nearer her. But he wasn't going to do that. Not even after he closed the paper and retired. For better or worse, he was going to end his days in Medicine Creek and be buried in the cemetery out on the Deeper Road, beside his wife.

He glanced at his watch. What had generated these thoughts of mortality? He had a deadline to make, even if it was self-imposed, and the time had come for him to go home and write up the story.

He made his stealthy way to the open doors of the hall. Beyond, late afternoon light illuminated the broad green lawn of the church. The heat was unbroken as it lay over the grass, the parking lot, and the cornfields like a suffocating blanket. But despite the heat—and, in fact, despite everything—a part of Smit Ludwig felt relieved. He could have fared a lot worse at the hands of his fellow townsfolk; he had Maisie, and perhaps Pendergast, to thank for that. And on a less selfish note, he'd be able to write an upbeat piece about the Sociable without dissembling. It had started with a certain grimness, he felt: a stoic sense that the show must go on, despite everything. But the gloom and oppression had seemed to lift. The town had become itself again, and not

even Chauncy's stultifying lecture, which still droned on behind him, could change that. The thirty-third annual Gro-
Bain Turkey Sociable was a success.

Ludwig fetched a deep, slow breath as he looked out
from the steps of the church. And then, suddenly, he froze.

One by one, the people around him began to do the same,
staring out from the wooden doorway. There was a gasp, a
low murmur. Like an electric current, the murmur began to
jump from person to person, running back into the crowds
within the hall itself, growing in volume until Chauncy's ex-
egesis of variegated corn kernels came under threat.

"What is it?" Chauncy said, stopping in mid-sentence.
"What's going on?"

Nobody answered. All eyes were fixed on the horizon
beyond the open doors of the hall, where, against the yellow
sky, a lazy column of vultures wheeled in ever tightening
circles above the endless corn.

Fourteen

When Corrie Swanson pulled up to the church, people were standing on the front lawn, huddled together in groups, murmuring anxiously. Now and then somebody would break away from one of the groups and stare out in the direction of the cornfields. There must have been fifty people out there, but she didn't see Pendergast among them. And that made no sense, because he'd asked her to come right away. He'd been most insistent on it, in fact.

It was almost a relief to find him missing. Pendergast was going to get her into even worse trouble than she already was in this town—she could feel it in her bones. She was already the town's A-number-one pariah. Once again, she wondered what the hell she'd gotten herself into. The money was still burning a hole in her glove compartment. He'd get her in trouble, and then he'd be gone, and she'd still be stuck in Medicine Creek dealing with the consequences. If she were smart, she'd give him back the money and wash her hands of the whole thing.

She jumped involuntarily as a black figure seemed to materialize out of nowhere beside the car. Pendergast opened the passenger door and slid in as sleekly as a cat. The way he moved gave her the creeps sometimes.

She reached for the dashboard, turned down the blaring sound of "Starfuckers, Inc." by Nine Inch Nails. "So, where to, Special Agent?" she said as casually as she could.

Pendergast nodded toward the cornfields. "Do you see those birds?"

She shaded her eyes against the glow of the sunset. "What, those turkey vultures? What about them?"

"That's where we're going."

She revved the engine; the car shuddered and coughed black smoke. "There's no roads out that way, and this is a Gremlin, not a Hummer, in case you hadn't noticed."

"Don't worry, Miss Swanson, I will not get you mired in a cornfield. Head west on the Cry Road, please."

"Whatever." She stamped on the accelerator and the Gremlin pulled away from the curb, shuddering with the effort.

"So how was the Turkey Sociable?" she asked. "That's like the big event of the year in Shit Creek."

"It was most instructive—from an anthropological point of view."

"Anthropological? Yeah, right, Special Agent Pendergast among the savages. Did they introduce that guy from KSU, the one who wants to grow radioactive corn around here?"

"Genetically modified corn. They did."

"And what was he like? Did he have three heads?"

"If he did, two must have been successfully removed in infancy."

Corrie looked at him. He looked back from the broken seat with his usual placid, mild, unsmiling expression. She could never tell whether or not he was cracking a joke. He had to be the weirdest adult she'd ever met, and with all the characters wandering around Medicine Creek, that was saying something.

"Miss Swanson? Your speed."

"Sorry." She braked. "I thought you FBI guys drove as fast as you wanted."

"I'm on vacation."

"The sheriff goes everywhere at a hundred miles an hour even when he's off duty. And you always know when there's fresh eclairs at the Wagon Wheel. Then he goes a hundred and twenty."

They hummed along the smooth asphalt for a while in silence.

"Miss Swanson, take a look up the road, if you please. Do you see where the sheriff's car is parked? Pull in behind it."

Corrie squinted into the gathering dusk. Ahead, she could see the cruiser pulled over onto the wrong shoulder, lights flashing. Overhead, and maybe a quarter mile into the corn, she could see the column of turkey vultures more clearly.

It suddenly clicked. "Jesus," she said. "Not another one?"

"That remains to be seen."

Corrie pulled up behind the cruiser and put on her flashers. Pendergast got out. "I may be a while."

"I'm not coming with you?"

"I'm afraid not."

"No problem, I brought a book."

She watched Pendergast push his way into the corn and disappear, feeling vaguely annoyed. Then she turned her attention to the back seat. She always had five or six books flung about willy-nilly back there—science fiction, horror, splatterpunk, occasionally a teen romance that she never,

ever let anybody catch her reading. She glanced over the pile. Maybe, while she waited, she'd start that new techno-thriller, *Beyond the Ice Limit*. She picked it up, then paused again. Somehow, the idea of sitting in the car, reading, all alone, didn't seem quite as appealing as it usually did. She couldn't help but glance again at the column of vultures. They had soared higher now. Even against the gathering dusk, she could see they were agitated. Perhaps the sheriff had scared them off. She felt a twinge of curiosity: there might be something out there in the corn a whole lot more interesting than anything she'd find in one of her escapist novels.

She tossed the book in the back seat with a snort of impatience. Pendergast wasn't going to keep her away like that. She had as much a right as anyone to see what was going on.

She flung open the car door and headed off into the corn. She could see where the sheriff had tramped through the dirt. There was another, narrower pair of tracks that ran back and forth over the sheriff's clown shoes: probably his well-meaning but brain-dead deputy, Tad. And near them, Pendergast's light step.

It was very hot and claustrophobic in the corn. The husks rose high over Corrie's head, and as she passed by they rattled, showering her with dust and pollen. There was still some light in the sky, but in the corn it seemed that night had already fallen. Corrie felt her breath coming faster as she walked. She began to wonder if this was such a good idea after all. She never went into the corn. All her life she had hated the cornfields. They started in the spring as so much endless dirt, the giant machines tearing up the earth, leaving behind plumes of dust that coated the town and filled her bed with grit. And then the corn came up and the only thing anyone talked about for four months was the weather. Slowly the roads got closed in by claustrophobic walls of corn until you felt like you were driving in a tunnel of green. Now the corn was yellowing and pretty soon the giant machines would be back, leaving the land as naked and ugly as a shaved poodle.

It was awful: the dust filled her nose and stung her eyes and the moldy, papery smell made her sick. All this corn, probably growing not to feed people or even animals, but cars. Car corn. Sick, sick, sick.

And then, quite suddenly, she broke through into a small trampled clearing. There were the sheriff and Tad, holding flashlights and bending over something. Pendergast stood to one side, and as she entered the clearing he turned toward her, his pale eyes almost luminous in the gathering twilight.

Corrie's heart gave an ugly lurch. There was something dead in the middle. But when she forced herself to look she realized it was only a dead dog. It was brown and so bloated with the gases of rot that its hair stood on end, making it look horribly strange, like a four-legged blowfish. An awful, sweetish smell hung in the still air and there was a steady roar of flies.

The sheriff turned. "Well, Pendergast," he said in a genial voice, "looks like we got all riled up for nothing." Then his eyes flickered over Pendergast's shoulder, and landed on her. He stared at her for a few uncomfortable seconds before looking back at Pendergast. The agent said nothing.

Pendergast had slipped a small light out of his own pocket and was playing its bright beam over the bloated corpse. Corrie felt sick: she recognized the dog. It was a chocolate Lab mutt belonging to Swede Cahill's son, a nice freckled kid of twelve.

"Okay, Tad," said the sheriff, slapping his hand on the gangly deputy's shoulder, "we've seen all there is to see. Let's call it a day."

Pendergast had now moved in and was kneeling, examining the dog more closely. The flies, disturbed, were swarming above the corpse in a wild cloud.

The sheriff walked past Corrie without acknowledging her, then turned at the edge of the clearing. "Pendergast? You coming?"

"I haven't completed my examination."

"You finding anything interesting?"

There was a silence, and then Pendergast said, "This is another killing."

"Another killing? It's a dead dog in a cornfield and we're two miles from the site of the Swegg homicide."

Corrie watched in vague horror as the FBI agent picked up the dog's head, moved it back and forth gently, laid it down, shone his light in the mouth, the ears, down the flank. The angry drone of flies grew louder.

"Well?" asked the sheriff, his voice harder.

"This dog's neck has been violently broken," said Pendergast.

"Hit by a car. Dragged himself out here to die. Happens all the time."

"A car wouldn't have done that to the tail."

"What tail?"

"Exactly my point."

Both the sheriff and Tad directed their lights to the dog's rump. Where the tail had been there was nothing but a ragged pink stump with a white bone at the center.

The sheriff said nothing.

"And over there"—Pendergast shone his light into the corn—"I imagine you will find the footprints of the killer. Bare footprints, size eleven, heading back down toward the creek. Same as the footprints found at the site of the first homicide."

There was another silence. And then the sheriff spoke. "Well, Pendergast, all I can say is, it's kind of a relief. Here you thought we were dealing with a serial killer. Now we know he's just some sicko. Murdering a dog and cutting off the tail. Jesus Christ."

"But you will note the difference here. There was no ceremony to this killing, no feeling that the corpse has been arranged *en tableau.*"

"So?"

"It doesn't fit the pattern. But of course, that simply means we're dealing with a *new* pattern—in fact, a new type altogether."

"A new type of what?"

"Of serial killer."

Hazen rolled his eyes theatrically. "As far as I'm concerned, we're still dealing with a single murder. A dog doesn't count." He turned to Tad. "Call the M.E. and let's scoop this dog up to Garden City for a necropsy. Get the SOC boys out here to work over the site and especially take a look at any prints they find. And get the Staties to post a guard. I want this site sealed. No unauthorized personnel. Got it?"

"Yes, Sheriff."

"Good. And now, Pendergast, I'm hoping you will escort all *unauthorized* personnel from the site immediately." Corrie jumped as he abruptly shone his light on her.

"Sheriff, you're not referring to my assistant, are you?"

There was a thunderous silence. Corrie glanced at him, wondering what his game was now. Assistant? Her old suspicions began to return; next thing she knew, he'd be trying to assist himself into her pants.

After a moment the sheriff spoke. "Assistant? Are you referring to that delinquent standing next to you who's facing a charge of larceny in the second degree, which, by the way, happens to be a felony in the state of Kansas?"

"I am."

The sheriff nodded. And when he spoke again, his voice was unnaturally mild. "I'm a patient man, Mr. Pendergast. I will say this to you, and this only: there *is* a limit."

In the ensuing silence, Pendergast said, "Miss Swanson, would you kindly hold the flashlight while I examine the posterior of this dog?"

Holding her nose against the rising stench, Corrie took the flashlight and aimed it at the desired spot, aware of Sheriff Hazen standing behind her, staring so hard at the back of her neck that she could feel the hairs curling.

Pendergast turned, rose, and laid a hand on the sheriff's shoulder. The man looked down at the hand, seemed about to brush it off. "Sheriff Hazen," said Pendergast, his voice suddenly deferential, "it may seem that I have come here expressly to annoy you. But I assure you there are good reasons behind everything I do. I do hope you will continue to exercise the patience you've so admirably demonstrated already, and bear with me and my unorthodox methods—and my unorthodox assistant—a little longer."

The sheriff seemed to digest this for a moment. When he spoke again, his voice sounded ever so slightly mollified. "I can't say I honestly like the way you're handling the case.

You FBI boys always seem to forget that once we catch the perp we've got to *convict* him. You know how it is these days: screw up the evidence *in any way* and the perp walks." He glanced at Corrie. "She better have scene-of-crime authorization."

"She will."

"And keep in mind what kind of impression she's going to make in front of a jury with that purple hair and the spiked dog collar. Not to mention a felony on her record."

"We will cross that bridge when we come to it."

The sheriff stared hard at him. "All right then. I'll leave you to Fido here. Remember what I said. Come on, Tad, let's go make those calls."

Then he turned away, lit a cigarette, and disappeared into the wall of corn, followed by Tad. As the sound of crashing diminished, a silence descended on the site.

Corrie took several steps back from the stench of decay. "Agent Pendergast?"

"Miss Swanson?"

"What's this 'assistant' crap?"

"I assumed you were willing to take the job by the fact that you disobeyed my orders and came here, thereby displaying an interest in the forensic aspects of crime."

Was he kidding again? "I just don't like being left behind. Look, I don't know jack about detective work. I can't type, I can't handle the phones, and I'm sure as hell not going to take dictation or do whatever it is that assistants do."

"That is not what I require. This may surprise you, but I've actually given this matter some thought and I've concluded that you'll make an excellent assistant. I need someone who knows the town, knows the people, knows their secrets, but who is also an outsider, beholden to no one.

Someone who will tell me the unvarnished truth as she sees it. Are you not exactly that person?"

Corrie considered it. Outsider, beholden to no one . . . Depressingly, she seemed to fit the bill.

"The promotion comes with a raise to a hundred and fifty dollars a day. I have all the paperwork in the car, including a limited scene-of-crime authorization. It means obeying my orders to the letter. No more jumping out of the car on a whim. We will discuss your new responsibilities in more detail later."

"Who's paying me? The FBI?"

"I shall be paying you out of my own pocket."

"Come on, you know I'm not worth it. You're throwing your money away."

Pendergast turned and looked at her, and once again she was struck by the intensity that lay behind those gray eyes. "I already know one thing: we are dealing with an extremely dangerous killer and I do not have time to waste. I must have your help. If one life is saved, what is that worth?"

"Yeah, but how can I possibly help? I mean, the sheriff's right. I'm just a dumb delinquent."

"Miss Swanson, don't be fatuous. Have we got a deal?"

"All right. But *assistant* is where it begins and ends. Like I said before, don't get any ideas."

He looked at her. "I beg your pardon?"

"You're a man. You know what I'm talking about."

Pendergast waved his hand. "Miss Swanson, the inference you are making is quite unthinkable. We come from two different worlds. There is a vast difference between us in terms of age, temperament, upbringing, background, and relative positions of power—not to mention your pierced tongue. In my opinion such a relationship, while it might afford both of us considerable diversion, would be most unwise."

Corrie felt vaguely irritated by his explanation. "What's wrong with my pierced tongue?"

"Perhaps nothing. Females of the Wimbu tribe of the Andaman Islands pierce their labia and dangle strings of cowry shells from them. The shells jingle under their skirts when they walk. The men find it most attractive."

"That's totally foul!"

Pendergast smiled. "So you are not the cultural relativist I had assumed."

"You're a seriously weird person, you know that?"

"The alternative, Miss Swanson, does not appeal to me at all." He took the light from her and shone it back on the dog. "And now, as my assistant, you can begin by telling me whose dog this is."

Her eyes flickered unwillingly back to the bloated corpse. "It's Jiff. He belonged to Andy, Swede Cahill's son."

"Did Jiff wear a collar?"

"Yes."

"Did he normally run free?"

"Most of the dogs in town run free, despite the leash laws."

Pendergast nodded. "I knew my confidence in you was not misplaced."

Corrie looked at him, feeling amused. "You're a real piece of work, you know that?"

"Thank you. We seem to have something in common."

A silence descended on the rude clearing while Corrie wondered if she'd been insulted or complimented. But as she followed the beam with her eyes, she felt a sudden stab of pity: pity that transcended the awful stench, the drone of flies. Andy Cahill was going to be heartbroken. Somebody had to tell him, and it looked like that somebody would have to be her. She certainly couldn't leave it to the sheriff or his assistant, who could be counted on to say the wrong thing. Nor did she think Pendergast, for all his courtesy, was the right person to break the news to the kid. She looked up and, to her surprise, found Pendergast looking at her.

"Yes," he said, "I think it would be an act of kindness for you to break the news to Andy Cahill."

"How did—?"

"At the same time, Miss Swanson, you might find out, in an offhand way, when Andy last saw Jiff, and where the dog might have been heading."

"You want me to play detective, in other words."

Pendergast nodded. "You are, after all, my new assistant."

Fifteen

Margery Tealander sat behind the old wooden desk of her spartan office, industriously clipping coupons while keeping one eye on *The Price Is Right*. The picture on the old black-and-white was so poor that she'd cranked the volume up so as not to miss any of the action. Not that there was all that much action today; rarely had she seen such a sorry group of contestants. Bidding high, bidding low, bidding every which way except within a mile of the real price of anything. She paused in her clipping to peer at the screen and listen. Everybody else had bid on the latest item except for the final contestant, a skinny Asian girl who couldn't be more than twenty.

"I'll bid one thousand four hundred and one dollars, Bob," the girl said with a shy smile and a duck of her head.

"Man alive." Marge clucked disapprovingly and returned to her clipping. Fourteen hundred dollars for an over-under Maytag? What planet could these people be living on? Couldn't be more than nine hundred fifty, tops. And the audience wasn't any help either, yelling encouragingly at every wrong guess. Now, if *she* was on the show, the audience would see some *serious* cleaning up. She always seemed to guess the right price, always seemed to pick the right door. And she wouldn't settle for any of those cheesy prizes, either, the redwood utility sheds or the knickknack cabinets or the year's supply of floor wax. She'd hold out for the fifteen-foot Chris-Craft; she had a cousin up near Lake Scott with a dock and mooring. The pity of it was that she'd finally talked Rocky into taking her out to Studio City, and then a week later he was diagnosed with emphysema. And now, she couldn't very well go alone, God rest his soul, it would be much too much for . . . Now *this* was interesting: twenty percent off Woolite with a grocery purchase of $30 or more. That hardly *ever* went on sale, and with triple coupons on weekends that meant she could buy it for almost half price. She'd have to stock up. You just couldn't beat the Shopper's Palace in Ulysses for prices. The Red Owl in Garden City was closer, of course, but if you were serious about saving a little money you just couldn't beat the Palace. And on Super Saturdays she'd get ten cents off a gallon on regular gas—that more than made up for the extra mileage right there. Of course, she felt a little bad about not patronizing Ernie, but these were lean times and a body just had to be practical . . . Now, if that didn't beat all. Nine hundred twenty-five for the Maytag. Sure would have looked nice right next to her slop sink. Maybe she'd talk to Alice Franks about looking into a bus excursion that could—

All of a sudden she realized that a strange man was standing before her desk.

"Good gracious!" Marge quickly turned down the sound on the television. "Young man, you startled me." It was that man in the black suit she'd seen out and about recently.

"My apologies," the man replied in a voice redolent

of mint juleps, pralines, and cypress trees. He gave a formal little bow, then stood before her, hands at his sides. He had slender, tapered fingers with nails that—she noticed with some surprise—were subtly but very professionally manicured.

"Don't apologize," she said. "Just don't be sneaking up on a body like that. Now, what can I do you for?"

The man nodded toward the coupons. "I hope I haven't caught you at a bad time."

Marge barked out a laugh. "Hah! A bad time! That's a good one." She pushed the coupons to one side. "Mr. Stranger, you have my *un*divided attention."

"I must apologize again," the man said. "I've neglected to introduce myself. The name's Pendergast."

Marge suddenly remembered the article in the paper. "Of course. You're that fellow from down south who's looking into the murder. I could tell you weren't from around here, of course. Not talking like that, you aren't."

She looked at him with fresh curiosity. He was rather tall, with hair so blond it was almost white, and he returned her look with pale eyes full of mild inquisitiveness. Although he was slender, he gave no sense of being frail; quite the opposite, really, although his suit was so unrelievedly black it was hard to tell. He was really very attractive, in a Southern Comfort kind of way.

"Nice to meet you, Mr. Pendergast," she said. "I'd offer you a seat, but this swivel chair of mine's the only one. The people who come here aren't usually inclined to stay very long." She barked another laugh.

"And why is that, Mrs. Tealander?" The question was phrased so politely that Marge didn't notice he already knew her name.

"Why do you think? Unless you happen to be partial to paying taxes and filling out forms, of course."

"Yes, of course. I do see." The man named Pendergast took a step forward. "Mrs. Tealander, it's my understanding that—"

"Five hundred dollars," Marge interrupted.

The man paused. "Pardon me?"

"Nothing." Marge pulled her eyes from the now-silent TV.

"It's my understanding that you are the keeper of public records for Medicine Creek."

Marge nodded. "That's right."

"And that you function as town administrator."

"A part-time job. Very part-time, these days."

"That you run the public works department."

"Oh, that just means keeping tabs on Henry Fleming, who drives the snow plow and changes the bulbs in the streetlamps."

"And that you levy real estate taxes."

"Yes, and *that's* the reason I don't get invited to Klick Rasmussen's canasta parties."

Pendergast paused again for a moment. "So one could say that, in essence, you run Medicine Creek."

Marge grinned widely. "Young man, I couldn't have put it better myself. Of course, Sheriff Hazen and Art Ridder might not share your view."

"We'll leave them to their own opinion, then."

"Man alive, I *knew* it!" Marge's eyes had strayed back to the television, and with an effort she returned them to her guest.

Pendergast slipped a leather wallet from his jacket pocket. "Mrs. Tealander," he said, opening it to display the gold shield inside, "you're aware that I'm an agent with the Federal Bureau of Investigation?"

"That's what they said over at the Hair Apparent."

"I would like to get a better, shall we say, *bureaucratic* perspective on the people of Medicine Creek. What they do, where they live, what their economic status might be. That manner of thing."

"Then you've come to the right place. I know everything legal there is to know about every blessed soul in town."

Pendergast waved one hand. "Technically, of course, such an inquiry requires a warrant."

"Where do you think you are, young man? Great Bend? Wichita, maybe? I'm not going to stand on ceremony with an officer of the law. Besides, we've got no secrets here. At least, none that would interest you."

"Then you see no difficulty in, ah, making me better acquainted with the inhabitants."

"Mr. Pendergast, I've got nothing on my calendar until August twenty-second, when I have to type up the property tax bills for the fourth quarter."

Pendergast glided a little closer to the desk. "Let's hope it doesn't take quite that long."

Another bark of laughter. "Take that long! Hoo-*eee!* Man alive, that's a good one."

Marge turned her swivel chair to the back wall of the office, where an old-fashioned safe stood. It was massive and decorated around the edges with faded gold leaf. Aside from the desk and a small bookshelf, it was the only article of furniture in the room. She twirled its large central dial back and forth, entering the combination, then grasped the handle and pulled the iron door open. Inside was a smaller box, closed with a padlock. She unlocked the padlock with a key that she drew from around her neck. Reaching inside, she removed an even smaller, wooden box. Then she turned around in her swivel chair again and placed it on the desk between herself and Pendergast.

"There you go," she said, patting the little box with satisfaction. "Where do you want to start?"

Pendergast looked at the box. "I beg your pardon?"

"I said, where do you want to start?"

"Do you mean to tell me that—" For a very brief moment, the man's face seemed to go completely blank before once again assuming its look of casual curiosity.

"What, did you think it took a computer to run a town the size of Medicine Creek? I've got everything I need right in this little box. And what isn't there is up here." She tapped her temple. "Look, I'll show you." She opened the box, drew out an index card by random. It contained perhaps a dozen lines of neat handwriting, followed by a row of numbers, a couple of squiggles and symbols, and a few stickers of various colors: red, yellow, green. "You see?" she said, waving it under Pendergast's nose. "This is the card of Dale Estrem, the cranky young farmer. His father was a cranky old farmer. And his grandfather—well, we won't mention *him.* Dale and the rest of those troublemakers in the Farmer's Co-operative, always standing in the way of progress. See, it shows here that he's two quarters behind in his taxes, that his oldest kid had to repeat ninth grade, that his septic tank's not in compliance with the code, and that he's applied for farm relief seven years out of the last seven." She clucked disapprovingly.

Pendergast looked from her, to the card, and back to her again. "I see," he said.

"I've got ninety-three cards here, one for each family in

Medicine Creek and in the unincorporated areas around it. I could talk for an hour on each, maybe two hours if necessary." Marge felt herself growing excited. It wasn't every day that somebody official took an interest in her records. And with Rocky passed on, God knows, she had precious few people to chat with. "I promise, you'll know all there is to know about Medicine Creek when I'm done with you."

This was greeted by a profound silence.

"Of course," Pendergast said after a few moments, as if re-collecting himself.

"So I ask again, Mr. Pendergast. Where do you want to start?"

Pendergast thought a moment. "I suppose we should start with the A's."

"There are no last names starting with 'A' in Medicine Creek, Mr. Pendergast. We'll start with David Barness, out on the Cry Road. So sorry I can't get you a chair. Maybe when we start in again tomorrow I'll bring one along for you from my kitchen." And she returned the card she was holding to its spot, licked her finger eagerly, plucked the first card from the box, and began to talk. At her elbow the television flickered on, the game show now completely forgotten.

Sixteen

Deputy Sheriff Tad Franklin guided his cruiser into the gravel parking lot between the big old Victorian house and the gift shop. He crunched to a halt, pushed open the car door, and unfolded himself into the hot August sun. He paused to stretch, scratch at his black crew cut, and to peer, a little warily, at the house. The white picket fence that surrounded it was falling apart, paint peeling, slats hanging every which way. Beyond lay the overgrown yard. The giant old gabled house looked like it hadn't been painted in fifty years. Kansas dust storms had sandblasted it right down to weatherbeaten wood and were now stripping the wood down to tarpaper. The "Kraus's Kaverns" sign, off-kilter, with its great strips of peeling red and white paint, looked like something out of a grade-B horror flick. The whole place depressed him. He had to get out of Medicine Creek. But to do that, he needed to put in his time, get some more experience under his belt. And he dreaded the idea of telling Sheriff Hazen. The sheriff, Tad knew, was grooming him, in his rough paternal way, to take his place. Tad didn't like to think about what the sheriff would say when he told him he was taking a job in Wichita or Topeka. Anywhere but Medicine Creek.

He forced himself through the gate, along the weed-choked sidewalk, and up the steps onto the crooked wrap-around porch. His leather boots made a hollow sound as he walked up to the door. The air was still, and in the corn he could hear the cicadas droning. He paused, then rapped on the door.

It opened so quickly that he jumped. Special Agent Pendergast.

"Deputy Sheriff Franklin. Please come in."

Tad took off his hat and came into the parlor, feeling uncomfortable. The sheriff had wanted him to quietly check up on what Pendergast was up to, what else he had learned about the dog killing. But now that he was here, he felt embarrassed. He couldn't imagine any way to broach the subject without making the reason for his visit painfully obvious.

"You're just in time for lunch," said the agent, closing the door behind him. The shades were drawn and it was a little cooler here, out of the sun, but without air conditioning it was still uncomfortably hot. Not far from the front door sat two oversized suitcases—wardrobe trunks, really—overnight express labels still affixed to the expensive-looking leather exteriors. It seemed that Pendergast was settling in for a longer stay.

"Lunch?" Tad repeated.

"A light salad with antipasti. Prosciutto di San Daniele, pecorino cheese with truffled honey, baccelli, tomatoes, and rucola. Something light for a hot day."

"Er, sure. Great." If they were going to eat Italian, why not stick with pizza? He advanced another step, not knowing what to say. It was one o'clock. Who ate lunch at one o'clock? He had eaten at the normal time of eleven-thirty.

"Miss Kraus is feeling poorly. She's taken to bed. I've been filling in."

"I see." Tad followed Pendergast into the kitchen. In one corner a stack of Federal Express and DHL boxes had been neatly piled halfway to the ceiling. The counter was littered with at least a dozen food packages sporting foreign-sounding names: Balducci's, Zabar's. Tad wondered if maybe Pendergast wasn't Italian or French. He sure didn't eat like an American.

Pendergast had busied himself in the kitchen, his movements deft and economical, quickly arranging odd-looking food onto three plates—salami and cheese and what had to be some kind of lettuce. Tad watched, shifting his hat from one hand to the other.

"I'll just bring this plate back to Miss Kraus," said Pendergast.

"Right. Okay."

Pendergast disappeared into the back recesses of the house. Tad could hear Winifred's soft voice, Pendergast's murmured responses. A moment later, the agent returned.

"Is she okay?" Tad asked.

"Fine," Pendergast said in a low voice. "It's more psychological than physical. These delayed reactions are common in such cases. You can imagine the kind of shock she had, learning about the murder."

"We were all shocked."

"Of course you were. I recently wrapped up a rather unpleasant case myself in New York, where killings are regrettably more common. I am used to it, Mr. Franklin, or as used to it as a creature can ever be. For all of you, I have no doubt this was—and is—a most unwelcome new experience. Please sit down."

Tad sat down, put his hat on the table, decided that wasn't a good place, laid it on a chair, then snatched it up again, afraid he might forget it.

"I'll take that," said Pendergast, placing it on a hat rack nearby.

Tad shifted in his chair, feeling more awkward by the minute. A plate was put in front of him. *"Buon appetito,"* Pendergast said, gesturing for Tad to dig in.

Tad picked up a fork and stabbed into a piece of cheese. He cut some off and tasted it gingerly.

"You'll want to drizzle a little of this *miele al tartufo bianco* on there," Pendergast said, offering him a tiny jar of odd-smelling honey.

"I'll stick to it plain, thanks."

"Nonsense." Pendergast took a pearl spoon and dribbled some honey over the rest of Tad's cheese.

Tad took another bite, and discovered it wasn't bad.

They ate in silence. Tad found the food much to his liking, especially some small slices of salami. "What's this?" he asked.

"Cinghiale. Wild boar."

"Oh."

Now Pendergast was pouring olive oil all over everything, as well as some liquid as black as tar. He poured some on Tad's own plate as well. "And now, Deputy, I imagine you are here for a briefing."

Somehow, having it stated so baldly made everything much less awkward. "Well, yes. Right."

Pendergast dabbed his mouth and sat back. "The dog was named Jiff and he belonged to Andy Cahill. I understand that Andy is quite an explorer and that he used to roam all over the place with his dog. My assistant will be providing me soon with the results of an interview."

Tad fumbled for his notebook, brought it out, and started taking notes.

"It appears the dog was killed that previous night. You may recall it was overcast for a few hours after midnight, and that appears to be when the killing occurred. I have the results of the necropsy right here, which I just received. The C 2, 3, and 4 vertebrae were actually *crushed*. There was no indication that any kind of machine or instrument was used, which is problematic, since if only one's hands were employed, such crushing would require considerable force. The tail appears to have been hacked off with a crude implement and removed from the scene, along with the collar and tags."

Tad took notes furiously. This was good stuff. The sheriff would be pleased. Then again, he'd probably gotten the same report. He continued taking notes, just to be sure.

"I followed the bare footprints leading to and from the scene. The same corn row was used in both cases, leading away from, and then back to, Medicine Creek. Once in the creek, it was no longer possible to follow the tracks. So I spent the morning with Mrs. Tealander, the town administrator, acquainting myself with the local residents. I fear that this task will take much longer than I'd originally—"

A tremulous voice came from the rear of the house. "Mr. Pendergast?"

Pendergast held his finger to his lips. "Miss Kraus is out of bed," he murmured. "It wouldn't do for her to hear us talking this way." He turned, and said in a louder tone, "Yes, Miss Kraus?"

Tad saw the figure of the old woman appear in the

doorway, muffled despite the heat in a nightgown and robes. Tad quickly rose.

"Why, hello, Tad," said the old lady. "I've been poorly, you know, and Mr. Pendergast has been kind enough to take care of me. Don't stand on my account. Please, take your seat."

"Yes, ma'am," said Tad.

She sat down heavily in a chair at the table, her face care-worn. "I have to tell you, I'm getting awfully tired of that bed. I don't know how invalids do it. Mr. Pendergast, would you mind pouring me a cup of that green tea of yours? I find it settles my nerves."

"Delighted." Pendergast rose and moved toward the stove.

"It's just terrible, isn't it, Tad?" she said.

The deputy sheriff didn't quite know how to respond.

"This killing. Who could have done it? Does *anyone* know?"

"We've got some leads we're following up," Tad replied. It was the line the sheriff always used.

Miss Kraus drew the robe more tightly around her throat. "I feel dreadful, just dreadful, knowing someone like that's on the loose. And maybe even one of our own, if the papers are to be believed."

"Yes, ma'am."

Pendergast served tea all around and the table fell silent. Through the gauze curtains Tad could see the great fields of corn stretching out toward the horizon, a monochromatic rusty yellow. It made the eyes tired just looking at it. For the first time, the idea occurred to him that working on this case—if it had a successful resolution—could be just the ticket out he'd been waiting for. All of a sudden, checking up on Pendergast didn't seem like a chore. It seemed, instead, like something he should do regularly. But Miss Kraus was speaking again, and he politely turned to listen.

"I fear for our little town," Winifred Kraus was saying. "With this murderer out there, I fear for it truly."

Seventeen

Corrie Swanson brought the Gremlin to a shuddering halt, sending up a swirl of dust that spiraled slowly into the air. God, it was hot. She looked over at the passenger seat. Pendergast returned the glance, eyebrows slightly raised.

"This is the place," she said. "You still haven't told me why we're here."

"We're going to pay a visit to one James Draper."

"Why?"

"I understand he makes certain claims regarding the Medicine Creek Massacre. I think it's time I learned more about them."

"Brushy Jim makes a lot of claims."

"You doubt him?"

Corrie laughed. "He can't say hello without lying."

"I have found that liars in the end communicate more truth than do truth tellers."

"How's that?"

"Because truth is the safest lie."

Corrie eased the car forward, shaking her head. No question about it: weird, weird, weird.

Brushy Jim's place was an eighth-section of land out on the Deeper Road, fenced in with barbed wire. The plankboard, two-room house stood well back from the highway, a lone cottonwood in front offering a semblance of privacy. The house was surrounded by a sea of junked cars, old trailers, rusted boilers, abandoned refrigerators, washing machines, old telephone poles, compressors, a couple of boat hulls, something that appeared to be a steam locomotive, and other things too sunken into decrepitude to be recognizable.

As Corrie rolled into the dirt driveway she gave the car just a bit too much gas, and the Gremlin shuddered, backfired thunderously, and died. For a moment all was still. Then the door of the house banged open and a man appeared in the shade of the porch. As they got out of the car, he advanced into the light. Like most people in Medicine Creek, Corrie went out of her way to avoid meeting Brushy Jim, yet he looked just the same as she remembered: a mass of pale red hair and beard that sprouted from his entire face, leaving nothing visible but two beady black eyes, a pair of lips, and a patch of forehead. He was dressed in thick denim jeans, big chocolate-colored roper boots, a blue shirt with fake pearl snaps, and a battered felt cowboy hat. A bolo tie with a chunk of turquoise big enough to split the skull of a mule hung around his thick neck, the knotted leather partially obscured by the heavy beard. He was well over fifty, but with all the hair managed to look a decade younger. He gripped the post and peered at them suspiciously.

Pendergast strode toward the porch, suit coat flapping.

"Just hold it right there," Brushy Jim called out, "and state your business. Now."

Corrie swallowed. If something bad was going to happen, it was going to happen now.

Pendergast halted. "I understand you are Mr. James Draper, great-grandson of Isaiah Draper?"

At this, Brushy Jim straightened slightly. The look of mistrust did not go away. "And?"

"My name is Pendergast. I'm interested in learning more about the Medicine Creek Massacre of August 14, 1865, of which your great-grandfather was the lone survivor."

The mention of the massacre wrought a dramatic change in Brushy Jim's countenance. The suspicious glare in his eye softened somewhat. "And the young lady, if that's what she is? Who's she?"

"Miss Corrie Swanson," Pendergast replied.

At this, Jim stood even straighter. "Little Corrie?" he said in surprise. "What happened to your pretty blond hair?"

Ate too much eggplant, Corrie almost said. But Brushy Jim was unpredictable, and he had a hair-trigger temper, so she decided that a shrug was the safest response.

"You look terrible, Corrie, all dressed in black." He stood there a moment, looking at the two of them. Then he nodded his head. "Well, you might as well come in."

They followed Brushy Jim into the stuffy confines of his house. There were few windows and it was dark, a house crammed full of shadowy objects. It smelled of old food and taxidermy gone bad.

"Sit down and have a Coke." The refrigerator threw out a rectangle of welcome light as Brushy Jim opened it. Corrie perched on a folding chair, while Pendergast—after a quick scan of the premises—took a seat on the only portion of a cowhide sofa not stacked with dusty copies of *Arizona Highways.* Corrie had never been inside before, and she looked around uneasily. The walls were covered with old rifles, buckskins, boards with arrowheads glued on, Civil War memorabilia, plaques displaying different types of barbed wire. A row of moldering old books ran along one shelf, bookended by huge pieces of unpolished petrified wood. An entire stuffed horse, an Appaloosa, worn and moth-eaten, stood guard in one corner. The floor was littered with dirty laundry, broken saddle trees, pieces of leather, and other bric-a-brac. It was remarkable: the entire place was like a dusty museum devoted to relics of the Old West. Corrie had expected to see mementos of Vietnam: weapons, insignia, photographs. But there was absolutely nothing, not a trace, of the war that reputedly had changed Brushy Jim forever.

Brushy Jim handed Corrie and Pendergast cans of Coke. "Now, Mr. Pendergast, just what do you want to know about the massacre?"

Corrie watched Pendergast set the Coke can aside. "Everything."

"Well, it started during the Civil War." Brushy Jim threw his massive body into a big armchair, took a noisy sip. "You know all about Bloody Kansas, I'm sure, Mr. Pendergast, being a historian."

"I'm not a historian, Mr. Draper. I'm a special agent for the Federal Bureau of Investigation."

There was a dead silence. Then Brushy Jim cleared his throat.

"All right, then, Mr. Pendergast. So you're FBI. May I ask what brings you to Medicine Creek?"

"The recent homicide."

Brushy Jim's look of suspicion had returned, full force. "And what, *exactly,* does that have to do with me?"

"The victim was a relic hunter named Sheila Swegg. She'd been digging in the Mounds."

Brushy Jim spat on the floor, twisted it into the dust with his boot. "Goddamned relic hunters. They should leave the stuff in the ground." Then he looked quickly back at Pendergast. "You still haven't said what the murder has to do with me."

"I understand the history of the Mounds, and the Medicine Creek Massacre, are intertwined. Along with something I've heard referred to locally as the 'curse of the Forty-Fives.' And as you may know, a large number of Southern Cheyenne arrows were found arranged with the body."

A long time passed while Brushy Jim seemed to consider this. "What kind of arrows?" he finally asked.

"They were of cane, feathered with bald eagle primaries and tipped with a type II Plains Cimarron style point of Alibates chert and Bighorn red jasper. A matched set, by the way, in almost perfect condition. They date to around the time of the massacre."

Brushy Jim issued a long low whistle, and then fell into silence, his brow furrowed with thought.

"Mr. Draper?" Pendergast prompted at last.

For another moment, Brushy Jim was still. Then, with a slow shake of his head, he began his story.

"Before the Civil War, southwestern Kansas was completely unsettled, just Cheyenne and Arapaho, Pawnee and Sioux. The only white folks were those passing through on the Santa Fe Trail. But settlement was rolling this way from the frontier, which at that time was eastern Kansas. Folks had their eye on the good range in the valleys of the Cimarron River, the Arkansas, Crooked Creek, and Medicine Creek. When the Civil War broke out all the soldiers went off, leaving the territory defenseless. The settlers had been brutalizing the Indians and now it was payback time. There was a whole string of Indian attacks along the frontier. Then when the Civil War ended, a lot of soldiers came back, armed and bitter. They'd seen war, Mr. Pendergast. And I mean *war*. That kind of violence can do something to a man. It can damage the mind."

The man paused, cleared his throat.

"So they came back here and began forming vigilante groups to push the Indians west so they could take the land. 'Clearing the country,' they called it. There was a group formed over in Dodge, called the Forty-Fives. 'Course, it wasn't Dodge then, just the Hickson Brothers ranch. Forty-five men, it was, some of the worst dregs of humanity, murderers and crooks pushed out of settled towns farther east. My great-grandfather Isaiah Draper was just a boy of sixteen, barely in long pants, and he got sucked into it. I guess his thinking was he'd missed the war, so he'd better hurry up and prove his manhood damn quick while he still could."

Brushy Jim took another noisy sip.

"Anyway, in June of '65 the Forty-Fives went on a rampage, heading down the criks south of the Canadian and Cimarron and into the Oklahoma panhandle. These were Civil War veterans who knew all about fighting a mounted enemy. They were hardened men, tough, survivors of the very worst sort. They'd been through the fires of hell, Mr. Pendergast. But they were also cowards. If you want to survive a war, nothing helps like being a chicken-livered, yellow-bellied poltroon. They waited until the warriors had gone off on the hunt and then attacked Indian settlements at night, killing mostly women and children. They showed no mercy, Mr. Pendergast. They had a saying: nits make lice.

They even killed the babies. Bayoneted them to save ammunition."

Another sip. His low gravelly voice in the dark cool room was hypnotic. It almost seemed to Corrie that he was describing something he himself had seen. Maybe he had, in a way . . . She averted her eyes.

"My great-grandfather was sickened by what he saw. Raping and killing women and cutting up babies wasn't his idea of becoming a man. He wanted to leave the group, but with the Indians all riled up it would've been certain death to peel off and try to get home alone. So he had to go along. One night they got drunk and beat the hell out of him 'cause he wouldn't join in the fun. Busted a few ribs. That's what saved his life in the end—those broken ribs.

"Toward the middle of August they'd rampaged through a half dozen Cheyenne camps and driven the rest of them north and west out of Kansas. Or so they thought, anyways. They were returning to the Hickson ranch when they came through here. Medicine Creek. It was the night of August fourteenth they camped up at the Mounds—you been to the Mounds, Mr. Pendergast?"

Pendergast nodded.

"Then you'll know it's the highest point of land. There weren't any trees back then, just a bare rise with three scrub-covered mounds on top. You could see for miles around. They posted pickets, like always. Four sentries at the compass points, posted a quarter mile from camp. Sun was setting and the wind had kicked up. A front was coming in and the dust was a-blowing.

"My great-grandfather had those broken ribs and they'd laid him down in a little holler right there behind the Mounds, maybe a hundred yards away. With the broken ribs he couldn't sit up, see, and the dust at ground level was just about driving him crazy. So they put him in this little brush shelter out of the wind. I guess they felt sorry for what they'd done to him.

"Just as the sun was setting and the men were getting ready to eat dinner, it happened."

He tilted his head back, took a long swig.

"There was a sound of beating hooves right on top of them. Thirty warriors on white horses, painted with red ochre, came out of the dust. The Indians were all duded up with painted faces and feathers and rattles—and they came howling, arrows flying. Right out of nowhere. Surprised the hell out of the Forty-Fives. Made a couple of passes and killed them all, every last man. The sentries saw nothing. They hadn't seen any sign of riders approaching, hadn't heard a sound. The sentries, Mr. Pendergast, were among the *last* to be killed. Now that's just the opposite of what usually happens, if you know your western military history.

"It weren't no cakewalk for the Cheyennes, though. The Forty-Fives were tough men and fought back hard and killed at least a third of the attackers and a bunch of their horses. My great-grandfather saw the whole thing from where he was lying. After . . . after killing their last man, the Indians *rode back into* the huge clouds of dust. Disappeared, Mr. Pendergast. And when the dust cleared there were no Indians. No horses. Just forty-four white men, dead and scalped. Even the Indians' dead warriors and horses had vanished.

"A patrol of the Fourth Cavalry picked up my great-grandfather two days later near the Santa Fe Trail. He took 'em back to the site of the massacre. They found the blood and piles of rotting guts from the Indian horses, but no bodies or fresh graves. There were hoofprints all around the hilltop but nowhere else. No tracks went beyond where the sentries had been killed. There were some Arapaho scouts with the Fourth, and they were so terrified at the lack of tracks coming and going that they began wailing that these were ghost warriors and refused to follow the trail. There was a big uproar and several more Cheyenne villages were burned by the cavalry for good measure, but most folks were glad the Forty-Fives were gone. They were a bad bunch.

"That was the end of the Cheyenne in western Kansas. Dodge City was settled in 1871 and the Santa Fe Railroad came through in 1872, and pretty soon Dodge became the cowboy capital of the West, the end of the Texas Trail, shootouts, Wyatt Earp, Boot Hill, and all that. Medicine Creek was settled in 1877 by the cattleman H. H. Keyser, cattle brand bar H high on the left shoulder, horse brand flying H on the right. The blizzard of '86 wiped out eleven thousand head and the next day Keyser leaned his head against the barrels of his shotgun and pulled both triggers. They said it was the curse. Then sodbusters and nesters came and the days of the cattle barons were over. First it was wheat and sorghum, then the dust bowl, and after that they replanted in feed corn and now gasohol corn. But in all that time no one ever solved the mystery of the Ghost Warriors and the Medicine Creek Massacre."

He took one final sip and dramatically clunked down his can.

Corrie looked at Pendergast. It was a good story, and Brushy Jim told it well. Pendergast was so still he might have been asleep. His eyes were half closed, his fingers tented, his body sunken into the sofa.

"And your great-grandfather, Mr. Draper?" he murmured.

"He settled down in Deeper, married and buried three wives. He wrote up the whole thing in a private journal, with a lot more detail than what I just gave you, but the journal got sold off with a lot of his other valuables in the Great Depression and now sits in some library vault back east. Never could figure out where. I heard the story from my dad."

"And how did he manage to see everything, in the middle of a dust storm?"

"Well, all I know is what my dad said. When you get a dust storm in these parts, sometimes it blows on and off, like."

"And the Cheyenne, Mr. Draper, weren't they already known to the U.S. Cavalry as the 'Red Specters' because of the way they could sneak up on even the most vigilant sentry and cut his throat before he even realized it?"

"For an FBI agent, you seem to know quite a lot, Mr. Pendergast. But you got to remember this happened at sunset, not at night, and those Forty-Fives had just fought as Confederates and lost a war. You know what it's like to lose a war? You can damn well be sure they were keeping their eyes open."

"How was it that the Indians didn't discover your great-grandfather?"

"Like I said, the men felt bad about whomping him and had erected a little windbreak for him. He pulled that brush over himself to hide."

"I see. And from that vantage point, lying in a hollow, covered with brush, at least a hundred yards downhill from the camp, in a dust storm, he was able to see all that you just described in such vivid detail. The Ghost Warriors appearing and disappearing as if by magic."

Brushy Jim's eyes flashed dangerously and he half rose

from his seat. "I ain't selling you anything, Mr. Pendergast. My great-granddaddy ain't on trial here. I'm just telling you the story as it came down to me."

"Then you have a theory, Mr. Draper? A personal opinion, perhaps? Or do you really think it was *ghosts?*"

There was a silence.

"I don't like the tone you're taking with me, Mr. Pendergast," Brushy Jim said, now on his feet. "And FBI or not, if you're insinuating something, I want to hear it flat out. *Right now.*"

Pendergast did not immediately reply. Corrie swallowed with difficulty, her gaze moving toward the door.

"Come now, Mr. Draper," Pendergast said at last. "You're no fool. I'd like to hear your *real* opinion."

There was an electric moment in which nobody moved. Then Brushy Jim softened.

"Mr. Pendergast, it appears you've smoked me out. No, I don't think those Indians were ghosts. If you go out to the Mounds—it's hard to see now with all the trees—but there's a long gentle fold of land that comes up from the crik. A group of thirty Cheyenne could come up that fold, hidden from the sentries if they walked their horses. The setting sun would have put them in the shadow of the Mounds. They could've waited below for the dust to come up, mounted real quick, and rode in. That would explain the sudden hoofbeats. And they could've left the same way, packing out their dead and erasing their tracks. I never heard of an Arapaho who could track a Cheyenne, anyway."

He laughed, but it was a mirthless laugh.

"What about the dead Cheyenne horses? How did they vanish, in your opinion?"

"You're a hard man to please, Mr. Pendergast. I thought

about that, too. When I was young I saw an eighty-year-old Lakota chief butcher a buffalo in less than ten minutes. A buffalo's a damn sight bigger than a horse. Indians ate horsemeat. They could've butchered the horses and packed the meat and bones out with their dead or hauled them out by travois. They left the guts behind, you see, to lighten the loads. And maybe there weren't more than two or three dead Cheyenne horses, anyway. Maybe Great-Granddaddy Isaiah exaggerated just a little when he said a dozen of their horses had been killed."

"Perhaps," Pendergast said. He rose and walked over to the makeshift bookshelf. "And I thank you for a most informative story. But what does the story of the massacre have to do with the 'curse of the Forty-Fives' that you mentioned, which nobody seems willing to talk about?"

Brushy Jim stirred. "Well, now, Mr. Pendergast, I don't think 'willing' is the right word there. It's just not a pretty story, that's all."

"I'm all ears, Mr. Draper."

Brushy Jim licked his lips. Then he leaned forward. "All right, then. You know how I said that the sentries were among the last to be killed?"

Pendergast nodded. He had picked up a battered copy of *Butler & Company's New American First Reader* and was leafing through it.

"The very last to be killed was a fellow named Harry Beaumont. He was the leader of the Forty-Fives and a real hard case, too. The Indians were furious at what had been done to their women and children, and they punished Beaumont for it. They didn't just scalp him. They *rounded* him."

"I'm not familiar with that term."

"Well, let's just say that they did something to Harry Beaumont that would make sure none of his family recognized him in the afterlife. And after they were done they cut off his boots and skinned off the soles of his feet, so his spirit couldn't follow them. Then they buried the boots on either side of the Mounds, as a backup, like, to trap his evil spirit there forever."

Pendergast returned the book, pulled out another, even more battered, titled *Commerce of the Prairies*. He flipped through the pages. "I see. And the curse?"

"Different people will tell you different things. Some say Beaumont's ghost still haunts the Mounds, looking for his missing boots. Some say still worse things that I'd just as soon not repeat in front of a lady, if it's all the same to you. But the one thing I can tell you for sure is that, right before he died, Beaumont cursed the very ground around him—cursed it for all eternity. My great-granddaddy was still hidden in the hollow, and he heard him with his own ears. He was the only living witness."

"I see." Pendergast had pulled out another volume, very narrow and tall. "Thank you, Mr. Draper, for a most interesting history lesson."

Brushy Jim rose. "Not a problem."

But Pendergast seemed not to hear. He was staring closely at the narrow book. It had a cheap cloth cover, Corrie noticed, and its ruled pages seemed filled with crude drawings.

"Oh, that old thing," Brushy Jim said. "My dad bought that off some soldier's widow, years and years ago. Swindled. I'm ashamed he was taken in by such a fake. Always meant to throw it out with the trash."

"This is no fake." Pendergast turned a page, then another,

with something close to reverence. "To all appearances, this is a genuine Indian ledger book. Fully intact, as well."

"Ledger book?" Corrie repeated. "What's that?"

"The Cheyenne would take an old Army ledger book and draw pictures on the pages—of battles, courtship, the hunt. The pictures would chronicle the life of a warrior, a kind of biography. The Indians thought decorated ledger books had supernatural powers, and if you strapped one to your body they would render you invincible. The Natural History Museum in New York has a ledger book done by a Cheyenne Indian named Little Finger Nail. It wasn't as magical as Little Finger Nail would have liked: it still bears the mark of the soldier's carbine ball that passed through both the ledger book *and* him as well."

Brushy Jim was staring, wide-eyed. "You mean . . ." he began in an incredulous tone. "You mean to say that, all this time . . . The thing's real?"

Pendergast nodded. "Not only that, but unless I'm much mistaken, it's a work of singular importance. This scene, here, seems emblematic of the Little Bighorn. And this, at the end of the book, appears to be a depiction of the Ghost Dance religion." He closed the volume with care and handed it to Brushy Jim. "This is the work of a Sioux chief. And here perhaps is his glyph, which might be interpreted as Buffalo Hump. It would take additional scholarship to be sure."

Brushy Jim held the book at arm's length, trembling, as if afraid to drop it.

"You realize that it's worth several hundred thousand dollars," Pendergast said. "Perhaps more, should you want to sell it. It is in need of conservation, though. The ground-wood pulp in ledger book paper is highly acidic."

Slowly, Brushy Jim brought the book closer, turned the pages. "I want to keep this here book, Mr. Pendergast. The money's no good to me. But how do I get it, um, conserved?"

"I know a gentleman who can work wonders with books as damaged and frail as this one. I'd be happy to have it taken care of, gratis, of course."

Brushy Jim looked at the book for a minute. Then, without a word, he extended it to Pendergast.

They said their goodbyes. As Corrie drove back to town, Pendergast fell into silence, eyes closed, deep in thought, the carefully wrapped ledger book held very gently in one hand.

Eighteen

Willie Stott moved across the slick concrete floor, sweeping the hot mixture of bleach and water back and forth, propelling stray gizzards, heads, crests, guts, and all the other poultry effluvia—collectively known as "gibs" by the line workers—toward the huge stainless steel sink in the floor below the Evisceration Area. With the expertise of years, Stott flicked his hose hand left and right, sending additional strings of offal skidding away under the force of the cleanser, rolling them all up neatly together as they were forced toward the center. Stott worked the jet like an artist works a brush, teasing everything into a long bloody rope before giving it one final signature blast that propelled it down the drain with a wet swallow. He gave the floor a once-over, snaking the jet here and there to catch a few stray strings and wattles, the odd beak, causing the stragglers to jump and dance under the play of the hose.

Stott had given up eating turkey within days of starting work at Gro-Bain, and after a few months had given up meat altogether. Most everybody else he knew who worked there was the same. At Thanksgiving, Gro-Bain gave free turkeys to all its employees, but Stott had yet to meet anyone who actually ate it.

Work complete, he switched off and racked the nozzle. It was ten-fifteen and the last of the second shift had left hours before. In years past there would have been a third shift, from eight until four in the morning, but those days were gone.

He felt the comforting pressure in his back pocket from the pint bottle of Old Grand-Dad. As a reward for finishing, he slipped out the flask, unscrewed the cap, and took a pull. The whiskey, warmed to body temperature, traced a nice warm tingling line right down to his belly and then, a few moments later, back up to his head.

Life wasn't so bad.

He took a final pull and emptied the bottle, shoved it back into his pocket, and picked up the big squeegee that hung on the tiled wall. Back and forth, back and forth—in another five minutes the floor, workers' platform, and conveyor belt overhead were all so clean and dry you could eat off them. And the stench of turkey shit, fear, blood, and sour guts had been replaced by the clean, astringent smell of bleach. Another job well done. Stott felt a small stab of pride.

He reached for the bottle, then remembered it was empty. He glanced at his watch. The Wagon Wheel would be open for another thirty minutes. If Jimmy, the night guard, arrived on schedule, he would make it with plenty of time to spare.

It was a wonderfully warming thought.

As he was racking up the last of the cleaning equipment, he heard Jimmy coming into the plant. The man was actually five minutes early—or, more likely, his own damn watch was running slow. He walked over to the docks to wait. In a minute he heard Jimmy approaching, jangling like an ice cream truck with his keys and all his other crap.

"Yo, Jimmy-boy," Stott said.

"Willie. Hey."

"All yours."

"Whatever."

Stott walked into the deserted employee parking lot, where his dusty car sat beneath a light at the far end, all alone. Since he arrived at the height of the second shift, his car was always the farthest away. The night was hot and silent. He walked through the pools of light toward his car. Beyond the lot, cornfields stretched into darkness. The nearest stalks—the ones he could make out—stood very still and straight. They seemed to be listening. The sky was overcast and it was impossible to tell where the corn stopped and night began. It was one huge black sinkhole. He quickened his pace. It wasn't natural, to be surrounded by so much goddamn corn. It made people strange.

He unlocked the car and got in, slamming the door behind him. The violent motion sent the thin blanket of dust and corn pollen that had settled on the roof skittering down the windows. He locked the door, getting more dust on his hands. The shit was everywhere. Christ, he could already taste Swede's whiskey, burning the back of his throat clean.

He started his car, an old AMC Hornet. The engine turned over, coughed, died.

He swore, looked out the windows. To his right, darkness. To his left, the empty parking lot with its regular intervals of light.

He waited, turned the key again. This time the engine caught. He gave the accelerator a few revs and then put the thing into drive. With its habitual clank of protesting metal, the car moved forward.

Wagon Wheel, here we come. A warm feeling invaded him as he thought of another pint, another pull, just something to see him back to Elmwood Acres, the sad little mini-development where he lived on the far end of town. Or maybe he'd make it two pints. It felt like that kind of a night.

The lights of the Gro-Bain plant flashed past, and then Stott was humming along in the darkness, two walls of corn blurring past on either side, his headlights illuminating a small section of the dusty road. Up ahead it curved, angling lazily toward Medicine Creek. The lights of town lay to the left, a glow in the sky above the corn.

As he rounded the curve the engine clanked again, more ominously than before. And then, with a wheeze and cough, it went dead.

"Shit," Willie Stott muttered.

The old Hornet glided to a stop along the road. Stott put it in park and turned the key, but there was nothing. The car was dead.

"Shit!" he cried again, slamming the wheel. "Shit, shit, *shit!*"

His voice died away in the confines of the car. Silence and darkness surrounded him. Whatever had happened in his car just now sounded pretty fucking final, and he didn't even have a flashlight to look under the hood.

He pulled out his flask, opened it, tipped it up, drained the last fiery drop. He licked his lips, turning the bottle over in his hands, staring at it. He didn't have any more at home.

He flung it out the window into the corn and checked his watch. Twenty minutes until the Wagon Wheel closed. It was about a mile. He could still make it on foot if he walked fast.

Then, hand on the door handle, he paused, thinking about the recent murder, about the unpleasant details the newspaper had hinted at.

Yeah, right. Five billion acres of corn and some nutcase is lying in wait, right between here and the Wagon Wheel.

Muggy night air flowed in as he opened the door. Christ, twenty minutes to eleven and it was still hot as bejesus. He could smell the corn, the moisture. Crickets chirped in the darkness. Heat lightning flickered on the distant horizon.

He turned back toward the car, wondering if he should put on the emergency blinkers. Then he decided against it. That would just add a dead battery to his problems. Besides, nobody would come along the road until the pre-shift, at seven.

If he was going to get to the Wagon Wheel in time, he'd better get moving.

He walked fast, lanky legs eating up the road. His job at the plant paid seven-fifty an hour. How the hell was he supposed to fix his car on seven-fifty an hour? Ernie would give him a break, but parts cost a fortune. A new starter might be three fifty, four hundred. Two weeks of work. He could hitch a ride to work with Rip. Like last time, he'd have to borrow Jimmy's car to get home, and then come back at seven to pick him up. Problem was, Jimmy expected him to pay for all the gas during the arrangement, and gas cost a fucking fortune these days.

It wasn't fair. He was a good worker. He should be paid more. Nine bucks an hour, eight-fifty, at least.

He walked even faster. The warm glow of yellow light in the Wagon Wheel, the long wooden bar, the plaintive jukebox, the bottles and glasses glistening on their shelves before the mirror—the images filled his heart and propelled his legs.

Suddenly he stopped. He thought he'd heard a rustling in the corn to his right.

He waited a moment, listening, but all was silent. The air was dead still. The heat lightning flickered, then flickered again.

He resumed walking, this time moving to the center of the road. All was silent. Some animal, coon probably. Or maybe his imagination.

Again his thoughts turned to the Wagon Wheel. He could see the big friendly form of Swede with his red cheeks and handlebar mustache moving behind the counter: good old Swede, who always had a friendly word for everyone. He imagined Swede setting the little shot glass down in front of him, the generously poured whiskey slopping over the side; he imagined raising it to his lips; he imagined the golden fire making its way down his gullet. Instead of a pint, he'd pay a little more and drink at the bar. Swede would give him a ride home, he was good to his customers. Or maybe he could just rack out in the back room, go on over to Ernie's first thing in the morning. Wouldn't be the first time he'd slept one off in the Wagon Wheel. Beat going home to the ball and chain, anyway. He could call her from the bar, make some excuse—

There was that sound in the corn again.

He hesitated only for a moment, then continued walking, his work shoes soft on the warm asphalt. And then he heard the sound again, closer now, close enough to be recognized.

It was the rustle of someone brushing through the dry corn.

He peered to his right, trying to see. But he could only see the tops of the corn against the faint sky. The rest was a wall of darkness.

Then, as he stared, he saw a single cornstalk tremble against the sky.

What was it? Deer? Coyote?

"Hah!" he cried, shooing his hands in the direction of the sound.

His blood froze at the reply. It was a grunt, human yet not human.

Muh, came the sound.

"Who the hell is that?"

No sound now.

"Fuck you," said Stott, quickening his pace and veering to the far side of the road. "I don't know who the hell you are, but *fuck you.*"

There was a rustling sound, of someone moving through the corn, faster now, keeping pace with him.

Muh.

Stott began to jog along the far side of the road.

The rustling in the corn kept pace. The voice, the strange gasping voice, rose in volume and insistence. *Muh! Muh!*

Now Stott broke into a run. There was a corresponding crashing in the corn to his right. He could see, against the faintest sky, the tops of the corn alongside the road thrashing and snapping. More crashing, and then he saw what he thought was a dark shape coming out of the corn, very fast, first moving parallel to him, then angling closer.

In a second, some atavistic instinct drove Willie Stott to jump the ditch on the left side of the road and crash headlong into the corn. As the tall ears swallowed him up, he glanced back for only a second. As he did so he saw a large, dark shape scuttling across the road behind him at a terrible speed.

Stott crashed through the next row, and the next, forcing himself as deeply as possible into the dark, suffocating corn, gasping out loud. But always he heard the crash of dry ears being trampled behind him.

He took a ninety-degree angle and ran down a row. Behind, the crashing stopped.

Stott ran. He had long legs and in high school he'd been on the track team. That had been years ago, but he still knew how to run. And so he ran, thinking of nothing else except planting one foot before the other, outrunning whatever it was behind him.

Despite the encircling corn, he was not yet fully disoriented. Medicine Creek lay ahead of him, just over a mile away. He could still make it . . .

Behind him now, he could hear the loud slapping of feet against earth. And with each step, a rhythmic grunt.

Muh. Muh. Muh.

The long row of corn made a slow curve along the topography of the land, and he flew along it, running with a speed born of sheer terror.

Muh. Muh. Muh.

Christ, it was getting closer. He swerved, desperately crashing through another row, still running.

He heard an echoing crash behind him as the pursuer broke through the row, following him, closing in.

Muh. Muh. Muh. Muh.

"Leave me the fuck alone!" he screamed.

Muh. Muh. Muh. Muh.

It was getting closer, so close he almost imagined he could feel puffs of hot breath on his neck, keeping time with the thudding feet. A sudden wet warmth flooded his thighs as his bladder let go. He swerved, crashed through yet another row, swerved, veered back. The thing kept right behind him, closer, ever closer. *Muh! Muh! Muh! Muh!* It was still gaining, and gaining fast.

Stott felt something grab his hair, something horribly strong. He tried to jerk his head away, the sudden pain awful, but the grip held fast. His lungs were on fire. He could feel his legs slackening with terror.

"Somebody, help me!" he screamed, diving to one side, jerking and thrashing his head so violently he could feel his scalp begin to separate from his skull. The thing was now almost on top of him. And then he felt a sudden, viselike grip on the back of his neck, a brutal twist and snap, and suddenly it seemed as if he had left the ground and was flying, flying, up into the dark sky, while a triumphant voice screamed:

Muuuuuuuuuuuuuuuuuuhhhhhhhhhhhhhhhhhh!!

Nineteen

Smit Ludwig locked the door to the *Cry County Courier* and dropped the keys into his pocket. As he angled across the street he glanced up at the early morning sky. Big sterile thunderheads were piling up on the northern horizon, just as they had done every day for the past two weeks. They would spread across the sky by nightfall and be gone by morning. One of these days the heat would break and there would be one hell of a storm. But it looked as if the heat would grip the town for a while more, at least.

Ludwig had a pretty good idea what Art Ridder and the sheriff wanted to talk to him about. Well, tough: he'd already written the story about the dog, and it was going to run that very afternoon. He strode down the sidewalk, feeling the heat soaking through the soles of his shoes, feeling the pressure of the sun on his head. Magg's Candlepin Castle was only a five minute walk, but two minutes into it Ludwig realized his mistake in not driving. He would arrive sweaty and disheveled: a tactical error. At least, he told himself, Magg's was air-conditioned to tundra-like temperatures.

He pushed through the double doors into a blast of icy

air, and was greeted by silence: at this time of the morning the alleys were dark, the pins like tall white teeth in the gloom, the racking machines mute. At the far end of the alley he could see the lights of the Castle Club, where every morning Art Ridder held court with his paper and his breakfast. Ludwig adjusted his collar, straightened his shoulders, and started forward.

The Castle Club was not so much a club as a glassed-in eating area with red fake-leather banquettes, Formica tables made to look like wood, and beveled mirrors shot through with faux gold marbling. Ludwig pushed through the door and approached the corner table, where Ridder and Sheriff Hazen were seated, talking in low tones. Ridder caught sight of Ludwig, rose with a big smile, held out his hand, and guided the reporter into a chair.

"Smitty! Real good of you to come."

"Sure, Art."

The sheriff had not risen, and now he simply nodded through a wash of cigarette smoke. "Smit."

"Sheriff."

There was a short silence. Ridder looked around, his polyester collar stretching this way and that. "Em! Coffee! And bring Mr. Ludwig some bacon and eggs."

"I don't eat much of a breakfast."

"Nonsense. Today's an important day."

"Why's that?"

"Because Dr. Stanton Chauncy, the professor from KSU, will be joining us in fifteen minutes. I'm going to show him the town."

There was a short pause. Art Ridder was wearing a pink short-sleeved shirt and light gray doubleknit trousers, his white blazer thrown over the back of the chair. He was rounded, but not especially soft. All those years wrestling turkeys had put muscles on his arms that, it seemed, would never wither. He glowed with ruddy good health.

"We don't have much time, Smitty, so I'll be direct. You know me: Mr. Direct." Ridder gave a little chuckle.

"Sure, Art." Ludwig leaned back to allow the waitress to slide a greasy plate of bacon and eggs in front of him. He wondered what a real reporter would do at this point. Walk out? Politely decline?

"Okay, Smitty, here's the deal. You know this guy, Chauncy, is looking for a place to put in an experimental cornfield for Kansas State. It's either us or Deeper. Deeper's got a motel, Deeper's got two gas stations, Deeper's twenty miles closer to the interstate. Okay? So you might ask, where's the contest? Why us? You following me?"

Ludwig nodded. *You following me?* was Art Ridder's signature phrase.

Ridder raised the coffee mug, flexed his hairy arm, took a sip.

"We've got something Deeper doesn't. Now listen to me good, because this isn't the official KSU line. We've got *isolation.*" He paused dramatically. "Why is isolation important? 'Cause this cornfield's going to be used for testing *genetically—altered—corn.*" He hummed the *Twilight Zone* theme, then grinned. "You following me?"

"Not really."

"We all know that genetically modified corn is harmless. But there are a bunch of ignorant city folks, liberals, enviros—you know who I'm talking about—who think there's something *dangerous* about genetically altered corn." He hummed *Twilight Zone* again. "The real reason Medicine Creek is in the running is because we're isolated.

No hotel. Long drive. No big mall. Closest radio and television station one hundred miles away. In short, *this is the world's lousiest place to organize a protest.* Of course, Dale Estrem and the Farmer's Co-op aren't too pleased about it, either, but they're just a few and I can handle them. You following me?"

Ludwig nodded.

"But now we've got a small problem. We've got a son-ofabitch wacko running around. He's killed a person, killed a *dog,* and God knows what the hell else he's up to, maybe he's fucking sheep, too. Right when Stanton Chauncy, project director for the Agricultural Extension Program of Kansas State University, is in town to see if Medicine Creek is the right place to site these fields. And we want to show him it *is* a good place. A calm, law-and-order town. No drugs, no hippies, no protests. Sure, he's heard about the murder, but he figures it's just some random, one-time thing. He's not concerned, and I want him to stay that way. So I need your help with two things."

Ludwig waited.

"First, take a break from these goddamn articles about the killing. Okay, it happened. Now take a breather. And whatever you do, for *chrissakes* don't do a story on the dead dog."

Ludwig swallowed. There was a silence. Ridder was staring at him with a pair of red eyes, dark circles under them. He was really taking this seriously.

"That story qualifies as news," Ludwig said, but his voice cracked when he said it.

Ridder smiled, laid a big hand on Ludwig's shoulder. He lowered his voice. "I'm *asking* you, Smitty, as a *favor,* to just take a few days off from the story. Just while the KSU guy is here. I'm not telling you to kill it, or anything like that." He gave Ludwig's shoulder a little squeeze. "Look, you and I both know the Gro-Bain plant isn't exactly a sure thing. When they cut the night shift back in '96, twenty families left town. Those were good jobs, Smitty. People got hurt, had to uproot themselves and leave homes their granddaddies built. I don't want to live in a dying town. *You* don't want to live in a dying town. This could make a real difference for our future. One or two fields is just a start, but genetic crop engineering is the coming wave, it's where the big money's going to be, and Medicine Creek could be part of it. There's a lot riding on this, Smitty. A lot more than you might think. All I'm asking, *all* I'm asking, is a two-, three-day break. The guy's announcing his decision on Monday. Just save it up and publish it when the guy leaves. Tuesday morning. You following me?"

"I see your point."

"I care about this town. So do you, Smitty, I know you do. This isn't for me. I'm just trying to do my civic duty."

Ludwig swallowed. He noticed that his eggs were congealing on the plate and his bacon had already stiffened.

Sheriff Hazen spoke at last. "Smitty, I know we've had our differences. But there's another reason not to publish anything on the dog. The forensic psychology guys in Dodge think the killer might be feeding off the publicity. His goal is to terrorize the town. People are already dredging up the old rumors about the massacre and the curse of the Forty-Fives, and those damn arrows just seemed calculated to revive the whole thing. It seems the killer might be acting out some weird fantasy about the curse. They say articles in the paper just encourage him. We don't want to do anything that might trigger another killing. This guy's no joke, Smitty."

There was a long silence.

Ludwig finally sighed. "Maybe I can put the dog story off a couple of days," he said in a low voice.

Ridder smiled. "That's great. Great." He squeezed Smitty's shoulder again.

"You mentioned two things," Ludwig said a little weakly.

"That's right, I did. Okay. I was thinking—again, this is just a suggestion, Smitty—that you could fill the gap with a story on Dr. Stanton Chauncy. Everybody loves a little attention, and this guy's no exception. The project—maybe it's better not to go into that too much. But a story on *him,* who he is, where he comes from, all his big degrees, all the great things he's done up at KSU—you following me, Smitty?"

"It's not a bad idea," Ludwig murmured. And, in fact, it really wasn't a bad idea. If the guy proved to be interesting it would make a good story, and it was just the kind of thing people wanted to read. The future of the town was always the number one topic of conversation in Medicine Creek.

"Great. He's going to be here in five minutes. I'll introduce you, then leave you two alone."

"Fine." Ludwig swallowed again.

Ridder finally released his grip on Ludwig's shoulder. He felt a cold patch where the warm, moist hand had been. "You're a good guy, Smitty."

"Right."

Just then the sheriff's radio crackled to life. Hazen pulled it off his belt and pressed the receive button. Ludwig could hear Tad's tinny voice giving the sheriff the morning's incident report. "Some joker let the air out of the tires of the football coach's car," came Tad's voice.

"Next," said Hazen.

"Another dead dog. This one reported by the side of the road."

"Christ. Next."

"Willie Stott's wife says he didn't come home last night."

The sheriff rolled his eyes. "Check with Swede at the Wagon Wheel. He's probably sleeping it off in the back room again."

"Yes, sir."

"I'll check out the dog myself."

"It's two and a half miles out the Deeper Road, on the west side."

"Check."

Hazen shoved the radio back into his belt, ground out his cigarette in an ashtray, swept his hat off the empty seat next to him, fitted it to his head, and stood. "See you, Art. Smitty, thanks. Gotta run."

The sheriff left, and then, as if on cue, Dr. Stanton Chauncy materialized at the far end of the bowling alley, glancing around.

Ridder called, waved at him through the glass. Chauncy nodded and walked past the alleys and into the Castle Club. He had the same stiff walk Ludwig had noticed at the Sociable. The man peered at the plastic decor and Ludwig thought he could see a flicker of something in his eyes: amusement? contempt?

Ridder rose and so did Ludwig.

"Don't get up on my account," Chauncy said. He shook their hands and they all sat down.

"Dr. Chauncy," Ridder began, "I want to introduce to you Smit Ludwig from the *Cry County Courier,* our local paper. He's the publisher, editor, and reporter. It's a one-man band." He laughed.

Ludwig found a pair of rather cool blue eyes turned on him. "That must be very interesting for you, Mr. Ludwig."

"Call him Smitty. We don't go on ceremony in Medicine Creek. We're a friendly town."

"Thank you, Art." Chauncy turned to Ludwig. "Smitty, I hope you'll call me Stan."

Ridder spoke before Ludwig could answer. "Stan, listen. Smitty wants to do a story on you and I have to run, so I'll leave you here. Order what you like; bill's on me."

In a moment Ridder was gone, and Chauncy had turned his two dry eyes back on Ludwig. For a moment, Ludwig wondered what he was waiting for. Then he remembered he was supposed to do an interview. He pulled out his steno book, fished out a pen.

"If you don't mind, I prefer to work with questions presented to me ahead of time," said Chauncy.

"I wish we were that organized," said Ludwig, mustering a smile.

Chauncy did not smile. "Tell me what kind of story you had in mind."

"It would be a profile, basically. You know, the man behind the project and all that."

There was a silence. "We're dealing with a sensitive subject. It has to be handled *just so*."

"It would be a favorable, uncontroversial article, focusing on you, not on the details of the experimental field."

Chauncy thought a moment. "I'll have to see the piece before it runs."

"We don't usually do that."

"You'll just have to make an exception in my case. University policy."

Ludwig sighed. "Very well."

"Proceed," said Chauncy. He sat back in the chair.

"Would you like a coffee, some breakfast?"

"I ate hours ago, back in Deeper."

"All right, then. Let's see." Ludwig opened the steno book to a blank page, smoothed it, readied his pen, and tried to think of a few pithy questions.

Chauncy looked at his watch. "I'm really a very busy man, so if you could keep this to fifteen minutes, I'd appreciate it. Next time, you should bring questions instead of making them up on the spot. It's a simple courtesy when interviewing someone whose time is valuable."

Ludwig exhaled. "So, tell me about yourself, where you went to school, how you got interested in agriculture, that sort of thing."

"I was born and raised in Sacramento, California. I went to high school there, and attended the University of California at Davis, where I majored in biochemistry. I graduated Phi Beta Kappa, summa cum laude, in 1985." He paused. "Would you like me to spell 'summa cum laude'?"

"I think I can manage it."

"Then I attended graduate school at Stanford University, graduating in four years—that would be 1989—with a doctorate in molecular biology. My dissertation was awarded the Hensley Medal. That's H-E-N-S-L-E-Y. I shortly thereafter joined the biology department of Kansas State University on a tenure-track position. I was awarded the chair of Leon Throckmorton Distinguished Professor of Molecular Biology in 1995 and, in addition, became director of the Agricultural Extension Program in 1998."

He paused for Ludwig to catch up.

Ludwig had done enough boring stories to know what one smelled like, and this reeked to high heaven. The *Hensley* Medal, Jesus Christ. Was this guy a prick or what?

"Right, thanks. Stan, when did, ah, genetic engineering

really capture your interest? When did you know what you wanted to become?"

"We don't refer to it as genetic engineering. We refer to it as genetic *enhancement.*"

"Genetic enhancement, then."

A pious look briefly settled on Chauncy's features. "When I was twelve or thirteen, I saw a picture in *Life* magazine of a crowd of starving Biafran children all crowding around a UN truck, trying to get a bit of rice. I thought, *I want to do something to feed those starving children.*"

What a crock. But Ludwig dutifully wrote it all down.

"And your father? Mother? What did they do? Does science run in the family?"

There was a brief silence. "I would prefer to keep the focus on myself."

Father probably drove a truck and beat his wife, thought Ludwig. "Fine. Tell me, have you published any papers or books?"

"Yes. A great many. I will have a copy of my curriculum vitae faxed to your office if you will give me the number."

"No fax machine. Sorry."

"I see. Frankly, I find it a waste of time to answer questions like this when it would be far simpler for you to get the information yourself from the KSU public relations department. They have a file on me a foot thick. And it would be much better if you *read* some of my papers before interviewing me. It just saves everyone so much time." He checked his watch again.

Ludwig shifted to another tack. "Why Medicine Creek?"

"May I remind you, we haven't necessarily chosen Medicine Creek."

"I know, but why is it in the running?"

"We were looking for an average place with typical growing conditions. Medicine Creek and Deeper came out of a comprehensive, two-hundred-thousand-dollar computerized study of almost a hundred towns in western Kansas. Thousands of criteria were used. We are now in phase three of the study, determining the final choice for the project. We have already struck agreements with the appropriate agribusinesses for possible access to their land. All we need now is to make a decision between the two towns. And that is why I am here: to make that final decision and announce it on Monday."

Ludwig wrote it all down, all the while realizing that when you really parsed what the man had said, he in fact had said nothing.

"But what do you think of the *town?*" he asked.

There was a brief silence, and Ludwig could see that this was one question Chauncy did not have a ready answer for.

"Well, I . . . Unfortunately there's no hotel here, and the only place where I could stay had already been booked by a man, a difficult man it would seem, who took the entire floor and categorically refused to relinquish a room." His lips pursed, bristling the short hairs around his mouth. "So I've had to stay in Deeper and make an inconvenient drive of twenty-five miles every morning and evening. There isn't anything here, really, except a *bowling* alley and a diner . . . No library, no cultural events, no museum or concert hall. Medicine Creek really hasn't got anything particular to recommend it, frankly." He smiled quickly.

Ludwig found himself bristling. "We've got good, solid, small-town, old-fashioned American values here. That's worth something."

Chauncy shuddered faintly. "I have no doubt of that. Mr.

Ludwig, when I make the final decision between Deeper and Medicine Creek, you will no doubt be among the first to know. And now, if you don't mind, I have important business to tend to." He rose.

Ludwig rose with him and grasped the extended hand. Out of the corner of his eye, he saw the sun-reddened, stubble-headed form of Dale Estrem and two other farmers looking at them through the glass front of the bowling alley. They had seen Chauncy inside and were obviously waiting for him to come out. Ludwig suppressed a smile.

"You can fax or e-mail the piece to the KSU public relations department," said Chauncy. "The number is on my card. They will vet it and return it to you by the end of the week." He snapped his card on the table and stood up.

By the end of the week. Ludwig watched the little prick walk stiffly past the bowling lanes, his head up, his back very straight, his small legs moving as briskly as machinery. Chauncy pushed open the door to the street and now Dale Estrem was striding toward him, his big farmer's arms swinging. The sound of his raised voice was enough to penetrate even the inner sanctum of the Castle Club. It looked like Chauncy was in for a verbal mauling.

Ludwig smiled. Dale Estrem: now there was someone who was always willing to speak his mind. Screw Chauncy, screw Ridder, and screw the sheriff. Ludwig had a paper to publish.

The dog would stay.

Twenty

*T*ad walked back out of the Wagon Wheel into the blast-furnace heat. So far, no luck, no Willie Stott sleeping it off in the back room. Still, Tad was mighty glad he'd taken the time to check. He popped a mint into his mouth—his second—to cover up any possible beer breath from the ice-cold Coors Swede had slipped him under the bar. It sure tasted good on a day as hot as this one. Swede Cahill was one hell of a nice guy.

Tad's cruiser was sitting outside the sheriff's office, baking in the sun, and Tad made a beeline for it. He slid inside and started the engine, careful to let the minimum amount of back and buttcheek come in contact with the blistering leatherette. If he could land a desk job in Topeka or Kansas City, he wouldn't have to spend his days hopping in and out of the suffocating heat, forced to drive a cruiser that carried its own little hell around inside it.

He switched his radio to the frequency of the county dispatcher.

"Unit twenty-one to Dispatch," he said.

"Hiya, Tad," came the voice of LaVerne, who worked

the day shift. She was sweet on Tad and, had she been maybe twenty years younger, perhaps he might have felt the same way.

"LaVerne, anything new?" he asked.

"Someone at Gro-Bain just reported a vehicle parked by the side of the approach road. Seems abandoned."

"What's the model?" Tad didn't have to ask for the make. Except for Art Ridder's Caprice and the police '91 Mustangs, bought secondhand from the Great Bend PD, just about every car in town was AMC. It had been the only dealership within an hour's drive. Like so much else, though, it had closed down years ago.

"Hornet, license plate Whiskey Echo Foxtrot Two Niner Seven."

He thanked LaVerne before slipping back into more formal jargon. "Unit twenty-one, moving," he said, replacing the radio.

That would be Stott's Hornet. No doubt the guy was sleeping in the back, like he had the last time his shitbox broke down outside of town. He'd curled up and made a nice little evening out of it, just the two of them, him and Old Grand-Dad.

Tad put the cruiser in gear and pulled away from the curb. It was the work of fifteen seconds to leave the town behind. Four minutes later, he turned into the plant road. There was a huge semi-load of live turkeys lumbering ahead of him, laying down a stink of turkey shit on the road so thick you could almost see it. Tad overtook the semi as quickly as he could, glancing over at the stacked cages full of terrified turkeys, their eyes bulging.

Tad's job had carried him into the Gro-Bain plant a couple of times. His first visit was right before Thanksgiving, and that year he and his widowed mother had enjoyed a nice pork roast. It had been pork roast ever since. Tad was glad he had never seen a pig farm.

There it was: Stott's Hornet, parked by the side of the road, almost invisible in the shadow of the corn. Tad stopped behind it, switched on his flashers, and got out.

The windows were open, the car was empty. There was no key in the ignition.

The turkey truck blasted by, rocking the corn on either side of the road and leaving behind the stench of diesel and panicked poultry. Tad turned away with a wince. Then he pulled his radio from his belt.

"Yeah?" came Hazen's response when he called.

"I'm here at Stott's car. It's parked on the access road leading to Gro-Bain. It's empty, no sign of Stott."

"Figures. He's probably sleeping it off in the corn."

Tad looked out into the sea of corn. Somehow, he didn't think anyone would choose to sleep in there, even drunk. "You really think so?"

"Sure I do. What else?"

The question hung in the air.

"Well . . ."

"Tad, Tad. You can't let this craziness get to you. Not every missing person turns up murdered and mutilated. Look, I'm out here at the dog. And guess what?"

"What?" Tad felt a constriction in his throat.

"It's just a dog hit by a car. Still got its tail and everything."

"That's good."

"So listen. You know Willie as well as I do. His car breaks down and he sets off on foot to wet his whistle at the Wagon Wheel. He's got his usual hip flask in his back pocket, and he nips it until it's gone. On the way, he decides to take a little snooze in the corn. And that's where you'll find him, hungover as hell but otherwise intact. Cruise back along the road slow, you'll probably find him in the shade of the ditch. Okay?"

"Okay, Sheriff."

"That's a boy. You be careful, huh?"

"Will do."

As Tad was about to get back in the cruiser, he noticed something gleaming in the dirt beside Stott's Hornet: an empty pint bottle. He walked over, picked it up, sniffed. The smell of fresh bourbon filled his nose.

It was just as the sheriff had said. Hazen seemed to know everything in town, almost before it happened. He was a good cop. And he'd always acted like a second father to him. Tad should be grateful to be working for a guy like that, he really should.

Tad put the pint into a plastic evidence bag and flagged the spot. The sheriff appreciated thoroughness, even in the little things. As he was heading back toward his cruiser, another truck passed. But this was a refrigerated truck coming from the plant, full of nice, sanitized, frozen Butterballs. No odor, no nothing. The driver waved cheerfully. Tad waved back, lowered himself into his car, and started back down the road, looking for Stott.

Two hundred yards later, he stopped. To the left, the cornstalks had been broken. And on the right-hand side the corn was broken as well, a few stalks angled sharply to one side. It looked to Tad like someone had pushed into the corn on the left, while someone else had come out and crossed the road from the right.

He stopped the cruiser, his sense of unease returning.

He got out of the car and looked at the ground under the corn on the left side of the road. There was a disturbance in the dry clods. A disturbance that suggested someone had walked—or, more likely, run—through the dirt between two corn rows. A little deeper in, Tad could see some broken stalks and a couple of dry cobs that had been torn away and were now lying on the ground.

Tad pushed into the first row, eyes on the ground. His heart was beating uncomfortably fast. It was hard to make out marks in the clumpy, dry earth, but there were depressions that looked like footprints, scuffed areas, places where clods had been overturned, showing their dark undersides. He paused, suppressing an urge to call the sheriff. The trail went on, and here it broke through another row of corn, flattening five or six stalks.

There seemed to be more than one set of blurred, incomplete tracks. Tad didn't want to articulate, even to himself, what this was starting to resemble. It looked like a chase. Jesus, it was really looking like a chase.

He continued walking, hoping it would turn out to be something else.

The trail went through another row, ran along the corn for a while, then broke through yet another. And then Tad came suddenly upon an area where there had been some thrashing in the dirt. A dozen stalks were broken and scattered. The ground was all torn up. It was a mess. It looked like something violent, really violent, had happened here.

Tad swallowed, scanning the ground intently. There, finally—on the far side of the disturbance—was a clear footprint in the dry earth.

It was bare.

Oh, God, thought Tad, a sick feeling rising in his stomach. *Oh, God.* And his hand trembled as he raised the radio to his lips.

Twenty-One

Corrie Swanson brought the shuddering Gremlin into the dirt lot of Kraus's Kaverns, parking it amidst a swirl of dust that spiraled up and away. She glanced at the dashboard clock: six-thirty exactly. God, it was hot. She snapped off the blaring music, threw open her door and got out, scooping up her new notebook as she did so. She walked across the lot and mounted the steps to the old, decaying Victorian pile. The oval windows in the door revealed little of the gloom beyond. She raised the big iron knocker and let it drop, once, twice. The soft creak of footsteps, then Pendergast appeared at the door.

"Miss Swanson," he said. "Punctual, very punctual. We, on the other hand, are running late. I must admit to a certain difficulty adjusting to the early dinner hour of this town."

Corrie followed him into the dining room, where the remains of what looked like an elaborate dinner could be seen beneath the glow of candles. Winifred Kraus sat at the head of the table, wiping her mouth primly with a lace napkin.

"Please sit down," said Pendergast. "Coffee or tea?"

"No, thanks."

Pendergast disappeared into the kitchen, coming back with a funny-looking metal teapot. He filled two cups with a green liquid, handing one to Winifred and keeping the other himself. "Now, Miss Swanson, I understand you've completed your interview with Andy Cahill."

Corrie shifted uncomfortably in her chair, laid her notebook on the table.

Pendergast's eyebrows shot up. "What's this?"

"My notebook," said Corrie with a defensiveness she didn't quite understand. "You wanted me to interview Andy, so I did. I had to write it down somewhere."

"Excellent. Let's have the report." The FBI agent settled into his chair, his hands clasped together.

Feeling awkward, Corrie opened the notebook.

"What lovely handwriting you have, my dear," said Winifred, leaning just a little too close.

"Thanks." Corrie edged the notebook away. Prying old gossip.

"I went to Andy's house yesterday evening. He'd been out of town, a 4-H trip to the state fair. I told him his dog had died, but I didn't say how. I kind of let him assume it was hit by a car. He was pretty upset. He loved that dog, Jiff."

She paused. Once again, Pendergast's eyes had drooped to mere slits. She hoped he wouldn't go to sleep on her again.

"He said that for the past couple of days, Jiff had been acting kind of strange. He wouldn't go outside and went whining and cringing around the house, had to be dragged out from under the bed when it was time for his dinner."

She turned the page.

"Finally, two days ago—"

"Exact dates, please."

"August tenth."

"Proceed."

"On August tenth, Jiff, er, took a dump on the living room rug." She looked up nervously into the silence that followed. "Sorry, but that's what he did."

"My dear," said Winifred, "you should say that the dog *dirtied* the rug."

"But he didn't just get the rug dirty, he, you know, *crapped* on it. Diarrhea, in fact." What was this meddling old lady doing anyway, listening to the report? She wondered how Pendergast could put up with her.

"Please continue, Miss Swanson," Pendergast said.

"So anyway, Mrs. Cahill, who's kind of a bitch, got pissed off and kicked Jiff out of the house and made Andy clean up the mess. Andy had wanted to take Jiff to the vet but his mom didn't want to pay for it. Anyway, that was the last he ever saw his dog."

She glanced over at Winifred and noticed her face was all pinched up. It took her a moment to realize it was because she had used the word "bitch."

"What time was this?" Pendergast asked.

"Seven o'clock in the evening."

Pendergast nodded, tenting his fingers. "Where do the Cahills live?"

"It's the last house on the Deeper Road, about a mile north of town, not far from the cemetery and just before the bridge."

Pendergast nodded approvingly. "And Jiff was wearing his collar when he was ejected from the house?"

"Yes," Corrie said, concealing a stab of pride that she'd thought to ask the question.

"Excellent work." Pendergast sat up. "Any news on the missing William Stott?"

"No," said Corrie. "They've got a search going. I heard they were bringing a plane down from Dodge City."

Pendergast nodded, then rose from the table, strolled to the window, folded his hands behind his back, and looked out over the endless corn.

"Do you think he was murdered?" asked Corrie.

Pendergast continued looking out over the corn, his dark figure accented against the evening sky. "I've been keeping an eye on the avian fauna of Medicine Creek."

"Right, sure," said Corrie.

"For example," Pendergast said, "do you see that vulture?"

Corrie drew up to his side. She could see nothing.

"There."

Then she saw it: a lone bird, silhouetted against the orange sky. "Those turkey vultures are always flying around," she said.

"Yes, but a minute ago it was riding a thermal, as it had been doing for the past hour. Now it's flying upwind."

"So?"

"It takes a great deal of energy for a vulture to fly upwind. They only do it under one circumstance." He waited, staring intently out the window. "Now, observe—it's made its turn. It sees what it wants." Pendergast turned toward her quickly. "Come," he murmured. "We don't have any time to lose. We must get to the site—just in case, you understand—before the state trooper legions descend and ruin everything." He turned toward Winifred and said, in a louder voice, "Excuse us, Miss Kraus, for the suddenness of our departure."

The old lady rose, her face white. "Not another—"

"It could be anything."

She sat down again, wringing her hands. "Oh dear."

"We can take the powerline road," Corrie said as she followed Pendergast out the door. "We'll have to walk the last quarter mile, though."

"Understood," Pendergast replied tersely, getting into the car and closing the passenger door. "This is one instance in which you can exceed the speed limit, Miss Swanson."

Five minutes later, Corrie was nosing the Gremlin down the narrow, rutted track that was known locally as the powerline road. She was familiar with this isolated, dusty stretch; this was where she came to read, daydream, or simply get away from her mother or the morons at the high school. The thought that a murderer might have lurked— might *still* be lurking—in these remote cornfields sent a shiver through her.

Ahead, the vulture had been joined by a couple of others, and they were now circling slowly, lazily. The car bumped and scraped over the washboard ruts. The last glory of the sunset lay in the west, an orgy of bloody thunderheads rapidly fading to darkness.

"Here," said Pendergast, almost to himself.

Corrie stopped and they got out. The vultures rose in the sky, apprehensive at their presence. Pendergast began to stride swiftly into the corn, and Corrie moved into step behind him.

Abruptly, Pendergast stopped. "Miss Swanson," he said. "You will recall my prior warning. We may well find something in the corn rather more disturbing than a dead dog."

Corrie nodded.

"If you wanted to wait in the car . . ."

Corrie fought to keep her voice sounding calm. "I'm your assistant, remember?"

Pendergast looked at her inquiringly for a moment. Then he nodded. "Very well. I do believe you are capable of it. Please keep in mind your restricted SOC access. Touch nothing, walk where I walk, follow my instructions precisely."

"Understood."

He turned and began slipping through the rows of corn, silently and swiftly, brushing past ears that hardly rustled at his passage. Corrie followed behind, struggling to keep up. But she was glad of the effort; it kept her mind from thinking about what might lie ahead. But whatever it was, the thought of staying in the car, alone, in the gathering dark, was even less pleasant. *I've seen a crime scene,* she thought. *I saw the dog. Whatever it is, I can take it.*

And then, suddenly, Pendergast stopped again. Ahead, the rows of corn had been broken and swept aside, forming a small clearing. Corrie froze at the agent's side, the sudden shock rooting her in place. The light was dim, but not dim enough to spare her any of the horror that lay splayed just ahead.

And still she was unable to move. The air lay still over the awful scene. Corrie's nose filled with the odor of something like spoiled ham. She felt a sudden constriction in her throat, a burning sensation, a spasm of the abdominal muscles.

Oh shit, she thought. *No, not now. Not in front of Pendergast.*

Abruptly, she bent to one side and vomited into the corn; straightened; then bent and vomited again. She coughed, struggling upright, wiping her mouth with the back of her hand. Mortification, fear, horror, all grappled within her.

But Pendergast seemed not to notice. He had moved ahead and was kneeling in the center of the clearing, completely engrossed. Somehow, the sheer physical act of retching seemed to have broken her paralysis, perhaps even prepared her a little better for the awful sight. She wiped her mouth again, took a cautious step forward, and stopped just inside the clearing.

The body was naked, splayed on its back, arms thrown wide, legs apart. The skin was an unreal, artificial grayish-white. There was a sticky sheen to everything. The corpse looked *loose,* somehow, as if the skin and flesh *were* liquefying, coming off the bones. And in fact they *were* coming off the bones, she realized with a shudder. The skin of the face was hanging loose, separating from the jaw and teeth; flesh was sagging and splitting at the shoulder and white bone could be seen poking through. An ear lay on the ground, misshapen and slimy, completely detached from the body. The other ear was missing entirely. Corrie felt her throat constrict again. She turned away, closed her eyes briefly, consciously slowed her breathing. Then she turned back.

The body was completely hairless. The masculine sexual organs had also fallen off, although again it looked as though an effort had been made to reattach them, or at least arrange them in the right place. Corrie had seen Stott around town, but if this was the body of the skinny drunk who ran the cleanup detail at Gro-Bain, there was no way to know. It didn't even look human. It was as bloated as a dead pig.

As the initial shock and horror began to ebb, she noticed other things about the site. Here and there, ears of corn had been arranged into strange geometrical shapes. There were a couple of objects fashioned in an extremely crude way out of corn husks. They might be bowls, or cups, or something else entirely; Corrie could not be sure.

All of a sudden, she became aware of a loud droning sound, directly overhead. She looked up. A small plane was circling the site, flying low. She had not even heard its approach. Now the plane waggled its wings, veered away, and headed quickly north.

She found Pendergast looking at her. "The search plane from Dodge. The sheriff will be here in ten minutes, and the state police shortly thereafter."

"Oh." She could hardly work her mouth.

Pendergast was holding his small flashlight in one hand. "Are you all right?" he asked. "Can you hold this light?"

"I think so."

"Excellent."

Corrie held her nose, took in a deep breath. Then she took the light, directed the beam as Pendergast indicated. The gloom was rapidly filling the air. A test tube had appeared out of Pendergast's suit coat and now the agent was kneeling, putting invisible things into it with a pair of tweezers. Then another test tube appeared, and another, specimens going deftly into each one. He worked swiftly, moving around the body in ever narrower circles, every now and then murmuring low instructions about the placement of the light.

She could already hear the faint siren of the sheriff's car drifting over the corn.

More quickly now, Pendergast was going over the body bit by bit, his face inches from the skin, plucking off something here, something there. The smell of rotting ham refused to go away, and she felt another twinge deep in her gut.

The siren got louder and louder, then finally stopped.

From beyond the fastness of corn, she heard a door slam, then another.

Pendergast straightened up. All the paraphernalia had vanished, almost miraculously, into the folds of his well-pressed black suit.

"Step back, please," he said.

They withdrew to the edge of the clearing just as the sheriff arrived, followed by his deputy. There were more sirens now and the sound of radios blaring in the corn.

"So it's you, Pendergast," said the sheriff, coming over. "When'd you get here?"

"I'd like permission to examine the site."

"As if you haven't already, I'll bet. Permission denied until we've completed our own examination."

Now more men were crashing through the corn: state troopers and grim-looking men in blue suits whom Corrie guessed were members of the Dodge City homicide squad.

"Set up a perimeter here!" bawled the sheriff. "Tad, lay out some tape!" He turned back to Pendergast. "You can stand behind the tape, like the others, and wait your turn."

Corrie was surprised at Pendergast's reaction. He seemed to have lost all interest. Instead, he began to steer an erratic course around the periphery of the site, looking for nothing in particular. He seemed to be wandering aimlessly off into the corn. Corrie followed. She stumbled once, then twice, and realized that the shock was still heavy upon her.

Suddenly, Pendergast stopped again, between two rows of corn. He took his flashlight gently from Corrie and pointed it at the ground. Corrie peered, but could see nothing.

"You see these marks?" Pendergast murmured.

"Sort of."

"They're footprints. Bare footprints. They seem to be heading down toward the creek."

Corrie took a step backward.

Pendergast switched off the light. "You've done—and seen—more than enough for one day, Miss Swanson. I'm very grateful for your help." He glanced at his watch. "It's eight-thirty, still early enough for you to get home without danger. Go back to your car, go straight home, and get a good rest. I'll continue here on my own."

"But what about driving you—?"

"I'll get a ride back with one of those fine, eager young policemen over there."

"You sure?"

"Yes."

She hesitated, strangely unwilling to leave. "Um, I'm sorry I puked back there."

She could barely see his smile in the gathering dark. "Think nothing of it. The same thing happened to a close acquaintance of mine, a veteran lieutenant of the NYPD, at a homicide site a few years back. It merely proves your humanity."

As she turned to go, he spoke again. "One last thing, Miss Swanson."

She stopped, looked back at him. "Yes?"

"When you get home, be sure to lock your house up tight. *Tight.* Agreed?"

She nodded, then turned again, making her way quickly through the corn, toward the striped red wash of police lights, thinking of Pendergast's words: *it's still early enough for you to get home without danger.*

Twenty-Two

Shading his light carefully, Pendergast followed the bare prints into the darkness of the cornfield. The tracks were now quite distinct in the dry dirt between the rows of corn. As he walked, the noise of the crime scene fell away. When the field began to slope ever so slightly down toward the creek, he stopped to look back. The row of skeletal powerline towers stood silhouetted against the last light of the sky, steel sentinels, the stars winking into view above them. Crows, coming to roost in the towers, were cawing fitfully. He waited as the noise of the crows gradually settled for the night. Then there was no sound at all. The air was still and close as the air of a tomb, and smelled of dust and dry cornhusks.

Pendergast slipped his hand into his jacket and removed his Les Baer custom .45. Carefully hooding his light, he examined the footprints again. They led straight on between the rows, unhurried, heading methodically toward the creek.

Straight toward Gasparilla's camp.

He turned off the light and waited, allowing his eyes to adjust. Then, as quietly as a lynx, he moved through the rows of corn, a shadow gliding among shadows. The corn rows made a gentle bend as he approached the creek, and he could just make out where the passage of the killer had knocked a few dry stalks awry. He turned sideways and slipped through the gap himself, and in another minute had reached the edge of the cornfield.

Below and beyond lay the bottomlands, the cottonwood trees along the banks throwing the creek itself into darkness. Pendergast moved forward along the edge of the cornfield, making the barest rustling noise, and in another minute gained the complete darkness of the trees.

He paused. The sound of the creek purling over its bed was barely audible. He checked his weapon once again, assuring himself there was a round in the chamber. Then he knelt and, cupping his hands carefully, turned on the light. The faint pool of yellow illuminated the tracks, now even clearer in the sand. They were still angling toward Gasparilla's camp. He knelt and examined the prints themselves. They were the same as before: male footprints, size eleven. But in the fine sand he could see that around the embossing made by the ball of the heel and the big toe there was a series of irregular impressions and cracks, as if the feet were unusually horny and tough. He made a few quick notes and sketches and then placed the tips of his fingers in one of the depressions. The prints had been made about twelve to fifteen hours before—just before dawn that same day. The pace had quickened a bit here: now the killer was moving at a good walk, not hurrying exactly, but rather moving with purpose. There was no sense of urgency or fear in the way he moved. He was relaxed. He was satisfied. It was as if he were going home.

Going home . . .

Gasparilla's camp was straight ahead, no more than a few

hundred yards away. Cupping his flashlight so that just enough light escaped to make out the prints, the agent crept forward with excruciating slowness.

He paused, listening intently, then moved forward again. Ahead, all was dark. There was no fire, no light. When he was within a hundred yards of the camp, he turned off the tiny ray of light and approached blindly. The camp was silent.

And then he heard it: a faint, almost indiscernible sound. He froze.

A minute passed.

There it was again, louder now: a long, drawn-out sigh.

Pendergast left the trail and circled around to the right of the camp, moving with exquisite care. As he approached the downwind sector, he smelled no smoke or food. There wasn't even a glow from a dying pile of coals.

And yet there was definitely someone, or something, in the camp.

The sound of exhaled air again. Wet, labored, almost a wheeze. Yet there was something strange about it: crude, animalistic, not quite human.

Careful to make no sound, Pendergast raised his gun. The noise was coming from the middle of Gasparilla's camp.

The noise came again.

Gasparilla—or whatever was making the noise—was no more than fifty feet away. The darkness was absolute. Pendergast could see nothing.

He leaned down, picked up a pebble. He then tossed it to the far side of the camp.

Tap.

A sudden silence. And then a guttural sound, like the growl of an animal.

Pendergast waited as a fresh silence stretched on into minutes. All his senses were on the highest alert, straining to determine whether or not anything was moving toward him. Gasparilla had already proven himself adept at moving through darkness. Was he doing it again?

Slowly, Pendergast picked up another pebble, tossed it in another direction.

Tap.

Once again, an answering snort came back: short, very loud, and in the exact same place. Whoever—whatever—it was had not moved.

Pendergast snapped on the light and squeezed the grip of his pistol simultaneously, activating the laser sight. The beam of the flashlight illuminated a human being lying on his back in the dirt, staring upward with huge bloodshot eyes. His face and head were completely covered in blood.

The red dot of the laser jitterbugged across the hideous face for a moment. Then Pendergast holstered the gun and took a step forward.

"Gasparilla?"

The face jerked back and forth. The mouth opened, blowing a bloody bubble of saliva.

In a moment Pendergast was kneeling over the man. It was unquestionably Gasparilla. Pendergast moved the flashlight across his face. All of the man's glossy black hair and heavy beard were gone, ripped out along with the scalp; the margins of flesh showed the cut marks of some crude implement: perhaps a stone knife. Pendergast quickly examined the rest of his body. Gasparilla's left thumb had been partly hacked through and then yanked off with a brutal tug that left behind a white nub of bone, a shred or two of cartilage. Beyond that and the hair, however, the man seemed physically intact. Except for the scalp, there was little loss of blood. The damage appeared not so much of the body as of the mind.

"Uhmm!" Gasparilla grunted, heaving upward. The eyes were wild, insane. He blew a spray of bloody saliva.

Pendergast bent closer. "It's all right now."

The eyes roved wildly, unable to fix on Pendergast or anything else. When they paused, they seemed to quiver violently, then return immediately to roving, as if the mere act of focusing was unbearable.

Pendergast took his hand. "I'm going to take care of you. We'll get you out of here."

He leaned back, flashed the light around. There was the place of attack: forty feet away to the north of the camp. There was the scuffle, the riot of footprints mingling with Gasparilla's own.

Pendergast stood now and approached the spot, licking the flashlight across the ground. There was the spot where Gasparilla had fallen, and from where—over the course of fifteen hours—he had dragged himself, in rolling fits, across the dirt. And there, on the far side of camp, were the footprints of the killer in the wet sand, well defined, heading into the creek.

The killer, carrying away his trophies.

The sand told the story.

Pendergast turned back and looked deeply into the wildly roving eyes. He saw nothing: no intellect, no memory, no humanity, nothing but the sheerest terror.

There would be no answers from Gasparilla; not now—and maybe not ever.

Twenty-Three

Sheriff Hazen entered the basement laboratory and took an unwilling look around. There was the same old sour smell, made worse by the overlay of disinfectants and chemicals; the same cinderblock walls painted diarrhea-tan; the same buzzing fluorescent lights. Breathing through the mouth did no good—the surgical mask did nothing but introduce a smell of antiseptic paper to the mix. What he needed was a frigging gas mask.

He summoned a variety of comforting sounds and images to mind: Hank Williams ballads; the taste of the first Grain Belt of an evening; going to the Harvest Festival as a kid with his dad and older brother. None of it helped. Sheriff Hazen shivered, and not just because of the smell of death.

He moved toward the bright end of the lab, scrubs rustling. The medical examiner was already there, swathed like himself in blue, and Hazen could hear the murmur of voices. There was a second figure beside the M.E., and despite the softness of the voice he recognized the southern cadence. Pendergast.

Pendergast had been right. It was a serial killer. And he was probably right that the killer was local. Hazen couldn't believe it, hadn't *wanted* to believe it. He'd laughed out loud when he'd heard that Pendergast was spending hours closeted with Marge Tealander, knowing the old busybody would eat up his time and have him chasing down red herrings all over town. But now, in the wake of this new killing, he was forced to admit things did point to a local killer. It was damned hard to come and go from Medicine Creek without people noticing. Especially at night, when a set of car headlights in the distance was enough to send people to the window to see who was coming. No, this wasn't the work of some drifter who killed and moved on. It seemed it was somebody who lived here in Medicine Creek. It was incredible, but there it was. Someone in town.

That meant he knew the killer.

"Ah, Sheriff Hazen, good to see you." McHyde nodded politely, even deferentially.

The guy had really changed his tune. No more Dr. Arrogant. The case was big now, and the M.E. could smell the publicity. This was a ticket out of western Kansas for anyone who wanted to hop aboard the train.

"Sheriff Hazen," said Pendergast, giving a little nod of recognition.

"Morning, Pendergast."

There was a short silence. The body lay covered on the gurney. It seemed the M.E. had not begun his work. Hazen bitterly regretted arriving so early.

The M.E. cleared his throat. "Nurse Malone?"

A voice came from offstage. "Yes, Doctor?"

"Are we ready to roll?"

"Yes, Doctor."

"Good. Run the video."

"Yes, Doctor."

They went through the preliminaries, each one giving their name and title. Hazen could not take his eyes off the shrouded corpse. He had seen it lying in the field, of course, but somehow seeing it in this sterile, artificial environment was different. Worse.

The M.E. grasped the cloth and slowly, carefully, raised the sheet. And there was Stott, bloated, the flesh literally falling off the bones.

Quickly, Hazen averted his eyes. Then, feeling self-conscious, he slowly forced himself to face the gurney again.

He had seen dead bodies in his time, but they sure as hell hadn't looked like this. The skin had split across the breast-bone and drawn back from the fatty flesh, as if it had shrunk. It had also split on the hips and across the face. Melted fat had dripped out in several places and run into little pools in the gurney, where it had congealed white and hard under re-frigeration. Yet there were no maggots—strange, very strange. And there seemed to be a piece missing from the body. Yes: a ragged chunk, torn away from the left thigh, the teeth marks still visible. Dog, it seemed. Man's best friend. Hazen swallowed.

The M.E. began to speak.

"We have here the body identified as that of William LaRue Stott, a white male thirty-two years old." He droned on for the benefit of the camera while they all stood around the corpse. Mercifully, the initial recitation was short. The M.E. turned to Pendergast and asked unctuously, "Any comments or suggestions, Special Agent Pendergast, before we proceed further?"

"Not at the moment, thank you."

"Very well. We performed a preliminary examination of the body earlier this morning and have noted several important anomalies. I will begin with the overall condition."

He paused, cleared his throat. Hazen saw his eyes flicker toward the videocamera positioned above the gurney. *Yeah, you look great, Doc.*

"The first thing I noticed was the lack of insect activity on the body, and the fact that decomposition had barely initiated, despite the fact that the victim has been deceased for at least eighteen hours in temperatures not less than ninety-five degrees, and in full sun for no less than twelve hours." He cleared his throat again.

"The second anomaly is more obvious. As can be seen, the flesh at the extremities has begun to separate from the bone. It is most pronounced here around the face, hands, and feet—the nose and lips almost appear to have melted. Both ears were missing; one was recovered at the scene. Here, across the hips and shoulders, the skin has ruptured, separated from, and ultimately withdrawn from the fatty tissue below. There is a preponderance of a sebaceous, tallowlike substance consistent with melting and subsequent cooling. The hair and scalp are gone—evidently removed postmortem and post-, er, processing—and the fatty tissue appears to have partially liquefied. All these and a whole suite of other anomalous characteristics can be explained by one simple fact only."

He paused and drew in some air.

"The body was boiled."

Pendergast nodded. "Just so."

For a minute Hazen couldn't quite grasp it. *"Boiled?"*

"The body was apparently immersed in water, brought to a boil, and left in that state for at least three hours, probably more. The autopsy and some biochemical workups will pin down the duration a little more precisely. Suffice to say the boiling was long enough to cause the separations you see here at the maxilla, mandible"—he touched the open mouth with a finger, moving the cheek away from the bone underneath—"and here, on the foot, you will note that most of the toenails are actually missing, having sloughed off. And on the hand, here, the fingernails are likewise all missing, and the left second and third digits missing down to the medial metacarpals. Note how the capsule of the proximal interphalangeal joint is sloughed away, here and here."

Hazen looked on with increasing disbelief. Damned if it didn't look just like a parboiled pig. "But, look—to boil a body like that would take days."

"Wrong, Sheriff. Once the temperature overall reaches one hundred degrees centigrade, an elephant will cook just as fast as a chicken. Cooking, you see, is essentially a process of breaking down the quaternary structure of the protein molecule through the application of heat—"

"I get the picture," Hazen said.

"The missing digits were not recovered at the scene of the crime," said Pendergast. "Therefore, one must assume they became separated at the time of boiling."

"That is a reasonable assumption. In addition, you will note what appear to be severe rope burns on the wrists and ankles. It suggests to me that the, ah, *boiling* might have started pre-mortem."

This was too frigging much. Hazen felt his little world spinning out of control. Upstairs in the hospital lay Gasparilla, an eccentric but harmless old coot, with all the hair scalped not only from his head, but from his chin, upper lip, underarms, even groin; and here, downstairs, lay the second victim—boiled alive, no less. And he was looking at a home-town mass murderer who went around in bare feet, hacked and scalped his victims, and arranged them like a crèche.

"Where is someone going to get a pot big enough to boil a body in?" he asked. "And wouldn't someone have smelled it cooking?"

He found Pendergast's cool gray eyes settling on him. "Two excellent questions, Sheriff, suggesting two fruitful routes of inquiry."

Fruitful routes of inquiry. Here was Stott, a guy he had lifted more than a few with at the Wagon Wheel.

"Needless to say," the M.E. went on, "I will verify this hypothesis with tissue sections and biochemical assays. I might even be able to tell you how long he was boiled. And now, I direct your attention to the eight-centimeter diagonal tear on the left thigh. It is deep, going through the vastus lateralis and into the vastus intermedius, exposing the femur."

Very unwillingly, Hazen looked closer at the bite mark. It was very ragged; the flesh, dark brown from the boiling, had been ripped away from the bone.

"A gross examination of this spot clearly reveals teeth marks," said the M.E. "This body has been partially eaten."

"Dogs?" Hazen could barely get the question out.

"I don't believe so, no. The dentition pattern, although showing remarkably advanced dental caries, is definitely human."

Hazen looked away again. No further questions came to mind.

"We've taken measurements and photographs and some tissue samples. The body was eaten post-cooking."

"Most likely, directly after cooking," Pendergast murmured. "Note that the first bites are small, exploratory, perhaps taken while waiting for the corpse to cool sufficiently."

"Er, yes. Well. Hopefully we snagged some DNA from the saliva of the, ah, person who did the eating. Despite the very poor condition of the teeth there is nonetheless evidence of exceptionally vigorous masticatory action."

The sheriff found himself studying the very interesting tile pattern of the floor, allowing Hank Williams's "Jambalaya" to drown out the M.E.'s drone. *Eaten.*

The tune played in his head for quite some time. When it was finished and he finally raised his eyes, he found that Pendergast himself was now bending over the corpse, his face not three inches from the bloated, mottled skin. Hazen heard several loud sniffs.

"May I palpate?" Pendergast asked, holding out a finger. The M.E. nodded.

Pendergast began prodding, *prodding,* the corpse with his finger, then rubbing his fingertip across the corpse's arm, his face. He then looked at his finger, rubbed it against his thumb, smelled it.

This was too much. Hazen looked back down at the tile and mentally cued up "Lovesick Blues." But just as the guitar intro began, he heard Pendergast's voice. "May I make a suggestion?"

"Of course," said the M.E.

"The skin of the body seems to have been coated in some oleaginous substance different from the liquefaction of human fat caused by the boiling. It almost seems as if the body has been coated deliberately. I'd recommend a series of chemical assays to determine the exact type of fats or fatty acids present."

"We will take all that into consideration, Agent Pendergast."

But Pendergast didn't seem to hear. He was staring intently at the body. The room fell into silence. Hazen was aware that everybody, including himself, seemed to be waiting to hear what Pendergast would say next.

Pendergast looked up from the table. "In addition, I note a second substance on the skin," he said, stepping back with an air of finality. "I would suggest testing for the presence of $C_{12}H_{22}O_{11}$."

"You can't possibly mean—?" The M.E. stopped abruptly.

Hazen glanced up. The M.E. looked astonished. But what in hell's name could be more outrageous than what they'd already discovered?

"I'm afraid so," said Pendergast. "The body, it appears, has been buttered and sugared."

Twenty-Four

The Gro-Bain turkey plant squatted low and long in the great sea of corn that lapped right up to its corrugated metal walls. It was the same color as the corn, too: a dirty tan that rendered it almost invisible from a distance. Corrie Swanson pulled her Gremlin into the big parking lot. It was crowded with hot glittering cars and she had to park some distance from the entrance. Pendergast opened the passenger door, unfolded his black-clad legs, and emerged in a single, lithe movement. He looked around.

"Have you ever been inside, Miss Swanson?"

"Never. I've heard enough stories."

"I confess I am curious to see how they do it."

"How they do what?"

"How they turn a hundred thousand pounds of live turkey into frozen Butterballs each day."

Corrie gave a snort. "I'm not."

A large semi-trailer approached the plant's loading dock, its air brakes squealing and squeaking as it backed up a huge load of stacked turkey cages. Beside the loading dock was an enormous bay, large black strips of rubber hanging over its mouth, like the ones Corrie had seen at the Deeper Car Wash. As she watched, the semi-trailer backed its load into the bay, the turkey cages disappearing five at a time between the rubber strips until only the cab of the semi remained in view. There was another chuff of brakes and the vehicle lurched to a halt.

"Agent Pendergast, can I ask what we're doing here?"

"You certainly may. We are here to find out more about William LaRue Stott."

"What's the connection?"

Pendergast turned to her. "Miss Swanson, in my line of work I have discovered that *everything* is connected. I must come to know this town, and everything and everyone in it. Medicine Creek isn't just a character in the drama, it is the *protagonist*. And here in front of us we have a business—a slaughterhouse, to be precise—on which the economic life-line of the town depends. The place of employment of our second victim. This plant is the beating heart of Medicine Creek, if you will pardon the metaphor."

"Maybe I should wait in the car. Dead turkeys are not my gig."

"I should have thought this fit in well with your *weltan-schauung*." Pendergast gestured at the Gothic appurtenances that littered the car. "And they are not dead when they ar-rive. In any case, you are free to do as you wish." And he set off cheerfully across the parking lot.

Corrie watched him for a moment. Then she yanked open the door of the Gremlin and hurried to catch up.

Pendergast was approaching a windowless steel door bearing a sign that read EMPLOYEE ENTRANCE—PLEASE USE KEY. He tried the handle but it was locked. Corrie watched as he began to reach into an inside pocket of his jacket. Then he withdrew his hand again, as if reconsidering.

"Follow me," he said.

They walked along the concrete apron to a set of cement stairs. The stairs led directly onto the loading dock where the semi-trailer stood, its load of turkeys now hidden within the plant itself. Pendergast ducked between the wide rubber strips at the edge of the bay and disappeared. Corrie swallowed, drew in her breath, and followed.

Beyond, the loading dock opened into a large receiving room. A man wearing thick rubber gloves was yanking the turkey cages off the bed of the semi and popping them open. A conveyor belt ran overhead, steel hooks dangling from its underside. Three other men were grabbing turkeys out of the open cages and hanging them, feet first, from the steel hooks. Already so filthy from their ride as to be barely recognizable as birds, the turkeys squawked and struggled feebly as they hung head downward, pecking at empty air, shitting themselves in terror. The belt went clanking off, very slowly, disappearing through a narrow opening in the far wall of the loading dock. The place was air-conditioned down to polar levels and it stank. God, it stank.

"Sir?" A teenage security guard came hustling over. "Sir?"

Pendergast turned toward him. "FBI," he said over the noise, flapping his identification wallet in the youth's face.

"Right, sir. But no one is allowed in the plant without authorization. At least, that's what they told me. It's the rules—" He broke off fearfully.

Of course," said Pendergast, slipping the wallet back into his suit. "I'm here to interview Mr. James Breen."

"Jimmy? He used to take the graveyard shift but after the, the killing, he asked for a transfer to days."

"So I've been told. Where does he work?"

"On the line. Look, you have to put on a hardhat and coat, and I have to tell the boss—"

"The line?"

"The line." The youth looked confused. "You know, the belt." He pointed upward at the row of dangling, writhing turkeys.

"In that case, we'll simply follow the line until we reach him."

"But, sir, it isn't allowed—" He glanced at Corrie as if beseeching her for help. Corrie knew him: Bart Bledsoe. Dingleberry Bart. Graduated high school last year, D average, and here he was. A real Medicine Creek success story.

Pendergast set off across the slick cement floor, his suit coat flapping behind him. Bledsoe followed, still protesting, and together they disappeared through a small doorway in the far wall. Corrie ducked quickly in behind them, holding her nose, careful to avoid the turkey shit that was dropping like rain from the conveyor belt overhead.

The room beyond was small, and housed only a long, shallow trough of water. Several yellow signs were placed above it, warning of electrical hazard. The turkeys moved slowly through a fine spray until they reached the trough. Corrie watched from a safe distance as their heads slid helplessly below the level of the water. There was a buzz, then a brief crackling sound. The turkeys stopped struggling, and emerged limp from the water.

"Stunned, I see," Pendergast said. "Humane. Very humane."

Corrie swallowed again. She could guess what came next.

The line now proceeded through a narrow port in the far

wall, flanked by two thick windows. Pendergast approached one of these windows and peered in. Corrie walked up to the other and gazed through it with trepidation.

The chamber beyond was large and circular. As the now-motionless turkeys moved slowly across it, a machine came forward and precisely nicked their necks with a small blade. Immediately, jets of blood shot out in pulsing streams, spraying the walls, which angled down toward what looked to Corrie like a lake of blood. A man with a machete-like weapon sat to one side, ready to administer the coup de grâce to any turkey the machine missed. She looked away.

"What is the name of this chamber?" Pendergast asked.

"The Blood Room," Bledsoe replied. He had stopped protesting, and his shoulders hung with a defeated air.

"Appropriate. What happens to the blood?"

"Gets siphoned off into tanks. Trucks take it away, I don't know where."

"To be converted into blood meal, no doubt. That blood on the floor looks rather deep."

"Two feet deep, maybe, this time of day. It gets backed up some as the shift goes on."

Corrie winced. This was almost as bad as Stott in the cornfield.

"And where do the turkeys go next?"

"To the Scalder."

"Ah. And what's your name?"

"Bart Bledsoe, sir."

Pendergast patted the bewildered youth on the back. "Very well, Mr. Bledsoe. Lead on, if you please."

They took a catwalk around the Blood Room—the smell of fresh blood was sickening—and went through a partition. All of a sudden, the building opened up around them and

Corrie found herself in a cavernous space, a single enormous room with the conveyor belt and its hanging turkeys going this way and that, up and down, disappearing in and out of oversized steel boxes. It resembled some infernal Rube Goldberg contraption. The noise was unbearable, and the humidity was beyond saturation: Corrie felt droplets condensing on her arms, her nose, her chin. The place smelled of wet turkey feathers, shit, and something even less pleasant she couldn't identify. She began to wish she had waited in the car.

The dead, drained birds emerged from the far end of the Blood Room, disappearing again into a huge stainless steel box from which issued a tremendous hissing noise.

"What happens there?" Pendergast asked above the roar, pointing at the steel box.

"That's the Scalder. The birds get blasted with steam."

At the far end of the Scalder the endless conveyor belt reemerged, now hung with steaming, dripping birds that were clean and white and partly defeathered.

"And from there?" Pendergast asked.

"They go to the Plucker."

"Naturally. The Plucker."

Bledsoe hesitated, then seemed to come to a decision. "Wait here, sir, please." And he was gone.

But Pendergast did not wait. He hurried on, Corrie following, and they passed through a partition that surrounded the Plucker, which was actually four machines in series, each sporting dozens of bizarrely shaped rubber fingers that whirred maniacally, plucking feathers off their appointed portions of the birds. Naked, pink-yellow corpses emerged dangling at the far end. From there, the conveyor belt rose up and turned a corner, disappearing out of sight. So far, everything had been automated; except for the man in the Blood Room, the only workers appeared to be people monitoring the machines.

Pendergast walked over to a woman who was watching some dials on the plucking console. "May I interrupt you?" he asked.

As she glanced at him, Corrie recognized Doris Wilson, a no-bullshit bleached-blonde in her fifties, heavy, red-scrubbed face, smoker's hack, who lived alone in the same trailer park she did, Wyndham Parke Estates.

"You're the FBI man?"

"And you are?"

"Doris Wilson."

"May I ask you a few questions, Ms. Wilson?"

"Shoot."

"Did you know Willie Stott?"

"He was the night cleaning foreman."

"Did he get along well here?"

"He was a good enough worker."

"I understood he drank."

"He was a nipper. Never interfered with his job."

"He was from away?"

"Alaska."

"What did he do up there?"

Doris paused to adjust some levers. "Fish cannery."

"Any idea why he left?"

"Woman trouble, I heard."

"And why did he stay in Medicine Creek?"

Doris suddenly grinned, exposing a rack of brown, crooked teeth. "The very question we all ask ourselves. In Willie's case, he found a friend."

"Who?"

"Swede Cahill. Swede is best friends with everyone who drinks in his bar."

"Thank you. And now, can you tell me where I can find James Breen?"

Her lips pointed down the conveyor line of turkeys. "Evisceration Area. It's up there, just before the Deboning Station. Fat guy, black hair, glasses. Loudmouth."

"Thanks again."

"No problem." Doris nodded to Corrie.

Pendergast moved up a metal staircase. Corrie followed. Ascending beside them, the conveyor line of dangling carcasses rumbled toward a high platform that was, finally, manned by people and not machines. Dressed in white, with white caps, they were expertly slicing open the turkeys and sucking out organs with oversized vacuum nozzles. The turkeys then jerked along toward another station, where they were blasted clean with high-pressure hoses. Farther down the line, Corrie could see two men lopping off the heads of the birds and dropping them into a big chute.

Thanksgiving will never be the same, she thought.

There was one black-haired fat man on the line, and he was talking loudly, relating a story at high volume. Corrie caught the word "Stott," then "last to see him alive." She glanced at Pendergast.

He smiled briefly in return. "I believe that is our man."

As they walked down the platform toward Breen, Corrie saw Bart returning, his hair mussed, practically running. And ahead of him was Art Ridder, the plant manager. He was charging across the concrete floor on stumpy legs.

"Why didn't anyone tell me the FBI was here!" he was shouting to no one in particular. His face was even redder than usual, and Corrie could see a wet turkey feather stuck to the crown of his blow-dried helmet of hair. "This is an off-limits area!"

"Sorry, sir." Bart was all in a panic. "He just walked in. He's investigating—"

"I know very well what he's investigating." Ridder climbed the ladder and turned to Pendergast, breathing hard, working to bring his trademark smile back onto his face. "How are you, Agent Pendergast?" He held out his hand. "Art Ridder. I remember seeing you at the Sociable."

"Delighted to make your acquaintance," Pendergast replied, taking the proffered hand.

Ridder turned back to Bart, his face losing its smile. "You go back to the dock. I'll deal with you later." Then he turned to Corrie. "What are you doing here?"

"I'm—" She glanced at Pendergast, waiting for him to say something, but he remained silent.

"I'm with him," she said.

Ridder cast a querying glance at Pendergast, but the agent was now absorbed in examining a variety of strange equipment that hung from the ceiling.

"I'm his assistant," said Corrie finally.

Ridder exhaled loudly. Pendergast turned and strolled over to where Jimmy Breen was working—he had shut up when the boss arrived—and began to watch him work.

Ridder spoke, his voice calmer. "Mr. Pendergast, may I invite you to my office, where you'll find it much more comfortable?"

"I have a few questions for Mr. Breen here."

"I'll send Jimmy right over. Bart will show you the way."

"There is no need to interrupt his work."

"It'll be much quieter in the office—"

But Pendergast was already talking to Jimmy. The man

continued to work, sticking a nozzle into a turkey and sucking out the guts with a great *schloock!* while he talked. He glanced at Ridder and then at Pendergast.

"Mr. Breen, I understand you were the last one to see Willie Stott alive."

"I was, I was," Jimmy began. "The poor guy. It was that car of his. I hate to say this, but the money he should've spent getting that crapmobile fixed up he spent down at Swede's instead. That hunk of junk was always breaking down—"

Corrie glanced at Art Ridder, who was standing behind Jimmy now, the ghastly smile once again fixed on his face.

"Jimmy," Ridder interrupted, "the nozzle goes *all the way up,* not like that. Excuse me, Mr. Pendergast, but it's his first day on this job."

"Yes, Mr. Ridder," said Jimmy.

"*Up,* like that. Up and in, as deep as it'll go." He shoved the hose in and out of the carcass a few times to demonstrate, then handed it back to Jimmy. "You following me?" Then he turned to Pendergast with a smile. "I started right here, Mr. Pendergast, in the Evisceration Area. Worked my way to the top. I like to see things done right." There was a note of pride in his voice that Corrie found creepy.

"Sure thing, Mr. Ridder," Jimmy said.

"As you were saying?" Pendergast kept his eyes on Breen.

"Right. Only last month Willie's car broke down and I had to drive him to and from work. I'll bet it broke down again and he tried to hoof it to Swede's. And got nailed. Jesus. I requested a transfer the very morning he was found, didn't I, Mr. Ridder?"

"You did."

"I'd rather be sucking gibs out of a turkey than ending up gibs in a field myself." Jimmy's lips spread in a wet grin.

"No doubt," said Pendergast. "Tell me about your previous job."

"I was the night watchman. I was in the plant from midnight to seven A.M., when the pre-shift arrives."

"What does the pre-shift do?"

"Makes sure all the equipment is working so's when the first truck arrives the birds can be processed right away. Can't leave birds in a hot truck that ain't moving while you fix something, otherwise you got a fine old truckload of dead turkeys."

"Does that happen very often?"

Corrie noticed Jimmy Breen shoot a nervous glance at Ridder.

"Almost never," said Ridder quickly.

"When you were driving to the plant that night," Pendergast asked, "did you see anything or anyone on the road?"

"Why d'you think I asked for the day shift? At the time, I thought it was a cow loose in the corn. Something big and bent over—"

"Where exactly was this?"

"Midway. About two miles from the plant, two miles from town. On the left-hand side of the road. Waiting, like. It seemed to dart into the corn as my headlights came around the bend. Almost scuttling, like on all fours. I wasn't sure, really. It might've been a shadow. But if so, it was a *big* shadow."

Pendergast nodded. He turned to Corrie. "Do you have any questions?"

Corrie was seized with panic. Questions? She found Ridder looking at her, his eyes red and narrow.

"Sure. Yeah. I do."

There was a pause.

"If that was the killer, what was he doing, waiting there? I mean, he couldn't have *expected* Stott's car to break down, could he? Might he have been interested in the plant, perhaps?"

There was a silence and she realized Pendergast was smiling, ever so faintly.

"Well, hell, I don't know," said Jimmy, pausing. "That's a good one."

"Jimmy, damn it," Ridder suddenly broke in. "You've let that turkey get past you." He shoved forward and grabbed a turkey as it was trundling away. With one great sweep, he reached inside and ripped out the guts by hand, flinging them into the vacuum container, where they were immediately swallowed with a horrible gurgling. Ridder turned back, shaking gore from his fingers with a savage snap of his wrist. He smiled broadly.

"In my day they didn't have vacuum hoses," he said. "You can't be afraid to get your hands a little dirty on this job, Jimmy."

"Yes, Mr. Ridder."

He clapped Jimmy on the back, leaving a heavy brown handprint. "Carry on."

"We've concluded here, I believe," said Pendergast.

Ridder seemed relieved. He stuck out his hand. "Glad to be of assistance."

Pendergast gave a formal bow, then turned to leave.

Twenty-Five

Corrie Swanson stood by the side of the road and watched, hands on her hips, as Pendergast pulled pieces of an odd-looking machine out of the trunk of her car and began screwing them together. When she'd picked him up at the old Kraus place, he'd been standing there by the road, waiting, the box of metal parts lying at his feet. He hadn't explained what his plan was then, and he seemed disinclined to do so now.

"You really like to keep people in the dark, don't you?" she said.

Pendergast screwed the last piece into place, examined the machine, and turned it on. There was a faint, rising hum. "I beg your pardon?"

"You know exactly what I'm talking about. You never tell anybody anything. Like what you're going to do with that thing."

Pendergast switched the machine off again. "I find nothing more tiresome in life than explanations."

Corrie had to laugh at this. How true it was; from her mother to the school principal to that dickwad of a sheriff, *You've got some explaining to do,* that's what they all said.

The sun was rising over the corn, already burning the parched ground. Pendergast looked at her. "Does this curiosity mean you're warming to the role of my assistant?"

"It means I'm warming to all the money you're paying me. And when somebody makes me get up at the crack of dawn, I want to know why."

"Very well. Today we're going to investigate the so-called Ghost Warrior Massacre up at the Mounds."

"That looks more like a metal detector than some kind of ghost-busting machine to me."

Pendergast shouldered the machine and began to walk up the dirt track that led through the low scrub toward the creek. He spoke over his shoulder. "Speaking of ghosts, do you?"

"Do I what?"

"Believe in them."

She snorted. "You don't really think there's some scalped, mutilated corpse wandering around up there, looking for his boots or whatever?"

She waited for an answer, but none came.

Within minutes, they entered the shade of the trees. Here, a faint, cool breath of night still lingered, mingling with the scent of the cottonwoods. Another few minutes brought them to the Mounds themselves, swelling gently out of the surrounding earth, rocky at the base, sparsely covered with grass and brush along the top. Pendergast paused to turn on the machine once again. The whine went up, then down as he fiddled with the dials. At last, it fell silent. Corrie watched as he slipped a wire out of his pocket, a little orange flag attached to one end, and stuck it in the ground at his feet. From another pocket, he took a thing that looked like a cell phone and started fiddling with it.

"What's that?"

"A GPS unit."

Pendergast jotted something down in his ever-present leather notebook and then, with the circular magnetic coil of the metal detector inches from the ground, began to slowly walk north, sweeping the coil back and forth. Corrie followed him, feeling a rising sense of curiosity.

The metal detector squawked sharply. Pendergast quickly dropped to his knees. He began scraping the soil with a palette knife, and within moments he had uncovered a copper arrow point.

"Wow," said Corrie. Without even thinking, she knelt by his side. "Is that Indian?"

"Yes."

"I thought they made their arrowheads out of flint."

"By 1865, the Cheyennes were just beginning to switch to metal. By 1870, they would have guns. This one metal point dates the site quite accurately."

She reached down to pull it up but Pendergast stayed her hand. "It stays in the ground," he said. Then he added, voice low, "Note the direction it is pointing in."

The notebook and GPS reappeared; Pendergast jotted some more notes; they disappeared once again into the jacket of his suit. He placed another little flag at the spot and then continued on.

They walked for perhaps two hundred yards, Pendergast sweeping as they went, marking every point and every bullet they found. It amazed Corrie how much junk there was under the ground. Then they returned to their point of origin and headed in another cardinal direction. Pendergast swept on. There was yet another squawk. He knelt, scraped, this time uncovering a 1970s-era pop-top.

"Aren't you going to flag that historic artifact?" Corrie asked.

"We shall leave it for a future archaeologist."

More squawks; more pop-tops, arrow points, a few lead bullets, a rusted knife. Corrie noticed that Pendergast was frowning, as if disturbed by what he was finding. She almost asked the question, and then stopped. Why was she feeling so curious, anyway? This was just as weird as everything else Pendergast had done to date.

"Okay," said Corrie, "I'm stumped. What does all this have to do with the killings? Unless, of course, you think the killer is the ghost of the Forty-Fiver who cursed the ground for eternity, or whatever."

"An excellent question," Pendergast replied. "I can't say at this point if the killings and the massacre are connected. But Sheila Swegg was killed digging in these mounds, and Gasparilla spent a lot of time hunting up at these mounds. And then there's all the gossip in town, to which you allude, that the killer is the ghost of Harry Beaumont come back for revenge. You may recall that they cut off his boots and scalped his feet."

"*You* don't believe that, do you?"

"That the killer is the ghost of Beaumont?" Pendergast smiled. "No. But I must admit, the presence of antique arrows and other Indian artifacts does suggest a connection, if only in the mind of the killer."

"So what's your theory?"

"It is a capital mistake to develop a premature hypothesis in the absence of hard data. I am trying my best *not* to develop a theory. All I wish to do now is collect data." He continued sweeping and marking. They were now on their third leg, which took them directly over one of the mounds. There was a cluster of points at its rocky base. At several scattered places Pendergast nodded to some fresh holes in the dirt, which someone had made a feeble attempt to hide with brush. "Sheila Swegg's recent diggings."

They continued on.

"So you don't have *any* ideas about who the killer might be?" Corrie pressed.

Pendergast did not answer for a moment. When he spoke, his voice was very low. "It is what the killer is *not* that I find most intriguing."

"I don't get it."

"We're dealing with a serial killer, that much is clear. It is also clear he will keep killing until he is stopped. What I find intriguing is that he breaks the pattern. He is unlike any known serial killer."

"How do you know?" Corrie asked.

"At the FBI headquarters in Quantico, Virginia, there's a group known as the Behavioral Science Unit, which has made a specialty of profiling the criminal mind. For the past twenty years, they've been compiling cases of serial killers from all over the world and quantifying them in a large computer database."

Pendergast moved ahead as he spoke, sweeping back and forth as they advanced down the far side of the mound and into the trees beyond. He glanced over at her. "Are you sure you want a lecture in forensic behavioral science?"

"It's a lot more interesting than trigonometry."

"Serial killing, like other types of human behavior, falls into definite patterns. The FBI has classified serial killers into two types: 'organized' and 'disorganized.' Organized offenders are intelligent, socially and sexually competent. They carefully plan their killings; the victim is a stranger, selected with care; mood is controlled before, during, and after the crime. The crime scene, too, is neatly controlled. The corpse of the victim is usually taken away and hidden. This type is often difficult to catch.

"The disorganized killer, on the other hand, kills spontaneously. He is often inadequate socially and sexually, does menial labor, and has a low IQ. The crime scene is sloppy, even random. The body is left at the crime scene; no attempt is made to conceal it. Frequently, the killer lives nearby and knows the victim. The attack is frequently what is known as a 'blitz' attack, violent and sudden, with little advance planning."

They continued moving on.

"It sounds like our killer is the 'organized' type," said Corrie.

"In fact, he is not." Pendergast paused and looked at her. "This is strong stuff, Miss Swanson."

"I can take it."

He gazed at her a moment, and then said, almost as if to himself, "I believe you can."

There was a whine from the machine, and Pendergast knelt and scraped, uncovering a small, rusted toy car. She saw him smile fleetingly.

"Ah, a Morris Minor. I had a Corgi collection when I was a child."

"Where is it now?"

A shadow passed across Pendergast's face and Corrie did not pursue the question.

"Superficially, our killer does seem to fit the organized type. But there are some major deviations. First, there is a sexual component to virtually *all* organized serial killings. Even if it is not overt, it is there. Some killers prey on prostitutes, some on homosexuals, some on couples in parked cars. Some killers perform sexual mutilations. Some killers rape first and then kill. Some killers just kiss the corpse and leave flowers, as if they had finished a date."

Corrie shuddered.

"These killings, on the other hand, have no sexual component whatsoever."

"Go on."

"The organized killer also follows a modus operandi, which forensic behavioral scientists call 'ritual.' The killings are done ritualistically. The killer will often wear the same clothes for each killing, use the same gun or knife, and perform the killing in exactly the same way. Afterwards, the killer will often arrange the body in a ritualistic fashion. The ritual may not be obvious, but it is always there. It is part of the killing."

"That seems to fit our serial killer."

"On the contrary, it does not. Yes, our killer performs a ritual. But here's the catch: *it's a totally different ritual each time.* And this killer doesn't just kill people: he kills animals. The killing of the dog is completely mystifying. There was no ritual at all involved there. It has all the earmarks of the 'disorganized' type. He simply killed the dog and ripped off its tail. Why? And the opportunistic attack on John Gasparilla was similar—no ritual, not even an effort to kill. He just, ah, seems to have taken what he needed—the man's hair and his thumb—and gone away. In other words, these killings share elements of both organized *and* disorganized serial killers. This has never been seen before."

He was interrupted by an explosive squawk from the metal detector. They had almost reached the end of the test line; ahead of them, the grassy slope descended through a fold of land to the great sea of corn below. Pendergast knelt and began to scrape away the dirt. This time he did not uncover anything. He placed the metal detector directly on the spot and adjusted some dials while the machine continued shrieking in protest.

"It's at least two feet down," he said. A trowel appeared in his hand and he began to dig.

In a few minutes, a sizable hole had been excavated. More carefully now, Pendergast trimmed the edges of the hole, going down scant millimeters at a time, until his trowel touched something solid.

A very small brush appeared in his hand and he began to sweep dirt from the object. Corrie watched over his shoulder. Something began emerging into view: old, twisted, curled up. A few more sweeps revealed it: a single cowboy boot with a hobnail sole. Pendergast lifted it out of the hole and turned it around in his hand. It had been neatly sliced down the back as if with a knife. He looked at Corrie and said:

"It appears Harry Beaumont wore a size eleven, does it not?"

There was a shout from behind. A figure was huffing his way out of the Mounds toward them, waving his hands. It was Tad, the deputy sheriff.

"Mr. Pendergast!" he was calling. "Mr. Pendergast!"

Pendergast rose as the red-faced, lanky figure came up to them, sweating and blowing.

"Gasparilla . . . in the hospital. He's regained consciousness, and—" Tad paused, heaving. "And he's asking for you."

Twenty-Six

Hazen sat in one of two plastic portable chairs set up outside Gasparilla's intensive-care room. He was thinking hard: about the first cool nights of fall; buttered corn on the cob; reruns of *The Honeymooners;* Pamela Anderson naked. What he tried very hard not to think about was the incessant moaning and the terrible smell that came from the room beyond, penetrating even the closed door. He wished he could go. He wished to hell he could at least head off to the waiting room. But no: he had to wait here, for Pendergast.

Jesus Christ.

And there was the man himself, in full undertaker's getup as usual, striding down the hall on those long black-clad legs. Hazen rose and reluctantly took the proffered hand. It seemed as if where Pendergast came from they shook hands five times a day. Great way to spread the plague.

"Thank you, Sheriff, for waiting," said Pendergast.

Hazen grunted.

Another long gibbering moan, almost like the cry of a loon, came from behind the door.

Pendergast knocked, and the door opened to reveal the attending physician and two nurses. Gasparilla lay in the bed, swathed like a mummy, only his black eyes and a slit for a mouth relieving the massive white swaddle of bandages. He had wires and tubes out the wazoo. All around, banks of machines ticked and blinked and chirped and buzzed like a high-tech orchestra. The smell was much stronger here; it hung in the air like a tangible presence. Hazen stayed near the door, wishing he could light up a Camel, watching as Pendergast strode across the room and bent over the prostrate form.

"He's very agitated, Mr. Pendergast," the doctor said. "Asking for you continuously. We hoped your visit might calm him."

For several moments, Gasparilla went on moaning. Then, suddenly, he seemed to spy Pendergast. "You!" he cried, his body suddenly struggling under the bandages.

The doctor laid a hand on Pendergast's arm. "I just want to caution you that if this is going to overly excite him, you'll have to leave—"

"No!" cried Gasparilla, his voice full of panic. "Let me speak!" A bony hand, swathed in gauze, shot out from underneath the covers and clutched at Pendergast's jacket, clawing and grabbing so frantically that a button popped off and rattled to the floor.

"I'm having second thoughts about this—" the doctor began again.

"No! No! I *must speak!*" The voice rose like the shriek of a banshee. One of the nurses quickly shut the door behind Hazen. Even the machines responded, with eager low beepings and a blinking red light.

"That's it," said the doctor firmly. "I'm sorry. This was a mistake; he's in no condition to speak. I must ask you to leave—"

"Noooo!" A second hand grasped Pendergast's arm, pulling him down.

Now the machines were really going apeshit. The doctor said something and a nurse approached with a needle, stabbed it into the drug-delivery seal on the IV, emptied it.

"Let me talk!"

Pendergast, unable to escape, knelt closer. "What is it? What did you see?"

"Oh, God!" Gasparilla's anguished voice strangled and choked, fighting the sedative.

"What?" Pendergast's voice was low, urgent. Gasparilla's hand had Pendergast by the suit, screwing it up, dragging the FBI agent still closer. The awful stench seemed to roll in waves from the bed.

"That face, *that face!*"

"What face?"

It looked to Hazen as if, lying on the bed, Gasparilla suddenly came to attention. His body stiffened, seemed to elongate. "Remember what I said? About the devil?"

"Yes."

Gasparilla began thrashing, his voice gargling. "I was wrong!"

"Nurse!" The doctor was now shouting at a burly male nurse. "Administer another two milligrams of Ativan, and get this man out *now!*"

"Noooo!" The clawlike hands grappled with Pendergast.

"I said *out!*" the doctor yelled as he tried to pull the man's arms away from Pendergast. "Sheriff! This man of yours is going to kill my patient! Get him out!"

Hazen scowled. *Man of yours?* But he strode over and joined the doctor in trying to pry off one of Gasparilla's skeletal hands. It was like trying to pry steel. And Pendergast was making no attempt to break his grip.

"I was wrong!" Gasparilla shrieked. "I was wrong, *I was wrong!*"

The nurse stabbed a second syringe into the IV, pumped in another dose of sedative.

"None of you are safe, *none* of you, now that *he* is here!"

The doctor turned toward the nurse. "Get security in here," he barked.

An alarm went off somewhere at the head of the bed.

"What did you see?" Pendergast was asking in a low, compelling voice.

All of a sudden, Gasparilla sat up in bed. The nasogastric tubing, ripped out of position with a small spray of blood, jittered against the bedguard. The clawed hand went around Pendergast's neck.

Hazen grappled with the man. Christ, Gasparilla was going to choke Pendergast to death.

"The devil! He's come! He's here!"

Gasparilla's eyes rolled upward as the second injection hit home. And yet he seemed to cling even more fiercely. "He does exist! I saw him that night!"

"Yes?" Pendergast asked.

"And he's a child . . . *a child* . . ."

Suddenly Hazen felt Gasparilla's arms go slack. Another alarm went off on the rack of machinery, this one a steady loud tone.

"Code!" cried the doctor. "We've got a code here! Bring the cart!"

Several people burst into the room all at once: security, more nurses and doctors. Pendergast stood up, disentangling himself from the now limp arms, brushing his shoulder. His normally pallid face was flushed but otherwise he seemed unperturbed. In a moment he and Hazen had been sent outside by the nurses.

They waited in the hall while—for ten, perhaps fifteen minutes—there was the sound of furious activity within Gasparilla's room. And then, as if a switch had been turned off, there came a sudden calm. Hazen heard the machines being shut down, the alarms stopping one by one, and then blessed silence.

The first to emerge was the attending physician. He came out slowly, almost aimlessly, head bent. As he passed them he looked up. His eyes were bloodshot. He glanced at Hazen, then at Pendergast.

"You killed him," he said wearily, almost as if he had passed the point of caring.

Pendergast laid his hand on the doctor's shoulder. "We were both only doing our jobs. There could have been no other outcome. Once he had me in that grip, Doctor, I assure you there would be no escape until he had his say. He had to talk."

The doctor shook his head. "You're probably right."

Nurses and medical technicians were now wandering out of the room, going their separate ways.

"I have to ask," Pendergast went on. "How exactly did he die?"

"A massive cardiac infarction, after a long period of fibrillation. We just couldn't stabilize the heart. I've never seen anyone fight sedation like that. Cardiac explosion. The heart just blew up."

"Any idea what caused the fibrillations to begin with?"

The doctor shook his head wearily. "It was the initial shock of whatever happened to him. Not the wounds themselves, which were not life-threatening, but the profound psychological shock that came with the injury, which he was unable to shake off."

"In other words, he died of fright."

The doctor glanced over at a male nurse who was emerging from the room, wheeling a stretcher. Gasparilla's body was now wrapped head to toe in white and bound tightly with canvas straps. The doctor blinked, passed the back of a sleeve across his forehead. He watched the body disappear through a set of double doors.

"That's a rather melodramatic way of putting it, but yes, that's about it," he said.

Twenty-Seven

Several hours later, and two thousand miles to the east, the setting sun burnished the Hudson River to a rich bronze. Beneath the great shadow of the George Washington Bridge, a barge moved ponderously upriver. A little farther south, two sailboats, small as toys, barely broke the placid surface as they sailed on a reach toward Upper New York Bay.

Above the steep escarpment of Manhattan bedrock that formed Riverside Park, the boulevard named Riverside Drive commanded an excellent view of the river. But the four-story Beaux Arts mansion that stretched along the drive's east side between 137th and 138th Streets had been sightless for many years. The slates of its mansard roof were cracked and loose. No lights showed from its leaded windows; no vehicles stood beneath its once-elegant porte cochère. The house sat, brooding and still, beneath untended sumacs and oaks.

And yet—in the vast honeycomb of chambers that stretched out like hollow roots beneath the house—something was stirring.

In the vaults of endless stone, perfumed with dust and

other subtler, more exotic smells, a strange-looking figure moved. He was thin, almost cadaverously so, with leonine white shoulder-length hair and matching white eyebrows. He wore a white lab coat, from whose pocket protruded a black felt marker, a pair of library scissors, and a glue pencil. A clipboard was snugged beneath one narrow elbow. Atop his head, a miner's helmet threw a beam of yellow light onto the humid stonework and rows of rich wooden cabinetry.

Now the figure stopped before a row of tall oaken cabinets, each containing dozens of thin, deep drawers. The man ran a finger down the rows of labels, the elegant copperplate script now faded and barely legible. The finger stopped on one label, tapped thoughtfully at its brass enclosure. Then the man gingerly pulled the drawer open. Rank upon rank of luna moths, pale green in the glow of the torch, greeted his gaze: the rare jade-colored mutation found only in Kashmir. Stepping back, he jotted some notes onto the clipboard. Then he closed the drawer and opened the one beneath it. Inside, pinned with achingly regular precision to the tack boards beneath, were a dozen rows of large indigo moths. Upon their backs, the strange silvery imprint of a lidless eye stared up from the display case. *Lachrymosa codriceptes,* wingèd death, the intensely beautiful, intensely poisonous butterfly of the Yucatan.

The man made another notation on his clipboard. Then he closed the second drawer and made his way back through several chambers, separated from each other by heavy cloth tapestries, to a vault full of glass cabinets. In the center, upon a stone table, a laptop computer glowed. The man approached it, set down the clipboard, and began to type.

For several minutes, the only sound was the tapping of

the keys, the occasional distant drip of water. And then a strident buzzing suddenly erupted from the breast of his lab coat.

The man stopped typing, reached into his pocket, and removed the ringing cell phone.

Only two people in the world knew he had a cell phone, and only one person had the number. The man lifted the phone, spoke into it: "Special Agent Pendergast, I believe."

"Precisely," came the voice on the other end of the line. "And how are you, Wren?"

"Ask for me tomorrow, and you shall find me a grave man."

"That I sincerely doubt. Have you completed your *catalogue raisonné* of the first-floor library?"

"No. I'm saving *that* for last." There was an undisguised shudder of relish in the voice. "I'm still assembling a list of the basement artifacts."

"Indeed?"

"Yes, indeed, *hypocrite lecteur.* And I expect to be at it several more days, at least. The collections of your great-grand-uncle were, shall we say, extensive? Besides, I can only be here during the days. My nights are reserved for the library. Nothing interferes with my work there."

"Naturally. And you've heeded my warning *not* to proceed into the final chambers beyond the abandoned laboratory?"

"I have."

"Good. Any surprises of particular interest?"

"Oh, many, many. But those can wait. I think."

"You think? Please explain."

Wren hesitated briefly in a way that his friends—had he any—would have called uncharacteristic. "I'm not sure, exactly." He paused again, looked briefly over his shoulder. "You know that I'm no stranger to darkness and decay. But on several occasions, during my work down here, I've had an unusual feeling. A most disagreeable feeling. A feeling as if"—he lowered his voice—"as if I'm being *watched*."

"I'm not particularly surprised to hear it," Pendergast said after a moment. "I fear even the least imaginative person on earth would find that particular cabinet of curiosities an unsettling place. Perhaps I was wrong to ask you to take on this assignment."

"Oh, *no!*" Wren said excitedly. "No, no, no! I would never forgo such a chance. I shouldn't even have mentioned it. Imagination, imagination, as you say. 'One sees more devils than vast hell can hold; such tricks hath strong imagination.' No doubt it's simply my knowledge of the, ahem, *things* these walls have borne witness to."

"No doubt. The events of last fall have yet to release their hold on my own thoughts. I'd hoped that this trip would in some measure drive them away."

"Without success?" Now Wren chuckled. "Not surprising, given your notion of getting away from it all: investigating serial murders. And from what I understand, such a strange set of murders, too. In fact, they're so unusual as to seem almost familiar. Your brother isn't vacationing in Kansas, by any chance?"

For a moment there was no answer. When Pendergast spoke again, his voice was chill, distant. "I have told you, Wren, *never* to speak of my family."

"Of course, of course," Wren replied quickly.

"I'm calling with a request." Pendergast's tone became brisk and businesslike. "I need you to locate an article for me, Wren."

Wren sighed.

"It's a handwritten journal by one Isaiah Draper, entitled *An Account of the Dodge Forty-Fives*. My research indicates that this journal became part of Thomas Van Dyke Selden's collection, acquired on his tour through Kansas, Oklahoma, and Texas in 1933. I understand this collection is now held by the New York Public Library."

Wren scowled. "The Selden Collection is the most riotous, disorganized aggregation of ephemera ever assembled. Sixty packing cases, occupying two storage rooms, and all utterly worthless."

"Not all. I need details that only this journal can provide."

"What for? What light could an old journal shed on these murders?"

There was no answer, and Wren sighed again.

"What does this journal look like?"

"Alas, I can't say."

"Any identifying marks?"

"Unknown."

"Just how quickly do you need it?"

"The day after tomorrow, if possible. Monday."

"Surely you jest, *hypocrite lecteur*. My days are taken up here, and my nights . . . well, you know my work. So many damaged books, so little time. Finding a specific item in that hurricane of—"

"There would be a special remuneration for your efforts, of course."

Wren fell quickly silent. He licked his lips. "Pray tell."

"An Indian ledger book in need of conservation."

"Indeed."

"It appears to be a particularly important one."

Wren pressed the phone close to his ear. "Tell me."

"At first, I thought it to be the work of the Sioux chief Buffalo Hump. But further examination convinces me it is the work of Sitting Bull himself, most likely composed in his cabin at Standing Rock, perhaps during the Moon of Falling Leaves in the final months before his death."

"Sitting Bull." Wren said the words carefully, lovingly, like poetry.

"It will be in your hands by Monday. For conservation only. You may enjoy it for two weeks."

"And the journal—if indeed it exists—will be in yours."

"It exists. But let me not disturb your work any further. Good afternoon, Wren. Be careful."

"Fare thee well." Replacing the phone in his pocket, Wren returned to his laptop, going over the physical layout of the Selden Collection in his mind, his veined hands almost trembling at the thought of holding, a day or two hence, Sitting Bull's ledger book.

From the pool of darkness behind the glass-fronted cabinets, a pair of small, serious eyes watched intently as, once again, Wren began to type.

Twenty-Eight

Smit Ludwig rarely attended church anymore, but he had the gut sense, as he rose that brutally hot Sunday morning, that it might be worth going. He couldn't say why, exactly, except that tensions had risen to a fever pitch in the town. The killings were all that people could talk about. Neighbors were glancing sidelong at each other. People were scared, uncertain. They were looking for reassurance. His reporter's nose told him that Calvary Lutheran was where they would seek it.

As he approached the neat brick church with its white spire, he knew he'd been right. The parking lot was overflowing with cars, which also spilled out along both sides of the street. He parked at the far end and had to walk almost a quarter mile. It was hard to believe so many people still lived in Medicine Creek, Kansas.

The doors were open and the greeters pushed the usual program into his hand as he entered. He eased his way through the crowd in the back and moved off to one side, where he had a decent view. This was more than a church service; this was a story. There were people in church who had never been inside the building their entire lives. He patted his pocket and was glad to see he'd brought his notebook and pencil. He removed them and surreptitiously began jotting notes. There were the Bender Langs, Klick and Melton Rasmussen, Art Ridder and his wife, the Cahills, Maisie, and Dale Estrem with his usual buddies from the Farmer's Co-op. Sheriff Hazen stood to one side, looking grumpy—hadn't seen *him* in church since his mother died. His son was beside him, an irritable look on his puffy face. And there, off in a shadowy corner, stood the FBI man, Pendergast, and Corrie Swanson, all spiked purple hair and black lipstick and dangly silver things. Now *there* was an odd couple.

A hush fell over the congregation as the Reverend John Wilbur made his fussy way toward the pulpit. The service began, as usual, with the entrance hymn, the prayer of the day. During the readings that followed, the silence was absolute. Ludwig could see that people were waiting for the sermon. He wondered just how Pastor Wilbur would handle it. The man, narrow and pedantic, was not known for his oratory. He larded his sermons with quotations from English literature and poetry in an attempt to show erudition, but the effect only seemed pompous and long-winded. The moment of truth had come for Pastor Wilbur. This was the time of his town's greatest need.

Would he rise to the occasion?

The reading from the Gospel was complete; the time for the sermon had arrived. The air was electric. This was it: the moment of spiritual reassurance that people had yearned for, had waited for, had come to find.

The minister stepped up to the pulpit, gave two delicate little coughs into his balled hand, pursed his thin lips, and smoothed with a crackle the yellowed papers that lay hidden behind the elaborately carved wood.

"Two quotes come to mind this morning," Wilbur said, glancing over the congregation. "One, of course, from the Bible. The other, from a famous sermon."

Hope leapt in Ludwig's heart. This sounded new. This sounded promising.

"Recall, if you will, God's promise to Noah in the Book of Genesis: *While the earth remaineth, seedtime and harvest, and cold and heat, and summer and winter, and day and night shall not cease.* And in the words of the good Doctor Donne, *God comes to thee, not as in the dawning of the day, not as in the bud of the spring, but as the sheaves in harvest.*" Wilbur paused to survey the packed church from over his reading glasses.

Abruptly, Ludwig's spirits fell, all the harder for having been falsely raised. He recognized these quotations all too well. Wilbur's air of practiced improvisation had fooled him. *Oh my God,* he thought, *he's not going to do the harvest sermon again, is he?*

And yet, beyond all understanding, that seemed to be Wilbur's intent. He spread his arms with magisterial pomp.

"Here we are, once again, the little town of Medicine Creek, surrounded by the bounty of God. Summer. Harvest. All around us are the fruits of God's green earth, God's promise to us: the *corn,* the stalks trembling under the weight of the ripe ears beneath the giving summer sun."

Ludwig looked around with a kind of desperation. It was the same sermon Wilbur always gave at this time of the year, for as long as Ludwig could remember. There was a time, when his wife still lived, that Ludwig found Wilbur's cycle of sermons—as predictable as the cycle of seasons—

comfortable and reassuring. But not now. Especially not now.

"To those who would ask for a sign of God's bounty, for those who require proof of His goodness, I say to you: go to the door. Go to the door and look out over the great sea of life, the harvest of corn that stands ready to be plucked and eaten, to provide physical nourishment to our bodies and spiritual comfort to our souls . . ."

"To be made into gasohol for our cars, you mean," Ludwig heard someone nearby mutter.

He waited. Maybe the minister was just warming up and was going to get onto the real topic soon.

". . . While Thanksgiving is the accepted time to thank God for the bounty of His earth, I like to offer thanks now, just before harvest, when the gift of God's goodness is made incarnate all around us, in the fields of corn that stretch from horizon to horizon. Let us all walk, as the immortal bard John Greenleaf Whittier impels us to, 'Up from the meadows rich with corn.' Let us all then pause, and look out over the great Kansas earth covered with the harvest and give thanks." He paused for effect.

The mood in the room remained one of suspension, of desperate hope that the sermon would take an unexpected turn.

"The other day," the minister began in a more jocular tone, "I was driving to Deeper with my wife, Lucy, when our car ran out of gas."

Oh, no. He told this story last year. And the year before.

"There we were, by the side of the road, completely surrounded by corn. Lucy turned to me and asked, 'Whatever are we going to do, dear?'

"I answered, 'Trust in God.' "

He chuckled, blissfully ignorant of the ugly undercurrent that was now beginning to ripple through the congregation. "Well, she got mad at that. Being the man, you see, I was supposed to have filled up the tank, and so it was my fault that we'd run out. 'You trust in God,' she said. 'I'm going to trust in my two good legs.' And she started to get out of the car—"

Suddenly a voice rang out: "and got the gas can out of the back and walked to the gas station!"

It was Swede Cahill himself who had completed the reverend's sentence: Swede Cahill, the nicest man in town. But there he was, on his feet, red-faced.

Pastor Wilbur compressed his lips so hard they almost disappeared. "Mr. Cahill, may I remind you that this is a church, and that I am giving a sermon?"

"I know very well what you're doing, Reverend."

"Then I shall continue—"

"No," said Cahill, panting heavily. "No, you will not."

"For heaven's sake, sit down, Swede," a voice cried from somewhere.

Cahill turned toward the voice. "There've been two horrible murders in this town and all he can do is read some sermon he wrote back in 1973? No, this won't scour. It won't scour, I say."

A woman had arisen: Klick Rasmussen. "Swede, if you have something to say, have the *decency* to wait until—"

"No, he's right," interrupted another voice. Ludwig turned. It was a worker from the Gro-Bain plant. "Swede's right. We didn't come here to listen to a damn sermon about corn. There's a killer on the loose and none of us are safe."

Klick turned her short, furious bulk on him. "Young man, this is a church service, not a town meeting!"

"Didn't you hear about what that man Gasparilla said on his deathbed?" Swede cried. His face had, if possible, grown even redder. "This is no joke, Klick. This town's in crisis."

There was a general murmuring of assent. Smit Ludwig scribbled madly, trying to get down Swede's words.

"Please, *please!*" Pastor Wilbur was saying, holding up two thin arms. "Not in God's house!"

But others were on their feet. "Yeah," said another plant worker. "I heard what Gasparilla said. I sure as hell heard it."

"I did, too."

"It can't be true, can it?"

The murmuring of voices rose dramatically.

"Pastor," said Swede, "why do you think the church is full? People are here because they're frightened. This land has seen bad times before, terrible times. But this is different. People are talking about the curse of the Forty-Fives, the massacre, as if the town itself is cursed. As if these murders are some awful judgment upon us. They're looking to you for reassurance."

"Mr. Cahill, as the local *tavern-keeper* I hardly think you're in a position to lecture me on my duties as a pastor," said Wilbur furiously.

"Look here, Reverend, with all due respect—"

"And what about this freakish corn they want to grow here?" called out a very deep voice. It was Dale Estrem, on his feet, raising a hoe in a knotted fist. "What about that?"

He brought that hoe here as a prop, thought Ludwig, writing madly. *He came prepared to make a scene.*

"It's going to cross-pollinate and pollute our fields! These scientists want to come here and play God with our food, Reverend! When are you going to talk about that?"

Now a far more hysterical voice rang out, trumping all.

An old man, skinny as a rail, with a huge bobbing Adam's apple that made his neck whiskers bristle like quills, had stood up and was shaking his fist furiously at Wilbur. It was old Whit Bowers, the recluse who managed the town dump. "The End Days are come! Can't you see it, you blind fool!"

Swede turned. "Look, Whit, that wasn't what I was—"

"You're all a pack of fools if you don't see it! The devil is walking among us!"

The man's voice was shriekingly high, raspy, cutting like a knife through the babel.

"The devil himself *is in this church!* Are you all blind? Can't you see it? Can't you *smell* it?"

Pastor Wilbur was holding up his hands and shouting something, but his dry, pedantic voice could not compete with the general hubbub. Now everyone was on their feet. The church was in chaos.

"He's here!" Whit shrieked. "Look to your neighbor! Look to your friend! Look to your brother! Is that the devil's eyes staring back at you? Look well! And take heed! Have you all forgotten the words of Peter? *Be sober, be vigilant; because your adversary the devil, as a roaring lion, walketh about, seeking who he may devour!!"*

Others were shouting to be heard. People were milling in the aisle. There was a cry and someone fell. Ludwig lowered his pad, strained to see. There was Pendergast, still as death in his shadowy corner. There was Corrie beside him, grinning with delight. The sheriff was yelling and gesturing. There was a sudden backward movement of the crowd.

"You son of a bitch!" someone shouted. There was a violent motion, the smack of a landed fist. My God, it was a fight, right here in the church. Ludwig was stunned. He hastily climbed up on the pew to get a better view, notebook in hand. It was Randall Pennoyer, a friend of Stott's, dusting it up with another plant worker. "Nobody deserved to die like that, parboiled like a hog!"

There was more confused shouting, and several men surged forward to separate the combatants. Ridder himself was now wading in, shouting, trying to reach the fight. Sheriff Hazen, too, was ploughing down the aisle like a bulldog, his head lowered. As Ludwig watched, Hazen fell over Bertha Blodgett and rose again, his face dark with fury. Horrified voices echoed off the vaulted ceiling. The people in the back had pushed open the doors and were exiting in a confused mass.

A pew came crashing down to the frightened screams of a woman.

"Not in the house of God!" Wilbur was shouting, his eyes bulging.

Above it all, the apocalyptic voice of Whit continued, piping out a shrill warning: *"Look into their eyes and you will see! Breathe the air and smell the brimstone! He's a crafty one, but you will find him out! Yes, you will! The killer is here! He's one of us! The devil has come to Medicine Creek and he's walking hand in hand with us. You heard it: the devil with the face of a child!"*

Twenty-Nine

Corrie Swanson sat in her car beneath the shade of the trees in the little turnout by the creek, where Pendergast had—in his mysterious fashion—asked her to drive him. It had just passed noon, and the heat was suffocating. Corrie shifted in her seat, feeling the beads of sweat gathering on her forehead, on the back of her neck. Once again, Pendergast was acting strange. He'd simply reclined in his broken seat and closed his eyes. He looked asleep, but of course Corrie knew enough by now to realize he wasn't sleeping. He was thinking. But about what? And why here? And whatever the hell it was, why had it taken half an hour, and counting?

She shook her head. He was a weird one. Nice weird, but weird all the same.

She picked up the book she was reading, *Beyond the Ice Limit,* found her dog-eared place at the beginning of chapter six, and began to read.

The sea horizon lay against the sky, blue against perfect blue, and it seemed to beckon the ship southward, ever southward.

She closed the book, put it down again. Not bad, but it lacked the punch of the original. Or maybe it was just that something else was on her mind. Such as what she'd just seen in church.

Her mother was not the church-going type, and Corrie had only been inside a few times. Even so, she realized that nobody in town, no matter how many times they'd set foot within Calvary Lutheran, had ever, *ever* seen anything like it. The whole town was falling apart. That Pastor Wilbur, who always passed her with his eyes averted and lips compressed in disapproval, had blown it big-time. What a self-righteous ass. She couldn't help but smile afresh at the images that reeled through her head: crazy old Whit shrieking hell and damnation, Estrem up there waving his hoe, everyone fleeing out the back and falling down the stairs, the plant workers fighting and knocking over pews. So many times in her fantasies she had imagined earthquakes leveling the town, bombs dropping, huge fires consuming everything, riots in the streets, the high school being swallowed by a bottomless pit. And now, in a way, it had come to pass. She was still smiling at the images, but the smile had grown fixed on her face. The reality wasn't quite so funny.

She glanced over at Pendergast and almost jumped. He was sitting there, at full attention, regarding her with his pale cat's eyes.

"To the Castle Club, if you please," he said quietly.

Corrie quickly composed herself. "Why?"

"I understand that Sheriff Hazen and Art Ridder will be lunching with Dr. Chauncy. As you know, Chauncy will make his announcement tomorrow as to which town will get the experimental field. No doubt citizens Hazen and Ridder are making a final pitch for Medicine Creek. Since

Chauncy's leaving the area tomorrow, there are certain questions I'd like to put to him first."

"You don't think *he's* involved?"

"As I've said, I am keeping my deductive faculties as quiescent as possible, and I'd advise you to do the same."

"You really think they'll be there? I mean, after what happened in church just now?"

"Chauncy was not in church. He may know nothing of what transpired. Regardless, the sheriff and Mr. Ridder will want to make a great show of normalcy. To reassure him, if need be."

"Okay," Corrie said, throwing the Gremlin in reverse. "You're the boss."

Although it galled her to do so, Corrie kept the car within the speed limit as Medicine Creek hove into view above the corn. In another moment they were pulling into the big parking lot of the bowling alley. It was almost empty, she noticed; but then, this was Medicine Creek, and emptiness was the norm.

Pendergast motioned her to precede him, and they entered the alley and made their way past the lanes to the glassed-in front of the Castle Club. Within, Chauncy, Ridder, and Hazen were seated at Ridder's usual table. The rest of the place was deserted. All three stared as they entered.

Hazen rose and quickly moved forward, intercepting them in the middle of the dining room.

"Pendergast, what is it now?" he said in a low voice. "We're in the middle of an important business meeting."

"Sheriff, I'm very sorry to interrupt your luncheon," the agent replied mildly. "I have a few questions for Dr. Chauncy."

"Now is not the time."

"Once again, I'm very sorry." Pendergast brushed past the sheriff, Corrie following.

As they approached the table, Corrie noticed that Art Ridder, too, had risen, an angry smile frozen on his smooth, plump face.

"Ah, Special Agent Pendergast," he said in a voice that almost managed to sound amiable. "Good to see you. If it's about the, ah, case, we'll be with you shortly. We were just finishing here with Dr. Chauncy."

"But it is Dr. Chauncy I've come to see." Pendergast held out his hand. "My name is Pendergast."

Chauncy, failing to rise, took the hand and gave it a shake. "I remember you now, the fellow that refused to relinquish a room to me." He smiled as if making a pleasantry, but irritation lurked in his eyes.

"Dr. Chauncy, I understand you will be leaving us tomorrow?"

"Today, actually," said Chauncy. "The announcement will be made at KSU."

"In that case, I have a few questions."

Chauncy folded his napkin into a neat square, taking his sweet time, then laid it down beside a plate of half-eaten stewed tomatoes. "Sorry, but I'm running late as it is. We'll have to have our chat some other time." He stood, shrugged into his jacket.

"I am afraid that won't be possible, Dr. Chauncy."

Chauncy turned and raked him with arrogant eyes. "If this is about the killings, naturally I know nothing. If this is about the experimental field, then you are out of your jurisdiction, Officer, you and your, ah, *sidekick*." He cast a pointed glace at Corrie. "Now, if you'll excuse me?"

When Pendergast spoke again, his voice was even milder.

"I determine whether or not questioning a person is relevant."

Chauncy reached into his suit coat, pulled out a wallet, took out a business card. He handed it to Pendergast. "You know the rules. I decline to be interviewed except in the presence of my attorney."

Pendergast smiled. "Of course. And your attorney's name?"

Chauncy hesitated.

"Until you give me the name and number of your attorney, Dr. Chauncy, I must deal with you directly. As you said, the rules."

"Look, Mr. Pendergast—" Ridder began.

Chauncy snatched the card out of Pendergast's hand and scribbled something on the back. He thrust it back. "For your information, Agent Pendergast, I am engaged in a confidential business of great importance to the Agricultural Extension at KSU, to Kansas, and indeed to the hungry people of the world. I will not be sucked into a local investigation of a couple of sordid murders." He turned. "Gentlemen, I thank you for lunch." He managed a brief pause before the word "lunch" that made it sound like an insult instead of a compliment.

But even before Chauncy had finished speaking, Pendergast had removed a cell phone from his suit and was dialing a number. This unexpected action caused everyone to pause. Even Chauncy hesitated.

"Mr. Blutter?" said Pendergast as he glanced at Chauncy's card. "This is Special Agent Pendergast of the Federal Bureau of Investigation."

Chauncy frowned sharply.

"I am here in Medicine Creek with a client of yours, Dr. Stanton Chauncy. I would like to ask him a few questions about the killings that have occurred here. There are two ways we could proceed. One is voluntarily, right now; and the other is later, through a subpoena, issued by a judge for cause, in a public proceeding. Dr. Chauncy seeks your advice."

He held the phone out toward Chauncy. The man grabbed it. "Blutter?"

There was a long silence and then Chauncy exploded into the telephone. "Blutter, this is pure harassment. It's going to drag KSU through the mud. I can't have any negative publicity. We're at a delicate moment here—"

There was another, longer silence. Chauncy's face darkened. "Blutter, damn it, I'm not going to talk to this cop—"

Another pause. Then "Christ!" He hung up and almost threw the phone back at Pendergast. "All right," he muttered. "You have ten minutes."

"Thank you, but I'll take as long as I need. My very capable *sidekick* will take notes. Miss Swanson?"

"What? Yeah, sure." Corrie was alarmed; she'd left her notebook in the car. But almost as if by magic a notebook and pen appeared in Pendergast's hand. She took them and flipped the pages, trying to look as if this was something she did every day.

Ridder spoke again. "Hazen? Are you just going to stand there and let this happen?"

Hazen looked back at Ridder, his face an unreadable mask. "And what would you have me do?"

"Stop this farce. This FBI agent is going to ruin everything."

Hazen's reply was quiet. "You know very well I can't do that." He turned to Pendergast and said nothing, his face neutral. But Corrie knew Hazen well enough to read the look in his eyes.

Pendergast spoke cheerfully to Chauncy. "Tell me, Dr. Chauncy, when did Medicine Creek first come up as a suggested host for the experimental field?"

"A computer analysis produced the name last year. In April." Chauncy spoke in a curt monotone.

"When did you first visit the town?"

"June."

"Did you make contact with anyone here at that time?"

"No. It was just a preliminary trip."

"Then what, exactly, did you do?"

"I fail to see—"

Pendergast held up the phone and said cheerfully, "Just hit redial."

Chauncy made a huge effort to control himself. "I had lunch at Maisie's Diner."

"And?"

"And what? It was the most revolting lunch it has been my misfortune to consume."

"And after?"

"Diarrhea, of course."

Before she could stop herself, Corrie burst out laughing. Ridder and Hazen looked at each other, not knowing how to respond. Chauncy's face broke into a mirthless smile; he seemed to be recovering his equilibrium, if not his arrogance. Then he continued. "I inspected a field owned by Buswell Agricon, the agricultural combine, who are our partners in this venture."

"Where?"

"Down by the creek."

"Where exactly by the creek?"

"Township five, Range one, the northwest quadrant of Section nine."

"What was involved in the inspection of these fields? How did you proceed?"

"On foot. I took samples of earth, corn, other samples."

"Such as?"

"Water. Botanicals. Insects. Scientific samples. Things you wouldn't understand, Mr. Pendergast."

"What day, exactly, was this?"

"I'd have to check my diary."

Pendergast folded his arms, waiting.

Scowling, Dr. Chauncy fished into his pocket, pulled out a diary, flipped the pages. "June eleven."

"And did you see anything unusual? Out of the ordinary?"

"As I've said, I saw nothing."

"Tell me, what *exactly* is this 'experimental field' going to experiment with?"

Chauncy drew himself up. "I'm sorry, Mr. Pendergast, but these scientific concepts are rather too complex for a non-scientist to comprehend. It's pointless to answer questions along that line."

Pendergast smiled in a self-deprecating way. "Well, then, perhaps you could simplify it in a way that any idiot could understand."

"I suppose I could try. We're trying to develop a strain of corn for gasohol production—you know what that is?"

Pendergast nodded.

"We need a strain that has high starch content and that produces a natural pesticide which eliminates the need for external pesticides. There's the idiot explanation, Mr. Pendergast. I trust you followed it." He gave a quick smile.

Pendergast leaned forward slightly, his face assuming a blank expression. He reminded Corrie of a cat about to pounce. "Dr. Chauncy, how do you plan to prevent cross-pollination? If your genetic strain escaped into this sea of corn around us, there would be no way of putting the genie back into the bottle, so to speak."

Chauncy looked disconcerted. "We'll create a buffer zone. We'll plough a hundred-foot strip around the field and plant alfalfa."

"And yet, Addison and Markham, in a paper published in the April 2002 issue of the *Journal of Biomechanics,* stated that cross-pollination by genetically modified corn had been shown to extend several miles beyond the target field. Surely you recall that paper, Dr. Chauncy? Addison and Markham, April—"

"I'm familiar with the paper!" Chauncy said.

"And then you must also know of the work of Engels, Traumerai, and Green, which demonstrated that the 3PJ-Strain 5 genetically modified plant produced a pollen toxic to monarch butterflies. Are you by chance working with the 3PJ strain?"

"Yes, but monarch mortality only occurs in concentrations greater than sixty pollen grains per square millimeter—"

"Which is present within at least three hundred yards downwind of the field, according to a University of Chicago study published in the *Proceedings of the Third Annual*—"

"I know the bloody paper! You don't have to cite it to me!"

"Well, then, Dr. Chauncy. I ask again: how are you going to prevent cross-pollination, and how are you going to protect the local butterfly population?"

"That's what this whole experiment is all about, Pendergast! Those are the *very* problems we're trying to solve—"

"So Medicine Creek will be, in effect, a guinea pig location to test possible solutions to these problems?"

For a moment, Chauncy spluttered, unable to reply. He looked apoplectic. Corrie could see he had lost it completely. "Why should I have to justify my important work to a—a—a fucking *cop*—!"

There was a silence as Chauncy breathed heavily, the sweat pouring off his brow and creeping through the underarms of his suit jacket.

Pendergast turned to Corrie. "I think we're done here. Did you get it all down, Miss Swanson?"

"Everything, sir, right down to the 'fucking cop.'" She slapped the notebook shut with a satisfying crack and jammed the pen into one of her leather pockets, then gave the group at the table a broad smile. Pendergast nodded, turned to go.

"Pendergast," Ridder said. His voice was low and very, very cold. Despite herself, Corrie shivered when she saw the look on his face.

Pendergast stopped. "Yes?"

Ridder's eyes glittered like mica. "You've disturbed our lunch and agitated our guest. Isn't there something you ought to say to him before you leave?"

"I don't believe so." Pendergast seemed to consider a moment. "Unless, perhaps, it is a quotation from Einstein: 'The only thing more dangerous than ignorance is arrogance.' I would suggest to Dr. Chauncy that in combination, the two qualities are even more alarming."

Corrie followed Pendergast out through the darkened bowling alley and into the strong sun. As they climbed into the car she couldn't hold herself back any longer and laughed.

Pendergast looked at her. "Amused?"

"Why not? You really ripped Chauncy a new one."

"That is the second time I've heard that curious expression. What does it mean?"

"It means, well, you made him look like the fool he is."

"If only it were so. Chauncy and his ilk are anything but fools and are, as such, decidedly more dangerous."

Thirty

It was nine o'clock when Corrie got back to Wyndham Parke Estates, the mobile home community just behind the bowling alley where she shared a double-wide with her mother. After leaving Pendergast she had driven to her secret reading place on the powerline road to kill time, but as soon as the sun had set she got spooked and decided to head on home.

She carefully opened the shabby front door and closed it behind her with a silence born of years of practice. By now, her mother should be out like a light. It was a Sunday, her mother's day off, and she would have started hitting the bottle as soon as she was up. Still, silence was always the wisest policy.

She crept into the kitchen. The trailer had no AC and was stiflingly hot. She eased open a cupboard, took out a box of Cap'n Crunch and a bowl, and carefully filled it. She poured in milk from the refrigerator and began to eat. God, she was famished. A second bowl disappeared before she felt sated.

She carefully washed the bowl, dried it, put it away, put away the cereal and the milk, and erased any sign of her presence. If her mother was really out cold, she might even be able to play an hour or two of the latest *Resident Evil* on her Nintendo before going to bed. She took off her shoes and began to sneak down the hall.

"Corrie?"

She froze. What was her mother doing awake? The raspy voice that issued from the bedroom boded ill.

"Corrie, I know it's you."

"Yes, Mom?" She tried to make her voice as casual as possible.

There was a silence. God, it was hot in the trailer. She wondered how her mother could stand being in here all day, baking, sweating, drinking. It made her sad.

"I think you have something to tell me, young lady," came the muffled voice.

"Like what?" Corrie tried to sound cheerful.

"Like your new job."

Corrie's heart fell. "What about it?"

"Oh, I don't know, it's just that I'm your mother, and I think that gives me a right to know *what's going on* in your life."

Corrie cleared her throat. "Can we talk about it in the morning?"

"We can talk about it right now. You've got some explaining to do."

Corrie wondered where to start. No matter how she put it, it was going to sound strange.

"I'm working for the FBI agent who's investigating the killings."

"So I heard."

"So you already know about it."

There was a snort. "How much is he paying you?"

"That's not your business, Mom."

"Really? Not my business? You think you can just live here for free, eat here for free, come and go as you please? Is that what you think?"

"Most kids live with their parents for free."

"Not when they have a good paying job. They *contribute*."

Corrie sighed. "I'll leave some money on the kitchen table." How much did it cost to buy Cap'n Crunch? She couldn't even remember the last time her mother had gone shopping or cooked dinner, except to bring home snacks from the bowling alley where she was a cocktail waitress during the week. Snacks and those miniature bottles of vodka. That's where the money went, all those vodka minis.

"I'm still waiting for an answer to my question, young lady. What's he paying you? It can't be much."

"I *said*, it's none of your business."

"You don't have any skills, what can you possibly be worth? You can't type, you don't know how to write a business letter—I can't imagine why he'd hire you, frankly."

Corrie replied hotly, "*He* thinks I'm worth it. And for your information he's paying me seven fifty a week." Even as she said it, she knew she was making a big mistake.

There was a short silence.

"Did you say seven *hundred* and fifty dollars *a week?*"

"That's right."

"And just what are you doing to earn that money?"

"Nothing." God, why did she let her mother goad her into the admission?

"Nothing? *Nothing?*"

"I'm his assistant. I take notes. I drive him around."

"What do you know about being an assistant? Who is this

man? How old is he? You *drive* him *around?* In *your* car? For seven hundred and fifty dollars a *week?*"

"Yes."

"Do you have a *contract?*"

"Well, no."

"No contract? Don't you know *anything?* Corrie, why do you think he's paying you seven fifty? Or do you already know why—is that what it's come to? No wonder you've been lying to me, hiding from me this little job of yours. I can just imagine what kind of *job* you do for him, young lady."

Corrie held her hands over her ears. If only she could get out, get into her car, get away. Anywhere. She could sleep in the car down by the creek. But she was scared. It was night. The killer was out there, somewhere, in the corn. "Mom, it's not like that, okay?"

"Not okay. Not okay. You're just a high school kid, you aren't worth anything, let alone seven fifty. Corrie, I've been around the block a few times. I know what's what. I know about men, I know what they want, how they think. I know what jerks they can be. Look at your father, look how he ran out on me, on us. Never paying a dime in child support. He was worthless, worse than worthless. And I can tell you right now that this man of yours is no FBI agent. What FBI agent would hire a delinquent with a record? *Don't you lie to me, Corrie.*"

"I'm *not* lying to you." If only she could get away, just this night. But tonight the whole town was as quiet as a tomb. Fallout from the riot at the church. Just driving home had really spooked her. Every house had been locked up and shuttered tight. And it was barely nine o'clock.

"If this is on the up and up, bring him here to me, then. I want to meet him."

"I'd die before I ever let him see this dump!" Corrie shouted, suddenly white-hot with rage. "Or *you!*"

"Don't you dare talk to me like that, young lady!"

"I'm going to bed."

"Don't you walk away while I'm talking to you—"

Corrie went into her room and slammed the door. She quickly put on some earphones and shoved a CD into her player, hoping that Kryptopsy would drown out the angry voice she could still hear yelling through the wall. The chances were good her mother wouldn't get out of bed. Standing up brought on a headache. She'd eventually get tired of yelling and, if Corrie were lucky, wouldn't even remember the conversation in the morning. But then again, maybe she would. She'd seemed alarmingly sober.

By the time the mangled thrashing of the last song had ended, all seemed to be quiet. She eased off the earphones and went to the window to breathe the night air. Crickets trilled in the darkness. The smell of night, of the corn just beyond the trailer park, of sticky heat, all flowed into the room. It was very dark outside; the streetlights on their lane had burned out long ago and had never been replaced. She stared out into the darkness for a while, wiping silent tears out of her eyes, and then lay down on her bed, in her clothes, and started the CD again from the beginning. *Look at your father,* her mom had said. *He was worthless.* As always, Corrie tried not to think about him. Thinking about her father only hurt more, because despite everything her mother said she only had good memories of him. Why had he left the way he did? Why had he never written her, not once, to explain? Maybe she really was worthless, useless, undeserving of love, as her mother had taken pains to point out many times.

She turned up the volume, trying to drive the train of thought from her mind. One more year. Just one more year. Lying on her bed in a dying town in the middle of nowhere, another year seemed like an eternity. But surely anyone could get through a year. Even her . . .

She woke up in blackness. The crickets had stopped trilling and it was now completely silent. She sat up, plucking off the dead headphones. Something had woken her. What was it? A dream? But she could remember no dream. She waited, listening.

Nothing.

She got up and went to the window. A sliver of a moon drifted from behind some clouds, then disappeared again. Heat lightning danced along the horizon, little flickers of dull yellow. Her heart was racing, her nerves strung tight. Why? Maybe it was the creepy music she'd fallen asleep to.

She moved closer to the open window. The night air, laden with the fragrance of the fields, came drifting in, humid and sticky. It was unrelievedly dark. Beyond the black outline of the trailer next door she could see the distant darkness of the cornfields, a single glowing star.

She heard a sound. A snuffle.

Was it her mother? But it seemed to have come from *outside*: out there, in the darkness.

Another snuffle, like someone with a bad cold.

She peered hard into the darkness, into the deep pools of shadow that lay alongside the trailer. The street beyond was like a dark river. She strained to see, every sense alert. There, by the hedge that lined the street: was there something moving? A shape? Was it just her imagination?

She placed her hand on the window and tried to draw it shut, but as usual it was stuck fast. She jiggled it, trying to free the mechanism with a feeling of rising panic.

She heard more snuffling, like the heavy panting of a large animal. It seemed very close now. But the act of listening caused her to pause for just an instant; then in a sudden panic she redoubled her struggle to get the window shut, rattling it in desperation, trying to free the cheap aluminum latch. Something *was* moving out there. She could feel it, she could sense it—and now, yes now, she was sure she could *see* it: a lumpen, malformed shadow, a mass, black against black, moving ever so stealthily toward her.

Instinct took over and she fell away from the window, abandoning her attempt to close it in favor of reaching for the light and banishing the darkness. She fumbled, knocked the CD player to the floor, found the light.

The instant it went on, the room lit up and the window became an opaque rectangle of black. She heard a sudden grunt; a dull thud; a frantic rustling sound. And then, silence.

She waited, taking a few slow steps back from the black window. Her body was shaking uncontrollably, and her throat was very dry. She could see nothing outside now, nothing at all. Was *it* there, in the window, looking at her? A minute ticked off, then another and another. Then she heard, in the middle distance, what sounded like a cough and groan: very low, but so replete with terror and pain that it chilled her to the marrow. It cut off abruptly, replaced with a strange wet ripping noise, and then a sound like someone dumping a bucket of water on the pavement down the street. Then, silence: utter, total silence.

Somehow, the silence was even worse than the noise. She felt a scream rising, unbidden, in her throat.

Then, all of a sudden, there was a snap, a gurgle, and a hissing sound, which slowly subsided to a steady swishing murmur.

She slumped, her body abruptly relaxing. It was just Mr. Dade's sprinkler system coming on, as it did every morning at exactly 2 A.M.

She glanced at her clock: sure enough, it read 2:00.

How many times had she heard that sprinkler system cough and splutter and gurgle and make all sorts of weird noises as it started up? *Get a grip,* she thought. Her imagination was really working overtime. Not surprising, given all that was going on in the town . . . and given what she'd seen, with Pendergast, out there in the cornfields.

She returned to the window and grabbed the latch, feeling a little sheepish. This time, a single, brutal thrust was enough to close it. She locked the window and climbed back into bed and turned out the light.

The sound of the sprinklers filtering through the glass, the caressing patter of raindrops, was like a lullaby. And yet it wasn't until four that she was finally able to fall back to sleep.

Thirty-One

Tad rolled over so hard that he fell out of bed. Staggering to his knees, he passed a hand across his face, then reached blindly for the ringing telephone. He found it, fumbled with it, lifted it to his face.

"Hello?" he mumbled. "Hello?" Through the sleep-heavy bars of his lashes, he could see that outside the bedroom window it was still dark, the stars hard in the sky, only the faintest streak of yellow on the eastern horizon.

"Tad." It was Hazen, and he sounded very awake indeed. "I'm over on Fairview, near the side entrance to Wyndham Parke. I need you here. Ten minutes."

"Sheriff—?" But the phone was already dead.

Tad made it in five.

Although the sun had yet to rise, a crowd from the nearby trailer park had gathered, clad mostly in bathrobes and flip-flops. They were strangely silent. Hazen was there, in the middle of the street, setting up crime-scene tape himself while talking into a cell phone propped beneath his jaw. And there, too, was the FBI man, Pendergast, standing off to one side, slender and almost invisible in his black suit. Tad looked around, an uneasy feeling growing in the pit of his stomach. But there was no body, no new victim; just a lumpy, irregular splotch in the middle of the street. Sitting next to it was a canvas bag, full of something. The uneasy feeling gave way to relief. Another animal, it seemed. He wondered what all the hurry was.

As he walked closer, Hazen snapped his phone shut. "Get back, all of you!" he shouted, waving the phone at the crowd. "Tad! Take over with this tape and *get these people back!*"

Tad moved forward quickly, grabbing the end of the tape. As he did so, he got a much closer glance at the pile on the street. It glistened redly, pearlescent, steaming in the predawn light. He looked away quickly, swallowing hard.

"All right, folks," Tad began, but his voice didn't sound quite right and he stopped, swallowing once more. "All right, folks, back up. More. More. Please."

The crowd huddled back, silent, their faces pale in the gloom. He strung the plastic tape across the road and tied it to a tree, wrapping it several times, completing the square that Hazen had begun. He saw that Hazen was now talking to the Goth, Corrie Swanson. Pendergast stood beside her, silent. Behind was her mother, looking like hell as usual, her thin brown hair plastered to her skull, a stained and frayed pink bathrobe wrapped tightly around her. She was chain-smoking Virginia Slims.

"You *heard* something?" Hazen was repeating. His voice was skeptical, but he was taking notes nevertheless.

Corrie was pale, and she was trembling, but her mouth was set in a hard line and her eyes were bright. "I woke up. It was just before two—"

"And how did you know what time it was?"

"I looked at my clock."

"Go on."

"Something woke me up, I wasn't sure what. I went to the window, and that's when I heard the sound."

"What sound?"

"Like snuffling."

"Dog?"

"No. More like . . . like someone with a bad cold."

Hazen jotted notes. "Go on."

"I had this sense there was something moving out there, right beneath my window, but I couldn't really see it. It was too dark. I turned on the light. And then I heard a different sound, like a groan."

"Human?"

Corrie blinked. "Hard to tell."

"Then?"

"I shut my window and went back to sleep."

Hazen lowered his notebook and stared at her. "You didn't think to call me or your, ah, boss?" He nodded at Pendergast.

"I—I figured it was just the sprinkler system, which goes on every night around two. It makes weird noises."

Hazen put away his notebook. He turned to Pendergast. "Some assistant you got there." Then he turned to Tad. "All right, this is what we've got. Somebody dumped a pile of guts on the road. Looks like cow to me, there's too much there for a dog or sheep. And that sack sitting next to it is full of ears of corn, freshly picked. I want you to check around all the local stock farms, see if anyone's missing a cow, pig, any large livestock." His eyes flitted back toward Corrie before returning to Tad. He lowered his voice. "This whole thing is starting to look more and more like a cult of some kind."

Over Hazen's shoulder, Tad watched Pendergast step forward and kneel before the pile of offal. He reached forward, actually prodded at something with his finger. Tad averted his eyes. Then he reached over and with one finger lifted the mouth of the canvas bag.

"Sheriff Hazen?" Pendergast asked without rising.

Hazen was already back on the cell phone. "What?"

"I would suggest looking for a missing person instead."

There was a shocked silence as the implication sunk in.

Hazen lowered the cell phone. "How do you know these are . . ." He couldn't quite bring himself to finish the sentence.

"Cows don't normally eat what appears to be Maisie's meatloaf, washed down with a glass of beer."

Hazen took a step forward and shone his light into the glistening pile. He swallowed hard. "But why would the killer . . ." He paused again. His face was dead white. "I mean, why take a body and leave the guts behind?"

Pendergast rose, wiping his finger with a handkerchief of white silk. "Perhaps," he said grimly, "to lighten his load."

Thirty-Two

It was eleven o'clock before Tad finally returned to the sheriff's office. The sweat was pouring off his brow, and his uniform was soaked to the cuffs. He was the last to return: the state troopers and Hazen, who had also been conducting searches, were there before him. The inner office had been turned into a command center, and a large group of Staties were standing around, talking on cell phones and radios. The press, naturally, had gotten wind of it, and once again the street was lined with TV vans, reporters, and photographers. But they were the only people in sight: all the residents had shut and locked themselves in their houses. The Wagon Wheel was closed and shuttered. Even the shift at Gro-Bain had been sent home for the day. Except for the hungry gaggle of media, Medicine Creek had become a ghost town.

"Any luck?" Hazen said immediately as Tad came through the door.

"No."

"*Damn!*" The sheriff pounded his fist on the desk. "Yours was the last quadrant." He shook his head. "Three hundred and twenty-five people, and every damn one of them accounted for. They're canvassing Deeper and the surrounding farms, but nobody's come up missing."

"Are you sure the, um, guts were human?"

Hazen looked sideways at Tad, his eyes red, rimmed by dark circles. Tad had never seen the sheriff under so much pressure. The man's muscular hands were balled into fists, the knuckles white.

"I wondered that, too. But the remains are now up at Garden City, and McHyde assures me they're human. That's all they know so far."

Tad felt sick to his stomach. The image of the meatloaf, poking out of that ragged tear in the ruined guts, the beer foam mixing with the blood—that was going to stay with him the rest of his life. He never should have looked. Never.

"Maybe it was someone passing through," he said weakly. "What local person would be out alone at that time of night, anyway?"

"I thought of that, too. But where's the car?"

"Hidden, like Sheila Swegg's?"

"We've checked everywhere. We've had a spotter plane up since eight."

"No circle cut in a cornfield?"

"Nothing. No hidden car, no circle, no dumped body, nothing. No footprints this time, either." Hazen wiped his forehead with the back of his hand and sat down with a heavy thump.

It was hard to concentrate, the state police were making so much noise with their radios and cell phones in the inner office. And worse, the press was camped right outside, a battery of cameras aimed point-blank at them through the glass door.

"Could it have been a traveling salesman?" Tad asked.

Hazen jerked his head toward the inner office. "The Staties are checking all the area motels."

"What about the sack of corn?"

"We're working on it. Christ, we don't know if it was left by the killer or if the victim was carrying it. But why the hell would someone be carrying a sackful of corn in the middle of the night? And each ear was tagged and numbered in some kind of weird code, to boot." He glanced at the sea of cameras beyond the front door. He started to rise, sat down, rose again. "Get me that can of whitewash and the brush from the storeroom, okay?"

Tad knew exactly what Hazen was going to do. When he returned, Hazen took the can from his hands, tore off the lid, dipped in the brush, and began to paint the glass.

"Bastards," he muttered as his arm swept back and forth, the paint running down and puddling on the doorsill. "*Bastards.* Photograph this and see how you like it."

"Let me help," Tad said.

But Hazen ignored him, slopping the paint up and down in big strokes until the door was covered. Then he shoved the brush in the can, jammed the lid back on, and sat down heavily again, closing his eyes. His uniform was flecked with white paint.

Tad sat down beside him, worried. Hazen's square face had a gray sheen to it, like a dead piece of fish. His sandy hair lay limp across his forehead. A vein pulsed in his right temple.

Suddenly, the sheriff's eyes popped wide open. It happened so fast that Tad jumped.

Hazen's lips parted, and he muttered just one word:

"*Chauncy!*"

Thirty-Three

Around noon, Sheriff Hazen decided he'd watched the dog-handler, Lefty Weeks, struggle with the dogs for just about as long as he could stand. Weeks was one of those types that really got on Hazen's nerves: a little man with white eyelashes, big ears, long thin neck, red eyelids, a wheedler and whiner who never stopped talking, even if his audience was a pair of useless dogs. The air under the cottonwood trees was hot and dead and Hazen could feel the sweat springing out on his forehead, the nape of his neck, his underarms, his back, leaking and running down through every fold and crease, even the crack of his ass. It must be over 105 frigging degrees. He couldn't smoke because of the damn dogs, but it was so hot he didn't even feel a craving. Now *that* was saying something.

Once again the two dogs were whining and cringing about in circles, their tails clamped down hard over their assholes. Hazen glanced at Tad, then looked back at the dogs. Weeks was yelling at them in a high-pitched voice, swearing and jerking ineffectually at the leashes.

Hazen went over, gave one of the dogs a swift kick in the

haunch. "Find that motherfucker!" he shouted. "Go on. Get going."

The dog whined and crouched lower.

"If you don't *mind,* Sheriff—" Weeks began, his red ears backlit and flaming in the heat.

Hazen spun on him. "Weeks, this is the third time you've brought dogs down here and every time it's been the same thing."

"Well, kicking them isn't going to help."

Hazen struggled to control his temper, already sorry he had kicked the dog. The state troopers were now looking at him, their faces blank, but no doubt thinking that he was just another redneck hayseed sheriff. He swallowed hard and moderated his voice. "Lefty, look. This is no joke. Get those dogs to track or I'm putting in a formal complaint up to Dodge."

Weeks pouted. "I know they've got a scent, I know it. But they just won't track."

Hazen felt himself boiling up all over again. "Weeks, you promised me *dogs* this time, and look at them, groveling like toy poodles in front of a mastiff." Hazen took a step forward at the dogs. This time one of them snarled.

"Don't," Weeks warned.

"She's not afraid of me, the bitch, although she should be. Give her another go, damn it."

Weeks took out the plastic bag holding the scent—an object retrieved from the second killing—and opened it with gloved hands. The dog backed away, whining.

"Come on, girl. Come on," Weeks wheedled.

The dog slithered back and forth almost on its belly.

Weeks crouched, the thin travesty of a goatee bobbing on his chin while he held the bag open invitingly. "Come on, girl. Scent it! Go!" He shoved the bag up to her nose.

The quivering, crouching dog let loose a stream of piss onto the dry sand.

"Oh, Christ," said Hazen, turning away. He crossed his arms and looked up the creek.

They had been up and down it now for three hours, dragging the unwilling dogs the whole way. Beyond, in the cornfields, Hazen could see the state police teams moving. Farther down, the SOC teams were on their hands and knees, combing the sandbeds along the creek for something, *any*thing. Above droned two spotter planes, criss-crossing back and forth, back and forth. Why couldn't they find the body? Had the killer taken off with it? There were state police roadblocks up, but the killer could have escaped during the night. You can drive a long way in a Kansas night.

He glanced up and saw Smit Ludwig approaching, notebook in hand.

"Sheriff, mind if I—"

"Smitty, this is a restricted area." Hazen had just about had it.

"I didn't see any tape, and—"

"You get out of here, Ludwig. On the double."

Ludwig stood his ground. "I have a right to be here."

Hazen turned to Tad. "Escort Mr. Ludwig to the road."

"You can't do this—!"

The sheriff turned his back on the entreaty. "Come on, Mr. Ludwig," he heard Tad say. The pair of them disappeared in the trees, Ludwig's protests increasingly muffled by the muggy air.

The sheriff's radio crackled. He hoisted it.

"Hazen here."

"Chauncy's been missing from his hotel since yesterday."

It was Hal Brenning, state police liaison officer, down in Deeper. "Didn't return last night. Bed wasn't slept in."

"Hallelujah, what else is new?"

"He didn't tell anyone what he was doing, where he was going. Nobody up here knows anything about his itinerary."

"We checked into that," Hazen replied. "Seems he had car problems, left his Saturn over at Ernie's Exxon. Insisted it be fixed that day, even though Ernie told him it was a two-day job. Chauncy was last seen eating a late dinner at Maisie's. Never picked up the car, though. Looks like he went into the cornfields and was doing a little last-minute research on the sly, collecting and labeling ears of corn."

"Collecting corn?"

"I know, I know. Insane, with a killer running loose. But this Chauncy liked to play his cards close to his vest. Probably didn't want anybody prying, asking awkward questions." Hazen shook his head, remembering how upset Chauncy had become at Pendergast's talk of cross-pollination.

"Well. Anyway, we're looking through Dr. Chauncy's papers now with some of Sheriff Larssen's boys. It looks like he was going to make some kind of announcement today at noon."

"Yeah. The experimental field project which Medicine Creek wasn't going to get. Anything else?"

"Some dean from KSU's coming down with their head of campus security. Should be here in half an hour."

Hazen groaned.

"On top of that, we've got a dust storm brewing. There's a weather advisory out for Cry County and the eastern Colorado plains."

"When?"

"The leading edge could come as early as tonight. They say it might be upgraded to a tornado watch."

"Great." The sheriff punched the radio off, holstered it, and glanced up. Sure enough: thunderheads, darker than usual, were piling up to the west, as if a nuclear war was being fought somewhere over the horizon. Any Kansan with half a brain knew what clouds like that meant. There was more than a dust storm coming. At the least, the creek would be up, scouring the whole creek bed. The fields would get drenched, maybe flooded. There'd probably be hail. And there would go all their clues. They'd get nothing more to go on until . . . until the next killing. And if there were indeed tornadoes, it would shut down the whole investigation while everyone dove for cover. What a frigging mess.

"Weeks, if those dogs aren't going to track, then get them the hell out of here. Your dragging them up and down the creek is just wrecking the site for everyone else. This is a disgrace."

"It's not my fault."

Hazen stalked off down the creek. It was a ten-minute walk to the spot where his cruiser and a dozen other vehicles, marked and unmarked, glittered alongside the road. He coughed, spat, breathed through his nose. There was definitely that curious stillness in the air that precedes a storm.

And there on the gravel shoulder was Art Ridder, getting out of his idling vehicle, standing and waving. "Sheriff!"

The sheriff walked over.

"Hazen, I've been looking all over creation for you," said Ridder, his face even redder than usual.

"Art, I'm having a bad day."

"I can see that."

Hazen took a deep breath. Ridder might be the town's big shot, but there was only so much crap he was going to take.

"I just got a call from a guy named Dean Fisk, up at the Agricultural Extension. KSU. He's on his way down with an entourage."

"I heard."

Ridder looked surprised. "You did? Well, here's something I'll bet you *don't* know. Listen, you're not going to believe this."

Hazen waited.

"Chauncy was going to announce today that *Medicine Creek* had been awarded the experimental field."

Just when he thought he couldn't get any hotter, Hazen felt a sudden flush burn its way through him. "Medicine Creek? *Not* Deeper?"

"It was going to be us all along."

Hazen just stared, stupid with heat and surprise. "I can't believe it."

"He may have hated the town, but that didn't change the fact that it's a perfect place for their field." Ridder wiped his greasy brow, tucked the soiled handkerchief back into his breast pocket. "We're a dying town, Sheriff. My house is worth sixty percent what it was twenty years ago. Sooner or later the turkey plant's going to lose another shift, maybe even close down. Do you know what this field would have meant for us? Genetic engineering, Hazen. One field would've just been the beginning. There'd have been more fields, a computer center, accommodations for visiting scientists and faculty, maybe a weather station. There would have been construction opportunities, real estate opportunities, more business for everyone, work for our children." His voice rose into the dead air. "That field would have *saved our town*."

"Let's not get ahead of ourselves, Art," Hazen said woodenly, still stunned.

"You're a fool if you don't see it! But do you think we're going to get it now? Now that their man just had his guts ripped out in the center of our town? Huh?"

Hazen felt an immense weariness settling on his shoulders. He began to walk past Ridder. "I don't have time for this, Art. I've got a body to find."

But Ridder blocked him. "Look, Sheriff. I've been thinking." He lowered his voice. "Have you looked into this guy Pendergast? Think about it. He showed up in town awfully goddamn fast after that first killing. We only have his word that he's FBI. How do you know *he* isn't involved? That *he* isn't the psycho? He's at every killing, poking his albino nose everywhere—"

But Hazen barely heard. Suddenly Ridder's voice seemed to have gone far away.

Hazen had an idea.

Ridder was right: Deeper would get the experimental field now, by default. But by rights it should have gone to Medicine Creek. Right on the eve of Chauncy's announcement—the very eve—he comes up murdered. And now Deeper would get the field.

Deeper would get the field . . .

It was suddenly coming together.

He tuned out Ridder's droning voice, trying hard to think. The first killing, Sheila Swegg, had occurred three days before Chauncy's arrival. The killer struck again the day after he arrived. In both cases, the killer had left all kinds of clues and bizarre shit behind, arrows and bare footprints and what-not, as if he were trying to capitalize on the legend of the Ghost Warriors, the curse of the Forty-Fives. But the strategy didn't work. Chauncy didn't pay a lot of attention to the murders, and he could care less about legends and curses. He wasn't even reading the papers. He was a scientific man looking at things long-term. Ghosts and murders might scare the residents of Medicine Creek, but they just didn't register with Chauncy.

And then, the night before Chauncy was to announce Medicine Creek got the field, he himself comes up dead.

Could it be any clearer? This wasn't a serial killer. And it wasn't someone local, like Pendergast believed. It was someone who had a lot to lose if the experimental field went to Medicine Creek. Someone from Deeper. Art was right: there was a shitload of money at stake here, maybe even the future of the town—*either* town. Deeper was hurting, too. Christ, in the last thirty years they were down fifty percent in population, worse than Medicine Creek. They were bigger, they had farther to fall, and they didn't even have the turkey plant.

It was kill or be killed. *Deeper.*

"You following me?" Ridder was shouting.

Hazen looked at him. "Art," he said abruptly, "I've got some important business to take care of."

"You haven't heard a goddamn word I've said!"

Hazen placed a hand on his shoulder. "I'm going to solve these murders, and maybe even get that field back for Medicine Creek. You just wait."

"And how the hell do you plan to do *that?*"

But Hazen was already walking back to his car. Ridder followed, waiting for an answer. Hazen paused, his hand on the door handle. "And another thing. You're right about that FBI agent. He's the source of the whole problem."

"He's the killer, you mean!"

The sheriff opened the door. "Art, don't be an idiot. He's

no killer. But he *is* the one who's screwed everything up. He's the one who came roaring in here, insisting it was a serial killer. Insisting it was someone local. He got the investigation off on the wrong foot right from the get-go. Got me so confused I wasn't thinking straight. Made me doubt my own instincts."

"What are you talking about?"

"I can't believe I didn't see it before."

"See what?"

Hazen grinned, gave Art's shoulder an affectionate squeeze. "Let me take care of this, Art. Trust me."

Hazen swung into his cruiser, unhooked the radio. Pendergast had shown up without a car and driver, no backup, and he hadn't liaised with the local Dodge office. The son of a bitch was freelancing. It was time to put an end to that, once and for all.

Hazen punched the radio, spoke into it. "Harry? Sheriff Hazen here from Medicine Creek. Listen, this is important. It's about the killings. You know anyone in the FBI field office in Dodge who's in a position to do me a favor? Yeah, I need to call in a big one." He listened for a moment, nodded. "Thanks a lot, Harry."

As he hung up the radio, Ridder leaned in the window, his face rashy from the heat. "I hope to hell you know what you're doing, Hazen. The future of Medicine Creek is at stake here."

Hazen grinned. "May all your dreams come true, Art."

He gunned the engine and pointed the big cruiser east, toward Dodge.

Thirty-Four

Smit Ludwig sat disconsolately at Maisie's counter, displaced from his usual corner booth by a loud group of AP reporters, or maybe they were *National Enquirer* or *Weekly World News*. It hardly mattered. The diner was full of reporters and townspeople, who seemed to have gravitated there as the place to go, to gossip, to get reassurance, to share news and speculate. Each new murder had brought more reporters, and each time they'd stayed a little longer. But it wasn't just reporters who were choking the usually quiet eatery. There was Mrs. Bender Lang and her gaggle of blue-rinsed beauties; there was Ernie the mechanic at another table with his buddies; there was Swede Cahill, who'd kept the Wagon Wheel closed for the day; there was the Gro-Bain contingent, workers at one table, management at the other. The place was full, the noise level like a New York City club. The only one who seemed to be missing was Art Ridder himself.

Where, Ludwig asked himself, was he going to turn for the rest of the story? He'd had a taste of being a real reporter—just a little taste, true, but he found himself liking it nevertheless. He'd recounted the curse of the Forty-Fives, he'd written up the Ghost Massacre, he'd covered all the gossip in town along those lines. The scalping of Gasparilla with some kind of primitive knife, on top of the arrows left with the Swegg corpse, had really gotten the rumor mill in high pitch. He had written up the killings and the church riot and he had the story on Chauncy's disappearance in the can. But he wanted to take it one step further. He needed something new and he needed it for tomorrow.

A real reporter wouldn't be sitting in a diner nursing his coffee. A real reporter would be out in the field talking to the cops, getting the lowdown. That bully, Hazen: there must be some kind of complaint he could make. What did you do if the police didn't cooperate, if they threatened to arrest you just for doing your job?

For the first time in his life, Ludwig had gotten a story between his teeth. It was real, and it was big. He had broken it and he was in the best position to finish it. My God, he'd *earned* that, at least. At sixty-two years old, it would be nice to go out with a bang. His grandkids could look over the yellowing issues of the *Courier,* turning the pages like precious parchment, and say, "Remember those murders back in '03? Our granddad covered them. Boy, he was some reporter."

This pleasant little daydream faded as a man climbed onto the stool next to his. Ludwig turned to find the man sticking out his hand in greeting. A young, fresh, eager face filled his field of view. There was the stubble, the butt hanging off the lip, the mussed-up hair, the skewed tie, but despite all the affectation he still looked like a kid trying to be a reporter.

Smit took the hand.

"Joe Rickey, *Boston Globe.*"

"Howdy-do." Smit shook the hand, a little surprised. *Boston Globe?* He was a long way from home.

"Smit Ludwig, right? *Cry County Courier?*"

Ludwig nodded.

"Hot enough for you?"

"I've seen it hotter."

"Yeah? Well, I haven't." The man plucked a paper napkin from the dispenser, dabbed it across his temples. "I've been here for two days and I can't get dick on this story. I promised my editor something different, you know; a little piece of Americana. That's my column: 'Americana.' People in Boston like to read about stuff that goes on in the rest of the country. Like these killings here, a man boiled, buttered, and sugared." He shuddered with pleasure.

Ludwig looked at the kid. In an odd way he reminded him of himself, forty years ago. The *Boston Globe?* The kid must have talent. He looked J-school, smart and eager but without real-life reporting skills.

"Anyway, that redneck sheriff of yours and those state police storm troopers won't give me the time of day. But you, you're local, you know where the bodies are buried. So to speak. Am I right?"

"Sure." Ludwig wasn't about to tell the kid he was in the same boat.

"I'm going to be in deep shit, after all the *Globe* paid to send me out here, if I come back empty-handed."

"It was your idea?" Ludwig asked.

"Yeah. It took a lot of persuading, too."

Ludwig felt for the kid. It could have been himself, if he'd taken that scholarship to Columbia instead of the copyboy job at the *Courier,* back when it was more than a one-man paper. A fateful decision, but one that curiously enough he'd never regretted making. Especially as he read the desperation, the ambition, the fear and hope in the young man's eyes.

The man leaned closer, dropping his voice. "I was just wondering. Is there anything you might like to share with me? I swear, I'd hold it back until you publish first."

"Well now," Ludwig paused. "To tell you the truth, Mr. Rickey—"

"Joe."

"Well, Joe, I don't really have anything new at this point myself."

"But surely you could get something?"

Ludwig looked at the kid. In a way he even looked like himself, forty years before. "I could always try," he said.

"I've got to file by eleven tonight."

Ludwig glanced at his watch. Three-thirty.

At that moment the door burst open and Corrie Swanson came barging into the diner, tossing back her purple hair, all the little chains and doohickeys pinned to her tank top astir.

"Two large iced coffees to go," she said, "one black, one with double cream and sugar."

Ludwig watched her, palm resting on her hip, elbow jutting out, tapping her change impatiently on the counter, ignoring everybody in the place. She was working for Pendergast, his girl Friday. And here she was, getting two coffees to go.

To go where?

But even as he asked the question, Ludwig guessed the answer. Once again, Pendergast would come to his rescue.

Maisie delivered the coffees. Corrie paid and turned away.

Ludwig gave Rickey a quick smile and stood up. "I'll see

what I can do." He started to take out some money but Rickey stopped him. "Coffee's on me."

Ludwig nodded and was up and out the door after her. As he left, he heard Rickey's voice: "I'll be here, Mr. Ludwig. And thanks. Thanks a lot."

Thirty-Five

All FBI buildings look the same, Hazen thought as he squinted up at the white, slablike facade with the smoked windows, burning in the afternoon sun: brick-shithouse ugly. He tucked in his shirt, straightened his tie, ground out his cigarette on the asphalt, and adjusted his hat. Then he passed through the double doors into a blast of cold air that, had it been wintertime, would have caused an uproar of complaint.

He paused at the desk, signed in, got directions, clipped a temporary ID to his lapel, and headed down the polished linoleum hall for the elevator. *Second floor, second right, third door on the left . . .* He repeated the directions in his head.

The elevator opened onto a long hall, decorated with government bulletins and typed lists of esoteric directives. As he walked along it, Hazen noticed that every door was open, and inside each office sat men and women in white shirts. Jesus Christ, there weren't enough crimes in the entire state of Kansas to keep this bunch busy. What the hell did they do all day?

Hazen threaded the hallways, finally locating an open door labeled PAULSON, J., SPECIAL AGENT IN CHARGE. Within, a woman in cat's-eye glasses was pecking away at her computer with robotic precision. She glanced up, then nodded him past into an inner office.

This office seemed as sterile as the rest of the building, but there was at least a framed photo on the wall of its occupant riding a horse, and another picture on the desk of the guy with his wife and kids. The man himself pushed his chair back from his desk, rose, and held out his hand.

"Jim Paulson."

Hazen grasped it and was just about crushed. Paulson indicated a seat, then settled back into his chair, threw one leg over the other, and leaned back.

"Well, Sheriff Hazen, what can I do for you?" Paulson said. "A friend of Harry McCullen is a friend of mine."

No bullshit, no small talk. Here was Mr. Straight-Shooter, crew-cut, fit, dressed in a decent suit, blue eyes, even dimples when he smiled. Probably had a dick as big as a bargepole. A wife's dream.

Hazen knew just how to play it. He was the small-town sheriff, just trying to do his job.

"Well, now, Mr. Paulson, it's right kind of you to see me—"

"Jim, please."

Hazen smiled a self-deprecating little smile. "Jim, you probably don't know Medicine Creek. We're a town down Deeper way."

"I've sure heard of it, what with the recent killings."

"Then you know we're a small town with solid American values. We're a close-knit community and we trust each other. And as sheriff, I'm the embodiment of that trust. You know that better than I. It's more than just law enforcement. It's about *trust*."

Paulson nodded sympathetically.

"And then these killings happened."

"Yes. Tragic."

"And being a little town, we can use all the help we can get."

Paulson smiled, dimpled. "Sheriff, we'd love to help you with this case, but we need evidence of interstate flight or other interstate or terrorist activity—well, Sheriff, you know when the FBI can justify involvement. Unless there's something I'm not aware of, my hands are tied."

Perfect, thought Hazen. He feigned surprise. "Oh, but Jim, that's just it. We're already getting help from the FBI. Right from the beginning. You didn't know?"

Jim Paulson's smile froze on his features. After a moment, he shifted position. "Right. Of course. Now that you mention it."

"That's what I'm here about. This Special Agent Pendergast of the FBI. He's been on the case since day one. You know all about him, right?"

Paulson shifted again, a little uneasily. "I have to tell you I wasn't fully aware of this man's activities."

"You weren't? He says he's out of the New Orleans office. I thought he'd liaised with you. Isn't that the usual courtesy?"

He paused. Paulson was silent.

"Anyway, Jim, I'm sorry. I just *assumed* . . ." he let his voice trail off.

Paulson picked up the phone. "Darlene? Pull me the jacket on a Special Agent Pendergast, New Orleans office. That's right, *Pendergast*." He hung up.

"Anyway, the reason I'm here is that, with all due respect, I wanted to ask the FBI to withdraw him from the case."

Paulson tilted his eye at him. "Is that so?" A reddish blush was creeping up his well-shaven neck.

"I told you that Medicine Creek can use all the help it can get. And, normally, that's true. Now, I know I'm just a small-town Kansas sheriff, but we've got help from the Dodge forensic unit and the state police, and—well, to tell you the truth, Special Agent Pendergast has been . . ." His voice trailed off, as if he was reluctant to criticize one agent to another.

"Has been what?"

"Just a little heavy-handed. And not respectful of local law enforcement."

"I see." Paulson was looking more pissed by the minute.

Hazen leaned toward the desk, lowered his voice confidentially. "To tell you God's own truth, Jim, he goes around in expensive suits and handmade English shoes quoting poetry."

Paulson nodded. "Right."

The phone buzzed and Paulson picked it up with alacrity. "Darlene? Great. Bring it in."

A moment later the secretary came in, a long computer printout trailing from one hand. She gave it to Jim, who touched her hand lightly in response.

Secretary's dream, revised Hazen, his eye falling on the picture on the desk of Paulson with his wife and kids. Cute wife, too. Nice to have two of them.

Paulson was scrutinizing the printout. A low whistle escaped his lips.

"Quite a guy, this Pendergast. First name Al—Al . . . Christ, I can't even pronounce it. FBI All-National

Pistol-Shooting, First Place, 2002; FBI Bronze Cluster for Distinguished Service, 2001; Gold Eagle for Valor, 2000 and 1999; Distinguished Service Cluster, '98; another Gold Eagle in '97; four Purple Heart Ribbons for injuries received in the line of duty. It goes on. Done a lot of casework in New York City—figures—and there's a bunch of earlier, classified assignments in here, with classified decorations to boot. Military, by the look of them. Who the hell is this guy?"

"That's what I was wondering," Hazen said.

Jim Paulson was really mad now. "And who the hell does he think he is, coming into Kansas like some kind of hot shot? The case isn't even FBI purview."

Hazen sat tight, saying nothing.

Paulson slapped down the printout. "Nobody in this office authorized him. He didn't even have the courtesy to stop by and present credentials." He picked up the phone. "Darlene, get me Talmadge in K.C."

"Yes, Mr. Paulson."

A moment later the telephone rang. Paulson picked it up. He glanced at Hazen. "Sheriff, if you wouldn't mind waiting in the outer office?"

Hazen passed the time in the outer office getting a better look at Miss Cat's Eyes. Behind those silly glasses was a pert little face; below them was a nice twitchy figure. It wasn't a long wait. Within five minutes, Paulson emerged. He was calm again, smiling. The dimples were back.

"Sheriff?" he said. "Leave your fax number with my secretary."

"Sure thing."

"In a day or two we'll be faxing you a cease-and-desist

order, which you will be asked to serve on Special Agent Pendergast. Nobody in the New Orleans office knows what he's up to. All the New York office would say is that he's supposed to be on vacation. He has peace officer status here, of course, but that's it. It doesn't appear he's actually broken any rules, but this is highly irregular, and these days we have to be exceptionally careful."

Hazen tried to maintain the look of grave concern on his face, although he could hardly keep himself from shouting for joy.

"This guy has got some big-time friends in the Bureau, but it seems he also has some big-time enemies. So just wait for the order, say nothing, and deliver it with courtesy when it comes in. That's all. Any problems, here's my card."

Hazen pocketed the card. "I understand."

Paulson nodded. "Thanks for bringing this to my attention, Sheriff Hazen."

"Think nothing of it."

Another flash of the dimples, a glance and wink at Miss Cat's Eyes, and the head of the field office withdrew.

A day or two, Hazen thought as he glanced at his watch. He could hardly wait.

It was now three o'clock. He had a trip to make to Deeper.

Thirty-Six

Corrie maneuvered her Gremlin over the dirt track at a crawl, one-handed, balancing the two iced coffees in her lap to keep them from spilling. The ice was mostly melted already, and her thighs were wet and numb. The car jounced over a particularly deep rut, and she winced: her muffler had been dangling rather loosely under the chassis lately, and she didn't want it torn off by one of these murderous gullies.

Ahead, the low shoulders of the Mounds reared above the surrounding trees, the light of the afternoon sun turning the grass along their crests into halos of gold. She got as close as she dared, then threw the car into park and eased her way gingerly out of the driver's seat. Coffees in hand, she climbed the grade into the trees. Bronze thunderheads loomed in the north, already covering a third of the sky, great towering air-mountains with dark streaks at their base. The air was dead, totally dead. But that wouldn't last long.

She entered the sparse scattering of trees and continued along the path toward the Mounds. There was Pendergast, dark and slim, looking around, his back partly to her. "Looking" really wasn't the word, she realized: more like staring.

Intently. Almost as if he was trying to memorize the very landscape around him.

"Coffee delivery!" she called out, a little too cheerfully. Something about Pendergast sometimes gave her the shivers.

He slowly turned, his eyes focusing on her, then he smiled faintly. "Ah, Miss Swanson. How kind of you. Alas, I drink tea only. Never coffee."

"Oh. Sorry." For a moment she felt disappointed, somehow, that she hadn't been able to please him the way she'd hoped. She shook the thought away: now she could drink both coffees herself. As she looked around, she noticed there were topographical maps and diagrams of all kinds spread out on the ground, held down with rocks. Under another rock was an old journal, its weathered pages full of spidery, childlike script.

"You are kind to think of me, Miss Swanson. I'm almost finished here."

"What are you doing?"

"Reading the *genius loci*. And preparing myself."

"For what?"

"You shall see."

Corrie sat on a rock and sipped her coffee. It was strong and cold and as sweet as ice cream: just the way she liked it. She watched as Pendergast walked about the area, stopping to stare for minutes at a time in seemingly random directions. Occasionally he would pull out his notebook and jot something down. At other times he would return to one of his maps—some of them looked old, at least nineteenth-century—and make a mark or draw a line. Once Corrie tried to ask a question, but he quietly raised his hand to silence her.

Forty-five minutes passed as the sun began to sink into a swirl of ugly clouds on the western horizon. She watched him, mystified as usual, but with a perverse kind of admiration she didn't really understand. She was aware of feeling a desire to help him; to impress him with her abilities; to gain his respect and trust. In recent years no teacher, no friend, and certainly not her mother had ever made her feel useful, worthwhile, needed. She felt that way now, with him. She wondered what it was that motivated Pendergast to do this kind of job, to investigate horrible murders, to put himself in danger.

She wondered if perhaps she wasn't just a little bit in love with him.

But no, that was impossible: not someone with those creepy long fingers and skin as pale as a corpse and strange blond-white hair and cold silver-blue eyes that always seemed to be looking a little too intently at everything, including her. And he was so *old,* at least forty. Ugh.

Finally Pendergast was finished. He came strolling over, slipping his notebook into his jacket pocket. "I believe I'm ready."

"I would be, too, if I knew what was up."

Pendergast knelt on the ground among his maps and documents, gathering them carefully together. "Have you ever heard of a memory palace?"

"No."

"It is a mental exercise, a kind of memory training, that goes back at least as far as the ancient Greek poet Simonides. It was refined by Matteo Ricci in the late fifteenth century, when he taught the technique to Chinese scholars. I perform a similar form of mental concentration, one of my own devising, which combines the memory palace with elements of Chongg Ran, an ancient Bhutanese form of meditation. I call my technique a memory crossing."

"You've totally lost me."

"Here's a simplified explanation: through intense research, followed by intense concentration, I attempt to recreate, in my mind, a particular place at a particular time in the past."

"In the past? You mean, like time travel?"

"I do not actually *travel* in time, of course. Instead, I attempt to reconstruct a finite location in time and space within my *mind*; to place myself within that location; and to then proceed to make observations that could not otherwise be made. It gives me a perspective obtainable in no other way. It fills in gaps, missing bits of data, that otherwise would not even be *perceived* as gaps. And it is frequently in these very gaps that the crucial information lies." He began removing his suit coat. "It's especially relevant in this particular case, where I have made absolutely no progress through the usual methods, the offices of the good Mrs. Tealander not excepting."

Pendergast carefully folded his suit coat and laid it across the gathered maps, charts, and journal. Corrie was startled to see a large weapon strapped beneath one arm.

"Are you going to do it now?" Corrie said, feeling a mixture of curiosity and alarm.

Pendergast lay down on the ground, like a corpse, very still. "Yes."

He folded his hands on his chest.

"But . . . but what am I supposed to do?"

"You are here to watch over me. If you hear or see anything unusual, wake me. A good hard shake should bring me back."

"But—"

"Do you hear those birds? Those chirping grasshoppers? If you hear them *stop,* you must also awaken me."

"Okay."

"Finally, if I do not come back in one hour, you must wake me. Those are the three circumstances under which I am to be awakened. No others. Do you understand?"

"It's simple enough."

Pendergast crossed his arms over his chest. If Corrie had been lying there like that, there was no way she could have thought of anything but the hard ground and the stubble underneath her. And yet he seemed to be becoming so *still.*

"So what time are you going back to?"

"I am going back to the evening of August 14, 1865."

"The Ghost Massacre?"

"Precisely."

"But why? What does this have to do with the serial murders?"

"The two are connected, that much I know. *How* they are connected is what I hope to discover. If there is no key to these new killings in the present, then that key must lie in the past. And the past is where I intend to go."

"But you're not really going anywhere, are you?"

"I assure you, Miss Swanson, the journey I make is strictly *within* my own mind. But even so, it is a long and dangerous interior journey to terra incognita, perhaps even more dangerous than a physical journey would be."

"I don't . . ." Corrie let her voice trail off. Any more questions would be useless.

"Are we ready, Miss Swanson?"

"I guess so."

"In that case, I shall now ask for your absolute silence."

Corrie waited. Pendergast remained absolutely still. As the minutes went by, he seemed even to have stopped breathing. The afternoon light poured through the trees as usual, the birds and grasshoppers chirped, the thunderheads continued to rear above the trees. Everything was as before—and yet, somehow, she herself could almost hear a faint whisper of that same late afternoon 140 years before, when thirty Cheyenne had come galloping out of a swirl of dust, bent on a most terrible revenge.

Thirty-Seven

Sheriff Hazen pulled into the big parking lot at the Deeper Mall, sped across the nearly empty blacktop, and slid his cruiser into one of the "Law Enforcement Only" spaces outside the Deeper sheriff's office. Hazen knew the Deeper sheriff, Hank Larssen, well. He was a regular guy, decent, if a little slow on the uptake. Hazen felt a twinge of envy as he walked through the hushed outer office with its humming computers and pretty secretaries. Christ, in Medicine Creek they couldn't even afford to recharge the AC in the squad cars. Where did these guys get the money?

It was almost five, but everyone was still busy propping up the decrepit Lavender empire. Hazen was well known here, and nobody stopped him as he made his way through the building toward Larssen's office. The door was shut. He knocked, and then, without waiting for a reply, opened.

Larssen was sitting in his wooden swivel chair, listening to two guys in suits who were both talking at once. They broke off when he entered.

"Perfect timing, Dent," Larssen said with a quick smile. "This is Seymour Fisk, dean of faculty at KSU, and Chester

Raskovich, head of campus security. This is Sheriff Dent Hazen, Medicine Creek."

Hazen took a seat, giving the two KSU people the once-over. Fisk was a typical academic, bald, jowly, reading glasses dangling from his neck. Chester Raskovich was a type, also: brown suit, heavyset, sweating all over, with close-set eyes and a handshake even more crushing than Agent Paulson's had been. A cop wannabe if he'd ever seen one.

"I don't have to tell you why they're here," Larssen went on.

"No." Hazen genuinely liked Hank and he was sorry about what he was going to have to do. He had done nothing but think about his theory, and it amazed even him how beautifully it came together.

"We were just talking about the ramifications for Medicine Creek and Deeper. Regarding the experimental field, I mean."

Hazen nodded. He was in no rush. Perfect timing, indeed: it was a major stroke of luck the KSU people were there to hear what he had to say.

Fisk leaned forward, resuming what he had been saying before Hazen entered. "The fact is, Sheriff, this tragic killing changes everything. I just don't see how we can proceed with Medicine Creek now as the site for the field. That leaves Deeper, by default. What I must have from you, Sheriff, are assurances that the negative effects won't spill over here. I can't emphasize enough that publicity will be intolerable. Intolerable. The whole point of locating the field in this, ah, quiet corner of the state was to avoid the kind of circus atmosphere and excess publicity generated by those with irrational fears of so-called genetic engineering."

Sheriff Larssen nodded sagely, his face a mask of seriousness. "Medicine Creek is twenty miles away and the crimes are strictly confined to that town. The authorities—and Sheriff Hazen will confirm this—believe the killer is local to Medicine Creek. I can assure you in the strongest terms that there will be no spillover to Deeper. We haven't had a homicide here since 1911."

Hazen said nothing.

"Good," said Fisk, with a nod that set his jowls shaking. "Mr. Raskovich is here to assist the police"—he nodded toward Sheriff Hazen—"in finding the psychopath who committed this horrendous crime, and also in finding Dr. Chauncy's body, which we understand is still missing."

"That is correct."

"He's also going to interface with you, Mr. Larssen, in making sure the publicity and security environment of Deeper is appropriately maintained. Of course, any announcement of the new location of the field has been put off until this situation settles down, but just among us I can say it will be Deeper. Any questions?"

Silence.

"Sheriff Hazen, any news on the investigation at your end?"

This was what Hazen had been waiting for. "Yes," he said mildly. "As a matter of fact, there is."

They all leaned toward him. Hazen settled back in his chair, letting the moment build. Finally, he spoke.

"It appears that Chauncy went down near the creek and collected some last-minute corn samples, which he tagged and labeled. They say he was waiting for the corn to get ripe or something."

All three of them nodded.

"The other news is the killer isn't local. Local to Medicine Creek, that is." Hazen said this as casually as possible.

This perked everybody up.

"It also appears that these killings aren't the work of some psychopathic serial killer, either. That's what they were *meant* to look like. The scalping, the bare feet, the hint of a connection to the old Ghost Massacre and the curse of the Forty-Fives—all that's just window dressing. No: these killings are the work of someone with a motive as old as the hills—money."

Now he *really* had their attention.

"How so?" Fisk asked.

"The killer struck first three days before Dr. Chauncy's scheduled arrival. Then he struck again the day *after* Chauncy arrived. Coincidence?"

He let the word hang in the air a moment.

"What do you mean?" Larssen was getting worried.

"The first two killings didn't have the desired effect. And that is why Chauncy had to be killed."

"I'm not following you," Larssen said. "What desired effect are you talking about?"

"To persuade Chauncy that Medicine Creek wasn't the right place for the experimental field."

He had dropped his bombshell. There was a stunned silence.

He continued. "The first two killings were an attempt to convince KSU to forgo Medicine Creek and site the field in Deeper. But it didn't work. So the killer had no choice but to kill Chauncy himself. Right on the eve of his big announcement."

"Now wait—" began Sheriff Larssen.

"Let him finish," said Fisk, placing his tweedy elbows on his tweedy knees.

"These so-called serial killings were nothing more than a way to make Medicine Creek look unsuitable for a sensitive project like this—a way to make sure the experimental field went to Deeper. The mutilations and Indian crap were all designed to stir up Medicine Creek, get everyone talking about the curse, make us all look like a bunch of superstitious yahoos." Hazen turned to Hank. "If I were you, Hank, I'd start asking myself: who had the most to lose with the field going to Medicine Creek?"

"Now hold on here," the Deeper sheriff said, rising in his chair. "You're not suggesting that the killer is from Deeper, I hope."

"That's exactly what I'm suggesting."

"You haven't a shred of proof! What you've got is nothing more than a theory. A *theory!* Where's the evidence?"

Hazen waited. Better to let Hank blow off a little steam.

"This is ridiculous! I can't imagine anyone here brutally murdering three people over a damn cornfield."

"It's a lot more than a 'damn cornfield,'" said Hazen coolly, "as I'm sure Professor Fisk can tell you."

Fisk nodded.

"This project is important. There's big money in it, for the town and for KSU. Buswell Agricon is one of the biggest agricultural companies in the world. There are patents, royalties, laboratories, grants, you name it, up for grabs here. So Hank, I'll ask you the question again: *who in Deeper had the most to lose?*"

"I'm not going to open an investigation on the basis of a crackpot theory."

Hazen smiled. "You don't have to, Hank. I'm in charge

of the case. *I'll* open the investigation. All I ask is your cooperation."

Larssen turned to Fisk and Raskovich. "Here in Deeper, we don't habitually send law enforcement off on wild-goose chases."

Fisk returned his gaze. "Frankly, what Sheriff Hazen is saying makes sense to me." He turned to Raskovich. "What do you think, Chester?"

When Raskovich spoke, the sound came from deep within his barrel chest. "I'd say it's definitely worth looking into."

Larssen looked from one to the other. "We'll look into it, of course, but I sincerely doubt the killer is going to turn up here. This is premature—"

Hazen broke in smoothly. "Dr. Fisk, with all due respect, I think you should keep your options open as to where the field should be sited. If the killer's been trying to influence your decision . . ." He paused significantly.

"I certainly see your point, Sheriff."

"But the decision's already been made," Larssen said.

"Nothing is engraved in stone," said Fisk. "If the killer's from Deeper—and I have to say the theory stacks up nicely—then, frankly, this is the *last* place we'd want to site the field."

Larssen shut up. He was smart enough to know when to do that, at least. He gazed at Hazen, his face dark. Hazen felt sorry for him. He wasn't a bad guy, really, even if he was a little short on both brains *and* imagination.

Hazen rose. "I have to get back to Medicine Creek—we've still got a body to find—but I'm coming back first thing tomorrow to start my investigation. Hank, I hope we can work together in a friendly way."

"Sure we can, Dent." Hank had to choke out the words.

Hazen turned to the KSU men. "Nice to meet you. I'll keep you posted."

"We appreciate that, Sheriff."

Hazen plucked a pack of cigarettes from his pocket and fixed an eye on Raskovich. "When you get to Medicine Creek, come by my office. We'll see about getting you temporary peace officer status. It's the modern-day equivalent of being deputized. We're going to need your help, Mr. Raskovich."

The campus security chief nodded as if this were the most normal thing in the world, his face a mask of stolidity, but Hazen knew he had just scored big with Chief Campus Doorshaker Chester Raskovich.

Thirty-Eight

The discipline of Chongg Ran, invented by the Confucian sage Ton Wei in the T'ang dynasty, was later transported from China to Bhutan, where it was further refined over a period of half a millennium at the Tenzin Torgangka monastery, one of the most isolated in the world. It is a form of concentration that marries utter emptiness with hyper-awareness, the fusion of rigorous intellectual study with pure sensation.

The first challenge of Chongg Ran is to visualize white and black *simultaneously*—not as gray. Only one percent of adherents are able to move beyond this point. Far more difficult mental exercises await. Some involve simultaneous, self-contradictory imaginary games of Go, or more recent studious pastimes such as chess or bridge. In others, one must learn to fuse knowledge with nescience, sound with silence, self with annihilation, life with death, the universe with the quark.

Chongg Ran is an exercise in antitheses. It is not an end in itself, but a means to an end. It brings with it the gift of inexplicable mental powers. It is the ultimate enhancement of the human mind.

• • •

Pendergast lay on the ground, maintaining acute awareness of his surroundings: the smell of dry weeds, the feeling of sticky heat, the stubble and pebbles pressing into his back. He isolated every individual sound, every chirp, rustle, flutter, whisper, down to the faint breathing of his assistant sitting some yards away. With his eyes closed, he proceeded to visualize the surrounding scene exactly as if he were seeing it with his own eyes, spread out below him: *sight without seeing.* Piece by piece he assembled it: the trees, the three mounds, the play of shade and light, the cornfields stretching out below, the towering thunderheads above, the air, the sky, the living earth.

Soon the landscape had taken complete form. And now, having isolated each object, one by one he could extinguish them from his awareness.

He started with scents. He removed, one by one, the complex perfumes of the cottonwood trees, humidity, ozone from the approaching storm, the grass and leaves and dust. Then, sensation: he proceeded to extinguish, one at a time, every feeling impinging on his consciousness: the pebbles under his back, the heat, the crawling of an ant over his hand.

Next came sound. The trillings of the insects disappeared first, then the rustling of the leaves, the desultory tapping of a woodpecker, the fluttering and calling of the birds in the trees, the faint movement of air, the distant rumble of thunder.

The landscape still existed, but now it was a tableau of absolute silence.

Next, he suppressed in himself the very sensation of corporeality, that innate feeling of having a body and knowing where that body is in space and time.

Now the real concentration began. One by one, Pendergast removed each object in the landscape. He stripped it away, in the reverse order of its arrival. First the road disappeared, then the corn, then the trees, the town, the grass, the rocks, then the very light itself. A mathematically pure landscape was left: bare, empty, dark as night, existing only in form.

He waited five minutes, then ten, holding this empty fractal perfection in his head, preparing himself. And then, slowly, he began to put the landscape back together; but it would not be the same landscape he had just stripped away.

First the light returned. Then the grass rolled over the landscape, virgin tallgrass prairie dotted with prairie aster, wild poppies, cornflowers, rocketweed, and lupine. Then he piled back the bronze mountains of cloud, the rocky outcrops, the shady creek wandering free across the Great Plains. Now other things began to take shape: a herd of buffalo in the far distance; shallow water pans blazing silver in the late afternoon light; and everywhere an infinite array of wild grasses, undulating from horizon to horizon like a great rippling sea of green.

A thread of smoke came up from below. There were black dots of people moving about, a few ragged tents. Fifty horses were grazing the bottomlands by the creek, their noses in the grass.

Slowly, Pendergast permitted first the sounds, and then the smells, to return: voices laughing and cursing; fecund humidity; the whiff of woodsmoke and roasting buffalo steaks; the distant whinny of a horse; the jingle of spurs and the clank of cast iron cookware.

Pendergast waited, watchful, all senses alert. The voices became clearer.

Didier's buckskin come up lame again, said a voice.

The chunk of wood on fire. *Chuck's about ready.*

That boy wouldn't know where to piss less'n his mammy aimed his dingus for him.

Laughter. Men were standing around, battered tin plates in hand. The scene was still vague, tremulous, not yet fully formed.

I can't wait to get to Dodge and strip off this goddamned dust.

Use this to clean out what's in your throat, Jim.

The late afternoon sun refracted through a bottle and there was the sloshing of drink. There was a clank, the sound of an iron lid settling. A gust of wind swept up a skein of dust, settled back down. A piece of wood popped in the fire.

When we get to Dodge I'll introduce you to a lady who can clean the dust off another part.

More laughter.

Whiskey over here, amigo.

What's this you've been feeding us, Hoss, boiled sheepshit?

No tickee no washee, Crowe.

Whiskey over here, amigo.

Gradually, the scene crystallized. Men were standing around a fire at the base of a mound. They were wearing greasy cowboy hats, frayed bandannas, ragged shirts, and pants that looked so stiff from dirt and grease they almost crackled as they walked. All had scraggly beards.

The hill was a dusty island in the sea of grass. Below, the land swept away, open and free. The thick scrub that then covered the base of the mounds cast long shadows. The wind was picking up, rippling the grass in restless, random waves. The clean scent of wildflowers drifted on the air, mingling the sweet smell of cottonwood smoke, simmering beans, unwashed humanity. In the lee of one mound the men had unrolled their bedrolls and upended their saddles, using the sheepskin linings as headrests. There were a couple of pitched pole tents, badly rotted. Beyond, partway down the hill, stood one of the pickets, alert, carrying a rifle. Another picket was on the far side.

As the wind picked up, more clouds of dust swirled upward.

Chuck's ready.

A man with a narrow face, narrow eyes, and a scar across his chin stood lazily and shook out his legs, causing his spurs to jingle. Harry Beaumont, the leader. *You, Sink, get Web and go relieve the pickets. You eat later.*

But last time—

Any more out of you, Sink, and I'll fish the crik with your balls.

There was some muffled laughter.

Remember back at Two Forks, that Lo with the giant balls? The javelina sure did fight over those, remember?

More laughter.

Musta had some kind of disease.

They're all diseased.

You didn't worry 'bout that when you went for the squaws, Jim.

Mind shutting the hell up while I eat my chuck?

From one side, a man began to sing in a fine low voice:

Feet in the stirrups and seat in the saddle,
I hung and I rattled with them long-horn cattle,
Last night I was on guard and the leader broke ranks,
I hit my horse down the shoulders, I spurred him in the flanks,

The wind commenced to blow, the rain began to fall,
Hit looked, by grab, like we was going to lose 'em all.

The two pickets came back and propped their rifles on
their saddles, then came over with their plates, shaking the
rising dust from their shirts and leggings. The cook ladled
the beans and stew meat and then went and sat cross-legged
in the dirt.

Damn you, Hoss, this stew is half dirt!

Aids the digestion.

Whiskey over here, amigo.

A broad sweep of prairie rippled now with the wind. The
wind could be seen as it approached, pressing the grass down,
exposing its paler side, a wave of lighter green. It struck the
bottom of the mounds, picking up dust, swirling it up into a
curtain. The sun, sitting on the horizon, dimmed abruptly.

There was a stasis, a suspended moment, and then the
sudden pounding of hooves.

What the hell?

The horses, something's spooked the horses.

Those ain't ours.

Cheyenne!

The guns get your guns get the guns.

Instant chaos. The cloud of dust, rising higher, parted and
a white horse, painted with blood-red handprints, appeared,
followed by another and another. A cry arose. The stream of
horses divided, one on either side of the scrambling men:
horses that, quite literally, had appeared out of nowhere.

Aieeeeeeeeeee—!

A sudden hissing in the air. The arrows came from two

directions, followed by a tattoo of thuds. Screams, groans, the rattle of spurs, the sound of bodies hitting the ground.

The dust had now rolled over them, enveloping them in a fog through which could be dimly glimpsed the shapes of men running, falling, spinning. There was a shot, then another, disorganized. A horse fell heavily against the ground. A vague figure fired point-blank into the head of the Indian atop it, sending up a small cloud of dark matter.

The dust rose and fell in cascading sheets; the wind moaned and muttered; the wounded screamed and choked. The sound of beating hooves faded, stopped momentarily, then resumed.

They're coming back.

Back, they're turning back, get ready men.

The ghostly shapes of the riders appeared again, a second dividing stream.

Aieeeee-yip-yip-yip-aieeeee!

Now there was a coordinated volley of shots from those still alive, kneeling on the exposed ground, taking careful aim. Another terrible twanging and hissing of death on the air, the sound of a hundred arrows thudding into dirt and bodies, more falling horses, the crash and clink of bridle and spur, men clawing at their clothes, more firing. A man suddenly appeared out of the dimness, staggering, gargling, trying to pull an arrow from his mouth; another spun around and around with four arrows in his chest; then, abruptly, three more emerged like magic from his back. A horse, standing absolutely still, head hanging, its guts in a steaming pile beneath.

Another pass, a turn, then another. The smell of blood rose, rivers of it running from the dead horses and men.

A fifth pass. Now only sporadic shots, quickly silenced

by the hiss of arrows. A field in which groaning, wailing, writhing men moved feebly between inert forms. This time the Indians reined in their horses, dismounted, and began walking casually among the wounded, knives out. They became dark forms, bending over dark shapes on the ground. Shrieks, begging, weeping; the wet sound of scalps being ripped away; and then silence.

A man, lying on the ground, faking death, was dragged to his feet. His pleading cut through the dust and the dying moans: Harry Beaumont. The dark forms of the Indians clustered about him, silent, wraithlike, unhurried. The pleading rose in pitch, incomprehensible. He was grasped firmly, his head pulled back. A flash of a steel knife against the dust; a scream. A piece of flesh tossed aside. The Indians worked on the man's head, arms making short sharp movements as if carving a piece of wood; the screams became hysterical, choked. More red pieces discarded. Another wet ripping sound, more protracted than the others. Another scream. Two final movements, two more pieces dropping to the ground. Another, shorter scream.

And then, with ropes and poles hooked to their saddles, the Indians were dragging their dead horses away into the curtains of dust, heaping their dead warriors on travois and dragging them away as well. In less than a minute, they had disappeared completely into the dust from which they came.

Only one man was left, staggering through the dust, crying. Harry Beaumont. He dropped to his knees at the center of the mounds. He had no face left; no nose, lips, ears, or scalp. Just an oval of raw, red meat where his features had once been.

Rounded.

He rocked on his knees, head drooping, the blood pooling around his ruined jaws and chin and dripping into the ground. A dark hole opened in the bloody oval and a shriek arose:

Thon of a bith I curth thith groun I curth thith groun may it forever be damned may it rain blood for my blood guth for my guth damn thith evil groun—

He fell slowly, gargling and twitching in the bloody dust.

As the wind abated, as the dust settled and vision slowly returned, nothing remained but dead white men. The Cheyenne dead, the dead horses, all were gone. Only the endless grass now, stretching from horizon to horizon. And then a lone figure could be seen rising from a brushy fold in the earth a hundred yards downhill—a boy, previously hidden, who now staggered up in terror and ran across the empty prairie, his little figure fading into the orange glow of the horizon until he could be seen no more.

And then, silence.

Corrie jumped as Pendergast's eyes flew open, silvery and luminous in the twilight. The hour was up, and she had been about to rouse him. She'd almost woken him earlier, when the birdsong suddenly stopped; but within a minute or two it had resumed and her anxiety had faded. She stood, unsure for a moment what to say. It was now dark under the trees and the muggy night air was filled with the sound of rasping insects.

"Are you all right?" she finally asked.

Pendergast rose, brushing the leaves, dust, and grass off his coat and pants. His face looked drawn, almost as if he was ill.

"I am fine, thank you," he answered. His voice was toneless.

Corrie hesitated. She desperately wanted to know what he had seen or discovered, but she found herself afraid to ask.

Pendergast checked his watch. "Eight o'clock."

He swiftly collected his documents, papers, and notes, and began striding down the track toward the car. She followed, stumbling in her effort to keep up. He was already in the passenger seat, waiting, when she reached her own door and fumbled in the twilight with the handle.

"Please take me back to the Kraus place, Miss Swanson."

"Right. Okay."

The car engine turned over, turned again, rattled and shook into life. She turned on the headlights and crept back down the bumpy track.

After a few minutes, she couldn't stand it anymore. "Well?" she asked. "How'd it go?"

Pendergast's eyes turned to her, glistening strangely in the night.

"I saw the impossible" was all he said.

Thirty-Nine

The light faded and twilight crept into the air. The silent leaves disclosed, in the open area between the mounds, infrequent glimpses of the man and the girl. They had been talking, their low voices a murmur at this distance, but now there was only silence. The man had lain down and the girl was now sitting on a rock maybe twenty yards away, once in a while getting up to look around. The light had died in the west and only a faint glow lay over the landscape, rapidly turning to night.

The cornfields, dark and still, stretched out beyond the copse of trees. A star had appeared. From his place of concealment, the watcher looked for another star, found it. Then another, and another.

His eyes turned back to the figure on the ground. What in the world was Pendergast doing? Lying there, silently, like a corpse. Two hours had passed—two hours, wasted. It was well after seven o'clock. And now that *Globe* reporter, Joe Rickey, was soon going to be coming up against his deadline. Not to mention Ludwig's own deadline for the next edition of the *Courier*. Was this some kind of psychic crap?

New Age communication with the spirits? Perhaps there *was* a story here after all, only it wasn't the story he was after. Still, it was the only story around, and he wasn't going to move until he saw it through.

Smit Ludwig shifted his cramped limbs, yawned. The night crickets stopped chirping at the movement, then resumed: a peaceful, familiar sound. The whole landscape was familiar to him. He had spent his boyhood up at these mounds, playing Cowboys and Indians with his brother or swimming down in the creek. They'd even camped up here a couple of times. The tale of Harry Beaumont and the Forty-Fives, the fact that the Mounds had a sinister reputation, only added to the boyish sense of adventure. He could remember one night in August, camped here, watching the shooting stars. They'd counted to a hundred and then quit. His brother had left Medicine Creek, was now a retired grandfather in Leisure, Arizona. That was a different era back then. Mothers never thought twice about letting their kids run off and play all day long out of sight. Today it was different. The ugly modern world had come to Medicine Creek, bit by bit. And now, these killings. A part of him was glad Sarah hadn't lived to see this. Even if they found the killer, the town would never be the same.

Ludwig peered again through the gloaming. Pendergast was still lying on the ground, totally motionless. Even a sleeping person shifted once in a while. And nobody slept like that, perfectly straight, legs together, hands folded on the chest. Christ, he was still wearing his shoes. It was very bizarre.

He cursed under his breath. Should he just stand up and interrupt them, ask them what was going on? But somehow he couldn't do that. He'd waited this long, he'd wait to see what happened when—

Abruptly, he saw Pendergast rise and dust himself off. Ludwig quickly shrank back into the deepest shadows. There was a murmuring of voices, then without further ado the two started walking back toward their car.

Ludwig swore again bitterly. It had been utter folly to follow Corrie: a self-delusion, born of an attempt to help a cub reporter and to find his own new angle on the story. Now the story was gone, the kid would be in trouble, and next day's *Courier* would be left high and dry.

He waited for them to leave, bitterness continuing to rise. What was the hurry? There was no story to write up, nobody to go home to. He might as well just sit here all night. Nobody would miss him or his paper . . .

But Ludwig's tolerance for self-pity was limited, and before long he, too, had risen. He'd hidden his car well behind Corrie's, down the road and in the corn, where he knew they would not see it on their way out. He dusted himself off and looked around. The light was now completely gone and the wind had started to pick up—wind at dusk was a sure sign of a coming storm. The leaves started to rustle above his head, then thrashed under a sudden gust. It was very dark, the moon now covered by quick-moving clouds.

He saw a flash of lightning and waited, counting. A faint rumble reached him after almost half a minute.

The storm had a ways to come still.

Hunching forward against the rising wind, he walked toward the spot where Pendergast had lain. There might be something there, some clue as to what he was doing. But there was nothing, not even a faint impression. Ludwig drew out his notebook to jot down a few notes, but then stopped himself. Who was he kidding? There was no story here.

Suddenly, the air seemed full of sound: rustling grass and

leaves, sighing branches, swaying trees. The smell of humidity and ozone came to him, mingled with the scent of flowers. Another faint rumble of thunder.

He'd better hurry back and break the bad news to the kid.

It was so dark now that he wondered briefly if he could follow the old track. But he'd been down it a thousand times as a child, and childhood memories never died. He walked down the path, huddled against the wind. Leaves blew past him and a flying twig got caught in his hair. The rush of wind was almost pleasant after the weeks of heat and stillness.

He paused, aware of a new sound to his right. The rustle of an animal, perhaps.

He waited, took a step, another—and then he heard the distinct crackle of dry leaves underfoot.

But not under *his* foot.

He waited, hearing nothing but the whisper of leaves, the rising wind. After a minute or so, he turned and continued walking quickly.

Immediately he could hear footsteps to his right again.

He stopped. "Who is it?"

The wind blew, the cottonwoods creaked.

"Pendergast?"

He resumed walking, and almost immediately he could hear, he could *feel,* that he was being paced. A chill hit him.

"Whoever it is, I know you're there!" he said, walking faster. He tried to sound loud, angry, but he was unable to keep the quaver from his voice. His heart was pounding in his chest.

The unknown thing kept pace.

Unbidden, the words old Whit had quoted in church that Sunday came back to Ludwig, here in the darkness: . . . *the devil, as a roaring lion, walketh about, seeking who he may devour . . .*

He felt breath come snorting through his nose, and he fought hard against a rising panic. Soon, he told himself, he'd be out of the trees, back between two walls of corn. From there it was only two hundred yards to the road, and only another two hundred to the car. The road, at least, would be safe.

But, oh God, those horrible, plodding, crunching foot-falls . . . !

"Get the hell out of here!" he yelled over his shoulder.

He hadn't meant to yell: it had burst out from some in-stinctual place within him. Just as instinctual was the dead run that he now broke into. He was too old to run, especially all-out, and his heart felt like it would break loose in his chest. But even if he'd tried he could not have stopped his feet.

In the darkness beside him, the thing kept pace. Now Ludwig could hear the breathing—short rhythmic grunts in time to each thudding footfall.

I could run into the corn, lose him, Ludwig thought as he dashed out of the trees. Before him, the dark sea of corn was being tossed by the wind, roaring and rattling. Dust stung his eyes. There was a brief flash of lightning.

Muh! The sudden bark, alarmingly near, sent terror breaking in waves over him: it seemed human, and yet at the same time so very inhuman.

"Get away from me!" he screamed, running even faster now, faster than he dreamed possible.

Muh, muh, muh, the thing grunted as it ran alongside.

Another flicker of lightning, and in the pale flash he could see the shape pacing him through the corn. He saw it very briefly, but with brutal distinctness. For a moment, he almost stumbled in shock. It was mind-warping, impossible. Oh, dear Jesus, that face, *that face*—!!

Ludwig ran. And as he ran, he heard the figure keeping pace effortlessly. *Muh. Muh. Muh. Muh. Muh.*

The road! The flash of headlights, a car just passing—!

Ludwig rushed out into the road with a banshee wail of terror, screaming and running down the center line, waving his arms at the receding taillights. His cries were swallowed by another rumble of thunder. He stopped, sagging forward, palms on his knees, feeling as if his lungs would rupture. Completely spent now, he waited, limp and defeated, for the sudden blow, the white-hot lance of pain . . .

But there was nothing, and after a moment he straightened up and looked around.

The wind tossed and agitated the corn on both sides of the road, drowning all sound, but in the dimmest light Ludwig could see the monster was gone. Gone. Frightened away by the car, perhaps. He looked about more wildly now, heaving, coughing, and trying to suck in air, dazed by his own good fortune.

And his own car was only two hundred yards down the road.

Half stumbling, half running, Smit Ludwig went wheezing, gasping down the middle of the road. His heart hammered with a wild abandon. Just one hundred yards now. Fifty. Ten.

With a final gasp he staggered into the turnaround where he had hidden the car. With a surge of relief so strong it threatened to buckle his knees, he could see the faint gleam of its metal side, within a ragged patch of volunteer corn. He was safe, thank the risen Lord, he was safe! With a sob and a gasp he seized the door handle, pulled open the door.

From the dark semicircle of surrounding corn, the thing launched itself out at him with a rising bellow.

MuuuuuuuuUUUUUHHHHHHHHHHHHH!

Ludwig's gargling scream was swallowed by the shrieking of the wind.

Forty

From his suite of rooms on the second floor of the old Kraus place, Pendergast watched a dirty red dawn break along the eastern horizon. Distant lightning had flickered and rumbled all night. And the wind was still rising, rippling the fields of corn, causing the "Kraus's Kaverns" sign to swivel and shiver on its weatherbeaten post. The trees along the creek, half a mile away, were tossing in the gusts, and dusty sheets rose from the dry fields, carried aloft in rolling folds before disappearing into the dirty sky.

He lowered his eyes from the window. For the hundredth time he went over the memory crossing in his mind, re-creating the preparation, the setting of the scene, the mental deconstruction and reconstruction of the Mounds region, the past events that had followed. It was the first time a memory crossing had failed him. Having had no luck in his investigation into present-day Medicine Creek, he had made the crossing in an attempt to understand the events of the past: to solve the riddle of the curse of the Forty-Fives, to understand what really happened on that day in 1865. But it was as the legends held: the Indians really had appeared out of nowhere, and then vanished back into nowhere.

Yet that was impossible. Unless it was at last time to contemplate a possibility he had always resisted: that there were, in fact, extranatural forces at work here, forces that he neither apprehended nor comprehended.

It was a most frustrating turn of events indeed.

There was a faint droning sound to the southeast. Raising his head, Pendergast saw the dot of a plane coming in high over the corn. It grew in size, flying across his field of vision, resolving into a Cessna crop duster. As it receded again toward the opposite horizon, it banked and came back—the spotter plane, still looking for Chauncy's body.

A second drone came from out of the lightening horizon, and Pendergast saw a second plane arrive to work the cornfields, flying back and forth at the other end of the landscape.

From downstairs came the rattle of a kettle being placed on the stove. Moments later, the aroma of percolating coffee reached him. Winifred Kraus would also be making his tea, in the exacting manner he had taught her. It wasn't easy to make a satisfactory cup of King's Mountain Oolong, getting the temperature of both the water and the pot precisely right, knowing the correct quantity of leaves to add, the right amount of time to let them steep. Most important was the quality of the water. He had quoted to her at length from the fifth chapter of Lu Yu's *Ch'a Ching,* the holy scripture of tea, in which the poet debated the relative merits of mountain water, river water, and spring water, as well as the various stages of boiling, and Winifred had seemed to listen with interest. And, to his surprise, the tapwater of Medicine Creek had proven fresh, cool, pure, and quite delicious, with a perfect balance of minerals and ions. It made an almost perfect cup of tea.

Pendergast thought about this while watching the two planes move back and forth, back and forth. And then, rather suddenly, one began to circle.

Just like the vultures had done, not so many days before.

Still thoughtful, Pendergast slipped his cell phone out of his coat pocket and dialed. A voice answered, thick with sleep.

"Miss Swanson? I will expect you here in ten minutes, if you please. It would appear we've found the body of Dr. Chauncy." He snapped the phone shut and turned from the window.

There would be just enough time for tea.

Forty-One

Corrie tried not to look, but somehow not looking seemed even more terrible than the real thing. And yet, every time she looked, it was worse.

The site was simple: a clearing carved in the corn, with the body and paraphernalia carefully arranged. The earth around the body had been painstakingly smoothed and patted down, and a many-spoked wheel had been drawn in the dirt around the corpse. Gusts of wind rattled the corn and raised a mantle of dust that stung her eyes. Angry-looking dark clouds gathered overhead.

Chauncy lay on his back at the center of the wheel, naked, arms carefully folded across his chest, legs arranged. His eyes were wide open, filmed over, pointed at unnervingly different angles toward the sky. His skin was the color of a rotten banana. A ragged incision ran from his chest to the base of his gut, and his stomach bulged obscenely where it had been crudely sewn up again with heavy twine. Something, it seemed, had been stuffed inside.

Why the huge wheel? Corrie stared at the body, unable to take her eyes off it. And was it her imagination, or was something actually *moving* inside the sewn-up belly, causing the skin to bulge and subside slightly? There was something alive inside him.

Sheriff Hazen had gotten there first, and was bending over Chauncy's body with the medical examiner, who'd arrived by helicopter. It was odd: Hazen had actually smiled at Corrie when they arrived and had greeted Pendergast with a hearty hello. He seemed a lot surer of himself all of a sudden. She glanced at him sidelong, chatting confidentially with the M.E. and the SOC crew, who were combing the dirt for clues. There were the usual bare footprints, but when they were pointed out to the sheriff he'd only chuckled knowingly. An SOC guy was bent over one of them now, making a plastic mold from an imprint.

Pendergast, on the other hand, hardly seemed to be there at all. He had barely spoken a word since she'd picked him up, and now he was gazing off into the distance, toward the Mounds, as if his thoughts were far away. As she stared, he seemed at last to rouse himself. He stepped closer.

"Come, come," said the sheriff in a hearty voice. "Have a look, Special Agent Pendergast, if you're interested. You too, Corrie."

Pendergast stepped closer, Corrie trailing behind.

"The M.E.'s about to open him up."

"I would advise waiting until the laboratory."

"Nonsense."

The photographer took some photos, the flashes blinding in the dim light of dawn, and then stepped back.

"Go ahead," Hazen said to the M.E.

The M.E. removed a pair of scissors and carefully worked one point under the twine. *Snip.* The belly bulged, and the twine began to unravel from the pressure.

"If you're not careful," Pendergast cautioned, "some of the evidence might, ah, *abscond*."

"What's inside," said the sheriff cheerfully, "is irrelevant."

"I should say it's most relevant."

"You can say it all you like," said the sheriff, his good humor adding insolence to the comment. "Cut the other end."

Snip.

The whole belly flopped open, and a collection of things came tumbling out, spilling across the ground. A foul stink rose up. Corrie gasped and backed away, holding her hand over her mouth. It took her a moment to take in what it was that had slid steaming into the dirt: a crazy-quilt assortment of leaves, twigs, slugs, salamanders, frogs, mice, stones. And there, among the offal, a slimy circlet that appeared to be a dog's collar. A wounded but still living snake uncoiled from the mass and sidewinded painfully into the grass.

"Son of a *bitch*," said Hazen, backing up, his face slack with disgust.

"Sheriff?"

"What?"

"There's your tail."

Pendergast was pointing at something protruding from the mess.

"Tail? What are you talking about?"

"The tail ripped from the dog."

"Oh, *that* tail. We'll be sure to bag and analyze that one." Hazen had recovered quickly and Corrie caught him winking at the M.E.

"And the dog collar."

"Yup," Hazen said.

"May I point out," Pendergast continued, "that it appears the abdomen was cut open with the same crude implement previously used for the Swegg amputations, the cutting off of the dog's tail, and the scalping of Gasparilla."

"Right, right," said the sheriff, not listening.

"And if I am not mistaken," Pendergast said, "there is the crude implement itself. Broken and tossed aside." He indicated something in the dirt to one side.

The sheriff glanced over, frowned, and nodded to the SOC man, who photographed it in situ, then picked the two pieces up with rubber tweezers and put them in evidence bags. It was a flint Indian knife, lashed to a wooden handle.

"From here I'd say it was a Southern Cheyenne protohistoric knife, hafted with rawhide to a willow-wood handle. Genuine, I might add, and in perfect condition until it was broken by clumsy use. A find of particular importance."

Hazen grinned. "Yeah, important. As another prop in this whole bullshit drama."

"I beg your pardon?"

There was a rustle behind them, and Corrie turned. A pair of glossy-booted state troopers were pushing their way out of the corn and into the clearing. One was carrying a fax. The sheriff turned toward the newcomers with a big smile. "Ah. Just what I've been waiting for." He held out his hand, snatched the fax, and glanced at it, his smile broadening. Then he handed it to Pendergast.

"It's a cease-and-desist, Pendergast, straight from the FBI's Midwestern Divisional Office. You're off the case."

"Indeed?" Pendergast read the document carefully. Then he looked up. "May I keep this, Sheriff?"

"By all means," Hazen said. "Keep it, frame it, hang it in your den." All of a sudden, his voice grew less affable. "And now, Mr. Pendergast, with all due respect, this is a crime scene and unauthorized personnel are not allowed." His red eyes swiveled toward Corrie. "That means you and your sidekick."

Corrie stared back at him.

Pendergast folded the sheet carefully and slipped it into his suit coat. He turned to Corrie. "Shall we?"

She stared at him in outrage. "Agent Pendergast," she began, "you aren't just going to let him get away with that—?"

"Now is not the time, Corrie," he said softly.

"But you just *can't*—!"

Pendergast took her arm and steered her gently but firmly away, and before she could recover they were out of the corn and on the narrow dirt service road beside her Gremlin. Wordlessly, she slid behind the wheel, Pendergast settling in beside her as she started up the engine. She was almost blind with rage as she maneuvered through the thicket of parked official vehicles. Pendergast had let the sheriff walk all over him, insult her—and he'd done nothing. She felt like crying.

"Miss Swanson, I must say the tapwater in Medicine Creek is exceptionally good. As you know, I am a drinker of green tea, and I don't believe I've ever found better water for making the perfect cup."

There was no answer she could make to this non sequitur. She merely braked the Gremlin at the paved road and stared at him. "Where are we going?"

"You are going to drop me at the Kraus place. And then I'd suggest you return to your trailer and seal all the windows. I understand that a dust storm is coming."

Corrie snorted. "I've seen dust storms before."

"Not one of this magnitude. Dust storms can be among the most frightful of meteorological events. In Central Asia, they are so severe the natives have given names to the winds that bear them. Even here, during the dust bowl, they were known as 'black blizzards.' People caught outside were known to suffocate."

Corrie accelerated onto the paved road with a screech of rubber. The whole scene had begun to take on a sense of unreality. Here Pendergast had just been humiliated, ordered peremptorily off a case he'd come all the way from New York to investigate . . . and all he could do was talk about tea and the weather?

A minute ticked away, then two. At last, she couldn't take the silence any longer. "Look," she blurted indignantly, "I can't believe you just let that sack-of-shit sheriff *do* that to you!"

"Do what?"

"What? Treat you that way! Kick you off the site!"

Pendergast smiled. "*Nisi paret imperat.* 'If he does not obey, he commands.' "

"You mean you're not going to obey the order?"

"Miss Swanson, I do not habitually talk about my future intentions, even with a trusted assistant."

She blushed despite her anger. "So we're just going to blow him off? Continue our investigation? To hell with the runty bastard?"

"What I do with regard to, as you so colorfully put it, 'the runty bastard' can no longer be your concern. The important thing is, I cannot have you defying the sheriff on my account. Ah, here we are. Pull up to the garages behind the house, if you please."

Corrie pulled behind the Kraus mansion, where a rickety row of old wooden garages stood. Pendergast went to one that sported a fresh padlock and chain, unlocked it, and flung open the doors. Inside Corrie could see the gleam of a car—a big car. Pendergast disappeared into the gloom and she soon heard the roar of an engine, followed by a low purring. Slowly, the car nosed out of the garage. Corrie could hardly believe her eyes as a gleaming, polished vision of elegance emerged into the gray dust of Medicine Creek. She had never seen a car like it before, except maybe in the movies. It came to an idling stop and Pendergast got out.

"Where'd this come from?"

"I always knew there was a chance I might lose your services, and so I had my own car brought out."

"This is *yours?* What is it?"

"A '59 Rolls-Royce Silver Wraith."

It was only then that the full meaning of his prior sentence sunk in. "What do you mean, lose my services?"

Pendergast handed her an envelope. "Inside is your pay up to the end of the week."

"What's this for? Aren't I going to stay on as your assistant?"

"Not after the cease-and-desist. I can't protect you from it, and I could not ask you to put yourself in legal jeopardy. Regrettably, as of this moment, you are discharged. I would suggest you go home and resume your normal life."

"What normal life? My normal life *sucks*. There must be something I can do!" She felt a rising tide of fury and helplessness: now that she was finally interested in the case, fascinated even; now that she felt she had finally met a person she could respect and trust—now that she finally had a reason to wake up in the morning—he was firing her. Despite her best efforts, she felt a tear escape. She angrily wiped it away.

Pendergast bowed. "You could help me one last time by

satisfying my curiosity on the source of Medicine Creek's excellent water."

She stared in disbelief. He really was impossible.

"It comes from wells that supposedly tap into some underground river," she said, trying to make her voice as stony as possible.

"Underground river," Pendergast repeated, his eyes blank, as if his gaze had turned inward with a sudden revelation. He smiled, bowed, took her hand, raised it to within an inch of his lips. And then he got into his car and glided off, leaving her standing in the parking lot beside her own junk heap, in a swirl of dust, consumed by a mixture of wrath, astonishment, and misery.

Forty-Two

The cruiser whipped past the rows of corn on the airline road at a nice, easy 110 miles per hour. The AC might not work, thought Hazen, and the upholstery might look like shit, but the 5.0 Mustang police package still had what it took under the hood. The heavy chassis rocked from side to side, and in the rearview mirror Hazen could see two rows of corn whipsawing in his wake.

Hazen felt better than he had all week. Pendergast was out of the picture. He had a firm handle on the case, and it was getting firmer all the time. He glanced over at Chester Raskovich, sitting next to him. The security honcho looked a little gray around the gills, and beads of sweat had popped out on his temple. The speed of the cruiser didn't seem to agree with him. Hazen had much rather it had been Tad sitting in the passenger seat than this campus grunt; the confrontation that was about to take place would have been good experience for him. For the thousandth time, Hazen found himself wishing that his own boy, Brad, had grown up more like his deputy: respectful, ambitious, less of a wise-ass. Hazen sighed. Wishful thinking wasn't important right now. What *was* important was keeping Raskovich in the loop, and by extension, Dr. Fisk. If he played this right, he was certain Medicine Creek would get the experimental field.

The first outlying farmhouses of Deeper flashed past, and Hazen slowed quickly to the speed limit. It wouldn't be too swift to flatten some Deeper kid just as the case was breaking and things were going his way.

"What's the plan, Sheriff?" Raskovich managed to say. He had begun to breathe again.

"We're going to pay a visit to Mr. Norris Lavender, Esquire."

"Who's that?"

"He owns half of the town plus a lot of these fields out here. Leases 'em out. His family owned the first ranch in these parts."

"You think he's involved?"

"Lavender's got his finger in every pie around here. Like I asked Hank Larssen: who's got the most to lose? Well, no mystery there."

Raskovich nodded.

Now the commercial district of Deeper hove into view. There was a Hardee's at one end of town and an A&W at the other; in between, a bunch of shabby or shuttered storefronts; a sporting goods store; a grocery; a gas station; a used car lot (all AMC shitboxes); a coin-op laundromat; and the Deeper Sleep Motel. Everything dated from the fifties. *Could be a movie set,* thought Hazen.

He turned into the parking lot behind the Grand Theater (long abandoned) and the Hair Apparent salon. In the rear sat a low, one-story building of orange brick, completely surrounded by a shimmering expanse of heaved asphalt.

Hazen drove to the glass-doored entrance and parked his car across the fire lane, illegally, in your face. Hank's cruiser was parked neatly nearby. Hazen shook his head. Hank just didn't know how to do things in a way that commanded respect. He left the cruiser with its pinball flasher going like mad, so everyone would know he was there on official business.

Hazen pushed through the double doors and strode into the chilly air of the Lavender Building, Raskovich at his heels. He glanced around the reception area. A rather ugly secretary, with a voice of such efficiency that it bordered on unfriendliness, said, "You may go straight through, Sheriff. They've been waiting."

He touched the brim of his hat and strode down the hall, right, and through some more glass doors. Another secretary, even dumpier than the first, waved them past.

They grow 'em ugly up here in Deeper, he thought. *Probably marry their cousins.*

Hazen paused at the threshold of the rear office and looked around with narrowed eye. It was pretty snazzy, with a slick cosmopolitan look: bits of metal and glass in various shades of gray and black, oversized desk, thick carpeting, potted figs. A couple of cheesy Darlin' Dolls prints, however, betrayed Lavender's white trash origins. Lavender himself sat, smiling, behind the giant desk, and when Hazen's eye fell on him the man rose easily to his feet. He was wearing a jogging suit with racing stripes, and a diamond ring in a platinum setting winked on one pinky. He was slender and rather tall, and he invested all his movements with what he no doubt assumed looked like aristocratic languor. His head, however, was overly large for his body and shaped like a pyramid, a very wide mouth smiling under two gimlet eyes set close together, tapering to a narrow forehead as smooth and white as a slab of sliced suet. It was the head of a fat man on a thin body.

Sheriff Larssen, who'd been sitting in a chair to one side, rose also.

Lavender said nothing, merely extending an arm with a very small white hand at the end of it, indicating a seat. It was a challenge: would Hazen obey, or choose a seat himself?

Hazen smiled, guided Raskovich into the seat, and then took his own.

Lavender remained standing. He placed his childlike hands on the desk and leaned forward slowly, still smiling.

"Welcome to Deeper, Sheriff Hazen. And this is, I believe, Mr. Raskovich of Kansas State University?" His voice was smooth, unctuous.

Hazen nodded quickly. "I figure you know why I'm here, Norris."

"Do I need to call my lawyer?" Lavender made it sound like a joke.

"That's up to you. You're not a suspect."

Lavender raised his eyebrows. "Indeed?"

Indeed. And here his grandfather was a damn bootlegger.

"Indeed," Hazen repeated.

"Well then, Sheriff. Shall we proceed? Seeing as how this is a voluntary interview, I reserve the right to end questioning at any moment."

"Then I'll get to the point. Who owns the Deeper land chosen as a possible site for KSU's experimental field?"

"You know very well that's my land. It's leased to Buswell Agricon, KSU's partner in the project."

"Did you know Dr. Stanton Chauncy?"

"Of course. The sheriff and I showed him around town."

"What'd you think of him?"

"Probably much the same as you." Lavender gave a little smile that told Sheriff Hazen all he needed to know about Lavender's opinion of Chauncy.

"Did you know in advance that Chauncy had chosen Medicine Creek for his site?"

"I did not. The man played his cards close."

"Did you negotiate a new lease with KSU for the experimental land?"

Lavender shifted his body languidly and leaned his heavy head to one side. "No. I didn't want to queer the deal. I said if they chose to go with Deeper, they could have it at the same rate as Buswell Agricon."

"But you were planning to increase the leasing fee?"

Lavender smiled. "My dear fellow, I *am* a businessman. I was hoping for higher fees for their future fields."

My dear fellow. "So you expected the operation would expand."

"Naturally."

"You own the Deeper Sleep Motel, am I right?"

"You know very well I do."

"And you own the Hardee's franchise?"

"It's one of my best businesses here."

"You own all the buildings from Bob's Sporting Goods to the Hair Apparent, right?"

"This is a matter of public record, Sheriff."

"And you own the Grand Theater building—currently empty—and you're the landlord of the Steak Joint and the Cry County Mini-Mall."

"More common knowledge."

"In the past five years, how many of your tenants have broken their leases and gone out of business?"

Lavender's wide face remained smiling, but Hazen noticed that the man had begun winding the diamond ring around his pinky.

"My financial affairs are my own business, thank you very much."

"Let me guess then. Fifty percent? The Rookery closed down, the Book Nook's long gone. Jimmy's Round Up went out of business last year. The Mini-Mall is about two-thirds empty now."

"I might point out, Sheriff, that the Deeper Sleep Motel is currently running at one hundred percent occupancy."

"Yes, because it's filled with media folks. What happens when the big story ends? It'll go back to being about as popular as the Bates Motel."

Lavender was still smiling, but there was no mirth now in those wet lips that stretched across the lower half of his face.

"How many tenants are behind on their rents? Trouble is, you're not really in much of a position to get tough and kick 'em out for missing a payment, are you? I mean, who's going to take their place? Better to lower the rents, stretch things out, write a note or two."

More silence. Hazen eased up, let the silence build, taking a moment to give the office another once-over. His eyes fell on a wall of photographs of Norris Lavender with various big shots—Billy Carter, brother of the president; a couple of football players; a rodeo star; a country-and-western singer. In several of them, Hazen could see a third figure: hulking, dark-complected, muscle-bound, unsmiling: Lewis McFelty, Lavender's sidekick. He hadn't seen him when he came in, although he'd been looking out for him. More evidence to back up his theory. Hazen took his eyes off the creepy-looking man and turned back to Lavender with a smile. "You and your family have owned this town for almost a hundred years, but it looks like the sun might be setting on the Lavender empire, eh, Norris?"

Sheriff Larssen spoke. "Look here, Dent, this is sheer bullying. I fail to see how any of this could possibly connect with the killings."

Lavender stayed him with a gesture. "I thank you, Hank, but I've known what Hazen's game has been from the beginning. This dog is all bark."

"Is that a fact?" Hazen shot back.

"It is. This isn't about the killings in Medicine Creek. This is about my grandfather supposedly shooting your poor old granddaddy in the leg." He turned toward the KSU security man. "Mr. Raskovich, the Lavenders and Hazens go back quite a ways here in Cry County—and certain people just can't get over it." He smiled back at Hazen. "Well, sir, it just isn't going to warsh. My grandfather never shot your grandfather, and I'm no serial killer. Look at me. Can you imagine me in a cornfield carving someone up like one of those turkeys you people turn out over there in Medicine Creek?" He looked around smugly.

Warsh. There it was, rising to the surface like fat in a stew. Norris Lavender might sprinkle his speech with all the "indeeds" and "my dear fellows" in the world and it still wouldn't cover up the smell of white trash.

"You're just like your grandfather, Norris," Hazen replied. "You get other people to do the dirty work for you."

Lavender's eyebrows shot up. "That sounded remarkably like an accusation."

Hazen smiled. "You know, Norris, I kind of missed your pal Lewis McFelty when I came in just now. How's he doing?"

"My assistant, poor boy, has a sick mother in Kansas City. I gave him the week off."

Hazen's smile broadened. "I certainly hope it's nothing serious."

Another silence.

Hazen coughed and continued. "You had a lot to lose with this experimental field going to Medicine Creek."

Lavender opened a wooden box full of cigars and pushed it across the table to Hazen. "I know you're a committed smoker, Sheriff. Help yourself."

Hazen stared at the box. Cubans, wouldn't you know it. He shook his head.

"Mr. Raskovich? Cigar?"

Raskovich also shook his head.

Hazen leaned back. "You had *everything* to lose, didn't you?"

"Does anyone mind if I indulge?" Lavender reached into the box and removed a cigar, holding it up like a question between two thick fingers.

"Go ahead," said Hank, casting Hazen a malevolent glance. "A man has a right to smoke in his own office."

Hazen waited while Lavender slid a little silver clipper off his desk, trimmed and clipped the end of the cigar, admired his handiwork, picked up a gold lighter and heated the end of the cigar, then licked the other end, placed it in his wide mouth, and lit it. The process took several minutes. Then Lavender rose and strolled to the window, folded his tiny hands behind him, and stared out across the parking lot, puffing languidly, from time to time removing the cigar to stare at its tip. Beyond his slender figure, Hazen could see a horizon as black as night. The storm was coming, and it was going to be a big one.

The silence stretched on until Lavender finally turned. "Oh," he said to Hazen, feigning surprise. "Are you still here?"

"I'm waiting for an answer to my question."

Lavender smiled. "Didn't I mention five minutes ago that this interview was over? How careless of me." He turned back toward the window, puffing on the cigar.

"Take care not to get caught in the storm, gentlemen," he said over his shoulder.

Hazen peeled out of the parking lot, leaving precisely the right amount of rubber behind. Once they were on the main drag, Raskovich looked over at him. "What was that story about your grandfather and his?"

"Just a smokescreen."

There was a silence and he realized, with irritation, that Raskovich was still waiting for an answer. He pushed the irritation aside with an effort. He needed to keep KSU on his side, and Raskovich was the key to that.

"The Lavenders started as ranchers, then made a lot of money in the twenties from bootlegging," he explained. "They controlled all the moonshine production in the county, buying the stuff from the moonshiners and distributing it. My grandfather was the sheriff of Medicine Creek back then, and one night he and a couple of revenuers caught King Lavender down near the Kraus place, loading a jack mule with clearwater moonshine—old man Kraus had a still in the back of his tourist cave in those days. There was a scuffle and my grandfather took a bullet. They put King Lavender on trial, but he fixed the jury and went scot free."

"Do you really think Lavender's behind the killings?"

"Mr. Raskovich, in policework you look for motive, means, and opportunity. Lavender's got the motive, and he's a god-damned son of a bitch who'd do anything for a buck. What we need to find out now is the means and opportunity."

"Frankly, I can't see him committing murder."

This Raskovich was a real moron. Hazen chose his words carefully. "I meant what I said in his office. I don't think he *did* the killings himself: that's not the Lavender style. He would've hired some hitman to do his scut work." He thought for a moment. "I'd like to have a chat with Lewis McFelty. A sick mother in Kansas City, my ass."

"Where're we going now?"

"We're going to find out just how *hurting* Norris Lavender is. First, we're going to take a look at his tax records down at the town hall. Then we're going to talk to some of his creditors and enemies. We're going to learn just how deep in the shit he was with this experimental field business. This was his last chance, and I wouldn't be surprised if he bet the farm on this field coming through."

He paused. A little public relations never hurt. "What do you think, Chester? I value your opinion."

"It's a viable theory."

Hazen smiled and aimed the car in the direction of the Deeper town hall. It sure as hell was a viable theory.

Forty-Three

At two-thirty that afternoon, Corrie lounged restlessly on her bed, listening to Tool on her CD player. It had to be at least a hundred degrees in her room, but after the events of the other night she didn't have the guts to open her window. It still seemed impossible to believe that guy from Kansas State had been killed just down the street. But then, the entire last week was beyond belief.

Her eyes strayed to the window. Outside, huge thunderheads were spreading their anvil-shaped tops across the sky and a premature darkness was falling. But the approaching storm only seemed to make everything muggier.

She heard her mother's voice through the bedroom wall and cranked up the volume in response. There were a few muffled thumps as her mother tried to get her attention by knocking on the wall. Jesus. Of all days for her mother to call in sick, when Pendergast no longer needed her and she was stuck at home with nothing to do and too freaked out for her usual retreat on the powerline road. She almost longed for Labor Day and the start of school.

The door to her room opened and there was her mother,

standing in her nightgown, too-skinny arms draped over a too-fat stomach. Smoking a cigarette.

Corrie slipped off her earphones.

"Corrie, I've been yelling myself hoarse. One of these days I'm going to take away those earphones."

"You *told* me to wear them."

"Not when I'm trying to talk to you."

Corrie stared at her mother, at her smudged mascara and the remains of last night's lipstick still staining the cracks of her lip. She'd been drinking, but not, it seemed, enough to keep her in bed. How could this alien be her mother?

"Why aren't you out *working?* Did that man get tired of you?"

Corrie didn't answer. It really didn't matter. Her mother was going to have her say regardless.

"As I figure it, you got paid for two weeks. That's fifteen hundred dollars. Is that right?"

Corrie stared.

"As long as you're living here, you're going to contribute. I've told you this before. I've had expenses up the wazoo lately. Taxes, food, car payments, you name it. And now I'm losing a day's tips because of this nasty cold."

Nasty hangover, you mean. Corrie waited.

"A fifty-fifty split is the least I can expect."

"It's my money."

"And whose money do you think's been supporting you these past ten years? Certainly not that shitbag father of yours. Me. I've been the one working my fingers to the bone supporting you, and by God, young lady, you're going to give something back."

Corrie had taped the money to the bottom of her dresser drawer and she wasn't about to let her mother see where it was. Why, oh why, had she ever told her mother how much she was making? She was going to need that money to pay for a fucking lawyer when her trial came up. Otherwise she was going to end up with some crappy public defender and find herself going to jail. That would make a terrific impression, mailing her college applications from jail.

"I told you I'll leave some money on the kitchen table."

"You'll leave seven hundred and fifty dollars on the kitchen table."

"That's way too much."

"For supporting you all these years, it's hardly enough."

"If you didn't want to support me you shouldn't have gotten pregnant."

"Accidents happen, unfortunately."

Corrie could smell the acrid scent of burning filter as the cigarette was inhaled right down to the butt. Her mother looked around, stubbed it out in Corrie's incense burner. "If you don't want to contribute, you can go find yourself another place to live."

Corrie turned roughly away and replaced her earphones, cranking up the music so loud her ears hurt. She faced the smudged wall, stone-faced. She could just barely hear her mother shouting at her. *If she so much as touches me,* Corrie thought, *I'll scream.* But she knew her mother wouldn't. She'd hit her once and Corrie had screamed so loud the sheriff came. Of course, the little bulldog did nothing—he actually threatened *her* with disturbing the peace—but it had the effect of keeping her mother's hands off her for good.

There was nothing her mother could do. She just had to wait her out.

Long after her mother had gone back to her room in a fury, Corrie continued lying there, thinking. She forced her mind away from her mother, from the trailer, from the depressing empty meaningless hell that was her life. She found her thoughts drifting toward Pendergast. She thought about his cool black suit, his pale eyes, his tall narrow frame. She wondered if Pendergast was married or had children. It wasn't fair, the way he'd just dumped her like that and driven off in his fancy car. But maybe, like everybody else, he was disappointed in her. Maybe in the end she just hadn't done a good enough job for him. She burned with resentment at the way the sheriff had come in and just laid those papers on Pendergast. But he wasn't the kind to roll over and play dead. And hadn't he hinted he was going to continue working on the case? He *had* to take her off the case, she told herself. It wasn't anything she'd done. He'd said it himself: *I cannot have you defying the sheriff on my account.*

Her mind drifted toward the case itself. It was still so weird to think of someone in Medicine Creek doing those killings. If it really was someone local, it meant it was someone she knew. But she knew everyone in Shit Creek, and she couldn't imagine any of them being a serial killer. She shuddered, thinking back over the crime scenes she'd witnessed firsthand: the dog, its tail hacked off . . . Chauncy, sewn up like some overdone turkey . . .

The weirdest of all was Stott, boiled like that. Why had the killer done that? And how did you boil someone whole, anyway? He'd have to have lit a fire, put on a big pot . . . It seemed impossible. Where could you get a pot like that? Maisie's? No, of course not: the biggest pot she had was the one she used for Wednesday night chili, and you couldn't even fit an arm in that. The Castle Club also had a kitchen— could it have happened there?

Corrie snorted to herself. The idea was nuts. Even the

Castle Club couldn't have a pot big enough to boil an entire person; for that you'd need an industrial kitchen. Or maybe he'd used a bathtub? Could someone have winched a bathtub onto a stove, cooked the body that way? Or set up a bathtub in some cornfield? But the spotter planes would have seen it. And the smoke from the fire would have been visible from all over. Someone would've smelled it cooking; smelled the *smoke,* at least.

No, there was nowhere in Medicine Creek the body could've been cooked . . .

Abruptly, she sat up.

Kraus's Kaverns.

It was crazy. But then again, maybe it wasn't. Everyone knew that, during Prohibition, old man Kraus had run a moonshine operation in the back of that cave of his.

She felt a crawling sensation along her back: a mixture of excitement, curiosity, fear. Maybe the old still was still in there. Stills had big pots, didn't they? And would that pot be big enough to boil a person? Maybe, just maybe.

She lay back in bed, her heart beating fast. As she did so, the ridiculousness of it came over her again. Prohibition had ended seventy years ago and the old still would be long gone. You just didn't leave something that valuable rotting in a cave. And how would the killer sneak in and out of the cave? That prying old woman, Winifred Kraus, kept it locked up tight and watched over it like a hawk.

She tossed restlessly. Locks could be picked. She herself had downloaded *The MIT Guide to Lock Picking* while surfing the Web on the school computers, and she'd even made a small pick of her own and experimented on the padlocks of school lockers.

If the killer was local he'd know about old man Kraus's

moonshine operation and the still. The killer might have brought the body in some night, boiled it, and been gone by morning. Old Winifred would never have been the wiser. Fact is, she hardly ever gave tours anymore.

Corrie wondered if she should call Pendergast. Did he know about the still? She doubted it—the bootlegging was just some ancient bit of Medicine Creek lore nobody would have thought to tell him about. That was why he'd hired her, to tell him just this kind of stuff. She should call him now and let him know. She felt in her pocket for the cell phone he'd given her, pulled it out, started dialing.

Then she stopped. The whole idea was absurd. Stupid. It was just a wild guess. Pendergast would laugh at her. He might even be angry. She wasn't supposed to be on the case at all.

She dropped the phone and turned toward the wall again. Maybe she should check it out first—just in case. Just to see if the still was there. If it was, then she'd tell Pendergast. If it wasn't, she wouldn't make a fool of herself.

She sat up, put her feet on the floor. Everybody knew the cave only had one or two small caverns beyond the tourist area. The still would be in one of those. It wouldn't be hard to find. She would duck in there, check it out, leave. And it would get her out of the house. *Anything* to get out of this hellhole.

She turned down the music and listened. Her mother had fallen silent.

She slipped off the earphones, paused to listen again. Then, ever so carefully, she got out of bed, pulled on some clothes, and slowly opened the door. All remained quiet. Shoes in hand, she began sneaking down the corridor. Just as she reached its end, she heard her mother's door bang open and her voice ring out.

"Corrie! Where in hell do you think you're going?"

She hopped through the kitchen and ran out the door, letting it bang behind her. She jumped into her car, threw her shoes onto the seat next to her, and turned the key, praying the thing would start. It thumped, choked, died.

"Corrie!" Her mother was coming out the door now, moving awfully fast for someone with a nasty cold.

Corrie cranked the key again, pumping the pedal desperately.

"Corrie—!!"

This time the engine caught and she screeched down the gravel lane of Wyndham Parke Estates, laying a spume of smoke, dust, and dancing pebbles in her wake.

Forty-Four

Marjorie Lane, executive receptionist for the ABX Corporation, was becoming increasingly agitated by the man in the black suit sitting in her waiting room.

He had been there ninety minutes. That in itself wasn't unusual, but during that time he had not picked up any of the magazines conveniently laid about; he had not used his cell phone; he had not opened a laptop or done any of the things people usually did while waiting to see Kenneth Boot, the company CEO. In fact, it seemed as if he hadn't moved at all. His eyes, so strange and silvery, always seemed to be looking out the glass wall of the waiting room across downtown Topeka, toward the green geometry of farms beyond the city's edge.

Marjorie had been with the company through a host of recent changes. First, it had jettisoned its old name, the Anadarko Basin Exploratory Company, in favor of the sleek new acronym and logo. Then it had begun buying new businesses that went far beyond oil exploration: energy trading, fiber optics, broadband (whatever that was), and a million other things she didn't understand and, when she asked around, nobody else seemed to, either. Mr. Boot was a very busy man, but even when he was not busy he liked to keep people waiting. Sometimes he kept people waiting all day, as he had done recently with some mutual fund managers who had come to ask questions about something or other.

She longed for the old days: when she understood what the company did, when people weren't kept waiting. It was unpleasant for her when people had to wait. They complained, they talked loudly on their cell phones, they banged away on their laptops, and they paced about furiously. Sometimes they used profane language and she had to call security.

But this—this was worse. This man gave her the creeps. She had no idea if Mr. Boot would see him soon, or in fact see him at all. She knew he was an FBI agent—he had shown her his shield—but Mr. Boot had kept important people waiting before.

Marjorie Lane busied herself with work, answering phones, typing, responding to e-mails, but always out of the corner of her eye she could see the black figure, as immobile as a Civil War statue. He didn't even seem to blink.

Finally, when she couldn't stand it any longer, Marjorie did something she knew she wasn't supposed to do: she buzzed Mr. Boot's personal secretary.

"Kathy," she said in an undertone, "this FBI agent's been here almost two hours and I really think Mr. Boot should see him."

"Mr. Boot is very busy."

"I *know,* Kathy, but I really think he should *see* this man. I'm getting a bad feeling here. Do me a favor, please."

"Just a moment."

Marjorie was put on hold. A moment later the secretary came back. "Mr. Boot has five minutes."

Marjorie hung up. "Agent Pendergast?"

His pale eyes slowly connected with her own.

"Mr. Boot will see you now."

Pendergast rose, bowed slightly, and without a word passed through the inner door.

Marjorie heaved a sigh of relief.

Kenneth Boot stood over the drafting table that served as his desk—he worked standing up—and only gradually became aware that the FBI agent had entered his office and seated himself. He finished typing a memo on his laptop, transmitted it to his secretary, and turned to face the man.

He was startled. This FBI agent didn't look at all like Efrem Zimbalist Jr., one of his boyhood heroes. In fact, he couldn't have been more different. Beautifully cut black suit, handmade English shoes, custom shirt—not to mention the white skin and slender hands. Five, six thousand dollars' worth of clothes on the man, not counting his underwear. Kenneth Boot knew good clothes when he saw them, just as he made it a point to know fine wine, cigars, and women—as every male CEO in America had to do if he wanted to get ahead in business. Boot didn't like the way the agent had made himself so very comfortable. The man's eyes were roaming around in a way that offended Boot—it was almost as if he were undressing the office.

"Mr. Pendergast?"

The man did not look at him or answer. His eyes continued to roam, examine, scrutinize. Who was he to act so casual around the chief executive officer of ABX, seventeenth largest corporation listed on the New York Stock Exchange?

"You've got five minutes and one has passed," said Boot

quietly, going back to his drawing table and rapping out another memo on his computer. He waited for the man to speak, but no words were forthcoming. Boot finished the document, checked his watch. Three minutes left.

Really, this was quite annoying: this man sitting in his office, more comfortable than ever, looking at the paneling on the far wall. Staring, in fact, at the far wall. What was he looking at?

"Mr. Pendergast, you've got two minutes left," he murmured.

The man waved his hand and spoke at last. "Don't mind me. When you've finished your work and can offer me your *undivided* attention, we'll chat."

Boot glanced over his shoulder. "You'd better say what you have to say, Agent Pendergast," he said as unconcernedly as possible. "Because you've got exactly one minute left."

Suddenly the man looked at him, and the look was so intense Boot almost jumped.

"The vault lies behind that wall, correct?" Pendergast said.

With a huge effort of will, Boot remained motionless. The man knew where the corporate vault was—something only three officers and the chairman of the board knew. Was there some sign of it on the paneling? But in ten years no one had ever suspected. Was he under FBI surveillance? This was outrageous. All these thoughts occurred deep within Boot's mind and did not surface on his face.

"I have no idea what you're talking about."

Pendergast smiled, but it was a faintly supercilious smile, that of an adult humoring a child. "You're in a business, Mr. Boot, in which certain documents must be kept highly confidential. These documents would be the crown jewels of your company. I am referring, of course, to your seismic survey maps of the Anadarko formation. These maps show the location of oil and gas deposits, compiled by you at great cost. Therefore, your having a vault is a given. Since you are a person who trusts nobody, it makes sense the vault would be in your office, where you could keep an eye on it. Now, on three walls of your office you have expensive Old Master paintings. On that portion of the fourth wall, there, you have inexpensive prints. Prints that can be moved, taken down, without fear of a ding or scratch. It is therefore behind the paneling of that wall that your vault lies."

Boot began to laugh. "You fancy yourself a real Sherlock Holmes, don't you?"

Pendergast joined in the laughter. "I would respectfully ask you, Mr. Boot—and, of course, this is strictly a voluntary request—to open that vault and give me your seismic exploration survey of Cry County, Kansas. The last one, completed in 1999."

Boot found he had to make an effort to control himself. As usual, he was successful. Boot had learned a long time ago that a quiet voice was menacing, and the tone he now spoke in was barely audible. "Mr. Pendergast, as you yourself said, those surveys—wherever their location may be—are the crown jewels of ABX. That geological information alone represents thirty years of seismic exploration and wildcatting, at a cost of perhaps half a billion dollars. And you want me to just *give* it to you?" He smiled coldly.

"As I said, the request was strictly voluntary. I could never obtain a warrant for information like that."

The man had nothing to go on, no cards to play, as he himself openly admitted. It was a joke—or a trick. There was something about the entire business that made Kenneth Boot distinctly uncomfortable. He managed a pleasant smile. "I'm sorry I can't satisfy you, Mr. Pendergast. If there is nothing else, I wish you good day."

Hc went back to working on his memo. But the black figure in the corner of his eye did not move.

Boot spoke without looking up from his work. "Mr. Pendergast, in ten seconds you will become a trespasser in this office, at which point I will call security."

He paused, waited the ten seconds, then pressed the intercom to his secretary. "Kathy, get a security detail up here to show Mr. Pendergast out ASAP." Boot resumed his work, typing a memo to his VP for finance. But he couldn't help but notice that the son of a bitch was still sitting, one finger tapping the arm of the chair, looking around in that same breezy way as if he were in a doctor's waiting room. Insolent bastard.

The intercom buzzed. "Security is here, Mr. Boot."

Before Boot could respond, the man rose with an elegant swiftness and glided toward the drafting table. Boot stared at him, retort dying in his throat as he noticed the expression on the agent's pale face.

Pendergast leaned over and murmured a number into his ear: *"2300576700."*

For a moment Boot was confused, but the number rang familiar, and as it dawned on him just what it was he felt his scalp begin to tingle. A knock came at the door and then three security guards entered. They paused, hands on their weapons. "Mr. Boot, is this the man?"

Boot looked at them, his mind blank with panic.

Pendergast smiled and waved dismissively at them. "Mr. Boot won't be needing your help, gentlemen. He wishes to apologize for the inconvenience."

They looked at Boot. After a pause the CEO nodded stiffly. "Right. Won't be needing you."

"If you would be so kind as to lock the door on your way out," said Pendergast, "and please tell the secretary to hold all calls and visitors for the next ten minutes. We need a little privacy here."

Again the guards looked toward Boot for confirmation.

"Yes," said Boot. "We need a little privacy here."

The men retreated, the lock turned, and the office fell silent. Pendergast turned to the chief executive officer of ABX and said cheerily, "And now, my dear Mr. Boot, shall we return to our discussion of the crown jewels?"

Pendergast strolled out to his Rolls-Royce, the long mailing tube under one arm. He unlocked the door, placed the tube on the passenger seat, and slid into the hot interior. Starting the engine, he let the compartment cool off while he slipped the survey out of the tube and gave it a quick overview, just to make sure it was what he needed.

It was all that and more. This tied everything together: the Mounds, the legend of the Ghost Warriors, the massacre of the Forty-Fives—and the inexplicable movements of the serial killer. It even explained Medicine Creek's excellent water, which had proven to be the connection he had needed. As he'd hoped, it was all here on the oil exploration survey, printed in crisp blue and white.

First things first. He picked up the phone, pressed the scrambler option, punched in a number with the area code of Cleveland, Ohio. The ring was answered immediately, but it was several seconds before a voice of exceeding thinness spoke.

"And?"

"I thank you, Mime. The Cayman Islands number did the trick. I expect the target to experience more than a few sleepless nights."

"Happy to be of assistance." There was a click.

Pendergast replaced the receiver and examined the map again, looking more closely at the complex subterranean labyrinths it exposed.

"Excellent," he murmured.

The memory crossing had *not* failed. Instead, as the map confirmed, it had succeeded beyond his highest expectations. He had merely failed to interpret it properly. He rolled up the survey and inserted it back into the tube, capping it with a deft tap.

Now he knew exactly where the Ghost Warriors had come from—and where they had gone.

Forty-Five

In New York City, it was a warm, brilliant late afternoon. But in the strangely perfumed vaults that lay deep underneath the mansion at Riverside Drive, it was always midnight.

The man named Wren walked through the basement chambers, thin and spectral as a wraith. The yellow light of his miner's helmet pierced the velvety gloom, illuminating a wooden display case here, a tall metal filing cabinet there. From all corners came the faint sheen of copper and bronze, the dull winking of leaded glass.

For the first time in many days, he did not carry the clipboard beneath his arm. It sat beside his laptop, half a dozen vaults back, ready to be taken upstairs. Because Wren, after eight weeks of exhausting, fascinating work, had at last completed the cataloguing of the cabinet of curiosities that Pendergast had charged him with.

It had proved a remarkable collection indeed, even more remarkable than Pendergast had intimated it would be. It was full of wildly diverse objects, the finest of everything: gemstones, fossils, precious metals, butterflies, botanicals, poisons, extinct animals, coins, weapons, meteorites. Every room, every new drawer and shelf, had revealed fresh discoveries, some wondrous, others deeply unsettling. It was, without question, the greatest cabinet of curiosities ever assembled.

What a shame, then, that the chances of the public ever setting eyes upon it were vanishingly small. At least, not in this century. He felt a pang of jealousy that it should belong to Pendergast, all of it, and nothing for him.

Wren walked slowly through the dim chambers, one following upon the next, looking this way and that, making sure that all was in order, that he had overlooked nothing, left nothing behind.

Now, at last, he reached his final destination. He stopped, the beam of his light falling over a forest of glass: beakers, retorts, titration setups, and test tubes, all returning his light from long dark rectangles of a dozen laboratory tables. His beam stopped at last on a door set into the far wall of the lab. Beyond lay the final chambers, into which Pendergast had expressly forbidden him entrance.

Wren turned back, gazing down the dim, tapestried chambers through which he had just passed. The long journey reminded him, somehow, of Poe's story "The Masque of the Red Death," in which Prince Prospero had arranged for his masked ball a series of chambers, each one more fantastic, bizarre, and macabre than the one before it. The final chamber—the chamber of Death—had been black, with blood-colored windows.

Wren looked back into the laboratory, shining his light toward that little closed door in the far wall. He had often wondered, during his cataloguing, what lay beyond it. But perhaps, in retrospect, it was best that he not know. And he did so want to get back to the remarkable ledger book that awaited him at the library. Working on it was a way to put these strange and disturbing collections behind him, at least for a while.

. . . There it was again: the rustle of fabric, the echo of stealthy tread.

Wren had lived most of his working life in dim, silent vaults, and his sense of hearing was preternaturally acute. Time and again, as he had labored in these chambers, he'd heard that same rustle, heard that furtive step. Time and again he'd had the sense of being watched as he pored over open drawers or jotted notes. It had happened far too often to be mere imagination.

As he turned and began moving back through the shadowy rooms, Wren's hand reached into his lab coat and closed over a narrow-bladed book knife. The blade was fresh and very sharp.

The faint tread paced his own.

Wren let his gaze move casually in the direction of the sound. It seemed to be coming from behind a large set of oaken display cases along the right wall.

The basement chambers were vast and complex, but Wren had come to know them well in his two months of work. And he knew that particular set of display cases ended against a transverse wall. It was a cul-de-sac.

He continued walking until he was almost at the end of the chamber. A rich brocaded tapestry lay ahead, covering the passage into the next vault. Then, with sudden, ferretlike speed, he darted to the right, placing himself between the set of display cases and the wall. Pulling the scalpel from his pocket and thrusting it forward, he shone his light into the blackness behind the cases.

Nothing. It was empty.

But as he slipped the book knife back into his pocket and moved away from the display case, Wren heard, with utter distinctness and clarity, a retreating patter of steps that were too light, and too swift, to belong to anybody but a child.

Forty-Six

Corrie drove past the Kraus place slowly, giving the ugly old house a good once-over. A real Addams Family pile if ever there was one. That meddlesome old woman was nowhere to be seen, probably taken to bed sick again. Pendergast's Rolls was still gone and the place looked abandoned, sitting all by its shabby self in the stifling heat, surrounded by yellowing corn. Overhead, the great anvil-shaped wedge of the storm was creeping farther across the sun. There were now tornado warnings on the radio from Dodge City to the Colorado border. When she looked to the west, the sky was so black and solid it seemed to be made of slate.

No matter. She'd be in and out of the cave in fifteen minutes. A quick check, that was all.

About a quarter mile beyond the Kraus place, she pulled onto a dirt track heading into the nearby fields. She parked her car in a turnaround where it couldn't be seen from the road. Over the tops of the corn to the east, she could just make out the widow's walk of the Kraus place; if she took a shortcut through the corn, nobody would see her.

She wondered briefly if it was such a good idea to be out in the corn like this. But then she remembered Pendergast being quite positive the killer worked only at night.

Pocketing her flashlight, she got out of the car and closed the door. Then she pushed into the corn and walked down the rows in the direction of the cave.

The heat of the corn pressed down on her almost to the point of suffocation. The ears were drying out—gasohol corn was harvested dry—and Corrie wondered mildly what would happen if the corn caught fire. She enjoyed that thought until she reached the broken-down picket fence that separated the Kraus place from the surrounding fields.

She followed the line of the fence until she was behind the house. She glanced back quickly, just in case the old lady had appeared in one of the windows, but they all remained dark and empty, like missing teeth. The house gave her the creeps, frankly: standing against the cruel-looking sky, rundown and alone, a couple of gnarled, dead trees at its back. The weak rays of the sun still illuminated its mansard roofs and ocular windows. But even as she watched, the shadow of the approaching front crept across the corn like a blanket and the house darkened against the background sky. She could smell ozone on the air, and the mugginess grew even more suffocating. The storm was worse than it had seemed from inside the trailer—far worse. She'd better hurry before all hell broke loose.

She turned and skirted the path to the cave, keeping low in case old lady Kraus glanced out an upper window. In a moment she was descending the cut in the earth and had arrived at the iron door.

She looked carefully at the ground before the door, but the dust was undisturbed. Nobody had been through here in at least a couple of days. She felt both relief and disappointment: the killer, if he'd been here at all, was obviously long gone, but the lack of prints made it all the more likely that her theory was just so much bullshit. Still, she'd come this far; might as well check the place out.

She glanced over her shoulder again, then leaned forward to inspect the padlock on the iron door. Perfect: an old pin tumbler lock, the kind they'd been making for over a hundred years, still basically unchanged. This was the same kind of lock as on the front door of her trailer, the lock she'd first practiced on; it was the same kind as in the padlocks on the school lockers. She smiled, remembering the gift-wrapped box of horseshit she had once deposited into Brad Hazen's locker with a card and a single rose. He never had a clue.

First, she tugged on the padlock hard, to make sure it was actually locked. That was the first rule of lock picking: don't try any keyway tools until you're sure you need them.

It was locked, all right. *Here we go,* she thought.

She pulled an envelope of green felt out of her pocket and unfolded it carefully. Inside was her small set of tension wrenches and the lifter picks she'd surreptitiously made in shop class. She selected the wrench that seemed the right size and inserted it in the keyway, applying tension in the unlocking direction. Lock picking, she knew, was basically a job of finding the mechanical defects of a particular lock: the individual pins were never machined to precisely the same size, there were always slight variations between them that could be exploited. Next, she inserted a pick and gingerly tested the wards, looking for the tightest fit, which would signify the thickest pin. Since the thickest pin of a lock binds first when a turning force is applied, it was important to pick the pins in order of fattest to thinnest. There it was: the pin that bound the most. Carefully, using the pick, she raised it until she felt it set at the shear line. Then she moved to the next thinnest pin and repeated the process, and then once again, careful always to maintain tension. At last, the driver pin set with an audible click; she gave a yank and the lock popped open.

Corrie stood back, unable to suppress a small smile of pride. She wasn't particularly fast at picking locks—and there were lots of other techniques, like "scrubbing" and "raking," that she hadn't mastered—but she was competent. Too bad it was a skill Pendergast would disapprove of. Or would he?

Putting the lock-picking tools back in her pocket, she removed the padlock and placed it to one side. The door squeaked open on rusty hinges; she moved through the entrance, then hesitated. She stood in the darkness a moment, wondering if she should turn on the lights or use her flashlight. If Winifred Kraus showed up, the lights would be a dead giveaway. But then she re-collected herself. It was three o'clock in the afternoon, past time for the last tour of the day according to the sign; and besides, Corrie was positive there hadn't been any tours at all since Pendergast had been forced to take one. The old busybody wasn't going to stir out of her house in a rising storm. Also, the watchful darkness was getting on her nerves. Better to save her batteries.

She felt along the damp stone wall, found the light switch, flicked it on.

It had been years since she'd been in the cave. Her father had taken her there once, when she was six or seven, not long before he'd run off. For another moment she remained still, looking down into the yawning tunnel. Then she began to descend the limestone steps, her waffle-stompers echoing against the stone.

After a long descent, the staircase gave onto a wooden

boardwalk that disappeared between stalagmites and stalactites. Corrie had forgotten just how strange the place was. As a kid going there, she'd been surrounded by adults. Now she was alone in the silence. She walked forward hesitantly, wishing her shoes didn't make such a hollow sound against the walkway. Bare bulbs, hanging from the uneven ceiling far overhead, threw spectral shadows against the walls. A forest of stalagmites, like jagged, giant spears, rose on both sides. There was no sound in the vast empty space but her footsteps and the distant drip of water.

Maybe coming here hadn't been such a good idea.

She shook off the feeling of dread. There was no one here. The puddles on the wooden walkway had a skimming of silt that registered her footprints. It was clear—just as it had been outside the iron door—that no one had walked through in days. The last person in here was most likely Pendergast himself being dragged through the tour.

Corrie hastened through the first cavern, ducked under a narrow opening, and entered the second cavern. Immediately, she remembered what it was called: the Giant's Library. She remembered that, as a kid, she'd thought the place really *was* a giant's library. Even now, she had to admit that the rock formations looked amazingly real.

But always, the silence felt watchful, somehow, and the dim light oppressive, and she hurried on. She passed the Bottomless Pit and reached the Infinity Pool, which glowed a strange green in the light. This was the farthest point of the tour; here the walkway looped back toward the Krystal Kathedral. Beyond lay only darkness.

Corrie turned on her flashlight and probed the darkness beyond the boardwalk, but could see nothing.

She climbed over the wooden rail and stood at the edge

of the pool. The walls of the caverns she'd passed through had been devoid of any passageway or portal. If anything lay beyond, she'd have to go through the pool to find it.

Corrie sat on the rail and unlaced her shoes, took them off, pulled off the socks and stuffed them into her shoes, and tied the laces together. Holding the shoes in one hand, she stuck a toe in the pool. The water was shockingly cold and deeper than it looked. She waded across as quickly as she could and pulled herself out the other side. Now her legs were wet, damn it. Barefooted, she clambered down the far side of the pool and shone her light into the darkness at its base. Here she could see a low tunnel going off to the right. The ground was soft limestone, well worn down by old comings and goings. She was on the right track.

She sat on a hump of limestone and pulled her socks over her wet feet, then laced up the heavy waffle-stompers. She should've thought to wear old sneakers.

She stood up and approached the tunnel. She had to duck— it was about five feet high—and as she progressed the ceiling got lower. Water trickled along the bottom. Then the ceiling rose again and the tunnel bent sharply to the right.

Her light shone on an iron door, padlocked just like the one at the front of the cave.

This is it, then. This must lead to the old still.

Once again, she took out her lock-picking tools and went to work. For some reason—perhaps because of the poor light, perhaps because her fingers felt unaccountably thick and uncoordinated—this lock took much longer. But after several minutes, she felt the unmistakable give as the driver pin set. Silently, she placed the lock to one side and swung the door open.

She paused in the entranceway, shining her light around

cautiously. Ahead, a dark passageway cored through the living rock of the cave, its walls smooth and faintly phosphorescent. She started forward, following it for perhaps a hundred feet, flashlight playing around the walls, until it suddenly widened into a chamber. But this space had none of the vastness or majesty of the earlier caverns, just a few stubbly stalagmites rising from the rough uneven floor. The air was chill and close, and there was a smell, an unusual smell: smoke. Old smoke, and something else. Something foul. She could feel the cool flow of air coming from the open door, stirring the hairs on the nape of her neck.

This had to be it: the old moonshine still.

She advanced into the gloom, and as she did so her flashlight picked up something at the far end—a dull gleam of metal. She took another step, then another. There it was: an old pot still, an almost cartoonlike relic from a vanished era, with an enormous copper cauldron sitting on a tripod stand and the ashes of an old fire underneath. Stacked on a shelf above the floor were some split logs. The top of the cauldron, with its long coil of copper tubing, had been removed and now lay on the floor, partially crushed. There were several smaller pots and cauldrons scattered about.

She paused to sweep the room with her light. Off to one side was a table with a couple of glasses on it, one broken. Pieces of a chair lay on the floor beside a rotting playing card; an ace, Corrie noticed. In one corner stood a pile of broken bottles and jugs of all kinds: wine bottles, mason jars, clay jugs, amidst moldy trash. She could just imagine the men tending the fire, playing cards, drinking, smoking.

Now she shone her light upward. At first she could see nothing, the ceiling was so black. But then she was able to make out some broken stalactites and a honeycomb of cracks that, apparently, had drawn off the smoke. Even so, they couldn't have drawn it off very fast: her breath was condensing in the air, surrounding her with a fog that the flashlight set aglow.

She approached the cauldron set upon its iron tripod. It was certainly big enough to boil a human being. It was hard to tell, with all the dampness, if it had been used recently. Would the place still smell of smoke from the long-ago days of the still? She wasn't sure. And then there was that other smell: the bad one. Not rotten, exactly; it was even worse than rot. It was that same smell of spoiled ham as at the crime scene.

Corrie stopped, feeling suddenly frightened. She'd come to see if the still was there. Well, it *was* there. She should turn around and get out. In fact, coming here at all now seemed like a really, really bad idea.

She swallowed. Once again, she reminded herself that she'd already come this far. Might as well take five more seconds to finish the reconnoiter.

She tiptoed up and looked inside the cauldron. A smell of rancid grease hit her as she shone her light inside.

At the bottom was something pale, almost transparent, like a pearly seashell. A human ear.

She gagged and staggered back, dropping her flashlight. It struck the hard limestone floor and rolled away toward a dark corner, beam revolving lazily across the floor and ceiling, finally coming to rest against a far wall with a heavy thud.

A second later, it went out, and the cavern was thrown into utter blackness.

Shit, Corrie thought. *Shit, shit.*

Carefully, she got down on her hands and knees and, moving slowly, feeling along the ground with her hands, crawled in the direction it had rolled. Within a minute her hands brushed the rock wall of the cave. She began to feel along it, looking for the flashlight.

It wasn't there.

She swallowed again, sitting up on her haunches. For a minute, she thought about trying to find her way out in absolute darkness. But the way back down was so long, it would be easy to get disoriented. She fought down a feeling of panic. She would find the flashlight. It must have gone off in the collision with the wall. She'd find it, shake the light back into it, and get the hell out of there.

She moved along the wall, first to the left, then to the right, feeling with her hands.

No flashlight.

Maybe she'd taken the wrong tack. Carefully, she crawled back to where she thought she'd started, and then tried again, crawling in the direction she remembered the light had rolled. Still, no matter how far she went along the wall, sweeping the ground with her hands, she could not find the flashlight.

Her breath began to come faster as she returned to the middle of the room. At least, she thought it was the middle of the room: she was quickly becoming disoriented in the utter blackness.

Okay, she thought. *Stop moving, breathe a little slower, get a grip.* Okay, so it was really stupid to come in here with one flashlight and no matches. But the cavern she was in was small and there was only one opening—wasn't there? She hadn't remembered any passageways going off, but then again, she hadn't really checked.

Her heart was beating so fast that she could barely breathe. *Just slow down,* she thought. Time to forget about the flashlight. It was probably busted, anyway. The important thing now was to get out, to keep moving; otherwise, she'd freeze up. She'd left the door unlocked, thank God, and the lights were still on back in the Kaverns. All she had to do was get out of this back room and down the passageway.

Stupid, stupid, stupid . . .

Carefully, she oriented herself toward where she thought the exit would be. Then, just as carefully, she began crawling forward. The floor of the cave was cold, rough, uneven, covered with greasy pebbles and puddles of water. It was absolutely terrifying, the pitch blackness. Corrie wasn't sure she'd ever been in a place completely without light. Even on the darkest night, there was some trace of starshine or moonlight . . . She felt her heart begin to beat even faster than before.

Then her head bumped painfully into something. She reached up, felt: the iron cauldron. She had crawled right into the dead coals.

Okay, so she'd gone in precisely the opposite direction. But at least now she had her bearings. She'd crawl along the wall until she reached the passage out. Once in the passage, she'd keep crawling, one hand on the wall, until she reached the iron door. From there, she could reach the pool, she felt sure—even in utter darkness. And in any case, on the far side of the pool lay light and the boardwalk. *It's not so far,* she repeated, *not so far at all . . .*

Forcing herself to relax, she began crawling forward, sliding her left hand along the wall: *slide, stop, slide, stop again, three, four, five.* Her heart began to slow. She bumped into a stalagmite, tried to visualize its orientation in the room. With relief she realized the exit should be straight ahead.

She kept on crawling, one hand on the floor, the other on the wall. *Six, seven, eight . . .*

In the dark, her hand touched something warm.

She instinctively snatched back her hand. The rush of fear and surprise came a moment later. Was it some cave-dwelling creature—a rat or a bat, perhaps? Her imagination, working overtime in the blackness?

She waited. There was no sound or movement. Then she carefully reached out, felt again.

It was warm, naked, hairless, and wet.

She shrank back, a sob rising involuntarily to her throat. The smell of something dirty, something indescribably foul, seemed to rise and envelop her. Was that noise she heard really the sound of her own breathing? It was: she was gasping with fear.

She gritted her teeth, blinked her eyes against the darkness, tried to regain control of her wildly beating heart.

The thing she had touched hadn't moved. It was probably just another bump or ridge in the floor. If she stopped in horror at every little thing she touched, she'd never make it out of the cave.

She reached out to move forward, and brushed against it again. It *was* warm, there was no imagining that: but it must be some freakish thing, volcanic or something. She felt it again, lightly, letting her hand brush here, there . . .

She realized she was touching a naked foot, with long broken toenails.

Ever so slowly, she withdrew her hand. It was shaking uncontrollably and her breath came as a rasp, completely beyond her control to silence it. She tried to swallow but her mouth had gone dry.

And then a coarse, singsong voice, a caricature lisping of human speech, came from the darkness.

"Wanna pway wif me?"

Forty-Seven

Hazen sat back in the well-upholstered chair, fingertips pressed lightly against the polished wood of the conference table. He wondered yet again why Medicine Creek couldn't afford a sheriff's office with nice comfortable chairs, or a table like this one; but then it occurred to him that the Deeper sheriff's office, like everything else in Deeper, was running on borrowed money. At least his department ran in the black, every year. Medicine Creek's time would come, thanks in no small part to him.

The voice of Hank Larssen droned on in the background, but Hazen was barely listening. Better to let the Deeper sheriff talk himself out. He glanced surreptitiously at his watch. Seven o'clock. They'd come a long way today, made some great progress. He'd done a great deal of thinking, and in his mind the case was now almost complete. There was only one detail that still bothered him.

Larssen, it seemed, was winding down. "It's just way too premature, Dent. I haven't heard any hard evidence, just a lot of conjecture and supposition."

Conjecture and supposition. Christ, Hank had been reading too many Grisham novels.

Larssen drew himself up with an air of finality. "I'm not going to cast a cloud of suspicion on one of Deeper's leading citizens without firm evidence. I'm not going to do it, and I'm not going to allow anyone else to do it. Not in my jurisdiction."

Hazen let the silence ripen, then turned to Raskovich.

"Chester? What do you think?"

Raskovich glanced at Seymour Fisk, the KSU dean, who had been listening intently in silence, a crease furrowed across his bald pate. "Well," Raskovich said, "I think that what Sheriff Hazen and I found is enough to justify continuing the investigation."

"All you've found out," Larssen replied, "is that Lavender's in financial trouble. A lot of people are in financial trouble these days."

Again Hazen withheld comment. Let Chester do the talking.

"Well," said Raskovich, "we found more than just financial trouble. He hasn't paid real estate taxes on some properties in years. Why there haven't been any tax seizures is something I'd be interested in knowing. And Lavender went around assuring everyone that the experimental field was coming to Deeper. He told everyone he had a plan. As if he knew something that nobody else knew. This 'plan' sounds pretty suspicious to me."

"For heaven's sake, it was just *talk* to appease his creditors," said Larssen, practically rising out of the comfortable Naugahyde to make his point.

This is great, thought Hazen. *Now Hank's arguing with the KSU guys.* Larssen always had been a few beers short of a six-pack.

"It's pretty clear," Raskovich went on, "that if Dr. Chauncy had announced on Monday that the field was going to Medicine Creek, Lavender's creditors would have moved in and he'd have been forced into bankruptcy. That's a powerful motive."

There was a silence. Larssen was shaking his head.

And now Fisk spoke at last, his reedy ivory-tower voice filling the office. "Sheriff, the intention is not to make accusations. The intention is merely to continue the investigation, looking into Mr. Lavender's affairs along with whatever other leads develop."

Hazen waited. It was politically important to "consult" with Larssen. Old Hank just didn't seem to get the fact that it was all pro forma, that nothing he said would stop the investigation into Lavender.

"Mr. Fisk," Larssen said, "all I'm saying is, don't focus on a suspect too early. There are plenty of other avenues that should be explored. Look, Dent, we all know Lavender's no saint, but he's no killer either, especially not *that* kind of killer. Even if he hired someone, how in hell did that person get from Deeper to Medicine Creek without being observed? Where'd he hide out? Where's his car? Where'd he spend the night? That whole area's been searched by air and on the ground, and you know it!"

Hazen exhaled quietly. This was precisely the point that still bothered him. It was the one weakness in his theory.

"It seems to me," he went on, "that it's more likely the killer's a resident of Medicine Creek, a Jekyll and Hyde type. If it was an outsider, somebody would've seen something. You can't come and go from Medicine Creek, time and again, unnoticed."

"Someone could be hiding in the corn," said Raskovich.

"You can see into the corn from above," said Larssen. "They've been flying spotter planes for days now. They've searched the creek for twenty miles, they've searched the Mounds, they've searched everywhere. There's no sign of anyone hiding, and nobody's been coming or going. I mean, where's this killer supposed to be hiding? In a hole in the ground?"

Listening, Hazen suddenly went rigid. He felt his limbs stiffening as the sudden, brilliant insight burned its way through his consciousness. *Of course,* he told himself. *Of course.* It was the elusive answer he'd been searching for, the missing link in his theory.

He breathed deeply, glanced around to make sure nobody had noticed his reaction. It was critical that it not seem like Hank had given it to him.

And then he delivered his revelation in an almost bored tone of voice. "That's right, Hank. He's been hiding in a hole in the ground."

There was a silence.

"How's that?" Raskovich asked.

Hazen looked at him. "Kraus's Kaverns," he said.

"Kraus's Kaverns?" Fisk repeated.

"On the Cry Road, that big old house with the gift shop. There's a tourist cave out back of it. Been there forever. Run now by old Winifred Kraus."

It was incredible how fast the pieces were coming together in his mind. It had been under his nose all along, and he just hadn't seen it. Kraus's Kaverns. *Of course.*

Fisk was nodding, and so was Raskovich. "I remember seeing that place," said Raskovich.

Larssen had turned white. He knew Hazen had nailed it. That's how perfect it was, how well it fit together.

Hazen spoke again. "The killer's been hiding in that cave." He looked at Larssen and couldn't help but smile. "As you know, Hank, that's the same cave where old man Kraus had his moonshine operation. Making corn whiskey for *King Lavender.*"

"Now that's *very* interesting," Fisk said, turning an admiring look on Hazen.

"Isn't it? There's a room back there, behind the tourist loop, where they boiled up their sour mash. In a big *pot still.*" He emphasized the last two words carefully.

He saw Raskovich's eyes suddenly widen. "In a pot still big enough to boil a human body?"

"Bingo," said Hazen.

The atmosphere became electric. Larssen had begun to sweat now, and Hazen knew it was because even he believed.

"So you see, Mr. Fisk," Hazen continued, "Lavender's man has been holed up in that cave, coming out at night with his bare feet and his other shenanigans, killing people and making it look like the fulfillment of the Ghost Mounds curse. During Prohibition, King Lavender financed that pot still for old man Kraus, got him set up in the business. It's what he did all over Cry County. He bankrolled all the moonshiners in these parts."

Hank Larssen removed a handkerchief and dabbed at the line of sweat that had formed on his brow.

"Lavender claimed his assistant, McFelty, went to visit his sick mother in Kansas City. It's one of the things Raskovich and I checked out today. We tried to get in touch with McFelty's mother. And we found out all about McFelty's mother."

He paused.

"She died twenty years ago."

He let that sink in, then continued. "And this man McFelty's been in trouble with the law before. Small stuff, mostly, but a lot of it violent: petty assault, aggravated assault, drunk driving."

The revelations had been coming fast, one almost piling up upon the other. And now Hazen added the kicker: "McFelty disappeared two days before the Swegg killing. I think he went underground. As Hank just pointed out, you can't come and go from Medicine Creek without being noticed: without neighbors noticing, without *me* noticing. He's been holed up in Kraus's Kaverns all this time, coming out at night to do his dirty work."

There was a long pause in which nobody spoke. Then Fisk cleared his throat. "This is first-rate work, Sheriff. What's the next move?"

Hazen stood up, his face set. "The town's been crawling with law officers and press. You can be sure McFelty's still laying low in those caves, waiting for a lull so's he can escape. Now that he's completed his job."

"And?"

"And so we go in there and get the son of a bitch."

"When?"

"Now." He turned to Larssen. "Conference us into state police HQ in Dodge. I want Commander Ernie Wayes on the horn himself. We need a well-armed team and we need it now. We need dogs, good dogs this time. I'll head over to the courthouse, get a bench warrant from Judge Anderson."

"Are you sure McFelty's still there, in the caves?" Fisk asked.

"No," said Hazen. "I'm not sure. But there's going to be physical evidence in there at the very least. I'm not taking any chances. This guy's dangerous. He may be doing a job for Lavender, but he's been enjoying himself just a little too much—and that scares the piss out of me. Let's not make the mistake of underestimating him."

He looked out the window at the blackening horizon, the rising wind.

"We've got to move. Our man may use the cover of the storm to make his exit." He glanced at his watch, then looked once again around the room.

"We're going in tonight at ten, and we're going in big."

Forty-Eight

The darkness was total, absolute. Corrie lay on the wet rock, soaked to the bone, her whole body shivering from terror and cold. Not far away, she could hear it moving around, talking to itself in a singsong undertone, making horrible little bubbling sounds with its lips, sometimes cooing, sometimes laughing softly as if at some private joke.

Her mind had passed through disbelief and stark terror, and come out on the other side cold and numb. The killer had her. *It*—she supposed it was a *he*—had tied her up and thrown her over his shoulder, roughly, like a sack of meat, and carried her through a labyrinth of passageways, sometimes climbing, sometimes descending, sometimes splashing across underground streams, for what seemed like an eternity.

And through darkness—always, through darkness. He seemed to move by feel or by memory.

His arms had felt slippery and clammy, yet strong as steel cables that threatened always to crush her. She had screamed, begged, pleaded, but her protests had met with obliviousness. And then, at last, they got to *this place*—this place with its unutterable stink—and he had dropped her sprawling onto the stone floor. Then the horny foot had kicked her roughly into a corner, where she now lay, dazed, aching, bleeding. The stench—the stench that before had been faint and unidentifiable—was here appalling, omnipresent, enveloping.

She had lain, numb and unthinking, for an unguessable period of time. But now her senses were beginning to return. The initial paralysis of terror was wearing off, if only slightly. She lay still, forcing herself to think. She was far back in the cave—a cave much bigger than anyone imagined. Nobody was going to find their way back here to save her . . .

She struggled with the panic that rose at this thought. If nobody was going to save her, then she'd have to save herself.

She shut her eyes tight against the darkness, listening. *He* was busying himself in the blackness somewhere nearby, gargling and singsonging unintelligibly to himself.

Was he even human . . . ?

He *had* to be human. He had a human foot—though as callused as a piece of rawhide. And he spoke, or at least vocalized, in a high, babylike voice.

And yet, if he was human, he was like none other that had ever walked the earth.

Suddenly she felt him near. There was a grunt. She froze in fear, waiting. A hand seized her roughly, dragged her to her feet, shook her.

"Muh?"

She sobbed. "Leave me alone."

Another shake, more violent this time. "Hoooo!" went the voice, high and babyish. She tried to wrench free, and with a grunt he flung her down.

"Stop . . . stop . . ."

A hand seized her ankle and gave a sharp jerk. Corrie screamed, feeling pain lance through her hip. And then she felt his arms around her, grabbing her by the shoulders, lifting her bodily. "Please, please stop—"

"Plisss," squeaked the voice. "Plisss. Hruhn."

She feebly tried to push him away, but he was holding her close to him, his foul breath washing over her.

"No—let me go—"

"Heeee!"

She was flung down again, and then she heard him shuffle off with a low, murmuring sound. She struggled wildly, tried to sit up. The ropes burned her wrists and she felt her hands tingling from lack of blood. He was going to kill her, she knew that. She had to get away.

With a great effort, she managed to flop herself upward into a sitting position. If only she knew who he was, or what he was doing, or why he was there in the cave . . . If only she understood, she might have a chance. She swallowed, shivered, tried to speak.

"Who . . . who are you?" she said. It came out as a bare whisper.

There was a momentary silence. This was followed by a shuffling sound. He was coming over.

"Please don't touch me."

Corrie could hear him breathing. She realized that maybe it hadn't been such a good idea to attract his attention again. And yet her only hope was to engage him somehow. She swallowed again, repeated the question.

"Who are you?"

She felt him leaning over her. A wet hand touched her face, broken nails scratching her skin, the huge fingers callused and warm. She turned away with a stifled cry.

Then she felt a hand on her shoulder. She tried to lie still, to ignore it. It squeezed her shoulder, then moved down her arm, stopping to feel here and there as it went, then sliding further: horny and rough, the broken nails like splintered ends of wood.

The hand withdrew, then came back, sliding and slipping up the ridge of her backbone. She tried to twist away but the hand suddenly gripped her shoulder blade with a horrible strength. Involuntarily, she cried out. The hand resumed its crawl. It grasped the nape of her neck, squeezed. She felt paralyzed with terror. The squeezing grew harder.

"What do you want?" she choked out.

The hand slowly relaxed. She could hear breathing, and then some humming, and an undertone of rapid, singsong words. He was speaking to himself again. The hand caressed the back of her neck and reached up and rubbed her head.

She wanted to twist away but she forced herself not to. The hand kept rubbing, sliding down now over her forehead. It rubbed her face, stroked her cheek, pulled at her lips, tried to open her mouth, stinking horny fingers like a golem's claw. She turned, but the hand followed the movements of her head, poking, always poking, as if inspecting a cut of meat.

"Please stop it!" she sobbed.

The hand stopped, and there was a grunt. Then the fingers slipped around her neck, from the front this time, and squeezed, first lightly, then a little harder. And then harder still.

Corrie tried to scream, but the squeezing had already closed off her windpipe. She thrashed, struggled, saw stars begin to flash in front of her eyes.

And still he squeezed. And as consciousness flickered

and her limbs began to relax involuntarily, Corrie desperately tried to reach out, to claw the darkness, to push him away . . .

His hand gradually relaxed and released her. She fell, gasping, drawing in air, her head pounding. His hand went back to her hair, petting it.

Then he suddenly stopped. His hand withdrew, and he stepped back.

Corrie lay there, terrified, silent. She heard a sniffing noise, then another, and another. He seemed to be snuffling the air. She noticed then that the faintest of breezes was moving through this section of the cave. She could smell the outside world: the ozone and moisture from the storm, the earth, the cool nocturnal smells, pushed aside—if only a little—the stench of this nightmarish place. The smell seemed to beckon him, call him away.

And he was gone.

Forty-Nine

It was 8:11 P.M.: normally the hour of sunset. Except that to western Kansas sunset had already come, four hours early.

Since early afternoon, a front of cool air one thousand miles long, pushing down from Canada, had been forcing itself across a region of the Great Plains that for several weeks had remained parched and dry. As the front moved, rising air before it began to pick up fine particles of dust. Soon this manifested itself in the form of dust devils: spiraling vortexes of dirt that rose sharply into the dark air. As the front moved on, it grew in intensity, raising the dry topsoil, feeding off itself until it had formed a massive wall of whistling, roiling dust. Quickly, it mounted to a height of ten thousand feet. On the surface, visibility was decreased to less than a quarter of a mile.

As the front moved from west to east across Kansas, dust storm warnings preceded it. The dark brown wall bore down on town after town, engulfing one after the other. As it went, the cold front, laden with dust, drove itself like a wedge into the hot, dry, dead air that had been suffocating the Great Plains. As they collided, the air masses of differing density and temperature struggled for supremacy. This disturbance caused a massive low-pressure system to form, wheeling counterclockwise over almost a hundred thousand square miles of the High Plains. Ultimately, the warm air rising from the ground penetrated the cooler mass above, boiling into towering cumulonimbus clouds that rose taller and taller, until they appeared as dark angry mountains against the sky, larger than the Himalayas. The great mountain chain of clouds flattened against the tropopause, spreading out into a series of massive, anvil-shaped thunderheads.

As the storm matured, it broke into several cells that moved together as a disorganized yet single unit: mature cells forming at the storm's center, with newer ones developing on the periphery. In the cells that approached Cry County, the anvil-shaped top of a cell began to bulge upward. This "overshoot" indicated that the rising torrent of air at the storm's center was so powerful it had broken through the tropopause into the stratosphere. On the underside of the storm, ugly, bulging mammatus pouches appeared: bellwethers for heavy rainfall, hail, windbursts, and tornadoes.

The National Weather Service had been tracking the system with radar, satellites, and the reports of pilots and civilian "spotters." The dust storm and thunderstorm bulletins were upgraded to include tornado watches. Regional offices of the National Weather Service began advising local authorities of the need for emergency action. And always it remained vigilant for that rarest, yet worst type of storm: the supercell thunderstorm. In this far more organized event, the main updraft—known as a mesocyclone—reaches speeds of close to two hundred miles per hour. Such storms could create three-inch hail, eighty-mile-per-hour downbursts of wind, and tornadoes.

And already, virgas of rain were hovering over the land-scape, evaporating as quickly as they fell, blasting the ground with localized microbursts that uprooted trees, flat-tened fields, and peeled the roofs off trailers. Hailstones spilled from the sky, stripping corn cars from their stems and ripping up fields, tearing the dry stalks to tattered sticks.

Many thousands of feet below this cell, almost lost in the ap-proaching storm front, a lone Rolls-Royce hurtled along at one hundred miles an hour, two and a half tons of precision-engineered steel cutting the darkness of a long and lonely ribbon of tar.

Inside, the driver kept one hand on the wheel while glancing at the laptop open on the seat beside him. The lap-top showed the real-time progress of the storm, a composite downloaded by a mosaic of weather satellites orbiting high above.

Coming from Topeka, he had exited Interstate 70 just past Salina, and was now passing the outskirts of Great Bend. From here on, the road to Medicine Creek would be-come far more local. That—and the approaching storm it-self—would force him to slow dramatically.

And yet time was of the essence. The killer would soon kill again. In all likelihood he would be attracted to the storm, the violence and darkness of it, and he was almost certain to kill again that night.

He picked up his cell phone and dialed. Once again a recorded voice told him that the party he was trying to reach was out of range.

Out of range. He pondered that phrase: out of range.

And he pushed the Rolls ahead even faster.

Fifty

Ever since he'd seen *The Wizard of Oz* as a child, Tad Franklin had been fascinated by tornadoes. It was a source of secret embarrassment that, living all his life in western Kansas, the very center of "tornado alley," he had never managed to see one. He'd seen the aftereffects more often than he'd liked—twisted trailer parks, trees blasted into toothpicks, cars lifted and thrown across the road—but somehow he'd never seen an actual funnel cloud with his own eyes.

Tonight he felt sure that was going to change. All day long there had been weather advisories. Every hour, it seemed, the weather service alerts had grown in intensity: thunderstorm watch; severe thunderstorm warning; tornado watch. A brutal dust storm had come screaming through an hour before that had torn away placards and shingles, sandblasted cars and houses, knocked down trees, and reduced visibility to a few hundred yards. And then at 8:11 that evening, with Tad alone in the sheriff's office, the news came: the whole of Cry County had just been placed under a tornado warning until midnight. F-scale tornadoes of magnitude 2 or even 3, with two-hundred-mile-an-hour winds and devastating force, were possible.

Ten seconds later, Sheriff Hazen was on the radio.

"Tad," he was saying, "I'm in Deeper, about to head back."

"Sheriff—"

"I don't have a lot of time. Listen to me. We've made a lot of progress on the case. We believe the killer is hiding in Kraus's Kaverns."

"The killer—?"

"For chrissakes, let me finish. It's most likely McFelty, Norris Lavender's henchman. He's been holed up in that moonshine room back of Kraus's Kaverns. But we've got to move fast in case he decides to pull out under cover of the storm. We're putting together a team to go in at ten o'clock. But we also just got word from the NWS about a tornado warning for all of Cry County—"

"I just got the call."

"—and I've got to put you on the tornado side of things. You know the drill?"

"Sure do."

"Good. You get the word out, make sure everything's battened down in Medicine Creek and the outlying areas. We'll be arriving around nine, and then all hell's going to break loose—and I don't mean the weather. Just be sure to have a couple strong pots of fresh coffee. You're not going in with us, so don't worry. Somebody's got to hold down the fort."

It was only when Tad felt himself relax that he realized he *had* begun to get a little nervous. He didn't mind handling a tornado alert—he'd done that often enough before—but the idea of going after a killer in a dark cave was something else.

"Right, Sheriff," he said.

"Okay, Tad. I'm relying on you."

"Yes, sir."

Tad hung up the radio. He knew the drill, all right. First thing, warn the citizenry. If there were any outside, get them indoors or into shelters.

He pushed out the back, careful to face away from the wind. The gusts, full of sand and grit, felt as if they had teeth. He opened the door to his squad car, slipped in, shook the dust from his hair and face, started the engine, and ran the wipers a few times. Then he started the siren and turned on his flashers. He slid out onto Main Street and cruised along, slowly, speaking into the horn. Of course, most of them would already have heard it over the radio, but it was important to go through the motions.

"This is the sheriff's office. A tornado warning has been declared for all of Cry County. Repeat, a tornado warning has been declared for all of Cry County. All citizens should take shelter immediately, below ground or in concrete-reinforced buildings. Stay away from windows and doors. I repeat, a tornado warning has been declared for Cry County . . ."

He hit the edge of town, drove past the last houses, stopped, and looked down the dust-covered road. The few farms he could make out were already shuttered up tight, no activity anywhere. The farmers would have had their ears glued to the radio for hours already, and they knew what to do better than anyone: move livestock, especially the young, to sheltered areas; haul extra feed; make sure they were well stocked with provisions in case of a power loss.

The farmers knew what to do. It was the damn-fool townies one had to worry about.

Tad ran his eye down the road until it reached the level of the horizon. Above, the sky was black, intensely black; the sun must have set already, and what little light was left was completely blocked by the storm. The wind was gusting fitfully, pushing shreds of corn shucks and dust-covered stalks past his windows. To the southwest he could see a deep reddish flickering that looked more like the front of a war than lightning. In Cry County, tornadoes almost always moved from southwest to northeast. It was so dark that if a tornado were coming they couldn't even see it. They wouldn't know it was on them until they *heard* it.

He turned around quickly and headed back into town.

The windows of Maisie's were twin rectangles of cheerful yellow standing against the murk. Tad pulled up in front and got out, holding his collar against the wind. The air smelled of dry earth and tree roots. Fragments of corn sheaves peppered his jacket.

He pushed through the door and looked around. The place fell silent as they realized he wasn't there for a cup of coffee.

Tad cleared his throat. "Excuse me, folks, but we've got a tornado warning in effect for all of Cry County. Force 2, even force 3, tornadoes possible. Time to head home."

The reporters and camera crews had already fled the coming storm, and he found himself looking upon a roomful of the usual. Melton Rasmussen; Swede Cahill and his wife, Gladys; Art Ridder. Smit Ludwig was absent, which was a little odd. He was the one person you'd most expect to find. Maybe he was out on some storm-related story. If so, he'd better get his rear end to shelter.

Rasmussen was the first to react. "Any news on the killings?" he asked.

The question hung in the air and Tad faced a roomful of expectant faces. He was taken aback: here, even with the threat of tornadoes, the killings were still the first thing on everyone's mind. This was why Maisie's was full: Tad had seen cows do it, bunching up when they got scared.

"Well, we've—" Tad stopped himself. The sheriff would definitely have his ass on a platter if he mentioned the upcoming operation.

"We're following up some excellent leads," he finished up with the usual line, knowing how lame it must sound.

"That's just what you've been saying for a goddamned week," said Mel, standing up, his face red.

"Easy, Mel," said Swede Cahill.

"Well, we've got a better lead now," Tad said defensively.

"A *better* lead. Did you hear that, Art?"

Art Ridder was sitting at the bar nursing a cup of coffee. His look was definitely not friendly. He eased his butt around on the chrome seat and faced Tad. "The sheriff said he had a plan, some way of catching the murderer and getting the experimental field back to Medicine Creek. Tad, I want to know what the hell this plan of his is, or whether he was just blowing smoke."

"I'm not at liberty to discuss his plans," said Tad. "And anyway, the important thing is that there's a tornado warning in effect for—"

"The hell with the warning," said Ridder. "I want to see some action on these killings."

"Sheriff Hazen's making progress."

"Progress? Where's he been? I haven't seen hide nor hair of him all day."

"He's been in Deeper, pursuing a lead—"

Suddenly the swinging doors to the kitchen burst open and Maisie appeared behind the counter. "Art Ridder, you shut your trap," she barked. "Lay off Tad here. He's just doing his job."

"Now look here, Maisie—"

"Don't 'look here, Maisie' me, Art Ridder. I'm wise to

your bullying ways and you won't do it in here. And you, Mel, you know better. Lay off."

The room fell into a guilty silence.

"There's a tornado warning out," continued Maisie. "You all know what that means. You got five minutes to clear out. You can settle up later. I'm shuttering my windows and heading down to the basement. The rest of you'd better do the same if you don't want to find yourselves over the rainbow before the night is out."

She turned and went back into the kitchen, smacking the swinging doors together and causing everyone to jump.

"Get to a safe place of shelter," Tad said, looking around at the assembly, remembering the list in his manual. "Get in the basement, under a worktable or concrete washtub or staircase. Avoid windows. Bring a flashlight, potable water, and a portable radio with batteries. The warning's in effect until midnight, but they may extend it, you never know. This is one heck of a storm."

As the place cleared out, Tad went into the back, looking for Maisie.

"Thanks," he said.

Maisie waved her hand dismissively. She looked more haggard than he remembered ever seeing her. "Tad, I don't know if I should mention this, but Smit's missing."

"I kinda wondered about that."

"There was a reporter who waited for him until closing last night. Smit wasn't here for breakfast or lunch. It's not like him to stay away like that, not without saying something. I called his home and the paper, but there's no answer."

"I'll look into it," Tad said.

Maisie nodded. "Probably nothing."

"Yeah. Probably nothing." Tad went back out into the

restaurant, shuttered the windows, then made for the door. Hand on the knob, he turned back. "You get in that basement now, Maisie, okay?"

"On my way," Maisie's voice came drifting back from down the stairs.

Just as Tad returned to the sheriff's office, the call came from the county dispatcher. Mrs. Fernald Higgs had called. Her boy had seen a monster in his room. When he screamed and turned on the light, the monster ran away. The boy was hysterical and so was Mrs. Higgs.

Tad listened incredulously until the dispatcher had finished.

"You've got to be kidding," he said.

"She wants the sheriff out there," the dispatcher ended lamely.

Tad could hardly believe it. "We've got a serial killer loose and a frontful of tornadoes on their way, and you want me to check out a *monster?*"

There was a silence. "Hey," said the dispatcher, "I'm just doing my job. You know I have to report everything. Mrs. Higgs says the monster left a footprint."

Tad lowered the radio momentarily. *Jesus Christ.*

He looked at his watch. Eight-thirty. He could be out to the Higgs place and back in twenty minutes.

With a sigh, he raised the radio once again. "All right," he said. "I'll check it out."

Fifty-One

By the time Tad arrived at the Higgs residence, old man Higgs had returned home and whaled his boy, and the kid was sitting angrily in the corner, eyes dry, little fists clenched. Mrs. Higgs was flitting about in the background, worried, wringing her hands, her mouth compressed. Higgs himself sat at the kitchen table, face set, eating a potato.

"I'm here about the, ah, report," Tad said as he came in, taking his hat off.

"Forget the report," said the old man. "I'm sorry you were bothered."

Tad went over to the boy and knelt down. "You okay?"

The boy nodded, his face flaming red. He had blond hair and very blue eyes.

"Hillis, I don't want any more talk of monsters, hear?" the farmer said.

Mrs. Higgs sat down, got up. "I'm sorry, Deputy Tad, do you want a cup of coffee?"

"No thanks, ma'am."

He looked at the kid again and spoke softly. "What'd you see?"

The kid said nothing.

"Don't be talking about any monsters," growled the farmer. Tad leaned closer.

"I *saw* it," said the boy defiantly.

"What'd you say?" the farmer roared.

Tad turned to Mrs. Higgs. "Show me the footprint, if you will, ma'am."

Mrs. Higgs rose nervously.

The farmer said, "He ain't talking about monsters still, is he? By jingo, I'll whale him a second time. Calling the police about a monster!"

Mrs. Higgs brought Tad through the small parlor to the back of the house and scuttled into the boy's room. She pointed at the window. "I *know* I shut the window before I put Hill to bed, but when he screamed and I came in I saw it was open. And when I went to shut it I saw a footprint in the flowerbed."

Tad could hear Higgs's voice raised in the kitchen. "It's goddamned embarrassing, having the sheriff come calling over a bad dream."

Tad raised the window. The moment he did so, the wind came shrieking in, grabbing the curtains and tossing them wildly around. Tad put his head out the window and looked down.

In the faint light from the room he could see a bed of carefully tended zinnias. Several of them had been roughly flattened by a large, elongated mark. It might be a footprint, but then again, it might not be.

He went back through the parlor, exited the side door, and walked around the edge of the house, leaning toward the clapboards for cover, until he'd reached the boy's window. Snapping on his flashlight, he knelt by the flowerbed.

The impression was smudged and had been eroded by the storm, but it did, in fact, strongly resemble a footprint.

He straightened up, angling his flashlight away from the house. There was another mark, then another and another. With his flashlight, he followed their direction. About a quarter mile distant—beyond the frenzied, tossing sea of corn—were the faint lights of the Gro-Bain plant. The storm warnings had shut the plant down early and it now lay empty.

As he watched, the lights abruptly winked out.

He turned. The lights in the Higgs house were out, too. But the glow of light from Medicine Creek was still visible.

Blackout.

He trudged around the side of the farmhouse again and went in the door.

"It appears there may, in fact, have been an intruder," he said.

The farmer muttered angrily but didn't say anything. Mrs. Higgs was already lighting candles.

"We're also under a tornado warning. I'm going to ask you to shut and lock your doors and windows. Head for the basement the moment the wind gets any worse. If you have a battery-powered radio, keep it tuned to the emergency channel."

The farmer grunted acknowledgment. He didn't need anybody telling him what to do in case of a twister.

Tad got back in his car and sat for a moment, thinking. The big cruiser rocked back and forth to the gusting of the wind. It was nine o'clock. Hazen and his team would be in town by now. He unhooked the radio and called in.

"That you, Tad?"

"Yeah. You back at the station, Sheriff?"

"Not yet. Storm blew down a tree on the Deeper Road and knocked out a couple of repeater stations."

Tad quickly explained the situation.

"Monsters, huh?" Hazen chuckled. There was an awful lot of noise in the background.

"You know 911, they have to report everything. I'm sorry if I—"

"Don't apologize. You did right. What's the upshot?"

"It appears there may have been an intruder. The kid's scream might have startled him. He seems to have headed away in the direction of the Gro-Bain plant. Which, by the way, just lost power."

"Probably that Cahill kid and his friends again. Remember that egging last month? We don't want those boys out on a night like this. They take advantage of a blackout to go helling around, they could end up getting skulled by a flying tree. As long as you're out there, why don't you check out the plant? There's still time. Keep in touch."

"Right."

"And Tad?"

"Yes?"

"You haven't seen that man Pendergast, have you?"

"No."

"Good. Looks like he blew town after I served him with that C-and-D."

"No doubt."

"We're going to hit the cave at ten. Get back by then to cover the office."

"Got it."

Tad signed off and started up the car. He felt a certain relief. Now he had an even better reason not to go into the cave after the killer. As for Gro-Bain, they hadn't had a night guard since the last one started working days. He would just check the entrances: as long as they were all locked, and there was no sign of activity, his job would be done.

He pointed the car south, toward the dark, low outline of the plant.

Fifty-Two

Tad eased his squad car into the plant's parking lot. Heavy gusts blasted across the empty asphalt, carrying with them bits of straw and ruined husks of corn. Ribbons of rain cascaded here and there, coming and going in sudden sheets. A line of fat raindrops passed over the cruiser, from front to back, with a machine-gun cadence. Beyond the parking lot, he could hear waves of wind ripping through the cornfields surrounding the plant. He peered out at the blackness over the corn, half hoping for, half dreading, the sight of a daggerlike funnel cloud. But he could see nothing.

The sheriff had said he suspected Andy Cahill and his friends of terrorizing the Higgs homestead. Privately, Tad thought Hazen's own son, Brad, and his gang were the more likely suspects. Scaring little kids, egging buildings, was more their style. The son would never be the man his father was. Tad wondered what he'd do if he ran into the sheriff's son outside the plant. Now, that could prove to be more than a little awkward.

He eased the car up to the low outline of the plant and stopped, engine idling. Even through the closed windows, the wind screeched and moaned like a beast in pain. The plant was dim against the murk, sunken in the corn, dark and deserted.

Looking at the low, sinister building, what had seemed like a routine check was beginning to seem less appealing to Tad. Why the heck hadn't Gro-Bain hired another night watchman? It wasn't fair that the burden of private security fell on the sheriff's department.

Tad passed a hand through his closely cropped hair. No help for it now. He'd just do a quick check to make sure none of the doors had been forced, then he'd check Smit Ludwig's place and head on back to the station.

He cracked the cruiser door open, and the wind pushed it back at him with an angry howl. Pulling his hat down and raising his collar, he pushed harder at the door, then ducked out, face against the storm, making for the loading docks. As he ran, he could hear something banging in the wind. Reaching the shelter of the building, he pushed his hat back on his head and switched on his flashlight, then made his way along the cinderblock wall. The banging got louder.

It was when he reached the top of the loading dock stairs that his light revealed an open door, swinging and banging on broken hinges.

Shit.

Tad stood there, the beam of the flashlight playing over the shattered lock and mangled hinges. Somebody had really done a number on it. Normally, he would call for backup. But where was he going to get backup on a night like this? Any law enforcement officers that weren't going into the cave after the killer would be out working the tornado watch. Maybe he should just forget about it, come back in the morning.

He imagined explaining that decision to the darkening face of Sheriff Hazen and decided it was not an acceptable option. Hazen was constantly harping on him that he needed more pluck, more initiative.

This was nothing, really, to be concerned about. The killer was safely bottled up in the cave. Kids like Brad Hazen were always breaking into the plant for fun, even when the night watchman was there. It had happened several times before, most notably last Halloween—half a dozen hoodlums from Deeper who thought it would be fun to T.P. their rival town's major employer.

Tad felt a wash of irritation. It was a hell of a night to pull crap like that. He pushed through the broken door, making as much noise as possible, and shone his light around the receiving area.

"This is the police," he called out in his sternest voice. "Please identify yourselves."

The only answer was the echo of his own voice coming back at him from the blackness.

Moving forward carefully, letting his light drift from left to right, he exited the loading bay and walked along the catwalk leading into the plant proper. It was very dark and smelled strongly of chlorine, and as he walked beneath a partition he felt, rather than saw, the ceiling suddenly rise to a great height. He paused to run the beam of his light along the conveyor belt that snaked through the plant like an endless metal road, back and forth, up and down, on at least three different levels. Emerging first from a small, tiled room attached to the stunning area, the "line" ran through several freestanding structures within the plant, buildings within buildings: the Scalder, the Plucker, the Box Washer. Tad remembered their names from his previous visits. It was the kind of thing you didn't forget too quickly.

He shone his light back toward the tiled room. This small structure, the first within the plant, was the Blood Room. Its door was ajar.

"This is the police," he rapped out a second time, advancing a few more steps. Outside, the shriek of the wind answered faintly.

Transferring his flashlight to his left hand, Tad unsnapped the leather guard on his service holster, let his palm rest lightly on the handle of his piece. Not that there would be any call for it, of course. But it felt reassuring, just the same.

He turned and shone his light around again, licking the beam off the gleaming assembly line, off the tubes and pressure hoses that snaked up the gray-painted walls. The plant was vast, cavernous, and his light penetrated less than a third of it. But the place was silent, and what he could see looked decidedly empty.

Tad felt a certain relief. The kids had probably run for it at the first sign of his cruiser.

He glanced at his watch: almost quarter after nine. Hazen would be at the sheriff's office by now, preparing for the ten-o'clock raid. He'd followed through, and found nothing. Any further time here would be wasted. He'd check out Smit Ludwig's place, then get back.

It was as he turned to leave that he heard the noise.

He paused, listening. There it was again: a kind of giggle, or wet snicker. It seemed to come from the Blood Room, queerly distorted by the stainless steel floor and tiled walls.

Christ, the kids were hiding in there.

He shone his flashlight at the open door of the Blood

Room. The conveyor belt emerged from a wide porthole above the door, dangling hooks winking in his beam, throwing cruel misshapen shadows over the entrance.

"All right," he said, "come out of there. All of you."

Another snort.

"I'm going to count to three, and if you don't come out you'll be in serious trouble, and that's a promise."

This was ridiculous, wasting his time like this in the middle of a tornado warning. He was going to throw the book at those kids. Deeper scum, he was sure of it now.

"One."

No response.

"Two."

He waited, but there was nothing but silence from the half-open door.

"Three." Tad moved swiftly and purposefully toward the door, his boots echoing on the slick tile floor. He kicked the door wide with a hollow boom that echoed crazily around the vast interior of the plant.

Feet set apart, he swept the Blood Room with his light, the beam shining off the polished steel, the circular drain in the middle of the floor, the gleaming tile walls.

Empty. He walked into the middle of the room and stood there, the smell of bleach washing over him.

There was a rattle overhead, and Tad quickly angled his light upward. A sudden furious sound, a clashing of metal. The hooks dangling from the conveyor line began to bounce and swing wildly, and his light just caught a dark shape scuttling along the line, disappearing out the porthole above the door.

"Hey! You!" Tad ran back to the door, stopped. Flashed his light. Nothing but the swinging and creaking of the line as it moved away into blackness.

No leniency, no soft touch, this time: Tad was going to lock these kids up, teach them a lesson.

He let the beam of his light linger on the line. It was still swinging and creaking, and it looked as if the kids had climbed along it through a curtain of plastic flaps into the next structure, an oversized stainless steel box. The Scalder.

Tad moved forward as silently as he could. The plastic flaps covering the entrance to the Scalder were still swinging slightly.

Bingo.

Tad circled around to the other end of the Scalder. The thin black shape of the line emerged here, but the plastic flaps on this end weren't swinging.

He had trapped the kids inside.

Tad stepped back, bobbing his light back and forth between the Scalder's entrance and exit points. He spoke, not loudly, but firmly. "Listen: you're already in big trouble for breaking and entering. But if you don't come out of there right now, you're going to be charged with resisting arrest and a lot more besides. No probation or community service, you'll do time. You understand?"

For a moment, silence. And then, a low murmur came from inside the Scalder.

Tad leaned forward to listen. "What's that?"

More murmuring, turning into a kind of singsong sound. There was a strange wet lisping to it all, as if of a tongue being razzed against protruding lips.

The kids were mocking him.

In a burst of anger and humiliation, Tad kicked the side of the Scalder. The steel wall let out a hollow boom that rolled and echoed back into the unseen vastness of the plant.

"Get out here!"

Tad took one breath, then another. And then, quickly, he ducked through the plastic flaps covering the entrance to the Scalder, careful not to bang his skull on the hooks that dangled from the line overhead. As he licked his flashlight around the insides of the metal box, he got a peripheral glimpse of a figure scrambling along the conveyor belt and out the slot in the far wall. It looked surprisingly big and ungainly: probably the overlapping image of two running boys. But there was nothing ungainly about the speed at which the image scurried away from him. In the blackness just beyond vision, the shape leapt from the line; there was a thump, then the quick patter of feet running toward the rear of the plant.

"Stop!" Tad cried.

He ran around the Scalder and took up the pursuit, the yellow pool of his flashlight bobbing ahead of him. The dark form bypassed the Plucker and went shooting up an emergency ladder toward the Evisceration Area, running along the elevated platform and disappearing behind a thick cluster of hydraulic hoses.

"Stop, damn you!" Tad yelled into the darkness. He climbed the ladder, gun now drawn, and charged down the metal catwalk.

As he passed the cluster of hoses something flashed in his field of vision and he felt a terrific blow to his forearm. He yelled out in surprise and pain. The flashlight flew out of his hand and went crashing to the floor, skidding and rolling off the elevated platform. There was a loud clunk as it hit the concrete floor, a rattle of glass, and then darkness.

From outside came the wail of wind, the patter of hailstones against the roof.

Tad crouched, service piece pointed into the darkness, a

pain shooting up and down his left forearm. Christ, his arm hurt. He couldn't clench his fist or move his fingers, and the pain just seemed to grow and grow, until his whole arm felt like it was on fire.

The son of a bitch had broken his arm. Broken it badly. With a single blow. Tad stifled a sob, clenched his jaw.

He listened intently, but there was no sound except the storm raging beyond the cinderblock walls.

This is no fucking kid.

The anger he'd felt, the humiliation, was gone. The pain and the sudden darkness had taken care of that. Now all Tad wanted to do was get out.

He strained to see in the blackness, tried to remember which way to go. The plant was huge, and without light it would be very difficult to find the exit. Maybe he should stay here, silent and unmoving, until the power returned?

No. He couldn't stay here. He had to move, to run, somewhere. Anywhere.

Get away. Just get away.

He rose to his feet and, gun drawn, his broken arm dangling, tried to feel his way with his feet back to the ladder, scarcely daring to breathe, terrified that at any moment another blow might come out of the darkness. One step, three, five . . .

In the blackness, his elbow bumped into something.

With his gun hand, he reached out gingerly, touched a surface that felt rough and scaly. Was it the high-pressure hoses? But it didn't feel like a hose. It felt like something else.

But there was nothing else that should feel like that; not up here in the Evisceration Area.

He bit his lip, suppressed a sob of terror.

It was the blackness that was making him act this way. He wasn't used to utter blackness. If he fired his gun, maybe he could see long enough to orient himself. One shot toward the roof wouldn't hurt anything.

He raised his piece and fired upward.

The brief flash revealed a figure, standing next to him, looking at him, smiling. The image was so unexpected, so strange and horrifying, that Tad could not even scream.

But the figure screamed for him: a hoarse, guttural ululation of surprise and anger at the gunshot.

Tad ran. He found the ladder and half fell, half scrambled down it, banging his knees cruelly against the metal rungs. He got tangled near the bottom and fell crashing to the floor, on top of his broken arm. And now he found he could scream, in both pain and terror. But at least he was back on the main floor of the plant. He scrambled to his feet, nauseous from pain and sobbing with terror, ran, tripped again, scrambled back to his feet. And that was when he realized his piece was still clutched desperately in his hand. He could use it, and he would use it. He reached back and fired, once, twice, blindly — and each time, the muzzle flashes revealing that the *thing* was scuttling toward him, pink mouth yawning wide, arms outstretched.

Muh!

He had to aim the gun, *aim* it, not just fire wildly. Two more rounds, and each flash showed it coming closer, closer. Tad scrambled backward, still screaming, and fired twice more, his hand shaking wildly.

Muh! Muh!

It was almost on him. He couldn't miss now. He aimed point-blank, pulled.

The hammer fell on an empty chamber. He fumbled for

his extra clip, but a second terrible blow struck him in the gut and he fell, unable to breathe, the gun skittering away across the floor. A third blow, this one to his gun arm. He found his wind, thrashing desperately, screaming and kicking, trying to slide himself backward, but it was impossible with both his arms unusable.

Muh! Muh! Muh!

Tad shrieked again and twisted wildly away, sliding on his back, kicking in the direction of the sound.

And then the thing caught his flailing leg. Tad felt a terrible pressure on his ankle, then a sudden give, accompanied by the snap of bone. *His* bone.

A moment later, a huge weight pressed down on his chest and something rough and hard gripped his face. There was a smell of earth, and mold, and something fainter but far worse. For a moment it seemed as if the grasp would be gentle, comforting, reassuring.

But then it tightened with a terrible, unforgiving pressure. And then, with ferocious speed, his entire face was twisted in the direction of the floor.

There was a grinding click; a burst of fire at the base of his neck; and then the terrible darkness became bright, so very, very bright . . .

Fifty-Three

Corrie lay in the putrid dark. In this terrible and disorienting blackness, it was impossible to tell how much time had passed since he had left. An hour? A day? It seemed like forever. Her whole body ached, and her neck was sore from where he had squeezed it.

And yet he had not killed her. No: he'd meant to torture her instead. And yet torture didn't seem to be quite the right word. It was almost as if he was toying with her, *playing* with her, in some horrible, inexplicable way . . .

But guessing about the killer was pointless. There was no way she could understand something so alien, so broken, so foreign to her own experience. She reminded herself that nobody was going to rescue her way back in this cave system. Nobody knew she was there. If she were to live, she had to do something herself. She had to do it before he came back.

She struggled once again to loosen the cords, succeeding only in chafing and tearing her wrists. The ropes had been tied wet and the knots were as hard as walnuts.

. . . When would *he* come back? The thought sent a wave of panic through her.

Corrie, get a grip.

She lay still a moment, focusing on her breathing. Then, slowly, with her hands tied behind her, she half crawled, half rolled over the sloping floor of the cave, exploring. The floor was relatively smooth here, but now and then she noticed rough rocks projecting in clusters from the floor of the cave. She stopped to feel one formation more closely with her fingers. Crystals, maybe.

She positioned herself and kicked hard at them with her feet. There was a sharp snapping sound as they broke away.

Now she explored with numb fingers until she found a fresh, sharp edge. Positioning herself laboriously over it, she placed her hands against the edge and began rubbing the ropes, back and forth, back and forth.

God, it hurt. Her wrists were raw circles of flesh where the ropes bound her, and she could feel the blood trickling down the insides of her palms as she worked. There was barely any feeling left in her fingers.

But she kept rubbing, pressing harder. The wet rope slipped, the sharp stone cut her hands.

She stifled a cry and kept rubbing. Better to lose her hands than her life. At least the rope was beginning to fray. If she could only get it off, she could . . .

She could what?

. . . When would *he* come back?

Corrie shivered; a shiver that threatened to become uncontrollable. She had never been so cold and numb and wet in her life. The stench seemed to permeate everything, and she could taste it on her tongue, in her nose.

Focus on the rope.

She rubbed, slipped, cut herself again, and, sobbing aloud, kept scraping and chafing, harder and harder. There was no longer any feeling at all in her fingers, but this just made her rub the harder.

Even if she got free, what would she do without light? She didn't have a match or a lighter. Even if she had a light, *he* had taken her so far back into the cave that she wondered if she could ever find her way out.

Sobbing, she jammed the rope against the sharp rock again and again. Perversely, the very hopelessness of her situation brought new strength to her limbs.

Suddenly her hands were free.

She lay back, gasping, sucking in air. Pain rushed in like a thousand needles pricking at her palms and fingers. She could feel blood flowing more freely now along her skin.

She tried to move her fingers, without success. With a groan, she leaned to one side, gently rubbing her palms together. She tried moving her fingers a second time and got a little response. They were coming back to life.

Slowly, painfully, she sat up. Propping her legs behind her, she reached down and felt the cords around her ankles. They seemed to be tied in the craziest way, wrapped around and around, with half a dozen crude but effective knots. She tried to pick at them, gasped at the pain, and let her hands drop away. Maybe she could saw them off on the sharp rock she'd used for her hands. She felt around for the edge—

A sound interrupted her. She paused, dread clutching at her.

He was coming back.

She could hear grunting, huffing noises echoing off the cavern walls not far away. It sounded like he was lugging something. Something heavy.

Hnuff!

Quickly she hid her hands behind her back, lay down on

the cold floor, and fell still. Even though it was pitch black,
she wasn't going to take the chance that he could see she
was no longer tied.

The shuffle of footsteps grew near. New smells, sour
smells, were suddenly introduced into the darkness: fresh
blood, bile, vomit.

She lay perfectly still. It was so dark, maybe he had forgotten about her.

There was a dragging sound, then the jangling of what
sounded like keys. And then something heavy hit the floor
of the cave next to her. The stench abruptly grew worse.

She stifled the scream that rose in her throat.

Now *he* began humming and talking to himself once
again. There was a rattle of metal, the scratch of a match,
and suddenly there was light: almost indiscernibly faint, but
light just the same. For a moment, Corrie forgot everything—her pain, her desperate condition—as she felt her
soul rise toward the dim yellow glow. It seemed to be coming from between the chinks of a strange-looking lantern,
very old, with sliding sides of rusted metal. The light was
placed in a way that left *him* in shadow—just a dark shape
moving, gray against black. He disappeared around a corner,
doing something in an alcove, humming and talking to
himself.

So he did need light, after all, if only a little bit.

But if he'd managed to do so much in utter darkness—
bring her here, tie her up—what kind of work would he
need light for?

Corrie did not want to follow this train of thought. It was
easy to let it go: the instinctual relief of the light made her
feel sluggish, torpid. Part of her just wanted to give up, re-
sign herself. She looked around. Dim as it was, the light

seemed to reflect back at her in a million crystal-like points, coming from everywhere and nowhere.

She waited, motionless, her eyes adjusting to the gloom.

She was in a smallish cavern. Its walls were covered with feathery white crystals that gleamed in the faint glow of the dark-lantern, and countless stalactites hung from the ceiling. From each stalactite hung a bizarre little ornament of sticks and bones, lashed together with twine. For a long time, her eyes traveled back and forth across them, uncomprehending. Eventually her eyes moved to the walls, scanned slowly across them, and then at last fell to the surrounding floor.

A body lay beside her.

She stifled a cry. Horror and fear surged through her again. How could the mere relief of vision, of the lack of blackness, have allowed her to forget, even for a moment . . . ?

She shut her eyes. But the renewed dark was even worse. She had to know.

At first, there was so much blood on the face that she couldn't make it out. And then, slowly, the outlines seemed to resolve themselves. It was the ruined face of Tad Franklin: staring back at her, open-mouthed.

She turned her head violently away; heard herself scream, then scream again.

There was a grunt and she now saw him for the first time, coming around the corner and advancing toward her, a long, bloody knife in one hand, something wet and red in the other.

He was smiling and singing to himself.

The scream died as her throat closed involuntarily at the sight.

That face—!

Fifty-Four

Hazen stood before the assembled law enforcement officers. What he had to say wouldn't take long: it was a good crew, and they had a good plan. McFelty wouldn't stand a chance.

There was only one problem. Tad hadn't yet returned from the plant, and radio communications were down. Hazen would have preferred to hand off control directly before leaving, but he could wait no longer. Medicine Creek was well secured and properly hunkered down: Tad had clearly seen to that already. It was already a few minutes to ten. He didn't want McFelty slipping away under cover of the storm. They had to go. Tad would know what to do.

"Where's the dogs?" he asked.

Hank Larssen spoke up. "They're bringing them straight to the Kraus place. Meeting us there."

"I hope to hell they got us some real dogs this time. Did you ask for that special breed they've been training up in Dodge, those Spanish dogs, what are they called?"

"Presa canarios," Larssen said. "I did. They said their training wasn't complete, but I insisted."

"Good. I'm through playing around with lap dogs. Who's the handler?"

"Same as last time. Lefty Weeks. He's their best."

Hazen scowled, shucked out a cigarette, lit it.

Now he raked the group with his gaze. "You all know the drill, so I'll be brief. The dogs go first, then the handler—Lefty—then me and Raskovich." He pointed at the KSU security chief with his cigarette.

Raskovich nodded, his jaw tightening with the gravity of the situation.

"Raskovich, you know how to use a twelve-gauge?"

"Yes, sir."

"Then I'll issue you one. Behind us, as backup, there'll be Cole, Brast, and Sheriff Larssen." He nodded to two state troopers dressed in full raid wear: black BDU pants bloused over Hi-Tec boots, blacked-out bulletproof vests. No more Boy Scout hats—this was going to be the real thing. Then he turned back to Larssen. "That okay with you, Hank?"

The Deeper sheriff nodded.

Hazen knew it was important to play the political game, keep Hank in the loop, make sure he was part of the team. Hank clearly wasn't happy about it, but there wasn't much he could do: this was Hazen's turf, and until the operation was finished and outside communication was restored, it was completely his show. In the end Hazen would make sure Larssen looked good. They'd all share credit—Raskovich, too—and there wouldn't be any backstabbing when it came to trial.

"The rules of engagement are simple. You've all got guns, but don't use them unless your life is *directly threatened.* Is that absolutely crystal clear?"

Everyone nodded.

"We're taking our man out *alive* and *unhurt*. We're going in nice and easy, disarm the guy, bring him out shackled and cuffed, but with kid gloves. He's our star witness. If he panics and starts shooting, you *stay back* and let the dogs take care of him. And dogs like these can take a major round or two and still work."

Silence, nods.

"If any of you's thinking of coming out a hero, forget it. I'll arrest you myself. We work together."

He glared at each one in turn. It was Raskovich he was most worried about, but so far the man had been cool. It was worth taking the chance. Hell, he was willing to let Raskovich take all the damn credit if it meant the experimental field came to Medicine Creek.

"Shurte and Williams, you two will stake out the cave entrance. I want you to give yourself a good field of action, which means no lounging in the entrance where you could be surprised. If we flush McFelty and he tries to take off, you need to be ready to take him. You, Rheinbeck, you're going into the Kraus mansion to serve the warrant and drink tea with Winifred. Be prepared to back up Shurte and Williams if they need it."

Rheinbeck's face betrayed nothing, just a faint twitching along the jawline.

"I know, Rheinbeck, it's a tough assignment, but the old lady's bound to be upset. We don't want any heart attacks, right?"

Rheinbeck nodded.

"Remember, we'll have no communication to the outside world down there. And if we get separated, there won't be any communication between us, either. So we stay together. Got it?"

He looked around. They got it.

"All right, Cole's going to tell us about the night-vision goggles."

Cole stepped forward. He was Mr. State Police himself, tall, muscular, crew-cut, deadpan face. Funny how the Staties were never fat. Maybe it was a rule. He was carrying a gray helmet with a large set of goggles fastened beneath it.

"In a cave," he said, "there's no light at all. None. For that reason normal NVGs won't work. So we're going in with infrared illumination. The infrared light works just like a flashlight. This is the bulb, right here, on the front of the helmet. Here's the switch. It's got to be turned on to work, just like a regular flashlight. You can't see the light with the naked eye, but when you put the NVGs on you'll see a reddish illumination. If your infrared headlamp goes off, your goggles go black. Understand?"

Everyone nodded.

"The purpose of the NVGs is so we don't make ourselves targets by carrying flashlights. He can't see us. We'll keep the overhead lights off and go in silent, and he won't know how many we are."

"Is there a map of the cave or something?" It was Raskovich.

"Good question," said Hazen. "No, there isn't. A wooden walkway's been erected through most of it. There are a few rooms in the back, two or three at most, beyond. One of these rooms has the old still in it, and that's probably where we'll find our man. This isn't Carlsbad Caverns we're talking about. Just exercise common sense, stay close, and you'll be all right."

The security chief nodded.

Hazen went to the weapons locker, removed a shotgun,

loaded it, and handed it to Raskovich. "You've all checked your weapons?"

There was a general shuffling, a murmur of assent. Hazen did a final check of his service belt, counterclockwise: extra shells, asp baton, cuffs, pepper spray, sidearm all in place. He took a breath, snugged his armored vest up tight beneath his chin.

At that moment the lights in the office flickered, brightened, and went out. A chorus of groans and murmurs went up.

Hazen glanced out the window. No lights on the main drag, or anywhere else for that matter. Medicine Creek was blacked out from front to back. No surprise, really.

"This doesn't change a thing," he said. "Let's go."

He opened the door and they stepped out into the howling night.

Fifty-Five

As he pulled into Medicine Creek, Special Agent Pendergast slowed the big Rolls, then plucked his cell phone from his pocket and made another attempt to call Corrie Swanson.

The only reply was a steady beeping, no longer even a recorded message. The relay stations were down.

He replaced the phone. The police radio was also down and the lights of the town were out. Medicine Creek was effectively cut off from the outside world.

He drove along Main Street. The trees were lashing back and forth in a frenzy under the angry wind. Sheets of rain swept across the streets, forming muddy whirlpools in drains that a few hours before had been choked with dust. The town was locked down tight: shades drawn, shutters closed. The only activity seemed to be at the sheriff's office. Several state police cars were parked outside, and the sheriff and state police were moving around outside, loading equipment into a state police van and getting into squad cars. It looked like some operation was afoot, something more than the usual storm detail.

He continued on, turning into the gates of Wyndham

Parke Estates. Within, the windows of the mobile homes were heavily taped, and large rocks had been placed on many of the roofs. Everything was dark, except for the occasional glimmer of a candle or flashlight beam glimpsed through a taped window. The wind tore through the narrow dirt lanes, rocking the trailers, pulling pebbles from the ground and throwing them against the aluminum sidings. In a nearby yard the swings of a child's playset were whipping crazily, as if propelled by manic ghosts.

Pendergast pulled into the Swanson driveway. Corrie's car was gone. He got out of his car, moved quickly to the door, and knocked.

No answer. The house was dark.

He knocked again, louder.

There was a thump from inside, and the movement of a flashlight beam. A voice called out: "Corrie? Is that you? You're in trouble, young lady."

Pendergast pushed at the door; it opened two inches and was stopped by the chain.

"Corrie?" the voice shrieked. A woman's face appeared.

"FBI," Pendergast said, flashing his badge.

The woman peered out at him from beneath slitted lids. A half-smoked cigarette dangled from rouge-smeared lips. She poked the flashlight out the crack and shone it directly into his eyes.

"I'm looking for Miss Swanson," said Pendergast.

The ravaged face continued to look out, and now a cloud of cigarette smoke issued from the chained crack.

"She's out," said the woman.

"I'm Special Agent Pendergast."

"I know who you are," the woman said. "You're the FBI creep who needed an *assistant*." She snorted more smoke.

"I'm wise to you, mister, so don't bullshit me. Even if I knew where Corrie was, I wouldn't tell you. Assistant, yeah, *right*."

"Do you know when Miss Swanson went out?"

"No idea."

"Thank you."

Pendergast turned and walked briskly back toward his car. As he did so, the door to the trailer opened wide and the woman stepped out onto the sagging stoop.

"She probably went out looking for *you*. Don't think you can hide the truth from me, Mr. Slick-ass in your fancy black suit."

Pendergast got into his car.

"Oh, and looky what we have here, a, what is that, a Rolls-Royce? Sheee-*it*. Some FBI agent."

He shut the door and started the engine. The woman advanced across the little patch of lawn, into the lashing rain, clutching her nightgown, the storm tearing her shouted words and flinging them away.

"You make me sick, mister, you know that? I know your type and you make me *sick*—"

Pendergast swung out of the driveway, headed back toward Main Street.

Within five minutes, he pulled into the parking lot of the Kraus mansion. Again, Corrie's car was nowhere to be seen.

Inside, Winifred sat in her usual chair, doing a cross-stitch by candlelight. She looked up as he came in and a wan smile creased her papery face. "I was worried about you, Mr. Pendergast, out in that storm. It's a doozy, it really is. I'm glad you're back safely."

"Has Miss Swanson been by today?"

Winifred lowered her cross-stitch. "Why no, I don't believe she has."

"Thank you." Pendergast bowed and turned back to the door.

"Don't tell me you're going out again!"

"I'm afraid so."

Pendergast walked back across the parking lot, his face grave. If he was aware of the storm that lashed and tore the landscape on all sides, he gave no sign. He reached his car, grabbed the door handle. Then he stopped and turned, thinking. Beyond the house with its dimly lit windows, the dark sea of corn swayed violently. The signboard advertising Kraus's Kaverns banged repeatedly in the wind.

Pendergast released the handle and walked quickly past the house, along the road. Within a hundred yards he came to a dirt road leading into the corn.

Two minutes later he was standing beside Corrie's car.

Now he turned and strode briskly back toward the road. But even as he did so, a row of headlights appeared in the distance, approaching through the murk at high speed. As the cars blasted past and their brake lights went on as they turned into the Kaverns parking lot, growing concern became conviction, and he realized that the unthinkable had happened.

By a terrible, ironic twist of fate, it seemed that all of them—first he, then Corrie, and now Hazen—had come to the same conclusion: that the killer was hiding in the cave.

Pendergast quickly cut back through the corn, making directly for the opening to the cave. If he could manage to get inside before . . .

He was one minute too late. As he emerged from the

corn, Hazen, standing before the cut leading down into the cave, saw him and turned back, a dark expression on his face.

"Well, well, if it isn't Special Agent Pendergast. And here I thought you'd left town."

Fifty-Six

Sheriff Hazen stared at Pendergast. There was a moment of confused silence in which Hazen felt himself swell with rage. The guy had an amazing knack for appearing out of nowhere at exactly the wrong moment. Well, he was going to face down this son of a bitch, once and for all. This FBI prick wasn't going to waste any more of his time.

He advanced toward the thin figure, managing a smile. "Pendergast, what a surprise."

The agent halted. His black suit was almost invisible in the stormy half-light, and his face seemed to float, pale and ghostlike. "What are you doing here, Sheriff?" He spoke quietly, but his voice carried an edge that Hazen hadn't heard before.

"It's my recollection you were served with a C-and-D this morning. You are in violation. I could have you arrested."

"You're going in after the killer," said Pendergast. "You've deduced he's in the cave."

Hazen shifted uneasily. Pendergast must be guessing. There's no way he could have heard; not yet.

The agent went on. "You have absolutely no idea of what you're getting into, Sheriff—neither in terms of the adversary you're facing, nor the setting."

This was too much. "Pendergast, that's it."

"You're at the edge of the abyss, Sheriff."

"You're the one on the edge."

"The killer's got a hostage."

"Pendergast, you're just blowing smoke out your ass."

"If you blunder in there, Sheriff, you're going to cause the death of that hostage."

Despite himself, Hazen felt a chill. It was every cop's nightmare. "Yeah? And just who is this hostage?"

"Corrie Swanson."

"How do you know?"

"She's been missing all day. And I just found her car, hidden in the corn a hundred yards to the west."

There was a moment of uneasy silence, and then Hazen shook his head in disgust. "Right from the beginning, Pendergast, you've done nothing but throw the investigation off track with your theories. We would already have this man in the bag if it weren't for you. So Swanson's car is parked in the corn. She's probably out in the cornfield with some guy."

"She went into the cave."

"Now there's a brilliant deduction for you. The cave door is solid iron. How did she get in? Pick the lock?"

"Take a look for yourself."

Hazen looked in the direction Pendergast was indicating, down along the cut in the ground. The iron door wasn't locked after all: a padlock lay at the bottom of the doorframe, half concealed in the dust and leaves.

"If you think Corrie Swanson sprung that lock, Pendergast, you're an even bigger fool than I thought. That's not the work of a kid; it's the work of a hardened felon. The man we're after, in fact. And that's more than you need to know about it."

"As I recall, Sheriff, you were the one to accuse Miss Swanson of—"

Hazen shook his head. "I've listened enough. Pendergast, turn over your piece. You're under arrest. Cole, cuff him."

Cole stepped forward. "Sheriff?"

"He's willfully disobeyed a standing cease-and-desist. He's hindering a police investigation. He's trespassing on private property. I'll take full responsibility. Just get him the hell *out* of my *face*."

Cole advanced toward Pendergast. In the next instant, Cole was lying on the ground, desperately trying to breathe, and Pendergast had vanished.

Hazen stared.

"Uff," Cole said, rolling into a sitting position and cradling his gut. "The son of a bitch sucker-punched me."

"Christ," Hazen muttered, shining his light around. But Pendergast was gone. Moments later he heard the roar of a big engine, the sound of tires pulling rapidly away from gravel.

Cole got up, his face red, and dusted himself off. "We'll tag him for resisting arrest and assaulting a police officer."

"Forget it, Cole. We've got bigger fish to fry. Let's take care of business here and deal with that tomorrow."

"The son of a bitch," Cole muttered again.

Hazen slapped him on the back and grinned. "Next time you make an arrest, keep your eyes on the perp, hey, Cole?"

There was the distant slamming of a door and Hazen could hear a shrill voice rising and falling on the wind.

A moment later, the pallid form of Winifred Kraus came running down the path from the old mansion. The fierce gusts whipped and tugged at her white nightgown, and to Hazen it almost seemed as if a ghost was flying through the night. Rheinbeck was following in her tracks, protesting loudly.

"What are you doing?" shrieked the old woman as she came up, her hair haggard in the rain, drops running down her face. "What's this? What are you doing on my property?"

Hazen turned to Rheinbeck. "For chrissakes, you were supposed to—"

"I've been trying to explain to her, Sheriff. She's hysterical."

Winifred was looking around at the troopers, her eyes rolling wildly. "Sheriff Hazen! I demand an explanation!"

"Rheinbeck, get her out of—"

"This is a *respectable* tourist attraction!"

Hazen heaved a sigh and turned to her. "Look. Winifred, we believe the killer's holed up in your cave."

"Impossible!" the woman shrieked. "I check it twice a week!"

"We're going in there to bring him out. I want you to stay in your house with Officer Rheinbeck here, nice and peaceable. He'll take care of you—"

"I will *not*. Don't you *dare* go into my cave! You have no right. There's no killer in there!"

"Miss Kraus, I'm sorry. We've got a warrant. Rheinbeck?"

"I already showed her the warrant, Sheriff—"

"Show it to her again and get her the hell out of here."

"But she won't listen—"

"Pick her *up* if you have to. Can't you see we're wasting time?"

"Yes, sir. I'm sorry, ma'am—"

"Don't you *dare* touch me!" Winifred took a swipe at Rheinbeck, who fell back.

She turned and advanced on Hazen, her fists balled up. "You get off my property! You've always been a bully! Get out of here!"

He grabbed her wrists and she writhed and spat at him. Hazen was amazed at the old lady's strength and ferocity.

"Miss Kraus," he began again, trying to be patient, to make his voice more soothing. "Just calm down, please. This is important law enforcement business."

"Get off my land!"

Hazen struggled to hold her, and felt a sharp kick to his shin. The others were all standing around, gawking like civilian spectators. "How about a little help here?" he roared.

Rheinbeck grabbed her by the waist while Cole waded in and managed to snag one of her flailing arms.

"Easy now," Hazen said. "Easy. She's still a little old lady."

Her shrieks became hysterical. The three men held her immobile for a moment, struggling, and then Hazen finally extricated himself. Rheinbeck, with Cole's help, picked her up off the ground. Her legs kicked and flailed.

"Devils!" she shrieked. "You have no right!"

Her shrieks died as Rheinbeck disappeared into the storm, carrying his thrashing burden.

"Jesus, what's with her?" Cole asked, panting.

Hazen dusted off his pants. "She's always been a loopy old bitch, but I never expected *this*." He gave one final slap. She had kicked him pretty good in the shin and it still smarted. He straightened up. "Let's get into the cave before someone else pops up to spoil our party." He turned to Shurte and Williams. "If that son of a bitch Pendergast comes back, you're authorized to use all means to keep him out of the cave."

"Yes, sir."

Hazen leading, the others moved down the dark slot in the ground. As they descended, the sounds of the storm became muffled, far away. They opened the unlocked door, switched on their infrared lights and night-vision goggles, and began descending the stairs. Within moments the silence became complete, broken only by the sound of dripping water. They were entering another world.

Fifty-Seven

The Rolls scraped and bumped up the dirt track, the head-lights barely penetrating the screaming murk, hail hammering on the metal. When the vehicle could go no farther, Pendergast stopped, turned off the engine, tucked the rolled map inside his suit jacket, and stepped out into the storm.

Here, at the highest point of land in Cry County, the mesocyclone had reached its highest pitch of intensity. The ground looked like a battlefield, littered with jetsam scattered by the ruinous winds: twigs, plant debris, clods of dirt picked up from fields many miles away. Up ahead, the still-invisible trees fringing the Mounds thrashed and groaned, leaves and limbs tearing at each other with a sound like the crashing of surf on rocks. The world of the Ghost Mounds had been reduced to sound and fury.

Turning his head and leaning into the wind, Pendergast made his way along the track toward the Mounds. As he approached, the roar of the storm became more intense, occasionally punctuated by the earsplitting sound of cracking wood and the crash of a branch hitting the ground.

Once in the relative shelter of the trees, Pendergast was

able to see a little more clearly. Wind and rain boiled through, scouring everything with pebbles and fat pelting drops. The great cottonwoods around him groaned and creaked. The greatest danger now, Pendergast knew, came not from rain and hail, but from the possibility of high-F-scale tornadoes that could form at any time along the flanks of the storm.

And yet there was no time for caution. This was neither the time, nor the manner, in which he'd intended to confront the killer. But there was no longer any choice.

Pendergast switched on his flashlight and arrowed it into the gloom beyond the copse of trees. As he did so, there came a terrific splitting noise; he leapt to one side as a giant cottonwood came tumbling out of the darkness, hurtling down with a grinding crash that shook the ground and sent up a maelstrom of leaves, splintered branches, and wet dirt.

Pendergast left the trees and stepped back into the teeth of the storm. He moved forward as quickly as he could, eyes averted, until he reached the base of the first mound. Placing his back to the wind, he played his light carefully around its flanks until he had fully established a point of reference. And then—in the pitch of night, in the howling storm—he straightened, folded his arms across his chest, and paused. Sound and sensation alike faded from his consciousness as, from a marbled vault within the Gothic mansion of his memory, he took up the image of the Ghost Warriors. Once, twice, three times he ran through the reconstructed sequence from his memory crossing—where they had first emerged from the dust, where once again they had vanished—carefully superimposing this pattern upon the actual landscape around him.

Then he opened his eyes, let his hands fall to his sides.

Now—walking slowly, taking precise steps—he moved across the central clearing to the far side of the second mound. Soon he stopped before a large limestone outcrop. He moved slowly around it, back to the storm, oblivious to the wind and pelting rain, inspecting rocks with great care, touching first one, then another, until he found what he was looking for: a half dozen small, loose boulders, casually lying caught in a crack of the rock. After examining them for a moment, Pendergast rolled the smaller boulders aside, one by one, exposing an opening. He rapidly shifted more rocks. The ragged opening exhaled cool, damp air.

The route through which the Ghost Warriors had first appeared, then vanished. And—unless he was sadly mistaken—the back door to Kraus's Kaverns.

Pendergast slipped through the hole, flicking his beam back around to the inside face of rockfall, behind and above him. It was as he suspected: the smaller opening was inside what had once been a much larger natural opening.

He turned away, raking his light into the passageway that sloped downward. Pebbles rattled away into the listening dark. As he started descending, the appalling fury of the storm faded away with remarkable quickness. Soon it was nothing more than a memory. Time, the storm, and the outside world all ceased to exist in the changeless environment of the cave. He had to reach Corrie before the sheriff and his impromptu little SWAT team did.

The passageway broadened as it descended, leveled out, then turned abruptly. Pendergast moved carefully up to the turn and waited, listening, gun drawn. Total silence. Quick as a ferret, he spun around the corner, illuminating the space ahead with his powerful flashlight.

It was a giant cavern at least a hundred feet across. An

astonishing but not unexpected sight met his view. The only moving things in the cavern were his pale eyes and the beam of his flashlight, passing back and forth over the bizarre spectacle that lay before him.

Thirty dead horses, in full Indian battle dress, were arranged in a kneeling position in a ring at the center of the cavern. They had shriveled and mummified in the air of the cave: their bones stuck out of their hides, their dried lips were drawn back from their yellow teeth. Each was decorated in the Southern Cheyenne style, with streaks of brilliant red ochre on their faces, white and red handprints along their necks and withers, and eagle feathers tied into their manes and tails. Some carried beaded, high-cantled Cheyenne rawhide saddles on their backs; others had a blanket merely, or nothing at all. Most had been sacrificed by a massive blow to the head with a studded club, leaving a neat hole punched directly between each pair of eyes.

Arranged in a second circle, inside the first, were thirty Cheyenne braves.

The Ghost Warriors.

They had laid themselves out like the spokes of a wheel—the sacred wheel of the sun—each one touching his dead horse with his left hand, weapon in his right. They were all there: those who were killed in the raid as well as those who had survived. These latter had been sacrificed like the horses: a single blow to the forehead with a spiked club. The last one to die—the one who had sacrificed the rest—lay on his back, one mummified hand still clutching the stone knife that stuck from his heart. The knife was identical to the broken knife found with Chauncy's body. And each brave had a quiver of arrows exactly like the arrows found near the body of Sheila Swegg.

They had been here, bearing witness beneath the earth of Medicine Creek, since the evening of August 14, 1865. Those warriors who survived the raid had sacrificed themselves and their horses here, in the darkness of the cave, choosing to die with dignity on their own land. Never would the white men herd them off to a reservation. Never would they be forced to sign a treaty, board railroad cars, send their children to distant schools to be beaten for speaking their own language, to be robbed of their dignity and culture.

These Ghost Warriors had seen the inexorable roll of the white men across their land. They knew what the future looked like.

Here, in this great cavern, was where they had hid in ambush. From here they had issued forth during the dust storm, as if out of nowhere, to wreak havoc and destruction on the Forty-Fives. And here was where they had returned to seek eternal peace and honor.

In both his oral recollections, and at far greater detail in his private journal, Brushy Jim's great-grandfather had said the Ghost Warriors seemed to rise up out of the ground. He had been exactly right. And—though in 1865 the mounds would have been covered in dense brush—Harry Beaumont, in the moments before his death, must have realized where the warriors came from. He had cursed the ground for a very specific reason.

Pendergast paused only long enough to examine his map. Then he hurried past the silent tableau toward the dark tunnel that led deeper into the cave system.

There was very little time left—if there was any time at all.

Fifty-Eight

Hazen followed Lefty and the dogs as they proceeded along the wooden walkway of Kraus's Kaverns. Unlike the last pair, these beasts were hot on the trail. They seemed a little too eager: pulling on their leashes, straining forward, issuing growls from deep within their chests. Lefty barely had them under control, being jerked this way and that as he whined and cajoled. They were big dogs, ugly as shit, with enormous puckered assholes and giant balls that hung low like a bull's. Presa canarios, dogs bred to kill dogs. Or anything else on two or four legs, for that matter. Hazen wouldn't want to face them, not even with a brace of Winchesters loaded with double-ought buck. He noticed that the troopers seemed to be hanging back, too. If he had any sense, McFelty would fall to his knees and pray for mercy the moment these ugly mutts turned the corner.

"Sturm! Drang!" Lefty shouted.

"What kind of dog names are those?" Hazen asked.

"No idea. The breeder names them."

"Well, slow 'em down, Lefty. This isn't the Indy 500."

"Sturm! Drang! Easy now!"

The dogs paid only the scantest of attention.

"Lefty—"

"I'm *taking* them as *slowly* as I can," Weeks answered, his voice pitched high. "I'm not exactly dealing with a couple of Pomeranians here, in case you didn't notice."

With the overhead lights off, the night-vision goggles illuminated the cave in a flat red wash. Hazen had never worn the goggles before and he didn't like the way they reduced the world to a monochromatic, creepy landscape. It was like watching an old TV. The wooden boardwalk ahead swam in the crimson light, like the pathway to hell.

They passed by the Krystal Kathedral, the Giant's Library, the Krystal Chimes. Hazen hadn't been in the cave since he was a kid on a school outing, but they used to come every year and he was surprised how much he remembered of it. Winifred had always done the tour. She hadn't been such a bad-looking woman back then. He remembered his friend Tony making vulgar gestures behind her back as she hammered out some tune on the stalactites. She'd turned into a queer old hag, though.

They reached the far end of the tourist loop, and Lefty, with a great deal of trouble, reined in the dogs. Hazen stopped well short, keeping a good ten feet between himself and the animals. The dogs were looking intently into the darkness past the Infinity Pool, growling, their tongues like big red diapers hanging out of their mouths. Dripping saliva showed red in the goggles, like blood.

Hazen waited for the troopers to assemble behind him, then he spoke in a low tone.

"I've never been beyond this point. From now on, silence. And Lefty, do you think you can get the dogs to tone it down?"

"No, I *can't,* okay? Growling's instinctual for them."

Hazen shook his head and signaled Lefty forward. He followed with Raskovich; Cole and Brast came next; Larssen brought up the rear.

They splashed through the pool, climbed down the far end, and then followed Lefty along a tunnel that narrowed, then rose again and took a sharp turn to the right. On the far side of the bend was a second iron door.

It was ajar, the iron padlock lying nearby on the ground. Hazen gave them a thumbs-up, signaled Lefty on.

The dogs were growling even more insistently now, deep throaty snarls that prickled the hair on the back of Hazen's neck. There would be no taking McFelty by complete surprise, but maybe that wasn't such a bad thing. The growling was enough to inspire even Rambo to throw down his weapons.

On the far side of the door, the tunnel widened into a cavern. The dogs snuffled ahead eagerly, dragging Lefty along. Hazen gestured for the group behind him to wait. Then he and Raskovich fanned out to the left and right, shotguns at the ready, scanning the room in infrared.

Bingo: the bootleggers' nest. Hazen panned his goggles slowly across the large space. An old table; candle stubs; battered lanterns; broken crockery and bottles. At the far end, the still itself rose out of the reddish murk, a cauldron big enough to boil a horse. So big that it must've been brought into the cave in pieces and soldered in place—no wonder it never left.

When Hazen had satisfied himself that the room was empty, he waved the rest forward and approached the still. The smell of smoke still hung faintly in the air, mixed with other, less pleasant odors. He leaned over the cauldron and looked inside. There was something in the bottom, small and vague in the night-vision goggles.

It was a human ear.

He turned, feeling a thrill of vindication mingling with disgust. "Don't anybody touch anything."

The others nodded.

Hazen continued examining the cavern. For a moment, he thought this was the end of the line—that the cave was empty and that McFelty had already escaped. But then he made out a low archway in the side wall, a mere patch of gray leading to deeper darkness. "It looks like there's another room that way," he said, pointing. "Let's go. Lefty, lead with the dogs."

They passed through the low archway into the next cavern. This had once been the garbage dump for the moonshiners, and it was still filled with rotting trash, broken bottles, scraps of paper and tin cans and refuse of every kind, all pushed up against one wall. He paused. The room was cold, and in an especially chill series of niches along one wall he could see a stock of recent food supplies. A larder of sorts. He shone his light in to reveal sacks of sugar, cereal, beans, bags of potato chips and other snacks, loaves of bread, packages of beef jerky, tubs of butter. There was also a stack of candles, boxes of kitchen matches, a broken lantern. At the far end, a trash heap of discarded sacks and butter wrappings and cans and candlebutts showed that McFelty had been down here a surprisingly long time.

Continuing to pan with his night-vision goggles, Hazen saw that the passageway continued, leading to another cavern beyond. McFelty, if he was in here at all, would have heard them by now and would be in that room, maybe with a gun drawn, waiting to surprise them.

He put a hand on Lefty's shoulder and spoke low into his ear. "Unleash the dogs and tell 'em to flush out the next room. Can they do that?"

"Of course."

Sheriff Hazen positioned his men around the mouth of the passage, ready to collar anyone who came out. Then he nodded to Lefty.

Lefty unhooked the bullsnaps from the collars and stepped back. "Sturm, Drang. *Clear.*"

The animals took off instantly, disappearing into the darkness. Hazen crouched by the opening, shotgun at the ready. He could hear the dogs in the next room, growling, snuffling, licking their wet chops. A few moments passed. The sounds grew fainter.

"Call 'em back," said Hazen.

Lefty gave a low whistle. "Sturm, Drang. *Return.*"

More snuffling and slobbering.

"Sturm! Drang! *Return!*"

The dogs came back, reluctantly. In the glow of the goggles they looked like the hounds of hell.

Hazen was now convinced McFelty had gotten out. And yet it wasn't a complete loss; quite the contrary, in fact. They'd find plenty of physical evidence to prove he'd been in the cave and to connect him to the crimes: fingerprints, DNA. And what was no doubt Stott's ear was a terrific find as well, itself worth the trip down. With this kind of evidence against McFelty it would be a piece of cake to plea-bargain the guy and nail Lavender.

Hazen straightened up. "All right, let's go see what's in there."

They entered the third cavern. It was smaller than the others. Hazen stopped in surprise. It looked like it had been used as some kind of living quarters, but as his eye traveled around the room he wondered just who it was who'd been living there. There was a bed against the wall, rotting and broken, the mattress ticking spilling out, but it was very small: a kid's bed. Above the bed was a broken picture of an apple tree, and another of a clown. A few broken wooden toys, rotting and furred with mold, sat in a corner. There was a wooden bureau, once painted fire-engine red, buckling and listing to one side, the drawers sprung. Some rotten clothing could be seen inside. At the far end, the cavern narrowed to a tiny crack.

Jesus, what a place. Hazen hiked up his pants, fished in his pocket for a Camel. "Looks like our bird flew. We probably just missed him."

"What's all this about?" Raskovich asked, shining his light around the room.

Hazen lit the cigarette, put the match in his pocket. "Something left over from moonshine days, I'd say."

There was a long silence. Everyone stood around, looking disappointed.

Hazen sucked in a lungful, exhaled. "Back there, in the pot, is Stott's ear," he announced quietly.

As expected, this perked them up.

"That's right. We've done well, men. We've got proof the killer was down here, proof this is where he boiled Stott. Proof this was his base of operations. This is a major break in the case."

Everyone nodded. There were some excited murmurs.

The dogs began to growl.

"We'll get the SOC team and forensic guys down here tomorrow to work the place over. I think our work's done for the night." Hazen took another deep drag on his Camel, then pinched off the glowing ash and dropped it into his pocket. "Let's go home."

As he turned, he noticed that Lefty was trying to pull the dogs away from the crack in the far wall. The dogs would have none of it: they were straining toward the crack, deep growls rumbling in their chests.

"What's with them?"

Lefty gave their leashes another savage jerk. "Sturm! Drang! *Heel!*"

"For chrissakes, let 'em check it out," said Hazen.

Lefty walked them over. With a yelp the dogs suddenly piled into the crack, jerking the protesting Lefty along behind them. In another moment they were gone.

Hazen stepped over and peered in. He saw the crack made a ninety-degree turn and ran sharply downhill for a few feet before coming to what looked like a dead end.

And yet it went on. It *had* to. He could hear Lefty's voice echoing back from the unknown darkness beyond, strangely distorted, calling uselessly for the dogs to heel.

"The dogs have a trail," Hazen said over his shoulder. "And it looks like a hot one!"

Fifty-Nine

Corrie lay still, her hands behind her back. He had laughed when she screamed: a horrible, high-pitched laugh that sounded like the squeal of a guinea pig. Now he was doing something to the corpse of Tad. She kept her head turned, eyes closed. She could hear the sound of rending cloth, then a horrible wet tearing sound. She scrunched her eyes tight shut and tried to mentally block out the sound. *He* was only a few feet from her, humming and talking nonsensically to himself in a singsong while he worked. Every time he moved, a terrible reek washed toward her: sweat, mold, rot, other things even worse.

The horror, the sheer unreality, was so intense that she found herself shutting down.

Corrie, just hold on.

But she couldn't hold on. Not anymore. The instinct for self-preservation that had prompted her to free her hands had faded with the reappearance of that *thing,* lugging the dead Tad Franklin.

Her mind began to wander, curiously numb. Fragmented memories drifted across her consciousness: playing catch as a young child with her father; her mother, wearing curlers and laughing into the telephone; a fat kid who was nice to her once in third grade.

She was going to die and her life seemed so empty, a wasteland stretching back as far as she could remember.

Her hands were untied, but what did it matter now? Even if she got away, where would she go? How would she find her way out of the cave?

A sob escaped her lips, but still the horrible thing paid no attention. He had his back turned. Thank God, thank God.

She opened one eye and let it fall on the lantern. He had placed it in an angle of rock, where its glow was almost completely obscured. Its ancient metal shutters were closed, letting out only the barest slivers of light. He didn't like light, it seemed. God, he was so *white*, so pasty white he was almost gray. And that face, the sight of that face, the wispy little beard . . .

A wave of terror washed over her, disordering her mind. He was truly a monster. If she didn't get out, what had happened to Tad Franklin was going to happen to her.

She felt her breath coming faster as the desperate need to take action returned. Her hands were already free. There was a lantern here: she had light. And at the far end of the little cavern, she could see a well-worn trail leading into the darkness. It might, it just might lead out of the cave.

Another memory came back to her with an almost piercing clarity. She was out in the grassy softball field behind the trailer park, learning how to ride the two-wheeler her father had just bought for her seventh birthday. She'd tipped and fallen into the sweet grass, again and again. She remembered how her father had wiped away her tears of frustration, had talked to her in the soothing voice that never seemed to grow angry or upset: *Don't give up, Cor. Don't give up. Try again.*

All right, she said to the darkness. *I won't give up.*

By inches, she began shifting her body around, searching for the sharp outcropping of rock, careful to keep her hands behind her back. Locating it, she raised her tied ankles and began rubbing them slowly back and forth across the edge, trying to be as quiet and inconspicuous as possible. But he was so engrossed in his work that he didn't seem to notice what she was doing. She watched his back through slitted eyes while she chafed the fraying rope against the sharp edge of calcite. He had temporarily left Tad's corpse and was now hunched over what appeared to be three small burlap bags, stuffing them full with . . . She turned away, deciding she'd rather not know any more.

She scraped and scraped, and at last felt the rope give. She twisted her feet back and forth, loosening it further. One foot slipped free, then the other.

She lay back again, thinking. She was free. What now?

Grab the lantern and make a run for it. She'd follow the trail. It had to go somewhere.

Yes: she'd grab the lantern and run like hell. He'd pursue her, of course, but she was fast, the second fastest girl in her class. Maybe she could outrun him.

She lay there, breathing deeply, her heart pounding with fear at what she was about to do. Now that she was about to take action, she began to think of a dozen reasons why it would be so much easier just to lie there quietly. He had something else to keep him busy. Maybe he'd just forget about her, and . . .

No. One way or another, she had to get out.

She glanced around once more, orienting herself. She took a deep breath, let it out, took another, held it.

And then she counted to three, leapt up, grabbed the lantern, and ran. A loud, inarticulate bellow sounded behind her.

She skidded on the wet stone; almost fell; found her feet again; and ran headlong into the dark vertical maw at the far end of the cavern. The slot led to a long crack that opened into a strange gallery of thin, dripping cave straws and evil-looking ribbons of hanging limestone. Beyond was a shallow pool where the ceiling dropped precipitously; she splashed across the water and scrambled through the low place, holding the lantern high. Then she emerged into a larger cavern, filled from floor to ceiling with thickly-tiered stalagmites, many joined with the stalactites overhead to form strange yellow and white pillars.

Was *he* following? Was he right behind, about to clutch at her again . . . ?

She caromed between the pale, glistening pillars, gasping with terror and exertion, light flashing off the great trunks of stone. The lantern banged and the candle flickered, and Corrie was seized with a new fear: if the candle went out, it would all be over.

Slow down. Slow down.

She scrambled around another pillar and collided with a crumpled block of calcite that had fallen from the ceiling, badly scraping one knee. She paused a minute and looked around, fighting for breath. She had reached the far end of the cavern. Here, a rubble-strewn trail led upward. As she glanced back and forth, she became aware that there were crude marks etched into the walls, as if with a stone: weird concentric ribbons, sticklike figures, great clouds of frantic scribbles. But this was no time for sightseeing, and she scrambled up the slope, slipping and falling as the loose rocks gave way. Her raw wrists were bleeding afresh. The trail grew steeper, and as she again lifted the lantern over her head she could make out a sill of rock at what appeared to be its upper edge. She grabbed it with her free hand, hoisted herself up.

Ahead ran a long glossy tunnel of limestone as blue as ice, feathery crystals sprouting from the ceiling. She ran on.

The tunnel was completely flat, and it snaked gently back and forth. A thin flow of water ran along a rill at its center. Once again, the blue walls were incised with strange, crude, disturbing images. Corrie dashed forward, her feet splashing through the water, her footfalls echoing strangely in the long tunnel. But there were no corresponding sounds of following footsteps.

She could hardly believe it, but she'd escaped. *She'd outrun him!*

She kept going, pushing herself as hard as she dared. Now she entered a large cavern, its floor covered in a blizzard of shattered and broken stalactites. She scrambled over and under this cyclopean masonry, following whenever possible the wear marks indicating a trail. And there it continued, almost vertically, at the far end of the cavern.

She gripped the lantern handle in her teeth and began to climb. The foot- and handholds were slippery and worn. But fear spurred her on, helped her forget the pain in her wrists and ankles. The farther she went, the farther she would get from him. And the trail had to lead somewhere, she was bound to find a way out sooner or later. At last, with a gasp of relief, she reached the top, hoisted herself up—

And there he was. Waiting for her. His monstrous body

covered with flecks of blood and flesh, the nightmarish impossible face fixed in a broken smile.

She screamed and the pallid features broke out into a high-pitched, squeal-like laugh. A laugh of childlike delight.

Corrie tried to wriggle past, but a great hand swept down and clubbed her to the ground. She fell on her back, stunned. His laughter echoed hysterically. The dark-lantern went rolling across the floor, candle guttering. He stood above her, clapping his hands and laughing, face distorted with merriment.

"Get away from me!" she screamed, pedaling herself backward.

He reached down, grabbed her shoulders, jerked her to her feet. The breath steamed from his rotten mouth like an abattoir. Corrie screamed and he squealed again. She twisted, trying to break out of his grip, but he held her with steel arms, laughing, squeezing.

"Don't hurt me!" she cried. "You're hurting me!"

"Hooo!" he said, his strange high voice sending out a spray of fetid-smelling spittle. He suddenly dropped her, scurried away, disappeared.

She tried to get up, picked up the lantern, looking around wildly. She was surrounded by a forest of stalactites. Where was he? Why had he run away? She started down the trail— and suddenly with a huge bellow he leapt from behind a stalagmite and swung at her, knocking her down, his laughter filling the cave. And then he was gone again.

She rose to her knees, panting hard, feeling stupid with terror and incomprehension, waiting for the pain to clear from her head. All was quiet and dark. The light had gone out.

"Heee!" came the voice from the darkness, and the sound of clapping.

She crouched in the black, cringing, desperate, afraid to move. A scratching sound, the flare of a match, and the lantern was relit. And there the monster was, standing over her, leering, drooling, exposing the stumps of his rotten teeth, the lantern casting a dull glow. He cackled, ducked behind a pillar.

And that's when Corrie finally understood. *He was playing hide-and-seek.*

She swallowed, trembling, tried to find her voice. "You want to play with me?"

He paused, then squealed a laugh, his wispy beard waggling, his thick lips wet and red, the two-inch nails flashing as his hands alternately opened and clenched. "Pway!" he cried, advancing toward her.

"No!" she screamed. "Wait! Not that way—!"

"Pway!" he roared, spittle flying, as he drew back a massive hand. *"Pway!"* Corrie shrank back, waiting for the inevitable.

And then, suddenly, the thing turned his head. His grotesque eyes swiveled wetly in their orbits, long brown lashes blinking. His hand hovered in the air as he looked off into the darkness.

He seemed to be listening.

Then he picked her up, slung her over his shoulder, and once again began moving with fearsome speed. Corrie was only dimly aware of the confusing procession of galleries and chambers. She closed her eyes.

And then she felt him stop. She opened her eyes to a small hole, a mere black tube at the base of a limestone wall. She felt herself sliding off his shoulder, felt him pushing her feet into the hole.

"Please, don't—" She tried to grab on to the sides,

clutching and scratching, nails tearing against the stone. He placed his hands on her shoulders, gave a brutal thrust, and she slid downward, falling the last few feet and landing hard on the stone floor.

She sat up, dazed and bruised. He leaned in from above, holding the lantern, and for an instant she had a glimpse of the smooth glassy sides of the pit that surrounded her.

"Hooo!" he called down, and puckered his lips grotesquely at her.

Then his head vanished with the light, and Corrie was left at the bottom of the pit, in utter darkness, alone in the wet, cold silence of the cave.

Sixty

Pendergast slipped silently through the dark galleries of stone, moving as quickly as possible, following the faint worn marks of a trail.

The cave system was enormous and his map showed only a sketchy outline of its true complexity. The map was wrong in many particulars, and there were entire levels of the cave not shown on it at all. The cave system was folded in over itself in exceedingly complex ways, making it possible for someone familiar with its secrets—the killer—to move in mere minutes between locations that on the map appeared to be a thousand linear yards apart. Still, despite its drawbacks, the map was a remarkable piece of work, proving what even the U.S. Geological Survey maps didn't show: that Kraus's Kaverns was the mere tip of a subterranean iceberg, a vast cave system that honeycombed the depths beneath Medicine Creek and the surrounding countryside—of which one node connected with the Ghost Mounds.

Ahead, Pendergast could hear the sound of water. Another minute brought him to the spot. Here, a phreatic passage, formed ages before by water under great pressure, cut laterally through the limestone cavern he was following. Along its floor ran a swift-moving underground stream, the lone remaining vestige of the forces that had originally sculpted these strange, deep corridors.

Pendergast paused at the water, knelt, scooped up a handful, and tasted it.

It was the same water he'd drunk at the Kraus mansion—the water the town tapped into. He tasted again. It was, as he'd expected, the very water Lu Yu's *Ch'a Ching*, the Book of Tea, considered perfect for brewing green tea: oxygenated, mineral-laden water from a free-flowing underground limestone stream. It was that tea, and the water, that had triggered the revelation that Kraus's Kaverns must be more extensive than the small portion open to the public. The trip to Topeka had proven him right, had armed him with the map he now held. But the knowledge had come at a cost. He had not anticipated Corrie acting on her own, and coming so far in her own deductions—although, in hindsight, it was all too clear that he should have.

He rose from the stream, then paused again. Something lay on the far side at the faintest perimeter of his flashlight beam, a canvas knapsack, torn apart roughly at the seams. He crossed the stream and knelt, taking a gold pen from his pocket and using it to pull apart the edges of the cloth. Inside was a road map, a couple of trowels, and several spare D batteries, the kind used in heavy flashlights and metal detectors.

Pendergast let his light play around the bag. Arrowheads and potsherds were scattered on the ground beside it. An old parfleche was decorated in the same Southern Cheyenne style he'd seen in the burial chamber beneath the mound . . .

. . . And then, a few feet away, his light stopped at a ragged clump of hair, bleached-blond with black roots.

Sheila Swegg. Digging in the Mounds, she had accidentally come across the rear entrance to the cave. It was well hidden, but easy enough to access if one knew which rocks to move. She must have been astounded at the burial chamber where the Ghost Warriors were entombed, and she'd then gone deeper into the cave, looking for even more treasures.

She found something else instead. She found *him* . . .

There was no time for additional examination. Taking one final look at the pathetic remnants, Pendergast turned and followed the small river along the smooth curves of the phreatic passage.

Within a few hundred yards, the river dropped away into a deep hole, filling the cave with a wash of mist. Here, Pendergast went upward, through narrower tubes and pipes. Now the faint marks made by the long-term passage of feet were becoming stronger: he was approaching the inhabited region of the cave.

Pendergast had believed from the beginning that the killer was local. His mistake had been in assuming the killer was a *citizen*. But no, he was not somebody to be found on Margery Tealander's tax rolls: he lived *with* them yet not *among* them.

From this realization, it was a relatively simple matter to determine the identity of the killer. But along with that determination came an understanding—or the beginnings of an understanding—of just how malformed and amoral a creature they were dealing with. He was a killer of extraordinary dangerousness, whose actions even Pendergast, with his long study of the criminal mind, could not predict.

He arrived at another narrow corridor. Along the floor, the calcite flow had recrystallized, forming a shimmering, glowing, frozen river. In the center, the soft flow had been worn down several inches by the passage of feet over a great many years.

At the end of the corridor the tunnel began to branch repeatedly, each branch showing signs of having been traversed many times. Narrow crawlspaces and vertical cracks also showed signs of passage: a delicate crystal crushed here, a smear on an otherwise snowy white dripstone there—the variety of ways a human could betray his movements through a cave were almost infinite. In the labyrinth of passages Pendergast lost his way—once, twice—each time managing to guide himself back with the aid of the map. As he rejoined the central trail the second time, his flashlight caught a glimpse of color: there, on a high shelf of dripstone, was a collection of Indian fetishes, left hundreds of years before.

Added to the fetishes were others of more recent vintage, made of bits of string and bark, gum, and Band-Aids.

Pendergast paused just a moment to examine them. They were strange, crude, and yet made with loving care.

Pendergast forced himself to hurry on, trying always to follow the most traveled route. Infrequently he would stop to jot something on the map or simply to fix in his mind the growing three-dimensional layout of the cave system. It was a stupendous maze of stone, with passageways twisting in every imaginable direction: splitting, joining, splitting again. There were shortcuts here, secret passageways, tunnels, stopes, and drifts that would take many years to explore and learn. Many years indeed.

The fetishes began to grow in number, supplemented by bizarre, complicated designs and images scratched into the rock walls. Ahead, how near or far he did not yet know, was the killer's living space. There, he felt sure, was where he would find Corrie. Dead or alive.

In all previous investigations, Pendergast had taken pains to understand, anticipate, the thoughts and actions of his adversary. In this case, the killer's psychology was so far outside the bell curve—for even serial killers had a bell curve—that such anticipation would be impossible. Here, in this cave, he would confront the most profound forensic mystery of his career.

It was a disagreeable feeling indeed.

Sixty-One

Hazen jogged down the broadening slope of the tunnel, trying to catch up to Lefty and the dogs. He could hear Raskovich huffing behind him and, farther back, the thudding footsteps and jangling equipment of the others. And up ahead, the awful bellowing of the dogs. Any pretense to stealth was long since shot: that barking could probably be heard miles away. The cave was a hell of a lot bigger than anyone had imagined. They'd left the still at least a quarter mile behind—it was hard to believe the dogs had dragged Lefty this far.

A moment later, as if in response to the thought, Lefty came into sight up ahead at last, leashes taut in his glove, speaking angrily. He had finally gotten the animals to heel.

Hazen slowed up, grateful for the chance to catch his breath, and Raskovich came puffing up beside him. "Lefty, hold up for a moment," Hazen said. "Let the others catch up."

It was too late. There was a sudden explosion of hysterical barking from the passage ahead.

"What's going on?" Hazen yelled.

"There's something here!" Lefty shrilled back.

The dogs were growing frantic now, lunging and howling, once again dragging the protesting Lefty down the tunnel.

"Damn you, Lefty, slow 'em down!" Hazen bellowed as he trotted forward.

"You want to swear at me? Take me back to the surface and swear at me. I don't like it down here. And I don't like these dogs. Sturm! Drang! *Heel!*"

The dogs were baying and growling horribly, echoes distorting to the sound of hell itself. Lefty gave the chain a brutal jerk and one of the dogs whirled around with a savage snarl. The handler shrank back, almost dropping the leash. Hazen could see Lefty was frightened. The lure of the trail was too strong now: if these dogs caught up with McFelty, they might kill him.

That would be a disaster.

He pushed himself harder to catch up, Raskovich at his side. "Lefty," he called out, "if you don't get those dogs under control, so help me I'll shoot them."

"These dogs are state property—"

As Hazen watched, the pale red shapes that were Lefty and the dogs dipped around a bend up ahead, suddenly vanishing from sight. A moment passed, then there was a shout. The frenzied baying of the dogs went up a notch: huge, meaty barks that rose at the end to a high-pitched shriek.

"Sheriff, just ahead!" came Lefty's breathless voice. "Christ, there's something moving—!"

Something? What was Lefty talking about? Hazen turned the bend, drawing in the wet air of the cave through his nose and mouth, trying to find his wind. And then he stopped abruptly.

Lefty and the dogs had disappeared into a virtual forest

of limestone pillars. Along the walls, strange curtainlike deposits hung down in heavy folds. Everywhere he looked there were openings to tunnels, cracks, yawning holes. He could hear the frantic barking, echoing back through the strange stony woods, but the sounds were so distorted that he had no idea where they were coming from.

"Lefty!" His own voice reverberated around the cavern, taking forever to die away. He leaned against a broken pillar, heaving, wondering where to go next.

Raskovich pulled up beside him, winded. Hazen could see an incipient panic in his eyes. "Where'd they go?"

Hazen shook his head. The acoustics were diabolical.

Once again, the sheriff started forward through the labyrinthine pillars, his feet splashing in shallow water, making for the spot where the echoes seemed loudest. Raskovich stayed close behind. The barking of the dogs was farther away now, as if they had moved down a distant tunnel; and yet the sound had ratcheted up to yet another notch of hysteria.

And then it changed abruptly. The barking of one of the animals morphed into a sound like the squealing of brakes. The distant screaming mingled with another sound: low, throaty, angry.

Even in the red wash of the night-vision goggles, Raskovich's face looked ashen. Now the terrible chorus was joined by the unmistakable screaming of a human being. Lefty.

"Mother of God," said Raskovich, darting looks to the left and right.

He was going to bolt.

"Hey, take it easy," Hazen said quickly. "The dogs have probably cornered McFelty. I think they've left this cavern and gone down some side tunnel. Come on, we've got to find them. Larssen!" he bawled out in a louder voice. "Cole! Brast! We're over here!"

The distorted screeching and gibbering continued. It was hard for Hazen to think straight. He wasn't worried for the dogs anymore: he was worried for McFelty.

"Raskovich, it's okay."

The man stumbled backward, face slack, clutching his shotgun. Hazen recognized the danger of the situation now: Raskovich was about to lose it, and he had a loaded weapon in his hand.

The terrible screams became mixed with a guttural choking, punctuated by gasps and coughs.

"Raskovich, it's all right, just take it easy, just lay the gun down—"

The gun went off with a deafening blast, and a shower of pebbles came down, tinkling and bouncing among the pillars of stone before landing in the shallow water.

The distant shrieking of the dogs . . . the slack, panicked face of Raskovich . . . Hazen realized that the operation was rapidly spinning out of control. "Larssen!" he bawled out. "On the double!"

Now Raskovich turned and ran, the gun lying where he'd dropped it, still smoking from the shot.

"Raskovich!" Hazen took off after him, yelling at the top of his lungs: "Hey! Wrong fucking way!"

And as he ran, the terrible threnody of both dog and man went on and on behind him—and then, silence: sudden, unnerving silence.

Sixty-Two

Pendergast paused, listening. He heard the sounds echoing through the galleries of stone, distorted beyond recognition. He waited, straining to hear, but it was impossible to make out anything beside a whisper of sound, so altered by the acoustical properties of the caverns that it seemed almost like distant surf, or wind among trees.

He redoubled his pace in what seemed the right direction, dodging over and between enormous toppled stalactites. At the end of the cavern, where the trails divided, he stopped again, listening.

The sounds continued.

Now he consulted his map, found his approximate location. He was in the middle of a particularly labyrinthine section of the cave system, riddled with multilevel cracks, passageways, and blind holes. Locating the sound within such a fiendish maze would be difficult. And yet he knew that in caves such as this, sound usually followed the flow of air. Pulling a slim gold lighter from his pocket, Pendergast lit it and held it at arm's length, carefully scrutinizing the direction in which the flame bent. Then he pocketed the lighter again and continued on, upwind, toward the sound.

But now, the sounds had ceased. The cave had returned to dripping silence.

Pendergast went on, through galleries and tunnels. With the absence of sound, he went back to following the map toward what appeared to be the central part of the cave system. At the end of a particularly narrow gallery he stopped, shining his light upon a far wall. There was one narrow vertical crack here, not on the map, that looked like it might give way onto another cavern on the far side. If so, it would cut off a considerable distance. He went to the crack and listened.

Once again, he heard faint sounds. The rush of water, overlaid by a human voice. At least, it appeared to be human, and yet it was so distorted that it was impossible to make out any words—if indeed there were any.

Shining his light on the ground before his feet, he noticed that he was not the first person to have taken this shortcut.

He edged into the crack, which soon widened enough for him to walk normally. Gradually the bottom of the crack dropped away and a crevasse opened below; yet the walls remained narrow enough that he could continue forward, one foot on either side of the crevasse, squeezing his torso through a narrow slot. It was a position that gave, strangely, the sensations of both claustrophobia and acrophobia at the same time.

Ahead, the crack opened into the blackness of space. He was standing on a narrow ledge almost a hundred feet up the wall of a domelike cavity. A stream of water plunged from above and feathered down toward the base far beneath his feet, filling the cavern with the echoing splash of water. A billion winking lights—reflections of feathery gypsum crystals—filled the cavern like fireflies.

Pendergast's flashlight beam could only barely reach the bottom.

There had been footprints at the entrance to the crack: that meant there must be a way down.

Below the lip of rock on which he stood, his light caught a series of hand- and footholds. Intermittent sounds came from below, clearer now.

Had Hazen and the troopers reached the killer and Corrie? The thought was almost too unpleasant to contemplate.

Pendergast crouched on the narrow ledge, shining his light into the blackness below. He could see nothing but a massive jumble of fallen stalactites, torn from the ceiling by some long-ago earthquake.

He took off his shoes and socks, tied the laces together, and draped them around his neck. He turned off his flashlight and slipped it into a pocket: it would be of no help now. Then, reaching down into the darkness, he grabbed the first handhold again and swung out into space, his bare feet finding slippery purchase. Five minutes of cautious climbing brought him to the bottom. He put on his shoes in complete darkness, listening.

The noise was coming from the blackness at the far end of the cavern. Whoever was making that sound had no light. It rose and fell in a strange, babbling way, but there could be no mistake: it was a man, and he sounded injured.

Turning on the flashlight again and pulling out his handgun, Pendergast moved forward swiftly.

A flash of color, and something flickered across the dim cone of light; he swung the beam around and saw something yellow on the ground, behind a fractured boulder.

He leapt catlike onto the rock, gun and light pointing downward together. He peered into the cavity beneath the boulder. And then, after staring for a moment, he holstered the gun, dropped down the far side, and laid a hand on the man who was curled in a fetal position in the lee of the rock. He was a small man, soaking wet, gibbering to himself. Lying next to him was a regulation-issue set of night-vision goggles and a helmet with an infrared spotter.

At the touch of Pendergast's hand the man crouched farther, covered his head, and squealed.

"FBI," said Pendergast quietly. "Where are you hurt?"

The man shivered at the sound of his voice, then looked up. Two red eyes peered uncomprehendingly out of a face completely covered with blood. The man's black jacket sported the yellow insignia of the Kansas State Police K-9 squad. His lips trembled above a wispy goatee, but the only sound that emerged was more incoherent sobbing. His pale eyelashes trembled.

Pendergast performed a quick examination. "It seems you're unhurt," he said.

The stammering reply did not succeed in reaching the level of intelligibility.

They were wasting time. Pendergast grabbed the man by the collar of his K-9 suit and hauled him to his feet. "Get a grip on yourself, Officer. What's your name?"

The sharp tone seemed to stun the man into sensibility.

"Weeks. Lefty Weeks. Robert Weeks." His teeth chattered.

Pendergast released his hold; Weeks staggered but managed to stay upright.

"Where did the blood come from, Officer Weeks?"

"I don't know."

"Officer," Pendergast said, "I don't have a lot of time.

There's a killer in here who's kidnapped a girl. It is vital that I find her—before your friends get her killed."

"Right," said Weeks, swallowing.

Pendergast retrieved the night-vision goggles, found them broken and inoperative, dropped them again. "You're coming with me."

"No! No, please—"

Pendergast grabbed his shoulders and gave him a shake. "Mr. Weeks, you *will* conduct yourself like a police officer. Is that clear?"

Weeks swallowed again, struggled to master himself. "Yes, sir."

"Stay behind, follow my lead, and keep quiet."

"My God, no! No, don't go that way . . . please, sir. *It's* there."

Pendergast turned and looked carefully into the man's face. He looked traumatized, ruined. "It?"

"It. That, that *man.*"

"Describe him."

"I can't, I *can't!*" Weeks buried his face in his hands as if to blot out the image. "White. Huge. All bunched up, like. Cloudy, cloudy eyes. Big feet and hands— And . . . *and the face!*"

"What about the face?"

"Oh, lord Jesus, the face—"

Pendergast slapped the man. "What about the face?"

"The face of a . . . oh, God, of a *baby,* so . . . so—"

Pendergast cut him off. "Let's go."

"*No!* Please, not that way—!"

"Suit yourself." Pendergast turned and strode off. With a yelp, the man scrambled to follow.

Leaving the tumult of broken columns, Pendergast

moved into a broad limestone tunnel littered with huge yellow mounds of dripstone. Weeks stayed behind, cringing and whimpering to himself, afraid to follow Pendergast, but still more afraid to remain alone. Pendergast's light roamed from dripstone to dripstone, once again following a trail.

And then he stopped. His light remained fixed on one mound that looked strikingly different from the others. Its deep yellow was heavily streaked with red, and at its base lay a pool of bright red water. Something was floating in the water: about the size of a human, but the shape was all wrong.

Weeks had fallen silent.

Pendergast played his light around the cavern wall that rose behind the dripstone mound. The dark rock was decorated in arcs of crimson, and gobbets of white, red, and yellow hung dripping here and there. His light finally came to rest on the giant forelimb of what could only be a dog, lodged in a crack about halfway up the wall. A piece of a lower jaw was wedged nearby, and something that might have been part of a muzzle had struck the sloping wall with enough violence to stick.

"One of yours?" Pendergast asked.

The man nodded dumbly.

"Did you see this happen?"

The man nodded again.

Pendergast turned, raising his light to the man's face. "What, precisely, did you see?"

Officer Weeks choked, stammered, and finally got the words out. "*He* did it." He paused, swallowed. And then his voice broke. *"He did it with his bare hands!"*

Sixty-Three

At a nexus of branching tunnels, Hazen waited for the state troopers and Larssen to catch up. Five minutes passed, then ten, as his labored breathing returned to normal. It seemed that either they hadn't followed the sound of his voice, or they'd taken a wrong turn somewhere.

Hazen swore, spat. Raskovich was gone, bolted like a rabbit. Although Hazen had briefly given chase, he'd been unable to find the guy. The way the man had been running, he was probably halfway back to KSU already.

Hell. If he couldn't regroup with Larssen and the troopers, he'd have to go after Lefty and the dogs alone. And that meant returning to the limestone forest, for a start.

But now, as Hazen looked back the way he had come, he wasn't sure just which of the branching tunnels he'd come out of. He thought it was the one on the right. But he wasn't sure.

Hazen swallowed, cleared his throat. "Lefty?"

Silence.

"Larssen?"

He cupped his hands in the direction of his backtrail and bellowed, "Hey! Anybody! If you can hear me, sing out!"

Silence.

"Anybody there? Respond!"

Despite the chilly air and the incessant wetness, Hazen felt a prickly sensation along his spine. He looked back the way he had come; looked around; looked ahead. The night-vision goggles gave everything a pale, reddish, unreal look, like he was on Mars. He checked his belt and confirmed what he already feared: he'd lost his flashlight during the chase.

The whole operation was fucked up. They'd gotten separated. Raskovich was lost, the whereabouts of Larssen unknown, the condition of Lefty and the dogs uncertain. At the very least, McFelty knew they were there. If he was dead, or injured . . . Hazen figured he had enough to deal with without dreaming up a lot of hypotheticals.

The thing to do was to get everyone back together, get a situation report, take stock.

Shit, it was hard to remember which of those holes he had come out of . . .

He examined the cave floor for footprints or marks, but it seemed as if each of the tunnels had been heavily trafficked. And that alone was very strange.

He ran over what had happened in his mind, trying to recall landmarks. It was all vague; he'd been concentrating on catching the fleeing Raskovich. Still, on balance it seemed to him that he'd most likely come from that passage on the right.

He walked down it about fifty feet. There were some broken stalactite pieces scattered here, like teeth. He didn't remember those. Had he just run past them too fast?

Son of a bitch.

He went farther, but still nothing looked familiar. With a

curse he returned to the pillared cave and took one of the other tunnels. He proceeded slowly, straining to remember, feeling his heart starting to beat a little fast. Nothing looked familiar. The dripping rocks, the feathery crystals, the banded, glossy humps—it all looked strange.

And then he heard a sound. Someone up ahead, humming.

"Hey!" He broke into a trot, turned a corner, paused at a fork in the passage.

The humming had stopped.

Hazen spun around, calling out. "Larssen? Cole?"

Still no sound.

"Answer me, goddamn it!"

He waited. Couldn't they hear him? He'd heard the sound as clear as a bell; why couldn't they hear him?

More humming, high-pitched and farther away, coming out of the left tunnel.

"Larssen?" He unshouldered his shotgun and walked down the left tunnel. The sound was louder, higher, closer. He moved more cautiously now, his senses on alert, trying to control his heart, which seemed to be pounding way too hard in his chest.

There was a flash of something at the periphery of his vision and he stopped and spun around. "Hey!"

He got just the briefest look before it darted away into the blackness. Brief as the glance was, it was enough to leave no doubt at all that it wasn't one of his team.

And it sure as hell wasn't McFelty.

Sixty-Four

Chester Raskovich turned a corner and stopped, the grotesque sight before him arresting his headlong flight. He stared, his mind reeling. Crouching in front of him, blocking his path, was a ragged, wispy-haired figure, staring up at him with hollow eyes, mouth yawning open as if to bite, teeth drawn back.

Raskovich leaned back with a neigh of terror, wanting to run and yet unable to do so, waiting for the thing to leap up and pounce on him. It was like a nightmare: his feet frozen to the ground, paralyzed, unable to flee.

He gulped in air—again, and then again—and, gradually, paralysis and fright ebbed and reason began to return. He leaned closer. It was nothing more than the mummified body of an Indian, sitting on the floor, bony knees drawn up, mouth open, shriveled lips drawn back from an enormous row of brown teeth. Placed around him was a semicircle of pots, each with a stone arrowhead in it. The mummy was wrapped in stringy rags that at one time might have been buckskin.

He looked away, swallowed, looked back again, and let

his breathing slow to a semblance of normality. What he was looking at was a prehistoric Indian burial. He could see the remains of beaded moccasins on the twisted feet, next to a painted parfleche and some tattered feathers.

"Fuck," said Raskovich out loud, ashamed at his panic, just now realizing what he'd done. He'd blown it. His first job as a real cop and he'd lost it completely, right in front of Sheriff Hazen. Running like a rabbit. And now here he was, lost in a cave, with a killer on the loose, and no idea which way to go. He felt a wave of shame and despair: he should've stayed at KSU, keeping kids off the water tower and giving out parking tickets.

Suddenly, he lashed out in rage and frustration, aiming a savage kick at the mummy. His foot connected with a hollow *thock* and the top of the head exploded in a ball of brown dust. A boiling stream of white insects came skittering out—they looked like albino roaches—and the mummy toppled sideways, the jaw coming loose and rolling a few turns across the ground before coming to a halt among broken pieces of skull. An ivory snake, hidden beneath the rags, uncoiled with a flash and shot off into the darkness like a thin ghost.

"Oh, *shit!*" Raskovich shouted, skipping back. "God *damn* it!"

He stood there, breathing hard, hearing the sound of air rattling in his throat. He had no idea where he was, how far he had run, where he should go.

Think.

He looked around, shining his infrared lamp around the damp surfaces of rock. He had been running through a narrow, tall crack with a sandy floor. The crack was so high he could not even make out the top. He could see his own footprints in the sand. He listened: no sound, not even water.

Retrace your steps.

Giving one last glance at the now-desecrated burial, Raskovich turned and walked back along the crack, keeping his eyes on the ground. Now he noticed what had been ignored in his headlong flight: almost every niche and shelf on both sides of the crack was piled with bones and other objects: painted pots, quivers full of arrows, hollow skulls rustling with cave life. It was a mausoleum, an Indian catacomb.

He shivered.

To his relief, he soon left the burials behind. The crack widened and the ceiling came down, and he could make out cruel-looking stalactites overhead. The sandy bottom gave way to shallow terraces of water, layered in strange accretions like rice paddies. As the sand fell behind, so did the trace of his footsteps.

Ahead were two openings, one tall and partly blocked with fallen limestone blocks, the other open. Which way now?

Think, asshole. Remember.

But for the life of him Raskovich could not remember which way he had come.

He thought of shouting, then decided against it. Why attract attention? The thing the dogs had found might still be around somewhere, looking for him. The cave was far bigger than it was supposed to be, but he could still find his way out if he took his time and didn't panic again. They would be looking for him, too. He had to remember that.

He chose the larger opening and felt reassured by the long tunnel ahead of him. It looked familiar somehow. And now he could see something else, an indistinct reddish blur in the goggles, up on a shelf of rock beside a dark hole. An arrangement of objects. Another burial?

He approached. There was another Indian skull, some feathers and arrowheads and bones. But these were arranged in a very unusual pattern on the shelf of rock. It was disquieting, somehow, like nothing he'd seen in books or museum displays. There were non-Indian objects, too: strange little figures made of string and twine; a broken pencil; a rotting wooden alphabet block; the fragmented head of a porcelain doll.

Jesus Christ, the little arrangement gave him the creeps. He backed away. *This* wasn't old. Somebody had taken the old bones and rearranged them with these other things. Raskovich felt a shiver convulse his back.

There was a grunt from the darkness over his shoulder.

Raskovich did not move. There were no more sounds: the silence that descended again was complete. A minute went by, then two, while Raskovich remained frozen, as the uncertainty and terror continued to mount within him.

And then the moment came when he was unable to stop himself from turning. Slowly—very slowly—he twisted around until he saw what had made the noise.

Raskovich fell still, paralyzed once again, not even a whisper of breath escaping his lips. *It* stood there, grotesque, misshapen, hideous. The sight was so terrible that every detail etched itself into his brain. Was that really a pair of handmade shorts and suspenders on those giant, twisted legs: suspenders decorated with rocking horses? Was that shirt, hanging in tatters from the roped and matted chest, really patterned with comets and rocket ships? And, above them, was that face really, *really,* so very . . .

The horrible figure took a step forward. Raskovich

stared, unable to move. A meaty arm lashed out and swatted him. He fell to the cave floor, the night-vision goggles flying.

The blow broke the spell of terror, and now, finally, he was able to move his limbs. He scrambled backward, blind, a loud keening sound issuing from his throat. He could hear the monster shuffling toward him, making sucking noises with his mouth. He managed to get to his feet and retreated a few steps, the final step dropping into nothingness. He lost his balance and toppled backward, tensing, expecting to land heavily against the hard stone floor of the cave, but there was nothing, nothing at all, just a great rush of wind as he hurtled into a dark void, endlessly down, down—

Sixty-Five

Hank Larssen turned to face Cole and Brast. The troopers looked like goggle-eyed monsters in the reddish light.

"I really don't think this is the way they went," Larssen said.

The sentence fell away into silence.

"Well?" Larssen looked from Cole to Brast. The two state troopers almost looked like twins: fit, wiry, crew-cut, taut jawlines, steely eyes. Or rather, once-steely eyes. Now, even in the pale wash of the night-vision goggles they looked confused and uncertain. It had been a mistake, he realized, to leave the huge cavern of limestone pillars looking for Hazen. The barking of the dogs had gone suddenly silent, and they'd taken off down one of the countless side passages in what seemed like the direction of retreating footsteps. But the passage had divided, once, then twice, before turning into a confusing welter of crisscrossing tunnels. Once he thought he'd heard Hazen calling out his name. But there had been no more sounds for the last ten minutes, at least. It was going to be a real chore just to find their way back out.

He wondered how he'd become the de facto leader of this happy little picnic. Cole and Brast were both part of the much-vaunted "high-risk entry team" and had trained for special situations like this. At the state police HQ they had a gym, workout facilities, a pool, shooting range, special training seminars, and weekend retreats. Larssen sure hoped he wasn't going to have to hand-hold these guys.

"Wake up, you two. Did you hear me? I said, I don't think this is the way they went."

"I don't know," said Brast. "It seems right to me."

"It seems right to you," Larssen repeated sarcastically. "And you, Cole?"

Cole just shook his head.

"All right, that settles it. We turn around and get out of here."

"What about Hazen?" Cole said. "Weeks?"

"Sheriff Hazen and Officer Weeks are trained law enforcement personnel who can take care of themselves."

The two troopers just looked at him.

"Are we all in agreement on this?" Larssen asked, raising his voice. Damned idiots.

"I'm with you," Brast said with evident relief.

"Cole?"

"I don't like leaving people down here," said Cole.

A real hero, thought Larssen. "Sergeant Cole, it's pointless to wander around down here any longer. We can go for backup. They could be anywhere in this maze. I wouldn't be surprised if they were already on their way out."

Cole licked his lips. "All right," he said.

"Then let's go."

They had been circling their way back toward the limestone forest for five minutes and had reached an unfamiliar-looking crossroads when Larssen first heard the sound. The others must have heard it, too, because they spun around with him. It was faint, but unmistakable: the sound of running footsteps, approaching at high speed. But not human, no: the tattoo of heavy footfalls was too rapid for that.

It was something big.

"Weapons!" shouted Larssen, dropping to one knee and raising the gun to his shoulder. He took aim down the intersecting tunnel.

The running came closer, accompanied by a metallic clanking. And now a big reddish form materialized out of the darkness. Whatever it was, it was huge.

"Ready!"

The thing bore down on them with terrible speed. It tore through a shallow puddle, raising a curtain of droplets in its wake.

"Wait!" Larssen said abruptly. "Hold your fire!"

It was one of the dogs.

The animal hurtled toward them, utterly heedless of their presence, the wide wild eyes staring fixedly ahead. The only sound it made was the drumming of its huge paws against the stone. As it flashed past, Larssen saw that the animal was covered with blood, and that one of the ears was torn away, as well as part of the lower jaw. Big black lips and tongue flapped loosely, dripping foam and blood.

In another second it was gone, the sound of its flight fading away. Then silence returned. It had all happened so quickly that Larssen almost wondered if he'd imagined it. "What the *fuck?*" Brast whispered. "Did you see—?"

Larssen swallowed, but no moisture came. His mouth felt dry as sawdust. "He must've slipped, fallen."

"Bullshit," said Cole, his voice unnaturally loud in the

confined space. "You don't lose half your jaw in a fall. Someone attacked that dog."

"Or some *thing*," Brast muttered.

"For chrissakes, Brast," said Larssen, "show some backbone."

"Why was he running like that? That dog was scared shitless."

Larssen said, "Let's just get out of here."

"No argument there."

They turned back, Larssen keeping his eyes on the damp tracks of the dog. They could probably follow those with confidence; that would make things a whole lot easier.

Brast spoke into the silence. "I heard something."

They paused once again.

"Something splashing through that puddle back there."

"Don't start again, Brast."

Then Larssen heard it, too: the faint splash of a footfall in water, followed by another. He stared down the dark tunnel behind them, the cavern walls a red wash in his goggles. He could make out nothing.

"Just dripping water, probably." He shrugged, turned back to follow the dog tracks.

Muh!

Brast gave a yell, and at the same time Larssen felt a sudden brutal shove from behind that sent him sprawling to the ground, his night-vision goggles flying. Brast was still yelling, and Cole gave a sudden, sharp scream.

Larssen was blind. In desperation he crawled around on his hands and knees, feeling the ground, and then with enormous relief felt his hands close on the goggles. He slipped them back onto his head with thick stupid fingers and looked around.

Cole was on the ground, yelling and clutching his arm. Brast was on his hands and knees against the cavern wall, scrabbling around for his goggles just like Larssen had been a second before, cursing and gasping.

"My arm!" Cole screamed. A spear of bone protruded from his arm at a strange angle and hot blood poured from the wound, almost white in the sheen of the goggles.

Larssen tore his eyes from the sight and looked around wildly for whatever had attacked them, shotgun at the ready, but there was nothing—nothing but the grim artificial glow of the cavern walls.

A single sound, like a hoot of laughter or perhaps triumph, came from the darkness somewhere. Larssen tightened his grip on the shotgun. Exactly where it had come from was impossible to tell.

He was sure of only one thing: it was close.

Sixty-Six

Corporal Shurte of the Kansas Highway Patrol fingered his shotgun and rocked back and forth on the balls of his feet. He checked his watch: eleven-thirty. Hazen and the rest had been gone for over an hour. How long did it take to corner McFelty, cuff him, and drag his ass out? It was unnerving, standing out here without any contact. Part of it, of course, was the weather. He'd lived in this part of Kansas all his life but he couldn't remember ever seeing a storm like this one. Usually, the really ugly weather came and went pretty quick. But this had been going on for hours, it seemed, and it was only getting worse. Unbelievable wind, pelting rain, lightning like to split the sky. Before radio communications had finally gone down there'd been early reports of an F-3 tornado chewing toward Deeper, all hell breaking lose, FEMA trying to get in, the highways blocked.

And the power: usually you'd get one grid segment, maybe two, down at a time. But tonight it had been like a giant hand pulling the plug on one tiny town after the next. After Medicine Creek it had been Hickok, DePew, Ulysses, Johnson City, Lakin, and finally Deeper, before his radio had stopped working altogether from the loss of repeater stations. Shurte was from Garden City and he was glad the other side of the county seemed to be taking the worst of it. Still, he worried about his wife and kids. It was a hell of a night to be away from home.

The hooded propane lamp they'd set up cast a faint glow around the mouth of the cave. Williams, standing on the far side of the cut, looked like a zombie, hunched against the rain, big dark hollows where his eyes should be. The only thing that made him look remotely human was the glowing cigarette that dangled from his lower lip.

Another bolt of lightning cracked the sky, tearing almost from horizon to horizon. Beyond the cave, it flashed a brief image of the big old Kraus mansion, all alone and dilapidated, darkened by the rain.

He glanced over at Williams. "So how long are we going to stake out the entrance? I mean, I'm getting soaked."

Williams dropped his cigarette, ground it under his boot, shrugged.

There was another flash. Shurte glanced at the dark slot that led down into the cave. Maybe they had the perp holed up and were trying to persuade him to come out . . .

And then from the mouth of the cave, over the sound of the wind, he heard the heavy galloping of feet.

He took a step forward, raising his shotgun. "You hear that?" he began sharply.

A dark form suddenly came hurtling up the passage toward them: a huge dog, running like mad, chain twitching and lashing behind like a whip, feet drumming.

"Williams!" Shurte shouted.

The animal blew out of the cave mouth and into the open. Just then there was another terrific rip of lightning, followed instantaneously by an earth-shaking crash. The dog hesitated, confused, turning around and around, snapping at the air, eyes rolling and wild. In the livid lightning Shurte saw that it was bright red, wet and glistening.

"Holy shit," he breathed.

The dog crouched toward the light of the lantern, still trembling violently—all without making a sound.

"Son of a *bitch*," said Williams. "You see his mouth? Looks like he caught a load of buckshot."

The dog staggered, the blood pooling underneath him, and then righted himself, massive limbs shaking uncontrollably.

"Catch him," said Shurte. "Grab his chain."

Williams crouched and slowly picked up the end of the chain. The dog just stood there, still now, trembling with pain and terror.

"Easy, boy. Easy. Good dog."

Williams slowly lifted the end of the leash toward the only suitable tie spot: a protruding pin on the door hinge of the cave. Suddenly the dog, feeling the gentle tug on his neck, whirled with a screech of fury and slashed out at Williams. The man went down with a howl, dropping the leash, and in a second the dog was gone, a black shape hurtling away into the cornfields.

"Son of a bitch bit me!" Williams cried, holding his leg.

Shurte rushed over and directed his flashlight at the fallen trooper. The pants were torn and blood welled from a gash in his thigh.

"Jesus, Williams," Shurte said, shaking his head. "And to think he did that with only half a jaw."

Sixty-Seven

*L*arssen bent over Cole, who was sitting on the ground, rocking back and forth and whimpering to himself. It was an ugly compound fracture, the jagged end of bone sticking out just above the elbow.

"I can't see!" said Brast loudly from somewhere behind him. "I can't see!"

"Cool it," Larssen replied. He looked around, scouring the ground with his own set of goggles. They had all lost their goggles in the attack. He saw one of the sets lying in a puddle of water, one of its lenses broken. The other set was nowhere to be found. Was he the only one still able to see? It seemed so.

"Help me find my goggles!" Brast cried.

"They're out of commission."

"No, *no!*"

"Brast? Cole's hurt. Pull yourself together."

Larssen took off his shirt and tore it into strips, doing his best to ignore the chill dampness of the cave. He looked around for something that would do as a splint but saw nothing usable. Better to bind the arm to the torso and leave it at that. The important thing now was to get the hell out of there. Larssen wasn't particularly frightened—he'd never had quite the right imaginative equipment for fear—but he perfectly understood the seriousness of their situation. Whoever attacked them, it was someone who *knew* the cave inside out. Someone who'd been down here a very long time. Someone who could come and go at will, and very quickly. He'd seen his outline: big, shambling, with a hunched back from years of living under low ceilings . . .

Hazen had only been half right. The killer was in the cave, but it sure as hell wasn't McFelty—or anyone connected with Lavender, for that matter. This was something a lot weirder and deeper than that.

He forced himself back to the problem at hand. "Cole?" he asked.

"Yes?" Cole's voice was weak and he could see the man was sweating. Shock.

"I don't have anything to splint your arm with, so I'm going to immobilize it by tying it to your chest."

Cole nodded.

"It's going to hurt."

Cole nodded again.

Larssen tied two of the strips into loops and hung them around Cole's neck to form a sling, and then, as gently as possible, took hold of his arm and slid it in. Cole winced, cried out.

"What was that?" Brast shouted in a panic. "Is *he* back?"

"It's nothing. Just stay calm, keep quiet, and do what I tell you." Larssen tried to make his voice sound reassuring. He would almost rather have ended up with Hazen. The sheriff might be an asshole, but nobody could accuse him of cowardice.

Larssen tore another couple of strips from the shirt and tied them around Cole's torso, binding up and immobilizing the broken arm. The broken bones grated against each other, and Cole winced. He was sweating profusely now, and shaking.

"Can you stand up?"

Cole nodded, rose, staggered. Larssen steadied him.

"Can you walk?"

"I think so," he grunted.

"You're not going, are you?" cried out Brast, groping for Larssen in the darkness.

"We're all going."

"But what about my goggles?"

"As I said, they're broken."

"Let me see them."

With a hiss of irritation Larssen picked them out of the water and handed them to Brast. The man felt them frantically, tried to turn them on. There was a spark and a hiss. He hurled them away, his voice high and panicky. "Sweet Jesus, how are we ever going to get out of—"

Larssen reached out and grabbed a fistful of Brast's shirt, gave it a good screw. "Brast?"

"Did you see it? *Did you see it—?*"

"No, and neither did you. Now shut up and do what I tell you. Turn around, I'll need to get at your pack a moment. I'm going to make a lifeline with your rope. I'll tie it around my waist and then pass it back to you and Cole. You hang on with one hand and help Cole along. Got it?"

"Yes, but—"

Larssen gave Brast a hard shake. "I said, *shut the hell up and do what I tell you.*"

Brast fell silent.

Larssen reached into the pack, found the rope, and tied it around his own waist. That left about ten feet or so of slack, and he made sure Brast and Cole grasped it tightly.

"Now we're getting out of here. Keep tension on the rope, don't drop it, and for God's sake keep quiet."

Larssen began moving slowly back through the long black passage. A trembling that had little to do with the chill air had settled into his bare limbs. Brast's desperate *Did you see it?* ran through his head despite his best efforts to block it. The truth was, Larssen had gotten just a glimpse; just a glimpse, but it had been enough . . .

Don't think about it. The important thing is to get out.

Behind him Cole and Brast, both blind, shuffled and stumbled. Once in a while Larssen would murmur warnings about obstacles, or stop to help the troopers through some tricky place. They moved slowly, and agonizing minutes passed before they reached the next fork in the tunnel.

Larssen examined the fork, noticed the direction of the bloody paw prints. They set off again, moving a little faster now. The floor was covered in rills and shallow pools, and the sound of their splashing echoed in the cave. The prints grew few and far between here. If they could just find their way back to the big cavern with the limestone pillars, they'd be all right; he was pretty sure he knew the way from there.

"Are you sure we came this way?" Brast asked, his voice high and tense.

"Yes," said Larssen.

"What the hell attacked us? Did you see it? *Did—?*"

Turning and reaching past Cole, Larssen backhanded Brast sharply across the face.

"I saw it! I saw it! *I saw it!*"

Larssen didn't answer. If Brast didn't shut up soon, he thought he might kill him.

"It wasn't human. It was some kind of Neanderthal. With a face like . . . oh, dear God, like a big—"

"I said, shut up."

"I *won't* shut up. You need to hear this. Whatever we're up against, it isn't *natural*—"

"Brast?" It was Cole, speaking through gritted teeth.

"What?"

With his good arm Cole aimed his shotgun down the dark tunnel and pulled the trigger. It erupted with a deafening crash. A shower of pebbles dislodged by the vibration danced off their shoulders while the sound echoed and re-echoed crazily, rolling back and forth in the deep spaces.

"Jesus, what the fuck was that!" Brast fairly screamed.

Cole grabbed for the rope and waited for the echoes to die down. Then he spoke again. "If you don't shut up, Brast, the next one's for you."

There was a moment of silence.

"Come on," Larssen said. "We're wasting time."

They continued on, stopping briefly at another intersection. The set of bloody dog prints led to the right, and they followed these into another low passageway. A few minutes later the tunnel opened up into a huge cavern, draped on two sides by curtains of limestone and filled with massive pillars. Larssen felt immense relief. They'd found it.

Cole stumbled, grunted, then half sat in a puddle of water.

"Don't stop," said Larssen, grabbing his good arm and helping him rise. "I know where we are now. We've got to keep going until we're out of here."

Cole nodded, coughed, took a step, stumbled, took

another. *He's going deep into shock,* thought Larssen. They had to get out before he collapsed entirely.

They made their way through the forestlike cavern. Several tunnels led away from the far wall, looking like yawning mouths in the pink wash of the goggles. Larssen didn't remember seeing that many tunnels. He looked on the ground for the dog tracks, but the shallow flow of water on the ground here had erased any trace.

"Wait," he said abruptly. "Quiet."

They stopped. There was a sound of splashing from behind that could not be explained by the echoes of the gallery. After another moment, it, too, stopped.

"He's behind us!" said Brast in a loud voice.

Larssen pulled them behind one of the trunklike pillars, readied his shotgun, then peered out with his goggles. The cavern was empty. Could it have been just an echo, after all?

Turning back, he saw Cole leaning unsteadily, half conscious, against the limestone pillar.

"Cole!" He hauled him to his feet. Cole coughed, swayed. Larssen quickly leaned him over, head between his legs.

Cole vomited.

Brast said nothing, trembling, his eyes wide with fear, uselessly searching the darkness.

Larssen reached down, cupped some water, splashed it over Cole's face. "Cole? Hey, Cole!"

The man sagged to one side, eyes rolling into the back of his head. He had passed out.

"Cole!" Larssen patted some more water into his face, gave him a few light slaps.

Cole coughed, retched again.

"Cole!" Larssen tried to keep the man on his feet, but his

limp form felt like a sack of cement. "Brast, help me, god-dammit."

"How? I can't see."

"Feel your way along the rope. Do you know the fire-man's carry?"

"Yeah but—"

"Let's do it."

"I can't *see,* and besides, we don't have time. Let's leave him here and get help from—"

"I'll leave *you* here," said Larssen. "How would you like that?" He found Brast's hands and locked them together with his in a basket grip. Larssen guiding, they stooped to-gether, embraced Cole's sagging form, tried to rise again.

"Christ, he weighs a ton," Brast said, gasping.

At that same moment Larssen heard a distinct splash, then another: heavy footfalls in the shallow pools they had come through just moments before.

"I tell you, there's something behind us," Brast said as he strained desperately to lift Cole. "Did you hear it?"

"Just *move.*"

Cole slumped backward, threatening to slide out of their grip. They maneuvered him into place again and moved for-ward painfully.

The splashing continued from behind.

Larssen looked back but saw only indistinct washes of pinks and reds. He looked forward again, chose a narrow passage in the far wall that looked like it might be the right one, made doggedly toward it. If he could get to a defensi-ble location, he could hold the thing off with his gun . . .

"God," said Brast, his voice breaking. "Oh God, oh God . . ."

They ducked into the low passage, carrying Cole

between them as quickly as they could. Larssen staggered as the rope caught his ankles; he straightened up, went forward again. After a short distance, the ceiling rose toward a weird formation of a thousand needlelike stalactites, some as thin as threads.

Oh God, I don't remember that, thought Larssen.

Another splash from the darkness behind them.

Suddenly, Brast tripped against a rock. Cole slumped from their grasp and fell heavily onto his broken arm. He groaned loudly, rolled over, and lay still.

Larssen let him go, fumbling with his gun, aiming into the darkness.

"What is it?" Brast cried. "What's there?"

At that moment a monstrous shape came hurtling out of the darkness. Larssen cried out, firing as he stumbled backward, while Brast stood in terror, feet rooted to the ground, his arms clawing at the darkness. "Jesus, don't leave me—!"

Larssen grabbed his hand, yanked him away. As he did so, the shape fell upon the supine form of Cole. The two figures blurred together, a reddish tangle in the goggles. Larssen staggered backward again, tugging at Brast while at the same time struggling to get his gun back up. He heard a rending sound like a drumstick being wrenched off a turkey. Cole screamed abruptly: a terrible falsetto squeak.

"Help me!" cried Brast, clutching at Larssen like a drowning man, knocking him back and spoiling his aim. Larssen savagely shoved him away while trying to raise the shotgun, but Brast was all over him again, sobbing, clutching at him.

The gun went off but the shot was wide, sending long needles of limestone crashing to the ground, and then the shape was up and facing them. Larssen froze in horror: it was holding Cole's severed arm in one fist, the fingers still pulsing spasmodically. Larssen fired again, but he had hesitated too long and the shape was rising toward them, and all he could do was turn and flee down the dank tunnel, Brast yelling incoherently and blindly at his back.

Farther behind, Cole was still screaming.

Larssen ran and ran.

Sixty-Eight

For a long time Corrie lay in the wet dark, confused and dreamy, wondering where she was, what had happened to her room, her bed, her window. And then she sat up, her head pounding, and with the return of the pain came the memory of the cave, the monster . . . and the pit.

She listened. All was silent save the dripping of water. She finally stood, swaying slightly, the pounding in her head subsiding. She reached out and her hands encountered the slick, smooth wall of the pit.

She made a circuit, running her hands up and down the wet wall, seeking handholds, cracks, anything she might use to climb out. But the walls were of the slickest stone, smoothed by water, impossible to climb. And what would she do once she got out? Without a light she was as good as trapped.

It was hopeless. There was no way out. All she could do was wait. Wait for the monster to come back.

Corrie felt overwhelmed with a feeling of helplessness and misery so powerful it made her physically sick. Her despair was all the worse for the hope that had been raised in her brief dash to escape. But here, in the pit, there was no hope left. No one knew where she was, that she'd gone into the cave. Eventually the thing would come back. Ready to *play*.

She sobbed at the thought.

It would be the end of her miserable, useless life.

Corrie leaned against the slick wall, sank to the ground. She began to cry. Years of bottled-up misery came pouring out. Images flashed through her mind. She remembered coming home from fifth grade, sitting at the kitchen table and watching her mother drink miniature vodka bottles, one after another, wondering why she liked them so much. She remembered, two years ago, her mother coming home at two o'clock in the morning on Christmas Eve, drunk, with some man. No stockings, no presents, nothing that Christmas. It was a late, rise-at-noon, hungover morning like any other. She remembered the triumphant day when she was able to buy her Gremlin with the money she had earned from working at the Book Nook before its demise—and how furious her mother had been when Corrie brought it home. She thought about the sheriff, his son, the smell of the high school halls, the winter snowstorms that covered the stubbled fields in unbroken blankets of white. She thought about reading books under the powerlines in the heat of summer, the snide whispered comments of the jocks passing her in the halls.

He was going to come back and kill her and it would all be gone, every miserable memory now crowding her head. They'd never find her body. There'd be a halfhearted search and then everyone would forget about her. Her mother would tear apart her room and eventually find the money taped to the underside of her bureau drawers, and then she'd be happy. Happy that it was now all hers.

She cried freely, the sound echoing and reechoing above her head.

Now her mind wandered further back, to her early childhood. She remembered one Sunday morning getting up early and making pancakes with her father, carrying the eggs around and chanting like the soldiers in *The Wizard of Oz*. All her memories of him seemed to be happy: of him laughing, kidding around, squirting her with the hose on a hot summer day or taking her down to swim in the creek. She remembered him polishing his Mustang convertible, polishing and polishing, a cigarette hanging from his mouth, his blue eyes sparkling, holding her up so she could see her reflection in it, then taking her for a ride. She remembered effortlessly, as clear as if it had been last week, how the cornfields parted with their passing; the exhilarating sensation of acceleration, of freedom.

And now, in the silence, in the absolute final blackness of the pit, she felt all the protective walls she had carefully built for herself over the years start to crumble, one by one. In this moment of extremis, the only questions that remained in her head were the ones she had rarely ever allowed herself to ask: Why had he left? Why had he never come back to visit? What was so wrong with her that he'd never wanted to see her again?

But the darkness would allow no self-delusion. She had another memory, not all that distant: of coming home and finding her mother burning a letter in the ashtray. Had it been from him? Why hadn't she confronted her mother? Was it out of fear that the letter wasn't, in fact, what she hoped it was?

This last question hung in the blackness, unanswered. There could be no answer, not now. It would soon end, here, in this pit, and the question would be moot. Maybe her father would never even know she was dead . . .

She thought of Pendergast, the only person who had ever treated her like an adult. And now she'd failed him, too. Stupidly going into the cave without telling anyone. Stupid, stupid, *stupid* . . .

She sobbed again, loudly, painfully, giving full vent to her feelings. But the sound echoed so horribly, so mockingly, around and above her that she swallowed, choked, and fell silent.

"Quit feeling sorry for yourself," she said out loud.

Her voice echoed and died away and then she caught her breath. There was a distinct whisper in the dark.

Was *he* coming back?

She listened intently. There were more sounds now, faint sounds, so distant and distorted they were impossible to make out. Voices? Yelling? Screaming? She strained, listening.

And then there was a long, echoing sound, almost like the roar of rolling surf.

A gunshot.

And suddenly she was on her feet, crying out, *"Here I am! Help me! Over here! Please! Please! Please! Please!"*

Sixty-Nine

Weeks struggled to keep up with Pendergast as the FBI agent hurried through the cave. The way the man flicked his flashlight around, Weeks wondered if he missed anything. Probably not. It felt a little reassuring.

The air of purpose that radiated from the agent had helped steady Weeks's shattered nerves. He even felt some vestiges of his old aggrieved self returning. And yet he could not get out of his mind the image of the dog being ripped limb from limb by that . . . *by that* . . .

He stopped.

"What's that?" he asked in a high, quavering voice.

Pendergast spoke without looking back. "Officer Weeks? I expect you to follow my lead."

"But I heard something—"

Pendergast's slender white hand landed on his shoulder. Weeks was about to say more but fell silent as the pressure on his shoulder grew more intense.

"This way, Officer." The voice spoke with a silvery gentleness, but it somehow chilled Weeks to the bone.

"Yes, sir."

As they proceeded, he heard the sound once again. It seemed to come from ahead, a drawn-out, echoing noise that reverberated back and forth through the endless caverns, impossible to identify. A scream? A shotgun blast? The one thing Weeks felt sure of was that, whatever the sound might be, Pendergast was going to head directly for it.

He swallowed his protest and followed.

They moved through a narrow warren of passages whose low ceilings were covered with glistening crystals. Weeks scraped his head against the needle-sharp crystals, cursed, and ducked lower: this wasn't the way he'd come with the dogs. Pendergast's light moved back and forth, exposing nests of cave pearls clustered together in chalky pools. The sounds had finally died away, leaving only the faint plash of their own steps.

Then Pendergast halted suddenly, his light shining steadily on something. Weeks looked. At first he couldn't make out exactly what it was: an arrangement of objects on a shelf of flat stone, clustered around some larger central object. It looked like a shrine of some kind. Weeks leaned closer. Then his eyes widened with shock and he stepped back. It was an old teddy bear, furred with mold. The bear was arranged as if it were praying: hands clasped before it, one beady black eye staring out from creeping tendrils of fungus.

"What the *hell*—?" Weeks began.

Pendergast's light shifted to what the bear had been praying to. In the yellow glow of the flashlight, it was little more than a mound of silky mold. Weeks watched as Pendergast bent over and, with a gold pen, carefully pulled away the mold, exposing a tiny skeleton underneath.

"*Rana amaratis,*" Pendergast said.

"What?"

"A rare species of blind cave frog. You will note the bones were broken peri-mortem. This frog was crushed to death in somebody's fist."

Weeks swallowed. "Look," he ventured one last time, "it's insane to keep going deeper into the cave like this. We should be getting out of here, getting help."

But Pendergast had returned his attention to the objects around the teddy bear. With care he exposed more small skeletons and partially decomposed insect bodies. Then he went back to the teddy bear, picked it up, brushed off the mold, and examined it carefully.

Weeks looked around nervously. "Come on, come *on*."

He shut up as the FBI agent turned toward him. Pendergast's pale eyes were distant, focusing on some inner thought.

"What is it?" Weeks breathed. "What does it mean?"

Pendergast returned the bear to its place and said merely, "Let us go."

The FBI agent was moving faster now, stopping only infrequently to check the map he was carrying. The sound of water was louder now, and they were now wading almost constantly. The air was so chill and damp that their breath left trails. Weeks tried to keep up, tried to keep his mind off what he'd seen. This was insane, where the hell were they going? When he got back—*if* he got back—the first thing he'd do was put in for disability leave, because he'd be lucky if post–traumatic stress syndrome was all he got from—

Then Pendergast halted suddenly. His light disclosed a body lying on the cave floor. The figure lay on its back, eyes wide open, arms and legs flung wide. The head was strangely elongated, like it had expanded and flattened, and the back of the skull had burst open like an overripe pumpkin. The eyes were bugged out, looking in two different directions. The mouth was wide open—*too* wide. Weeks looked away.

"What happened?" he managed to say, struggling to hold back the terror.

Pendergast raised his light toward the ceiling. There was a dark hole in the roof of the cavern. Then he let it fall once again to the body. "Can you identify him, Officer?"

"Raskovich. The campus security guy from Kansas State."

Pendergast nodded and looked back up into the narrow hole overhead. "It would seem Mr. Raskovich had a great fall," he murmured, almost to himself.

Weeks shut his eyes. "Oh, my God."

Pendergast motioned him forward. "We must go on."

But Weeks had had enough. "I'm not going one step more. Just what do you think you're doing, anyway?" The panic elevated his voice louder and louder. "The dog's dead, Raskovich is dead. You've seen them both. There's a monster down here. What more do you want? *I'm* the one that's still alive. *I'm* the one you should be worrying about right now. *I'm*—"

Pendergast turned back. And Weeks stopped in mid-rant, involuntarily, at the steady, contemptuous gaze of the FBI agent.

After a moment, Weeks averted his eyes. "Anyway, what I'm saying is, we're wasting our time." His voice cracked. "What makes you so sure this girl is still alive, anyway?"

As if in answer, he heard a response: faint, distorted, and yet unmistakable. It was the sound of someone crying for help.

Seventy

Larssen ran like hell, Brast behind him, holding on to the
rope, careering from rock wall to rock wall, somehow managing in his blindness to keep up. It had been a couple of
minutes since the screaming had stopped but Larssen could
still hear it in his mind, playing over and over again like
some infernal recording: the final scream of Cole ending
abruptly in the sound of cracking bones. Whatever had done
that—whatever was pursuing them now—wasn't completely human. It really was some kind of monster.

It couldn't be true. But he'd seen it. He'd *seen* it.

He paid no attention to where he was going, what tunnel
he was in, whether he was heading back toward the surface
or deeper into the caverns. He didn't care. All he wanted to
do was put distance between himself and the *thing*.

They came to a pool, pale, shimmering red in the goggles, and Larssen waded in without hesitation, the icy water
eventually reaching his bare chest before shoaling. Brast followed blindly, as best he could. On the far side, the ceiling
of the cave became very low. Larssen moved forward more
slowly, sweeping his gun back and forth, breaking off the

sharp stalactites that hung before his face. The ceiling dropped still farther, and there was an ugly noise, followed by a desperate curse, as Brast hit his head against it.

Then the ceiling rose again, revealing an odd, broken room with cracks leading off in myriad directions. Larssen stopped, looking up and down and sideways, and felt the scrabbling Brast blunder into his back.

"Larssen? *Larssen?*" Brast clutched at him as if to make sure he was real.

"Quiet." Larssen listened carefully. There was no sound of splashing behind them. The thing was not following.

Had they gotten away?

He checked his watch: almost midnight. God knows how long they had been running.

"Brast," he whispered. "Listen to me. We've got to hide until we can be rescued. We'll never find our way out, and if we keep wandering around we'll just run into that thing again."

Brast nodded. His face was scratched, his clothes muddy; his eyes were dumb, blank with terror. Blood was running freely from a nasty gash in his crew-cut scalp.

Larssen looked forward again, shining his infrared head-lamp around. There was a crack high up on the wall, larger than the others, vomiting a frozen river of limestone. It looked just big enough to admit a person.

"I'm going to check something. Give me a hand up."

"Don't leave me!"

"Keep your voice down. I'll only be gone a minute."

Brast gave him a fumbling hand up, and within moments Larssen was into the high crack. He looked around, bare arms shivering in the chill air. Then he untied the rope from around his waist and dropped one end back down to Brast and hissed for him to climb up.

Brast fumbled and·pulled his way up the slippery rock wall.

Larssen led them deeper into the crack. The floor was rough and strewn with large rocks. After a few yards, it became a tunnel that opened up enough for them to proceed in a crouched position.

"Let's see where it leads," Larssen whispered.

Another minute of crawling brought them to the edge of blackness. The tunnel simply ended in a sheer drop.

Larssen put a steadying hand on Brast. "Stay there."

He peered carefully out over the edge of the hole but could see no bottom. He reached for a pebble, lobbed it in, and began to count. When he reached thirty, he gave up.

Overhead was a sheer chimney, with a thin thread of water spiraling down at them through space. There was no way the thing could come at them from that direction. He could come up only from the crack through which they'd just come.

Perfect.

"Stay here," he whispered to Brast. "Don't go any farther, there's a pit."

"A pit? How deep?"

"As far as you're concerned it's bottomless. Just stay put. I'll be right back."

He returned to the crack's entrance and, lying on his stomach, began dragging over the surrounding rocks and fitting them into the hole. In five minutes he had piled the rocks high enough to completely seal off the crack. The killer, if he even got to the broken-up cavern below, would see only rock. No opening. They had found the perfect hiding place.

He turned to Brast, speaking very quietly. "Listen to me.

No sound, no movement. Nothing that could betray us. We'll wait here for a real SWAT team to come down and clear that bastard out of the cave. In the meantime, we stay put, and keep quiet."

Brast nodded. "But are we safe? Are you sure we're safe?"

"As long as you keep your mouth shut."

They waited, the silence and darkness growing ever more oppressive. Larssen leaned back against the wall, shutting his eyes and listening to his own breathing, trying not to dwell on the madman roaming the caverns beyond.

He heard Brast next to him, restless, shifting. He felt irritated: even the smallest noise might betray them. He opened his eyes, adjusted the goggles, and looked over.

"Brast! No!"

It was too late; there was a brief *scritch* and a match flared into light. Larssen smacked it out of his hand, and it dropped to the ground with a hiss. The sulfurous smell of the match lingered in the darkness.

"What the hell—?"

"You son of a bitch," Larssen hissed. "What the hell do you think you're doing?"

"I found matches." Brast was weeping openly now. "In my pocket. You said we were safe, that he couldn't find us. I can't take this darkness any longer. *I can't.*"

There was a faint scratching noise, then another match flared into light. Brast sobbed with relief, his eyes wide and staring.

And suddenly, Larssen, half-naked and shivering, realized he didn't have the will to douse the friendly yellow glow anymore. Besides, he had piled the rocks pretty deep. The feeble light from a tiny match surely wouldn't leak out into the cave beyond.

He pushed the goggles onto his forehead and looked around, blinking his eyes. For the first time, he could see things in crisp, clear detail. Tiny as it was, the flame gave out a welcome glow of warmth in this awful place.

They were in a small, compartmentlike space. Five or six feet beyond, the sheer drop began. Behind them and past the low ceiling was their exit, blocked with rubble. They were safe.

"Maybe I can find something we can burn," Brast was saying. "Something to give a little warmth."

Larssen watched as the state trooper felt among his pockets. At least it kept Brast quiet.

Brast cursed under his breath as the match burnt his fingers. As he lit a third, there was a faint sound from behind Larssen: the clink of a rock being moved. Then the sound of falling, rolling; first one rock, then another.

"Put it out, Brast!" he hissed.

But Brast had turned and risen with the match in his hand, and was now looking behind Larssen, his face slackening with fear. For a terrible moment, Brast did not move. And then, very suddenly, he turned and ran blindly, mindlessly, off the edge into the pit.

"Noooo—!" Larssen cried.

But Brast was already gone, into the abyss, the burning match that had been in his hand dancing and flickering on an updraft before winking out.

Larssen waited for what seemed forever, heart hammering, listening in the pitch blackness to the rough breathing that echoed his own. And then, with numb fingers, he slowly put his goggles on and turned inexorably to stare, himself, into the face of nightmare.

Seventy-One

Rheinbeck sat in the darkened parlor, rocking back and forth, back and forth in the old, straight-backed chair. He was almost glad the house was so dark because he felt ridiculous: sitting here in his blacked-out raid wear, Kevlar vest, and bloused BDU pants, surrounded by lace antimacassars, crochet work, and frilly doilies. Assignment: little old lady.

Shit.

The big old house still groaned and creaked under the howling of the storm outside, but at least the shrieks of the old lady from the basement tornado shelter had subsided. He had double-locked the massive storm door and it was pretty clear she wasn't going anywhere. She'd be safe down there, a lot safer than him if a tornado came along.

It was well past midnight. What the hell were they doing down there? He watched the feeble glow of the propane lantern, turning over various scenarios in his mind. They probably had the guy trapped and were negotiating him out. Rheinbeck had seen a couple of hostage negotiations in his time and they sometimes went on forever. Communications were down, trees lay across most of the roads, and nobody was going to respond to his call for an ambulance and doctor for the old lady: not with Deeper shredded and the whole county under a Force-3 tornado alert. This was a medical situation, not a law enforcement one; and damned awkward at that.

Jesus God, what a shitty assignment.

There was a shriek and the sudden pop of glass. Rheinbeck sprang to his feet, chair tilting crazily behind him, before he realized it was just whipsawing tree branches and another window getting blown out by the wind. Just what the place needed: more ventilation. Now that the cold front had passed over, it was remarkable how chilly the air had grown. The rain was already pouring in one broken window, puddles running across the floor. He righted the chair and sat back down. The boys back at HQ would never let him live this one down.

The propane lantern guttered and he looked over at it, scowling. It figured: some jackass hadn't bothered to screw in a fresh canister, and now the thing was about to go out. He shook his head, rose, and went to the fireplace. A fire was laid and ready to go; above the hearth, on the stone mantelpiece, he noticed an old box of kitchen matches.

He stood for a minute, thinking. *Hell with it,* he decided. As long as he was stuck in this creepy old place, he might as well make himself comfortable.

He ducked his head into the fireplace and made sure the flue was open. Then he reached for the box, removed a match, struck it, and lit the fire. The flames licked up the newspaper and immediately he felt better: there was something reassuring about the warm glow of a fire. As it took, it threw a nice yellow light into the parlor, reflecting off the framed embroidery, the glass and porcelain knickknacks.

Rheinbeck went and turned off the propane lantern. Might as well conserve its last few minutes of light.

Rheinbeck felt a little sorry for the old lady. It was tough having to lock her in the basement. But there was a major tornado warning out, and she'd been uncooperative, to say the least. He settled back in the rocker. It couldn't be easy for an old woman, having a bunch of strangers with guns and dogs descending on your property in the middle of the night, in a terrible storm. It would be a shock for anybody, especially a shut-in like old Miss Kraus.

He leaned back in the rocker, enjoying the warmth of the flickering firelight. He was reminded of the Sunday afternoons he and the wife occasionally spent visiting his mother. In the winter, she'd make a pot of tea and serve it by a fire just like this one. And with the tea would always come cookies: she had an old family recipe for ginger snaps she kept promising to give his wife, but somehow never did.

It occurred to him that the old lady had been down in the cellar for almost three hours without any kind of nourishment. Now that she'd calmed down, he should bring her something. Nobody could accuse him later of having starved the old woman or allowing her to dehydrate. He could make a pot of tea. There was no power, but he could boil the tea water over the fire. In fact, he wished he'd thought of it earlier.

He roused himself from the chair, turned on his flashlight, and went into the kitchen. The place was remarkably well stocked. There were boxes of funny-looking dry goods stacked up along the walls: herbs and spices he'd never heard of, exotic vinegars, pickled vegetables in jars. On the counters were silver canisters covered with Japanese lettering, or maybe Chinese, he wasn't sure which. Finally he found the teakettle, set near the stove between a pasta maker and some contraption like an oversized steel funnel with a crank. He rummaged in the cabinets, located some good old-fashioned tea bags. He hung the kettle on a hook above the fire, then returned to the kitchen. The refrigerator was also well stocked, and it was the work of a few minutes to arrange a little tray with cream and sugar, tea cakes, jam, marmalade, and bread. A lace doily and linen napkin with spoon and knife completed the refreshment. Soon the tea was ready, and he put the kettle on the tray and started down the stairs.

He paused at the storm door and, balancing the tea tray on one hand, tapped lightly. He heard a stir within.

"Miss Kraus?"

No sound.

"I have some tea and cakes here for you. It'll do you good."

He heard another rustle, and then her voice came through the door. "Just a minute, please. I need to arrange my hair."

He waited, relieved by how calm she sounded. It was amazing, the propriety of the older generation. A minute passed, and then the old lady spoke again. "I'm ready for you now," came the prim voice.

Smiling, he slipped the big iron key out of his pocket, inserted it in the lock, and eased open the door.

Seventy-Two

Sheriff Hazen could feel the sweat running off his hands and down the dimpled stock of his shotgun. He'd heard a welter of distant noises over the last ten minutes: gunshots, screams, cries—it sounded like a major confrontation. They'd seemed to come from one general direction, and Hazen was heading toward it as quickly as he could. Others might have run like rabbits, but he was personally determined to bring the guy out.

In the sandy floor he could now make out footprints: the bare ones he'd seen before.

He straightened. The bare feet of the killer.

He realized he'd been wrong about McFelty. The glance he'd had of the killer, brief as it was, had assured him of that. And maybe he was even wrong about Lavender's connection. But he was right about the most important thing: the killer was holed up in the cave. This was his base of operations. Hazen had made the connection and he was determined to follow through and bring the son of a bitch out.

Hazen followed the footprints in the sand. Who could he be? A question to be answered later. Find the guy, get him out. It was as simple as that. Once they had him, all else would become clear: whether he was connected to Lavender; the experimental field; whatever. All would become clear.

He turned a sharp corner, following the footprints. The walls and roof suddenly pulled back, stretching away into vastness, their outlines dim in the infrared beam of his light. The ground was littered with huge, glittering crystals. Even with the monochromatic goggles, Hazen could tell they were all different colors. The cave was gigantic, a lot bigger and more spectacular than the miserable three-room tourist trap that Kraus had opened up. With the right management, it could be turned into a major tourist site. And the Indian burials he'd seen—they'd draw archaeologists and maybe even a museum. Even if Medicine Creek didn't get the experimental field, this cave was big enough to attract people from all over. It occurred to him, distantly, that the town was saved. This was better than Carlsbad Caverns. All this time the town had been sitting on a goldmine and they never knew it.

Hazen set the musings aside. He could dream about the future once this creepy bastard was behind bars. One thing at a time.

Ahead yawned a hole in the rock floor, from which came the sound of rushing water. He stepped cautiously around it and continued on, following the prints in the sand.

They were clear. And they looked fresh.

He sensed he was drawing closer to his quarry. The tunnel narrowed, then widened again. Hazen was noticing more and more signs of habitation: strange designs scratched into the walls with a sharp rock; moldering Indian fetishes arranged with care inside niches and atop limestone pillars.

He tightened his grip on the shotgun and moved on. The freak, whoever he was, had been down here a long time.

Ahead, the tunnel widened into another cavern. Hazen turned the corner cautiously, then stopped dead, staring.

The cavern was a riot of ornamentation. Countless odd figures of twine and bone had been lashed together, and were hanging by strings from a thousand stalactites. Mummified cave creatures had been set together in little dioramas. Human bones and skulls of all shapes and sizes could be seen: some lined up along the rock walls; others laid along the floor in intricate, bizarre patterns; still others piled in rough heaps as if awaiting use. Ancient lanterns, tin cans, rusted turn-of-the-century gadgets, Indian artifacts, and detritus of all sorts lay along makeshift shelves. It looked like the den of some madman. Which, in fact, was exactly what it was.

Hazen turned slowly, aiming his infrared beam at the spectacle. This was weird; seriously weird. He swallowed, licked his lips, and took a step backward. Maybe it was a mistake, coming blundering in here like a single-handed posse. Maybe he *was* being too hasty. The exit to the cave couldn't be that far away. He could return to the surface, get reinforcements, get help . . .

And it was then that his eye fell on the far wall of the cave. The rocky floor was particularly uneven here, sloping down into deeper darkness.

Someone was lying, motionless, on the floor.

Raising the barrel of his shotgun, Hazen moved forward. There was a rough table of stone nearby, littered with moldy objects. Nearby were some empty burlap bags. And beyond, sprawled across the floor, was the figure, maybe asleep.

Shotgun ready, he approached the stone table with the

utmost care. Now that he was closer, he realized that the objects on the table weren't covered in mold after all. Instead, they appeared to be dozens of little knots of black hair: dark tufts of whiskers; curly locks, bits of scalp still attached; kinky clumps of hair and God only knew what else besides. The image of Gasparilla's scalped and stripped head came to mind. He pushed it away, focusing his attention back on the figure, which on closer inspection didn't look asleep after all. It looked dead.

He crept forward, tension abruptly knotting as he realized the body was gutted. Where the belly should be, there was a hollow cavity.

Oh, my God. Another victim.

He approached, hands slippery on the butt stock, stiff-legged with horror. The body had been arranged, its clothes mostly torn away, only a few ragged pieces left, its face covered with dried blood. It was gangly, not much more than a kid.

His arm shaking almost beyond his ability to control it, Hazen stopped and, taking his handkerchief, wiped the blood and dirt off the face.

Then he froze, handkerchief on the cold skin, a storm of revulsion and overwhelming loss erupting within him. It was Tad Franklin.

He staggered, felt himself sway.

Tad . . .

And then everything burst out of him at once, and with a howl of grief and fury he began turning, around and around and around, pumping the shotgun in every direction, while he raged at the darkness, the fiery blasts punctuated again and again by the sound of the shattering stalactites that fell like showers of crystal rain.

Seventy-Three

"What was that?" Weeks asked, screwing up his face, blinking rapidly against the dark.

"Somebody firing a twelve-gauge." Pendergast remained still, listening. Then he glanced at Weeks's gun. "Have you been trained in the proper use of that weapon, Officer?"

"Of course," Weeks sniffed. "I got a Distinguished Shooting in my unit at Dodge Academy." As it happened, there had been only three cadets in the K-9 unit at the time, but Pendergast didn't have to be told everything.

"Then chamber a round and get ready. Stay on my right at all times and pace me exactly."

Weeks rubbed the back of his neck; humidity always gave him a rash. "It's my informed opinion that we should get some backup before proceeding further."

Pendergast spoke without bothering to look over his shoulder. "Officer Weeks," he said, "we've heard the crying of the killer's intended victim. We've just heard shooting. Is it really your *informed* opinion we have the time to wait for backup?"

The question lingered briefly in the chill air. Weeks felt

himself flushing. And then another faint cry—high, thin, clearly female—echoed faintly through the caverns. In a flash Pendergast was off again, moving down the tunnel. Weeks scrambled to follow, fumbling with his shotgun.

The crying seemed to rise and fall as they moved on, becoming fainter from time to time before growing louder again. They had entered a section of the cave that was drier and more spacious. The level floor was partially covered by large patches of sand, riddled with bare footprints.

"Do you know who the killer is?" Weeks asked, unable to completely hide his querulous tone.

"A man. But a man in form only."

"What's that supposed to mean?" Weeks didn't like the way the FBI agent always seemed to speak in riddles.

Pendergast bent briefly to examine the footprints. "All you need to know is this: *identify* your target. If it is the killer—and you will know it, I can assure you—*then shoot to kill.* Do not trouble yourself with any niceties beyond that."

"You don't have to be nasty." Weeks fell silent when he saw the look that Pendergast darted at him.

A man in form only. The image of that, that *thing*—it hadn't looked much like a man to him—raising one of the thrashing dogs and tearing off its limbs came unbidden into Weeks's mind. He shivered. But Pendergast paid no attention, moving ahead with great swiftness, gun in his hand, only pausing infrequently to listen. The sounds seemed to have died away completely.

After a few minutes, Pendergast stopped to consult the map. Then, under his guidance, they retraced their steps. The sounds returned briefly, then faded away once again. Finally, Pendergast dropped to his knees and began examining the tracks, moving back and forth for what seemed an interminable length of time, peering closely, his nose sometimes mere inches from the sand. Weeks watched him, growing more and more restless.

"Below," Pendergast said.

Pendergast squeezed through a crack along the edge of one wall, then dropped into a narrow space that descended steeply. Weeks followed. They inched along for a while, arriving shortly at a veritable ants' nest of natural boreholes in the cave wall, some with frozen rivers of flowstone erupting from their mouths. Pendergast played his light across the honeycombed face for a moment, selected one of the holes, and then—to Weeks's consternation—crawled into it. The opening was dank and wet-looking, and Weeks considered protesting, but decided against it as Pendergast's light abruptly vanished. Scrambling after Pendergast down the sharply descending passage, Weeks half jumped, half tumbled into a tunnel so heavily used that a trail had been worn in the soft limestone of its bed.

He clambered to his feet, brushing the mud from his clothes and checking his weapon. "How long has the killer been living down here?" he asked, staring at the track in disbelief.

"Fifty-one years this September," said Pendergast. Already, he was moving again, following the trail down the narrow corridor.

"So you *know* who it is?"

"Yes."

"And just how the heck did you figure *that* out?"

"Officer Weeks, shall we save the colloquy for later?"

Pendergast flew down the passageway. The crying had stopped, but now the FBI agent seemed sure of the way . . .

And then, quite suddenly, they came to a standstill. Ahead, a huge curtain of crystallized gypsum flowed from a rend in the ceiling, completely blocking the passageway. Pendergast shone his light onto the floor of the passage, and Weeks noticed that the heavy track had disappeared. "No time," Pendergast murmured to himself, angling his light back down the tunnel, up over the walls and ceiling. "No time."

Then he took a few steps back from the curtain of gypsum. He seemed to be counting under his breath. Weeks frowned: maybe he'd been right the first time and Pendergast wasn't such a good choice to be tagging along with, after all.

Then the agent paused, moved his head close to the wall, and called out, "Miss Swanson?"

To Weeks's surprise, there was a faint gasp, a sob, and then a muffled shout: "Pendergast? Agent Pendergast? Oh, God—"

"Be calm. We're coming to get you. Is *he* around?"

"No. He left . . . I don't know how long ago. Hours."

Pendergast turned to Weeks. "Now's your chance to be useful." He moved back to the curtain of gypsum, pointed. "Direct a shotgun blast at this spot, please."

"Won't he hear?" said Weeks.

"He's already close. *Follow my orders, Officer.*"

Pendergast spoke with such command that Weeks jumped. "Yes, sir!" He crouched, aimed, and pulled the trigger.

The blast was deafening in the enclosed space. Pendergast's light exposed a pall of glittering gypsum dust and, beyond, a great hole in the diaphanous stone. For a moment, nothing further happened. And then the curtain broke apart with a great crack, dropping to the floor and sending glittering crystal shards skidding everywhere. Beyond was another passage-way, and beside it the narrow dark mouth of a pit. Pender-gast rushed to the edge and shone his light within. Weeks came up behind and peered cautiously over his shoulder.

There, at the bottom, he saw a filthy girl with purple hair, staring up with a muddy, blood-smeared, terrified face.

Pendergast turned to look at him. "You're the dog-handler. You must have a spare leash in your pack."

"Yes—"

He found himself, in one swift movement, relieved of his pack. Pendergast reached inside and pulled out the spare, a length of chain with a leather strap. Then he fixed the chain end around the base of a limestone column and threw the other end into the pit.

From below came the clank of the chain, the sobbing of the girl.

Weeks peered over again. "It doesn't reach," he said.

Pendergast ignored this. "Cover us. If *he* comes, shoot to kill."

"Now, wait just a minute—"

But Pendergast had already disappeared over the edge. Weeks hovered at the top, one eye on the passageway and the other on the pit. The FBI agent clambered down the chain with remarkable agility, and when he reached the end he hung from it, free arm down, offering the girl his hand. She reached for it, swiped, missed.

"Stand aside, Miss Swanson," Pendergast said to the girl. "Weeks, nudge some of those boulders into the pit. Try not to brain one of us. And keep a careful eye on that tunnel."

With his foot, Weeks pushed half a dozen large rocks over the lip of the pit. Then he watched as the girl, who understood immediately, stacked them against the wall and clambered to the top. Now Pendergast was able to grab her hand. He hoisted her upward, planted his free arm beneath her shoulders, brought the hand back to the chain, and slowly climbed up the stone face. Pendergast looked scrawny enough, but the strength it took to climb up that chain while carrying another person was remarkable.

They emerged from the pit and the girl immediately fell to her knees, clinging to Pendergast, sobbing violently.

Pendergast knelt beside her. Taking a handkerchief from his pocket, he gently wiped the blood and dirt from the girl's face. Then he examined her wrists and hands. "Do they hurt?" he asked.

"Not now. I'm so glad you came. I thought . . . I thought—" The rest of the sentence was lost in a sob.

He took her hands. "Corrie? I know what you thought. You've been very brave. But it's not over yet and I need your help." He spoke gently but rapidly, in a low, urgent whisper.

She fell silent, nodded.

"Can you walk?"

She nodded, then broke into a sob once again. "He was *playing* with me," she cried. "He was going to keep playing with me, until . . . until I *died.*"

He put a hand on her shoulder. "I know it's difficult. But you're going to need to be strong until we get out of here."

She swallowed, eyes down.

Pendergast stood and briefly examined his map. "There might be a quicker way out. We're going to have to risk it. Follow me."

Then he turned to Weeks. "I'll go first. Then Miss Swanson. You cover us from the back. And I mean *cover,*

Officer: he could come from anywhere, above, below, beside, behind. He will be silent. And he will be *fast*."

Weeks licked dry lips. "How can you be so sure the killer will be coming after us?"

Pendergast returned his gaze, pale eyes luminous in the darkness. "Because he won't give up willingly his only friend."

Seventy-Four

Hazen moved fast, pausing only briefly to reconnoiter at the twists and intersections of the cavern, not bothering to conceal the noisy sounds of his passage. He gripped his twelve-gauge with white knuckles, fingers resting against the trigger.

This bastard was as good as dead.

He passed another little arrangement, then another, tiny crystals and dead cave animals placed on a rock ledge. A psychopath. The cave was where he'd practiced his craziness before going topside to do it to real people.

The son of a bitch was going to pay. No Miranda rights, no call to a lawyer, just two loads of double-ought buck in the chest and then a third to the brainpan.

There was such a confusing welter of footprints that Hazen wasn't sure what trail he was following anymore, or even if it was fresh. But he knew the killer couldn't be far away, and he didn't care how long it took or where he had to go to find him. The corridors couldn't go on forever. He'd find him.

The rage prickled his scalp and made his face feel hot and

flushed despite the clammy air of the cave. *Tad . . .* It was like he had lost a son.

His grief was checked, at least for now, by a tidal wave of anger. He felt tears streaming down his cheeks but didn't feel the emotion behind them. All he felt was hatred. He was crying with hatred.

The tunnel suddenly ended in a rocky cave-in. There was a black hole above from which the boulders had fallen. His infrared beam revealed a little trail, winding up through the debris and disappearing into what looked like an upper gallery.

Hazen charged his way up the debris slope, head down, shotgun pointed ahead. He came out into a soaring vertical space. Overhead, feathery crystals hung on long ropes of limestone, swaying slightly in an underground current of air. Passageways wandered off in all directions. He scanned the ground, fighting to get his breathing and his emotions under control; found what looked like a fresh track; and began following it again, threading his way through a maze of tunnels.

After a few minutes he realized something was wrong. The tunnel had curved back on itself somehow, and returned him to where he'd started. He set off down another tunnel, only to find that the same thing happened. His frustration grew until the red wash of his goggles seemed to dim from sheer rage.

After returning to the chamber yet a third time, he stopped, raised his shotgun, and fired. The blast rocked the room, and feathery crystals tinkled gently down on all sides like giant broken snowflakes.

"Mother*fucker!*" he screamed. "I'm here, come show your face, freak!"

He fired again and again, screaming obscenities into the darkness.

The only answers that came back were the echoes of the blasts, rolling insanely through the honeycomb of chambers, again and again.

The chamber was empty. Breathing raggedly, Hazen reloaded. This wasn't helping, hollering and shooting like this. Just find him. Find him. *Find* him.

He plunged down yet another passageway. This one looked different: a long, glossy tunnel of limestone, little pools of water dotted with cave pearls. At least he had escaped the merry-go-round of endless returning passageways. He could no longer remember where he had been or where he was going. He simply plunged on.

And then, off to one side, he saw a dark, hulking figure.

It was the merest glimpse, just a shadow flitting across his goggles; but it was enough. He spun, dropped to one knee, and fired—long practice at the range paying off—and the figure dropped, tumbling to the ground with a crash.

Hazen followed immediately with a second shot. Then he scuttled forward, ready to pump out one final round.

He stared down, the red glow of the night-vision goggles revealing not a dead body but a lumpy stalagmite, cut in half by his gun, lying shattered on the cave floor. He resisted the impulse to curse, to kick the shattered pieces away. Slowly and calmly, he raised the shotgun and continued down the echoing tunnel. He came to a fork, another fork, and then he paused.

He saw movement ahead, heard a faint sound.

He moved forward more carefully now, gun at the ready. He swung around a rocky corner, dropped to his knee, and covered the empty tunnel ahead; and in doing so he never did see the dark shape that approached swiftly out of the shadows behind him until he felt the sudden blow to the side of his head, the brutal wrenching twist, but by then it was too late and black night was already rushing forward to embrace him and he didn't have enough air left in his lungs to make any sound at all.

Seventy-Five

Perhaps, Corrie thought, it was all just a dream: this breathless, desperate dash through an endless gallery of caverns. Perhaps Agent Pendergast had never arrived and she hadn't been rescued, after all. Perhaps she was still down at the bottom of the pit, in a nightmarish half-doze, waiting to be awakened by the return . . .

But then, the ache in her wrists and ankles, the throbbing pain in her temple, would remind her that this was, in fact, no dream.

Agent Pendergast raised his arm, signaling for them to stop. His flashlight bobbled as he consulted the strange, soiled map. This hesitation seemed to greatly agitate the man who was accompanying them. It had taken Corrie several minutes, in her near-stuporous state, to even notice that somebody besides Pendergast had been running along with them. He was a little man with a high voice, sandy hair, and a scraggly goatee. His police fatigues were splattered with mud and clotted pieces of something else she didn't want to think about.

"This way," Pendergast whispered. Corrie roused herself

to follow, feeling as she did so the vague, dreamlike sensation return.

They passed through a low, chilly cavity that took a series of turns, first to the left, then to the right. And then quite suddenly, the ceiling rose into blackness. Corrie sensed, more than saw, that a large chamber lay ahead. Pendergast hesitated once again at its mouth, listening. When he had satisfied himself that there was no noise besides their own, he led the way forward.

One step, then another, as the walls fell away from the beam of Pendergast's flashlight. Despite her shock and exhaustion, Corrie looked wonderingly around at the extraordinary space that was revealed, in bits and pieces, by the FBI agent's flashlight. It was an immensely tall chamber, of blood-red stone so wet and slick that it appeared in places almost to be polished. Pools of shallow water dotted the floor. Near the top of the chamber, the rock face was broken by a series of horizontal cracks, through which the long seeping action of water had built up veils of calcite. These immense white veils, draped over the red stone, gave the uncanny appearance of a richly appointed gallery in a theater.

The only problem was there wasn't any exit at the far end. The dazed sense of relief that had been settling over Corrie was suddenly lost beneath a fresh wash of fear.

"Where now?" the man in uniform said, panting. "I just knew it. This shortcut of yours led us to a dead end."

Pendergast peered at the map another moment. "We're no more than a hundred yards from the public area of Kraus's Kaverns. But a portion of that will be along the Z-axis."

"The Z-axis?" the man said. "The Z-axis? What are you talking about?"

"Our route lies up there." Pendergast pointed to a small

arched opening that Corrie had not noticed before, situated
about forty feet up one of the curtains of stone. A stream of
water poured from it, splashing down the huge masses of
flowstone and disappearing into a yawning crack at the cavern's base.

"Just how are we supposed to get up there?" the man
asked truculently.

Pendergast ignored him, searching the wall above with
his beam.

"You don't expect to climb that, do you? Without a
rope?"

"It's the only choice left us."

"You call that a choice? With that huge gaping hole at the
bottom? One slip, and we're as much as—"

Pendergast ignored this, turning to Corrie. "How are your
wrists and ankles?"

She took a deep, shuddering breath. "I can make it."

"I know you can. You go first. I'll follow and tell you
what to do. Officer Weeks will come last."

"Why me last?"

"Because you need to provide cover from below."

Weeks spat to one side. "Right." Despite the chill damp
air, the man was sweating: rivulets that traced clean lines
through the muck that covered his face.

Quickly, Pendergast glided toward the cave wall, Corrie
following close behind. She felt her heart begin to beat hard
and fast again, and she tried to keep her eyes off the rock
face above them. They stopped a few yards short of the wide
fissure in the floor. The spray of falling water formed a curtain of mist that coated the already slick rock. Without allowing her time for second thoughts, Pendergast gave her a
boost, directing his light toward the initial footholds.

"I'm right behind you, Miss Swanson," he murmured. "Take your time."

Corrie clung to the rock, trying to suppress the pain in her hands and the still greater burden of her fear. To reach the opening overhead they had to climb diagonally, out over the yawning fissure. The ribbed limestone offered plenty of good hand- and footholds, but the rock was wet and smooth. She tried to think of nothing, nothing except raising first a hand, then a foot, and then pulling herself up another six inches. From the noises below, she could tell that both men were now on the rock face and climbing as well. Pendergast murmured directions, once in a while using his hand to direct her foot to one ledge or another. It was more frightening than it was difficult—the handholds were almost like the rungs of a ladder. Once she looked down, saw the top of Weeks's head and the gulf that now lay directly beneath them. She paused and shut her eyes, feeling a reeling sense of vertigo. Again, Pendergast's hand steadied her, his smooth, gentle voice urging her along, urging her to look ahead, not down . . .

One foot, one hand, the other foot, the other hand. Slowly, Corrie crept up the rock. Now, blackness yawned both above and below, barely pierced by the glow of Pendergast's flashlight. Her heart was racing even faster now, and her arms and legs were beginning to tremble from the unaccustomed effort of climbing. Somehow, perversely, the closer she got to the lip of the passage overhead, the more desperate she felt. She did not dare look up anymore, and had no idea if there were five feet, or thirty feet, still to go.

"There's something down here!" Weeks suddenly shouted from below, his voice pitched high. "Something moving!"

"Officer Weeks, brace yourself against the rock and provide cover," Pendergast said. Then he turned back to Corrie. "Corrie, just another ten feet. Pretend you're climbing a ladder."

Ignoring the pain that shot through her wrists and fingers, Corrie grabbed the next handhold, found another foothold, pulled herself up.

"It's *him!*" she heard Weeks shout. "Oh my God, *he's here!*"

"Use your weapon, Officer," Pendergast said calmly.

Desperately, Corrie grabbed a fresh handhold, found a higher ledge for her foot. It slipped and her heart almost froze with terror as she lurched away from the wall. But Pendergast was there once more, his hand bracing her, steadying her, guiding her foot to a better hold. She stifled a sob; yet again, she was so frightened she could barely think.

"He's gone," Weeks said in a tight voice. "At least, I can't see him."

"He's still there," said Pendergast. "Climb, Corrie. *Climb.*"

Corrie, gasping with the effort and pain, pulled herself up. Peripherally, she was aware that Pendergast, with a lithe maneuver, had turned himself around on the ledge to face outward. His flashlight was in one hand and his gun in the other, its laser sight scanning the cavern below.

"There!" cried Weeks.

Corrie heard the deafening blast of his gun, followed by another. "He's fast!" Weeks screamed. "Too fast!"

"I'm covering you from above," Pendergast said. "Just hold your position and *fire with care.*"

There was another blast from the gun, then another.

"Jesus Christ, Jesus Christ," Weeks was saying, over and over, sobbing and gasping.

Corrie ventured a glance overhead. In the dim glow of Pendergast's flashlight she could see that she was now just five feet below the lip of the archway. But there did not seem to be any more handholds. She felt around, first with one hand, and then with the other, but the stone was smooth.

Another scream, another wild blast.

"Weeks!" Pendergast rapped out. "You're firing wild! *Aim your weapon.*"

"No, no, *no!*" The gun went off yet again. And then Corrie heard the clatter as Weeks threw his empty gun down in a panic and began climbing furiously.

"Officer Weeks!" Pendergast shouted.

Once again, Corrie reached out with her hands, fingertips splayed, looking for a purchase. She could find none. With a sob of terror, she looked down toward Pendergast, appealing for help. And then she froze.

A shape had flashed out of the darkness below, leaping upon the rock wall like a spider. Pendergast's gun cracked but the shape kept coming, scrambling up after them. For a moment, Pendergast's light fell directly on it, but it gave a grunt of rage and ducked away from the beam. And yet it was enough for Corrie to see, once again, that great moon-like face, inhumanly white; the wispy trailing beard; the little blue eyes flecked with blood, staring out from below long, effeminate lashes; that same strange, intent, fixed smile: a face that seemed as ingenuous as a baby's, and yet so very alien, rent by thoughts and emotions so bizarre as to scarcely seem human.

Even as she watched, the figure ascended the rock with terrible speed.

Pendergast's gun cracked again but Corrie saw that Weeks, climbing desperately, had come directly between him and the monster and the FBI agent no longer had a shot. She lay against the rock face, her heart like a hammer in her chest, unable to move, unable to look away, unable to do anything.

The killer reached the frantically climbing Weeks, brought his pistonlike arm back, and smashed the man in the back, cracking him like a bug. With a scream of pain Weeks peeled off the rock and began to slide. The massive arm cocked back again and this time struck a sideways blow that rammed Weeks's head against the rock. Corrie watched in frozen horror as Weeks simply dropped, down the wall and into the great fissure below, his body making no sound as it plunged out of sight through the veil of mist into the unguessable depths beneath.

Then immediately there came another shot from Pendergast's gun, but the man, with a great apelike leap, dodged sideways and once again began scuttling up the rock face with almost unbelievable agility. Before she could even draw breath he was on top of Pendergast. There was a blow and the agent's gun fell away, clattering onto the cavern floor below. Then the thing's hammerlike fist drew back to deliver another, fatal blow and Corrie, finding her breath, screamed, "No!"

But when the fist came down, Pendergast was no longer there, having jumped sideways himself. Now the agent raised his hand, fingertips curled tightly in against themselves, and thrust the meat of his palm violently up into the man's nose. There was a cracking sound and a jet of crimson blood. The man grunted in pain and lashed out again, knocking Pendergast roughly from the wall. The agent teetered, slid, then managed to halt his fall, reestablishing a grip on the stone several feet below.

But it was too late. The thing, bloodied and frothing, had gotten past Pendergast and was now scrambling up the rock face toward Corrie. She was helpless; she could not even release a hand to defend herself; it was all she could do to cling to the cliff.

He was on top of her in a heartbeat and the great calloused hands closed once again around her throat, with no hesitation now, no humanity in his dead eyes, nothing but a sense of anger and the desire to kill. And the sound of her gagging was drowned out by his own brutal roar.

Muuuuuuuhhhhhhhhhhh!

Seventy-Six

The wind was blowing even harder now, and Shurte and Williams had retreated into the shelter of the cut leading down into the cave. It wasn't exactly where the sheriff had ordered them to be, Shurte knew, but the hell with it: it was past one in the morning, and they'd been standing in the cold and rain for over three hours already.

He heard Williams groan, then swear. He glanced over. Williams was huddled farther down the cut, holding the propane lantern. Shurte had dressed his partner's bite, using the first-aid kit from the cruiser. It was an ugly wound, but not nearly as bad as Williams was making it out to be. The real problem was their situation. The police-band radios were silent, the power was out everywhere; even the few commercial radio stations that reached this far into the boondocks were off the air. As a result, they had no information, no orders, no news, nothing. Three hours Hazen and the others had been in the cave, and the only one to come out had been one of the dogs with half his jaw ripped off.

Shurte had a very bad feeling.

The cave exhaled a smell of dampness and stone. Shurte shivered. He couldn't stop thinking about the way the dog had come tearing out of the darkness, trailing blood. What could have ripped a dog apart like that? He glanced at his watch again.

"Jesus, what the hell are they *doing* down there?" Williams asked for the tenth time.

Shurte shook his head.

"I should be in the hospital," Williams said. "I might be getting rabies."

"Police dogs don't have rabies."

"How do you know? I'm getting an infection, for sure."

"I put plenty of antibiotic ointment on it."

"Then why does it burn so much? If this gets infected I'll remember who dressed it, *Doctor* Shurte."

Shurte tried to ignore him. Even the banshee-like moaning of the wind across the mouth of the cave was preferable to his whining.

"I tell you, I've got to get medical help. That dog took a chunk out of me."

Shurte snorted. "Williams, it's a dog bite. Now you can put in for a Purple Heart Ribbon for being wounded in the line of duty."

"Not until next week I can't. And it hurts *now,* damn it."

Shurte looked away. What a jerk. Maybe he should request a rotation. When the going got rough Williams had crapped out. A dog bite. What a joke.

A bolt of lightning tore the sky in half, briefly painting the mansion a ghostly white. The huge drops of rain were propelled like bullets in the howling wind. A river of water was running down the ramp into the cave.

"Fuck this." Williams got to his feet. "I'm going up to the

house to relieve Rheinbeck. I'll take a turn watching the old lady and send him on down here."

"That wasn't our assignment."

"Screw the assignment. They were supposed to be in and out of the cave in half an hour. I'm injured, I'm tired, and I'm soaked to the skin. You can stay out here if you want, but I'm going up to the house."

Shurte watched his retreating back, then spat on the ground. What an asshole.

Seventy-Seven

The roar of the monster was suddenly drowned out by a second roar, sharp and deafening in the confines of the cavern. Corrie felt the horrible weight of the brute suddenly slam against her, pressing her cruelly into the rock face. He was roaring violently in her ear as if in pain, the bellowing filling her nostrils with the smell of rotten eggs. The great paw around her neck loosened, then released, allowing her to turn her head and gasp for air. She had a brief glimpse of a face inches from hers: broad, unnaturally smooth, pasty white, little eyes, bulbous forehead.

There was another blast, and this time she heard the slap of buckshot against the rock face nearby. Corrie gulped in air, clinging hard at the slippery purchase. Someone was firing a shotgun at him from below.

The monster slid away from the rock, then regained his hold, scrabbling frantically and roaring like a bear in the direction of the blast.

Vaguely, she heard Pendergast's voice from below. "Corrie! Now!"

Corrie struggled to clear her head. She released one hand,

gave a desperate reach upward, and found the handhold that had been eluding her. Crying and gasping, she pulled herself up by her arms, moved her foot—and felt a viselike grip close around her ankle.

She screamed, trying to shake her leg free, but the brute tugged fiercely at her, trying to peel her away bodily from the rock face. She struggled to maintain her hold but the pull was too strong. Her fingers, already swollen and bleeding from her struggles in the pit, grew too painful to endure. Corrie cried out in fear and frustration, feeling her grip give way, her nails scraping across the stone.

There was another shotgun blast and the terrible grip abruptly relaxed. Corrie felt a sharp sting in her calf and realized that one or more of the shotgun pellets had hit her.

"Hold your fire!" Pendergast shouted down.

But the monster had fallen abruptly silent. The roar of the shotgun, the shrieks of pain and rage, echoed and fell away. Corrie waited, frozen in terror against the rock face. Almost against her will, she found herself looking downward.

He was there, the broad moon face now a mask of blood. He stared up at her a moment, his face horribly twisted, grimacing, his eyes blinking rapidly. Then his hands spasmodically released their holds. His eyes remained on hers as he swayed back, as if in slow motion, from the rock face. Then he gradually fell backward, his countenance serene as his huge body dropped away into space. Corrie watched in sickened horror as he hit the rock wall a dozen feet below, bouncing with a great smack and a spray of blood, then turning once and landing heavily at the mouth of the fissure. He lay still for a moment, and then another shotgun blast roared out, catching him in one shoulder and turning him over violently, swinging his body partway over the abyss. A man holding a shotgun stepped forward: Sheriff Hazen. He aimed it point-blank at the man's head.

For a moment, one of the monster's great hands clung to the edge. And then it relaxed and the thing slid down out of sight, dropping like a stone into the void. Corrie waited, listening, but there was nothing more: no splash, no cry of ultimate pain to mark the thing's final passing. He had disappeared, claimed by the dark bowels of the earth. The sheriff stood there, not having fired the final shot.

The first to speak was Pendergast.

"Easy does it," he said to Corrie, his voice low and firm. "Let one hand follow the other. I can see the rest of the path from here. The handholds are good, and the top is only a few feet away."

Corrie gasped, sobbed, her entire body shaking.

"You may cry when you reach the top, Miss Swanson. Now, you must climb."

The businesslike tone broke the spell of terror that froze her against the rock. She swallowed, moved a hand, found another handhold, secured it, moved a foot. And when she reached up again, her hand found the lip of the precipice: she had made it to the top. In another moment, she had pulled herself up and over. She stretched out on the cold floor of the passageway, face down, and gave herself over to sobbing. *She was alive.*

For a minute, maybe two, she remained alone. And then Pendergast was kneeling over her, his arm around her, his voice low and reassuring. "Corrie, you're fine. He's gone now, and you're safe."

She couldn't speak; all she could do was cry with relief.

"He's gone now, and you're safe," Pendergast repeated, the cool white hand stroking her forehead—and for a moment the image of her father returned, so strong it was almost a physical presence. He had comforted her this way once, when she had been hurt on the playground . . . The memory was so vivid that she swallowed the next convulsive sob, hiccuped, and struggled to sit up.

Pendergast stepped away. "I have to go down for Sheriff Hazen. He's badly hurt. We'll be right back."

"He—?" Corrie managed to say.

"Yes. He saved your life. And mine." Pendergast nodded, then was gone.

Corrie leaned back against the stone floor. And only now the true storm of feelings flooded through her: the fear, pain, relief, horror, shock. A breeze came wafting down from out of the darkness, stirring her hair. It carried with it a familiar, horrible smell: the smell of that cauldron, in the room where the killer had first grabbed her. But along with it was the faint smell of something else, something almost forgotten: fresh air.

Perhaps she fell asleep then, or perhaps she simply shut down. But the next thing she remembered was the ring of footsteps against rock. She opened her eyes and saw Agent Pendergast looking down at her, gun once again in his hand. Beside him, leaning heavily against the FBI agent, was the sheriff: bloody, clothes ripped, nothing but a knot of gristle where one of his ears had once been. Corrie blinked, stared. He looked as tired and battered as a human being could be and still remain standing.

Pendergast spoke. "Come. We're not far now. The sheriff needs both our help."

Corrie staggered to her feet. She swayed a moment and Pendergast steadied her. Then they began moving slowly down the tunnel. And as the smell of fresh, sweet air began growing stronger, Corrie knew for sure that they were finally on their way out.

Seventy-Eight

Williams toiled up the path, the bite smarting with each step. The corn in the fields along the road had been ripped to shreds, husks gone, ears scattered across the path, broken stalks rustling crazily against each other. He cursed extravagantly at the rain and the wind. He should've packed it in an hour ago. Now he was soaked *and* injured. Great combination for pneumonia.

He struggled up onto the porch, his feet crunching over broken glass from a window blown out by the wind. Now he could make out a faint glow from inside.

It was a fire in the fireplace. Nice. Rheinbeck, it seems, had been taking it easy up here while he and Shurte were down in the storm, guarding the cave entrance. Well, now it was his turn at the fire.

Williams stopped, leaning on the door and catching his breath. He tried the handle, found it locked. The firelight flickered through the leaded panes, making warm kaleidoscopic patterns in the glass.

He gave the knocker a few raps. "Rheinbeck! It's me, Williams!"

No response.

"Rheinbeck!"

He waited one minute, then another. Still no response.

Christ, Williams thought, he was probably in the bathroom. Or the kitchen, maybe. That was it. He was in the kitchen eating—or drinking, more likely—and couldn't hear with all the wind.

He went around the flank of the house and found another broken window panel in the side door. He put his mouth to it and shouted, "Rheinbeck!"

Very strange.

He pushed out the rest of the glass in the panel, reached inside to unlock the door, then eased it open, nosing his light ahead of him.

Inside, the entire house seemed to be alive with the creaking, groaning, and muttering of the storm. Williams looked around uneasily. It looked solid enough, but old places like this were sometimes full of dry rot. He hoped the whole structure didn't come crashing down on him.

"Rheinbeck!"

Still no answer.

Williams limped forward. The door from the parlor to the dining room was half closed. He pushed through, looked around. All was in order, the dining table covered with a lace tablecloth, a vase of fresh flowers in the middle. He shone his light into the kitchen, but it was dark and there was no smell of cooking.

Williams returned to the parlor entrance and stood there indecisively. Looked like Rheinbeck had left with the old woman. Maybe an ambulance had finally come. But why hadn't they notified him and Shurte? It was only a five-minute walk to the cave mouth. Typical Rheinbeck, looking after himself and to hell with everyone else.

He glanced over at the fire, at the cheery yellow glow it threw over the parlor.

Hell with it, he decided. As long as he was stuck in this creepy old place, he might as well make himself comfortable. After all, he'd been badly injured in the line of duty, hadn't he?

He hobbled over to the sofa and eased himself down onto it. Now this was more like it: there was always something reassuring about the warm glow of a fire. He fetched a contented sigh, noticing the way the firelight reflected off the framed embroidery, the glass and porcelain knickknacks. He sighed again, more deeply, then closed his eyes, still seeing the flickering warm light through his eyelids.

He awoke suddenly, wondering for a wild moment where he was. Then it all came flooding back. He had dozed off for a moment, it seemed. He stretched, yawned.

There was a muffled thump.

He froze for a moment before figuring it must have been the wind, coming through another broken window. He sat up, listening.

Another thump.

It sounded like it was inside the house. Down below, in the basement. And then Williams suddenly understood. Naturally, Rheinbeck and the old lady were down in the cellar because of the tornado warnings. That was why the house seemed deserted.

He exhaled with irritation. He should go down there, just to report. He rose from the comfortable sofa, cast a regretful eye on the warm fire, and hobbled toward the door to the cellar stairs.

At the top he hesitated, then began to descend. The treads protested under his weight, squeaking frightfully over the fury of the storm outside. Halfway down he paused, craned his neck to see into the pool of darkness.

"Rheinbeck!"

There was that thump again, followed by a sigh. He fetched a sigh of his own. Christ, why was he bothering? He was injured, damn it.

He shone his light down and around, the banister rails throwing alternating bars of yellow and black in the cluttered space. At one end, a huge storm door had been set into the stone wall. That was where they must be.

"Rheinbeck?"

Another sigh. Now that he was closer, it didn't really sound like wind coming in a broken window, after all. It sounded forced, sounded *wet* somehow.

He took another step down, and another, and then he was at the bottom. The door was straight ahead. He hobbled over to it, and slowly—very slowly—pushed open the door.

A candle guttered on a small worktable, where tea for two had been set up with a pot: cups, cream, tea cakes, and jam all neatly arranged. Rheinbeck was sitting in a chair facing the table, slumped over, hands hanging at his sides, blood pouring into his mouth from a terrible gash in his skull. A broken porcelain statue lay in pieces on the ground around him.

Williams stared, uncomprehending. "Rheinbeck?"

No movement. A muffled boom of thunder shook the foundations of the house.

Williams could not move, could not think, could not even reach for his service piece. For some reason, all he could do was stare in disbelief. Even down here the old house seemed almost alive with the fury of the storm, groaning and swaying, and yet Williams could not pull his eyes away from the tea tray.

Another thump behind him abruptly broke the spell. Williams turned, the flashlight beam spinning across the walls as he groped for his gun, and as he did so a figure seemed to come out of nowhere, rushing toward him, boxes and packing crates falling away in a blur: a wild ghostly woman in white, her arms upraised, her tattered nightgown streaming behind her, her gray hair wild, Rheinbeck's commando knife in one of her upraised fists. Her mouth was open, a pink, toothless hole, and from it issued a shriek:

"Devils!"

Seventy-Nine

The rain and wind had risen to such a furious pitch that Shurte began to worry that a new line of tornadoes might be making for Medicine Creek itself. The water was now pouring down into the cave, and he had just retreated into the cave entrance when he heard the sounds from within: footsteps, slow and shuffling, and coming his way.

Heart pounding, silently cursing Williams for leaving him alone, Shurte positioned himself to one side of the propane lantern and aimed his shotgun down the steps.

Silent, indistinct figures began materializing out of the gloom. Shurte remembered the dog and felt his skin crawl. "Who's that?" he called out, trying to keep his voice from quavering. "Identify yourselves!"

"Special Agent Pendergast, Sheriff Hazen, and Corrie Swanson," came the dry reply.

Shurte lowered his gun with overwhelming relief, picked up the propane lantern, and descended to meet them. At first he could hardly believe his eyes at the bloody spectacle that greeted him: Sheriff Hazen, barely distinguishable under all the blood. A young girl, bruised and mud-spattered. Shurte recognized the third figure as the FBI agent who had sucker-punched Cole, but he didn't have time to wonder how the man had gotten himself into the cave.

"We need to get Sheriff Hazen to a hospital," the FBI agent said. "The girl also needs medical attention."

"All communications are down," Shurte said. "The roads are impassable."

"Where's Williams?" Hazen slurred.

"He went up to the house to, ah, to relieve Rheinbeck." Shurte paused, almost afraid to ask the question. "What about the others?"

Hazen merely shook his head.

"We'll send down a search-and-rescue team as soon as communications are restored," Pendergast said wearily. "Help me get these two into the house, if you please."

"Yes, sir."

Shurte put an arm around Hazen and gently guided him up the last of the steps. Pendergast came behind, helping the girl. They exited the cave mouth and bent into the fury of the elements, the rain coming horizontally down the cut, lashing and whipping against them, pelting them with broken corn-stalks and husks. The Kraus mansion loomed ahead, dark and silent, just a faint light flickering in the parlor windows. Shurte wondered where Williams and Rheinbeck were. The place looked deserted.

They moved slowly up the walk and mounted the steps to the porch. He watched Pendergast try the front door, find it locked. And then Shurte heard it: a muffled crash from inside, followed by a scream and the sound of a gunshot.

In one smooth motion, Pendergast's gun was in his hand; a second later, he had kicked in the door. Gesturing for Shurte to stay with Hazen and the girl, he darted inside.

Shurte peered around the doorframe, shotgun at the ready. He could see two figures struggling in the hall at the top of the basement stairs, Williams and somebody else: a hideous figure in a bloody white nightgown, long gray hair wild. Shurte could hardly believe it: old lady Kraus. There was another scream, this one shrill and almost incoherent: *"Baby killers!"* Simultaneously, there was another flash and roar of a gun.

In three leaps Pendergast had reached and tackled the woman in white. There was a brief struggle, a muffled shriek. The gun skittered across the floor. The two rolled out of Shurte's view and Williams darted down the stairs. Perhaps thirty seconds ticked by. And then Pendergast reappeared, carrying the old woman in his arms, murmuring something in her ear. Moments later, Williams came up the basement steps, his arm around Rheinbeck, who was staggering and holding his bloodied head.

Shurte entered with Corrie and the sheriff, passing through the front hall into the parlor, where the flickering light Shurte had noticed from outside proved to be a fire. There, Pendergast arranged the old lady in a wing chair, still murmuring soothing indistinct words, cuffing her loosely. He rose and helped Shurte lay the sheriff down on the sofa in front of the fire. Williams took a seat on a sofa as far from the woman as possible, shivering. The girl had fallen in the chair on the other side of the fire.

Pendergast's gaze darted about the room. "Officer Shurte?"

"Yes, sir."

"Get a first-aid kit from one of the cruisers and see to Sheriff Hazen. He has an aggravated excision of the left ear, what looks to be a simple fracture of the ulna, pharyngeal trauma, and multiple abrasions and contusions."

When Shurte returned a few minutes later with the medical kit, he found that the room had been lit with candles and new logs laid on the fire. Pendergast had draped an afghan around the old woman, and she peered out at them balefully through a tangle of iron-gray hair.

Pendergast glided toward him. "Take care of Sheriff Hazen." He went over to the girl and spoke to her softly. She nodded. Then, taking supplies from the first-aid kit, he bandaged her wrists and doctored the cuts on her arms, neck, and face. Shurte worked on Hazen, who grunted stoically.

Fifteen minutes later, all had been done that could be done. Now, Shurte realized, they just had to wait for emergency help to arrive.

The FBI agent, however, appeared to be restless. He paced the room, his silver eyes moving among its occupants. And yet again and again, as the storm shook the old house, his gaze came back to rest on the bloodied old woman who sat motionless, handcuffed to the wing chair, her head bowed.

Eighty

The warmth of the fire, the steam rising from the cup of chamomile tea, the numbing effect of the sedative Pendergast had administered: all conspired to create in Corrie a feeling of growing unreality. Even her bruised and battered limbs seemed far away, the pain barely noticeable. She sipped and sipped, trying to lose herself in the simple mechanical action, trying not to think about anything. It didn't help to think, because nothing seemed to make sense: not the nightmare apparition that had chased her through the cave, not the sudden homicidal rage of Winifred Kraus, nothing. It was as senseless as a nightmare.

In a far corner of the parlor, the state troopers named Williams and Rheinbeck sat, the latter nursing a bandaged head and leg. The other trooper, Shurte, stood by the door, gazing through the glass down the darkened road. Hazen reclined on an overstuffed couch, his eyes half open, battered and bandaged almost beyond recognition. Beside him stood Pendergast, looking intently at Winifred Kraus. The old woman stared back at them all from her wing chair, looking from one to the next, malevolent eyes like two little red holes in her pale, powdered face.

At last, Pendergast broke the long silence that had settled over the parlor. His eyes remained on the old woman as he spoke: "I am sorry to tell you, Miss Kraus, that your son is dead."

She jerked and moaned, as if the announcement was a physical blow.

"He was killed in the cave," Pendergast went on quietly. "It was unavoidable. He didn't understand. He attacked us. There were a number of casualties. It was a matter of self-defense."

The woman was now rocking and moaning, repeating over and over again, "Murderers, murderers." But the accusatory tone seemed almost to drain from her voice: all that remained was sorrow.

Corrie stared at Pendergast, struggling to understand. "Her *son?*"

Pendergast turned to her. "You gave me the crucial hint yourself. How Miss Kraus, when she was young, was known for her, ah, free ways. She became pregnant, of course. Normally she would have been sent away to have the baby." He turned back to Winifred Kraus, speaking very gently. "But your father didn't send you away, did he? He had a different way of dealing with the problem. With the *shame.*"

Tears now welled out of the old woman's eyes and she bowed her head. There was a long silence. And in that silence Sheriff Hazen exhaled loudly, as the realization hit him.

Corrie looked over at him. The sheriff's head was swathed in bandages, which were soaked red around his missing ear. His eyes were blackened, his cheeks bruised and puffy. "Oh, my God," he murmured.

"Yes," Pendergast said, glancing at Hazen. "The father,

with his fanatical, hypocritical piety, locked her and her sin away in the cave."

He turned back to Winifred. "You had the baby in the cave. After a time, you were let out to rejoin the world. But not your baby. He, the sinful issue, had to remain in the cave. And that's where you were forced to raise him."

He stopped briefly. Winifred remained silent.

"And yet, after a time, it didn't seem like such a bad idea, did it? Completely sheltered from the wicked world like that. In a way, it was a mother's dream come true." Pendergast's voice was calm, soothing. "You would always have your little boy with you. As long as he was in the cave, he could never leave you. Never would he leave home or fall into the ways of the world; never would he leave you for another woman; never would he abandon you—as your mother once abandoned you. You were doing it to *protect* him from the opprobrium of the world, weren't you? He would always need you, depend on you, love you. He would be yours . . . forever."

The tears were now flowing freely down the old lady's cheeks. Her head was swaying sadly.

Hazen's eyes were open, staring at Winifred Kraus. "How could you—?"

But Pendergast continued in the same soothing tone of voice. "May I ask what his name was, Miss Kraus?"

"Job," she murmured.

"A biblical name. Of course. And an appropriate one, as it turned out. There, in the cave, you raised him. He grew to be a big man, a strong man, enormously strong, because the only way to move about in his world was by climbing. Job never had a chance to play with children his own age. He never went to school. He barely learned how to talk. In fact, he never even *met* another human being for the first fifty-

one years of his life except for you. No doubt he was a boy
with above-average intelligence and strong creative im-
pulses, but he grew up virtually unsocialized as a human
being. You visited him from time to time, when it was safe.
You read to him. But not enough for him to learn more than
rudimentary speech. And yet, in some respects, he was a
quick boy. A desperately creative boy. Look what he was
able to learn by himself—lighting a fire, making clever
things with his hands, tying knots, creating whole worlds
out of little things he found in the cave around him.

"Perhaps at some point you realized you were doing
wrong by keeping him in the cave—away from sunlight,
civilization, human contact, social interaction—but by then,
of course, it would have seemed too late."

The old lady remained bowed, weeping silently.

Hazen exhaled again: a long, pent-up breath. "But he got
out," he said hoarsely. "The son of a bitch got out. And that's
when the murders began."

"Exactly," said Pendergast. "Sheila Swegg, digging at the
Mounds, uncovered the ancient Indian entrance to the cave.
The back door. Which also happened to be used by the Ghost
Warriors when they ambushed the Forty-Fives. It had been
blocked off from the inside, when the warriors went back into
the cave and committed ritual suicide after the attack. But
Swegg, digging in the Mounds, found it. To her sorrow.

"It must have been a monumental shock for Job when
Swegg wandered into his cave. He had never met another
human being besides his mother. He had no idea they even
existed. He killed her, in fear, no doubt unintentionally. And
then he found the freshly cut opening Swegg had made. And
for the first time, he climbed out into a vast and wondrous
new world. What a moment that must have been! Because

you never told him about the world above, did you, Miss Kraus?"

She slowly shook her head.

"So Job emerged from the cave. It would have been night. He looked up and saw the stars for the first time. He looked around and saw the dark trees along the creek; heard the wind moving through the endless fields of corn; smelled the thick humid air of the Kansas summer. How different from the enclosing darkness in which he had spent half a century! And then perhaps, far away, across the dark fields, he saw the lights of Medicine Creek itself. In that moment, Miss Kraus, you lost all control of him. Just as happens to every mother. But in your case, Job *was over fifty years old.* He had grown into a powerful—and transcendentally warped—human being. And the genie could not be put back in the bottle. Job had to come out, again and again, and explore this new world." Pendergast's voice trailed off into the chill darkness.

A small sob escaped from the old lady. The room fell silent. Outside, the wind was slowly dying. A distant rumble of thunder sounded, like an afterthought. Finally, she spoke: "When the first lady was killed, I had no idea it was my Job. But then . . . Then he *told* me. He was so excited, so happy. He *told* me about the world he'd found—as if he didn't know I already knew of it. Oh, Mr. Pendergast, he didn't mean to kill anyone, he really didn't. He was just trying to play. I tried to explain to him, but he just didn't *understand*—" She choked on a sob.

Pendergast waited a moment and then continued. "As he grew, you didn't need to visit him as often. You brought him his food and supplies in bulk once or twice a week, I imagine, which would explain where he got the butter and sugar. By that time he was almost self-sufficient. The cave system was his home. He had taught himself a great deal over the years, skills that he needed to survive in the cave. But where he was most damaged was in the area of human morals. He didn't know right from wrong."

"I tried, oh, how I *tried* to explain those things to him!" Winifred Kraus burst out, rocking back and forth.

"There are some things that cannot be explained, Miss Kraus," Pendergast said. "They must be observed. They must be *lived*."

The storm shook and rattled the house.

"How did his back become deformed?" Pendergast finally asked. "Was it just his cave existence? Or did he have a bad fall as a child, perhaps? Broken bones that healed badly?"

Winifred Kraus swallowed, recovered. "He fell when he was ten. I thought he would die. I wanted to get him to a doctor, but . . ."

Hazen suddenly spoke, his voice harsh with disgust, anger, disbelief, pain. "But why the scenes in the cornfields? What was that all about?"

Winifred only shook her head wonderingly. "I don't know."

Pendergast spoke again. "We may never know what was in his mind when he fashioned those tableaux. It was a form of self-expression, a strange and perhaps unfathomable notion of creative play. You saw the scratched wall-etchings in the cave; the arrangements of sticks and string, bones and crystals. This was why he never fit the pattern of a serial killer. Because he *wasn't* a serial killer. He had no concept of killing. He was completely amoral, the purest sociopath imaginable."

The old lady, her head bowed, said nothing. Corrie felt sorry for her. She remembered the stories she had heard of how strict the woman's father was; how he used to beat her for the merest infraction of his byzantine and self-contradictory rules;

how the girl had been locked in the top floor of her house for days on end, crying. They were old stories, and people always ended them with a wondering shake of the head and the comment, "And yet she's such a *nice* old lady. Maybe it never really happened that way."

Pendergast was still pacing the room, looking from time to time at Winifred Kraus. "The few examples we have of children raised in this way—the Wolf Child of Aveyron, for example, or the case of Jane D., locked in a basement for the first fourteen years of her life by her schizophrenic mother—show that massive and irreversible neurological and psychological damage takes place, simply by being deprived of the normal process of socialization and language development. With Job it was taken one step further: he was deprived of the *world itself.*"

Winifred abruptly put her face in her hands and rocked. "Oh, my poor little boy," she cried. "My poor little Jobie . . ."

The room fell silent except for Winifred's murmuring, over and over again: "My poor little boy, my little Jobie."

Corrie heard a siren sound in the distance. And then, through the broken front windows, the lights of a fire truck striped their way across the walls and floor. There was a squealing of brakes as an ambulance and a squad car pulled up alongside. Then came the slamming of vehicle doors, heavy footsteps on the porch. The door opened and a burly fireman walked in.

"You folks all right here?" he asked in a hearty voice. "We finally got the roads cleared, and—" He fell silent as he saw Hazen covered with blood, the weeping old woman handcuffed to the chair, the others in shell-shocked stupor.

"No," said Pendergast, speaking quietly. "No, we are not all right."

Epilogue

The setting sun lay over Medicine Creek, Kansas, like a benediction. The storm had broken the heat wave; the sky was fresh, with the faintest hint of autumn in the air. The cornfields that had survived the storm had been cut, and the town felt freed of its claustrophobic burden. Migrating crows by the hundreds were passing over town, landing in the fields, gleaning the last kernels from among the stubble. On the edge of town, the spire of the Lutheran church rose, a slender arrow of white against the backdrop of green and blue. Its doors were thrown wide and the sound of evening vespers drifted out.

Not far away, Corrie lay on her rumpled bed, trying to finish *Beyond the Ice Limit*. It was peaceful in the double-wide trailer, and her windows were open, letting in a pleasant flow of air. Puffy cumulus clouds passed overhead, dragging their shadows across the shaved fields. She turned a page, then another. From the direction of the church came the sound of an organ playing the opening notes of "Beautiful Savior," followed by the faint sound of singing, Klick Rasmussen's warble, as usual, trumping all.

As Corrie listened, a faint smile came to her lips. This would be the first service by that young new minister, Pastor Tredwell, whom the town was so proud of already. Her smile widened as she recalled the story, as it had been described to her when she was still in the hospital: how Smit Ludwig, shoeless, bruised, and battered, had come shambling out of the corn—where he had lain, unconscious and concussed, for almost two days—and right into the church where his own memorial service was being held. Ludwig's daughter, who had flown in for the service, had fainted. But nobody had been more surprised than Pastor Wilbur himself, who stopped dead in the midst of reciting Swinburne and collapsed in an apoplectic fit, certain he was seeing a ghost. Now Wilbur was convalescing somewhere far away and Ludwig was healing up nicely, typing from his hospital bed the first chapters of a book about his encounter with the Medicine Creek murderer, who had taken nothing but his shoes and left him for dead in the corn.

She set her novel aside and lay on her back, staring out the window, watching the clouds go by. The town was doing its best to return to normal. The football tryouts were beginning and school would be starting in two weeks. There was a rumor that KSU had decided to site the experimental field somewhere in Iowa, but that was no loss. Good riddance, in fact: Pendergast seemed to feel Dale Estrem and the Farmer's Co-op had a point about the perils of genetic modification. Anyway, people could hardly care less, now that the town was alive with National Park people, cave experts, a team of *National Geographic* photographers, and hardcore groups of spelunkers, all of whom were anxious to get a glimpse of what was being called the greatest cave system to be discovered in America since Carlsbad Caverns. It seemed the town was standing at the edge of a new dawn that would bring wealth, or at least prosperity, to all. Time would tell.

Corrie sighed. None of it would make the slightest difference to her. One more year and then, for better or worse, Medicine Creek would become ancient history for her.

She lay in bed, thinking, while the sun set and night fell. Then she got up and went to her bureau. She slid open the drawer, felt along the bottom, and carefully peeled off the bills. One thousand five hundred dollars. Her mother still hadn't found the money, and after what had happened she'd stopped harping about it. She had even been nice to Corrie for the first day after she'd come back from the hospital. But Corrie knew that would not last long. Her mother was now back at work and Corrie had little doubt she'd return with her purse rattling with its usual quota of vodka minis. Give it a day or two and she'd bring up the money and everything would start all over again.

She turned the bills over thoughtfully in her hands. Pendergast had stayed in town the last week, working with Hazen and the state police to wrap up the evidentiary phase of the case. He had called to say he was leaving tomorrow, early, and said he wanted to say goodbye before he left—and collect his cell phone. That was what he really wanted, she knew, the cell phone.

He'd already been by the hospital several times to see her. He had been very solicitous and kind; and yet, somehow, she'd hoped for more. She shook her head. What did she expect—that he'd take her with him, make her his permanent assistant? Ridiculous. Besides, he seemed increasingly eager to leave, citing some pressing matter waiting for him back in New York. He'd taken several calls on his cell phone from a man named Wren, but then he'd always left the room and she'd never caught what was said. Anyway, it didn't really matter. He was going away, and in two more weeks high school would begin again. Senior year, her last in Medicine Creek. One last year of hell.

At least there wouldn't be any more trouble from Sheriff Hazen. Funny, he'd saved her life and now he seemed to have taken some kind of almost paternal interest in her. She had to admit he had been pretty cool when she'd visited him that day she left the hospital. He'd even apologized—not in so many words, of course, but still it just about floored her. She had thanked him for saving her life. He'd shed a few tears at that, said he hadn't done nearly enough, that he'd done nothing. The poor man. He was still really broken up about Tad.

She looked down at the money. Tomorrow, on her way out, she'd tell Pendergast what she planned to do with it.

The idea had formed slowly, over those days she'd spent in the hospital. In a way, she was surprised she hadn't thought of it before. She had two weeks before school, she had money, and she was free: the sheriff had dropped all charges. Nothing was keeping her here: she had no friends to speak of, no job, and if she stuck around, her mother would wheedle the money out of her sooner or later.

Not that she had any illusions, not even when the idea first came to her. She knew that when she found him he'd probably turn out to be one of those guys who couldn't seem to get it together: a loser. After all, he'd married her mother and then split, leaving both of them in the lurch. He'd never paid child support, never visited, never written—at least, that she could be sure of. He wouldn't exactly be a Fred MacMurray.

It didn't matter. He was her father. In her gut, this seemed like the right thing to do. And now she had the money and the time to do it.

It wouldn't be hard to find him. Her mother's endless complaints had the unintentional side effect of keeping her informed of his progress. After bouncing around the Midwest he had settled in Allentown, Pennsylvania, where he worked doing brake jobs for Pep Boys. How many Jesse Swansons could there be in Allentown? She could drive there in a couple of days. The money Pendergast had paid her would cover gas, tolls, motels, with a nice cushion in the very likely event that some unexpected car repairs came up.

Even if he turned out to be a loser, her memories of him were good memories. He wasn't a jerk, at least. When he was there he'd been a good father, taking her out to the movies and miniature golf, always laughing, always having fun. What did it mean, anyway, to be a loser? The kids at school thought she was a loser, too. He *had* loved her, she felt sure . . . even if he did leave her alone with a horrible drunken witch.

Don't get your hopes up, Corrie, she reminded herself.

She folded the bills, stuffed them into her pants pocket. From beneath her bed she pulled out her plastic suitcase, plopped it on the bed, opened it up, and began throwing clothes in. She'd leave first thing in the morning, before her mother woke up, say goodbye to Pendergast, and be on her way.

The suitcase was soon packed. Corrie shoved it back under her bed, lay down, and in an instant was asleep.

She awoke in the stillness of night. All was dark. She sat up, looking around groggily. Something had awakened her. It couldn't be her mother, she was working the night shift at the club, and—

From directly outside her window came a gurgle, a chattering noise, a soft thump. Instantly, the grogginess went away, replaced by terror.

And then there was a splutter and a hiss, and a patter of drops began falling lightly against the side of the trailer.

She glanced at the clock: 2 A.M. She sank back on the bed, almost laughing out loud with relief. This time, it really *was* Mr. Dade's sprinkler system.

She rose to shut the window. She paused for a moment, drinking in the cool flow of air, the fresh smell of wet grass. Then she went to slide the window shut.

A hand suddenly reached in from the darkness and caught the window's edge, stopping it from closing. It was bloody, with broken nails.

Corrie dropped her hands from the window and backed away wordlessly.

A white, moonlike face now appeared in the window: bruised, cut, streaked with filth and blood, with a wispy beard and a strange, childlike puffiness. Slowly the terrible hand pulled the window open until it would go no more. A terrible stench—all the more terrible for the memories that it stirred—flowed in and filled her nostrils.

Corrie backed toward the door, numb fingers feeling in her pocket for the cell phone. She found it, hit the send button twice, directing the phone to call the most recently dialed number. Pendergast's number.

With a jerk the huge hand ripped out the cheap aluminum window frame, shattering the glass.

Corrie turned and ran from her room, tearing down the hall in her bare feet, racing across the living room toward—

With a crash, the front door was flung open. And there stood Job: Job, still alive, one eye ruptured and weeping yellow liquid, his oversized child's clothing torn and filthy, crusted with blood, hair matted, skin sallow. One arm hung, useless and broken, but the other was reaching toward her.

Muuuh!

The arm was reaching out, clawing at her, and *he* took a step forward, his face distorted with rage, filling the room with his stink.

"No!" she screamed. "No, no, get away—!"

He advanced, slashing and roaring incoherently.

She turned and raced back down the hall to her room. He was after her, blundering down the hall. She slammed the door and shot the bolt home, but he came through with a shuddering crash that flattened the flimsy plywood against the wall. Without pausing to think, she dove out the window headfirst, rolled over the broken glass and wet grass, stood up, and began sprinting toward town. Behind came a crash; a roar of frustration; another crash. Lights were going on in the trailers around her. She glanced back to see Job roaring, literally clawing his way out the window, smashing and tearing.

If she could get to the main road, she might have a chance. She raced through the trailer park. The gate was just a few hundred yards ahead.

She heard a roar and glanced sideways to see the bent and wounded figure running crablike across the grass with horrible speed, cutting off her route into town.

She strained, gulping air, but now he was angling back toward her, leaving her no choice but to veer toward the back of the trailer park, toward the darkness of the naked fields. She jammed her hand into her pocket and pulled out the phone, pressing it to her ear as she ran. There was the voice of Pendergast, speaking calmly.

"I'm coming, Corrie, I'm coming right now."

"He's going to kill me, please—"

"I'll be there as soon as possible with the police. Run, Corrie. *Run.*"

She ran for all she was worth, jumping the back fence and flying into the field, the sharp corn stubble lacerating her bare feet.

Muh! Muh! Muuuuuh!

Job was behind her, closing in with a strange, brutal, ape-like gait, loping ahead on the knuckles with his good arm. She kept going, hoping he might tire, might give up, might find the pain too much—but he kept on, roaring in agony as he went.

She redoubled her effort, her lungs burning in her chest. It was no good. He was gaining, steadily gaining. He was going to catch her. No matter how fast she ran, he was going to catch her.

No . . .

What could she do? There was no way she'd reach the creek. And even if she did, what then? She was running directly away from the town, into the heart of nowhere. Pendergast would never arrive in time.

Muuuh! Muuuh!

She heard a distant siren. It just confirmed that Pendergast was way too far away. She was on her own. *He* was going to catch her, grab her from behind and kill her.

Now she could hear feet pounding like a frenzied accompaniment to his agonized cries. He couldn't be more than ten yards behind. She called up every ounce of energy but could already feel herself faltering, her legs weakening, her lungs almost bursting from the effort. And still he kept coming, closing the gap. In a second he would be on her. She had to do something. There had to be some way to reach him, to make him understand, to make him stop.

She turned back. *"Job!"* she yelled.

He came on, roaring, oblivious.

"Job, wait!"

In another instant she felt the blow, the terrible blow that threw her backward into the soft dirt. And then he was on top of her, roaring, spittle spraying into her face, his great fist raised to smash in her skull.

"Friend!" she cried.

She closed her eyes, turning away from the anticipated blow, and said again: "Friend! I want to be your friend." She choked, sobbed, repeating it over and over. "Your friend, your friend, your friend . . ."

Nothing happened. She waited, swallowed, and opened her eyes.

The fist was there, still raised, but the face looking down at her was completely different. Gone was the rage, the fury. The face was twisted into some new, powerful, and unfathomable emotion.

"You and me," Corrie croaked. "Friends."

The face remained horribly twisted, but she thought she could see hope, even eagerness, shine from his one good eye.

Slowly the great fist uncurled. "Fwiend?" Job asked in his high voice.

"Yes, friends," she gasped.

"Pway wif Job?"

"Yes, I'll play with you, Job. We're friends. We'll play together." She was babbling, choking with fear, struggling to get a grip on herself.

The arm dropped. The mouth was stretched in a horrible grimace that Corrie realized must be a smile. A smile of hope.

Job lumbered off her awkwardly, managed to stand unsteadily, grimacing with pain but still smiling that grotesque smile. "Pway. Job pway."

Corrie gasped and sat up, moving slowly, trying not to frighten him. "Yes. We're friends now. Corrie and Job, friends."

"Fwiends," repeated Job, slowly, as if recalling a long-forgotten word.

The sirens were louder now. She heard the distant screech of brakes, the slamming of car doors.

Corrie tried to stand, found her legs collapsing underneath her. "That's right. I won't run away; you don't need to hurt me. I'll stay here and play with you."

"We pway!" And Job squealed with happiness in the dark of the empty field.

2

The Rolls-Royce stood in the parking lot beside Maisie's Diner, covered with dust, its once-glossy surface sandblasted to dullness by the storm. Pendergast was leaning against it, dressed in a fresh black suit, his arms in his pockets, motionless in the crisp morning light.

Corrie turned off the road, eased her Gremlin to a stop

beside him, and threw it into park. The engine died with a belch of black exhaust and she stepped out.

Pendergast straightened. "Miss Swanson, I'll be driving through Allentown on my way back to New York. Are you sure you won't accept a ride?"

Corrie shook her head. "This is something I'd like to do on my own."

"I could run your father's name through the database and give you advance notice of anything, shall we say, *unusual* in his current situation?"

"No. I'd rather not know in advance. I'm not expecting any miracles."

He looked at her intently, not speaking.

"I'm going to be just fine," she said.

After a moment he nodded. "I know you will. If you won't accept a ride, however, you must at least accept this."

He took a step closer, withdrew an envelope from his pocket, and handed it to her.

"What's this?" she asked.

"Consider it an early graduation present."

Corrie opened it and a savings account passbook came sliding out. The sum of $25,000 had been deposited in an educational trust account in her name.

"No," she said immediately. "No, I can't."

Pendergast smiled. "Not only can you, but you must."

"Sorry. I just can't accept it."

Pendergast seemed to hesitate a moment. Then he spoke again. "Then let me explain why you must," he said, his voice very low. "By chance, under circumstances I'd rather not go into, last fall I came into a considerable inheritance from a distant and wealthy relation. Suffice to say, he did not make his money via good works. I am trying to rectify, if only partially, the blot he left on the Pendergast family name by giving his money away to worthy causes. Quietly, you understand. You, Corrie, are just such a cause. A most excellent cause, in fact."

Corrie lowered her eyes for a moment. She could make no answer. Nobody her whole life long had ever given her anything. It felt strange to be cared about—especially by someone as remote, as aloof, as unlike her as Pendergast was. And yet the passbook was there, in her hand, as physical proof.

She looked at the passbook again. Then she slid it back into its envelope.

"What does it mean, educational trust?" she asked.

"You have another year of high school to get through."

She nodded.

A twinkle appeared in Pendergast's eye. "Have you ever heard of Phillips Exeter Academy?"

"No."

"It's a private boarding school in New Hampshire. They're holding a place at my request."

Corrie stared at him. "You mean the money isn't for college?"

"The important thing is to get you out of here now. This town is killing you."

"But a *boarding* school? In New England? I won't fit in."

"My dear Corrie, what's so important about fitting in? *I* never did. I'm certain you'll do well there. You'll find other misfits like yourself—intelligent, curious, creative, skeptical misfits. I'll be passing through in early November, on my way to Maine; I'll drop in to see how you're getting on." He coughed delicately into his hand.

To her own surprise, Corrie took an impulsive step forward and hugged him. She felt him stiffen and, after a moment, relax and then gently disentangle himself from her embrace. She looked curiously at him: he seemed distinctly embarrassed.

He cleared his throat. "Forgive me for being unused to physical displays of affection," he said. "I was not raised in a family that . . ." His voice stopped and he colored faintly.

She stepped back, feeling a confusing welter of emotions, embarrassment foremost among them. For a moment he continued looking at her, a faint, cryptic smile slowly gathering once again on his face. Then he bowed, took her hand, brought her fingers close to his lips, and quickly turned and got into his car. In another moment the Rolls had turned onto the road and was accelerating toward the rising sun, the light winking briefly off its curved surface before it vanished down the long, level stretch of macadam.

Corrie waited a moment and then got into her own car. She looked around—at the suitcase, the tapes, the small pile of books—making sure she hadn't forgotten anything. She put the envelope with the passbook into her glove compartment, wired it closed. Then she started the Gremlin, let the engine rev a bit, giving it gas until she was sure it wouldn't stall. As she eased out of Maisie's parking lot, her eye fell on Ernie's Exxon across the street. There was Brad Hazen. The sheriff's son was filling the tank of Art Ridder's powder-blue Caprice, one hand on the gas nozzle, the other on the trunk. His jeans had slipped down and she could see faded, grayish underwear, the line of a butt crack beginning just above the belt. Brad was staring, gape-jawed, in the direction Pendergast's Rolls-Royce had vanished. After a minute, he turned away, shaking his head wonderingly and reaching for the squeegee.

She felt a sudden pity for the sheriff. Strange what a decent man he'd turned out to be. She'd never forget him lying in his hospital bed, his bulletlike head resting against the crisp pillow, his face looking ten years older, tears coursing down his cheeks as he talked about Tad Franklin. She looked back at Brad, wondering if perhaps, deep down, there was a spark of decency buried within him, too.

Then she shook her head and accelerated. She wasn't going to stick around to find out.

As the road rose up to meet her, she wondered where she would be next year, in five years, in thirty years. It was the first time in her life that such a thought had ever occurred to her. She had no idea of the answer. It was both a wonderful and a scary feeling.

The town dwindled in her rearview mirror until all she could see were stubbled fields and blue sky. She realized that she could no longer hate Brad Hazen any more than she could hate Medicine Creek. Both had moved from her present into her past, where they would gradually dwindle into nothingness. For better or worse she was off into the wide, wide world, never to return to Medicine Creek again.

3

Sheriff Dent Hazen, head still heavily bandaged and one arm in a cast, was standing at the end of the short corridor, talking to two policemen, when Pendergast arrived. He broke away and came over to the FBI agent, offering his left hand to shake.

"How's the arm mending, Sheriff?" Pendergast asked.

"Won't be able to fish again until after the season ends."

"I'm sorry to hear it."

"You heading out now?"

"Yes. I wanted to stop by one last time. I was hoping I'd find you here. I wanted to thank you, Sheriff, for helping to make this a most, ah, interesting vacation."

Hazen nodded abstractedly. His face was deeply lined and full of bitterness and anguish. "You're just in time to see the old lady say goodbye to her bundle of joy."

Pendergast nodded. He had come to see that, as well. Although he did not expect anything from the visit, he hated to leave a loose end, *any* loose end, behind him. And this case still had one remarkably large unanswered question.

"You can view the tender parting through the one-way glass. All the shrinks are there already, clustered like flies. It's this way." Hazen led Pendergast through an unmarked door and into a darkened room. A lone window, a long rectangle of white, was set into the far wall. It looked down into the "quiet room" of the locked unit of Garden City Lutheran Hospital's psychiatric wing. A group of psychiatrists and medical students were standing before the one-way glass, talking in low voices, notebooks at the ready. The room beyond was empty, its lighting dim. Just as Pendergast and Hazen stepped up to the window a set of double doors opened and two uniformed policemen wheeled Job in. He was heavily bandaged over his face and chest, and one arm and shoulder was in a cast. Despite the dimness of the room, Job blinked his one good eye against the light. An oversized leather belt was snugged tight around his haunches, and the handcuff for his wrists ran through a ring in its front. Both legs were shackled to the wheelchair with leg irons.

"Look at him, the bastard," said Hazen, more to himself than to Pendergast.

Pendergast watched intently as the policemen parked Job in the middle of the room, then took up positions on either side.

"I wish to hell I knew why the guy did what he did," Hazen went on in a quiet, dull voice. "What was he doing in those clearings out there in the corn? The crows arranged like that, Stott cooked like a pig, the tail sewed up in Chauncy . . ." He swallowed hard. "And Tad. Killing Tad. What the hell was going through that fucking head of his?"

Pendergast said nothing.

The doors opened again and Winifred Kraus came in, leaning on the arm of a third policeman. She was in a hospital gown and moved very slowly. A tattered book was tucked beneath one arm. Her face was pale and sunken, but as soon as she saw Job it brightened and her whole appearance seemed to transform.

"Jobie, dearest? It's Mommy."

Her voice came into the darkened observation room through a loudspeaker above the window, sounding harsh and electronic in the sudden silence.

Job raised his head, his face grimacing into a smile.

"Momma!"

"I brought you a present, Jobie. Look, it's *your* book."

Job let out an inarticulate sound of joy.

She came over and pulled up a chair next to her son. The policemen tensed, but neither Winifred nor Job took any notice. She seated herself beside him, put one frail arm around his bulk, pulled him close. She began to hum softly while Job beamed, leaning against her, his calflike face illuminated with joy and happiness.

"Christ," Hazen muttered. "Look. She's rocking him like a baby."

Winifred Kraus placed the book in his lap and opened to the first page. It was a book of nursery rhymes. "I'll start at the beginning, shall I, Jobie?" she crooned. "Just the way you like it."

Slowly, with a singsong, infantile voice, she began to read.

> Sing a song of sixpence,
> A pocket full of rye;
> Four and twenty blackbirds,
> Baked in a pie.
> When the pie was opened,
> The birds began to sing;
> Wasn't that a dainty dish,
> To set before the king?

Job's big head nodded to the rhythm of her voice, his mouth making an *ooooooo* sound that rose and fell with the cadence of her words.

"Jesus Christ," said Hazen. "The freak and his mother. It gives me the creeps just watching."

Winifred Kraus finished the rhyme, then slowly turned the page. Job beamed, laughed. And she began again.

> Davy Davy Dumpling,
> Boil him in a pot;
> Sugar him and butter him,
> And eat him while he's hot.

Hazen turned and grasped Pendergast's hand. "I'm out of here. See you in purgatory."

Pendergast took the hand without responding, without noticing. His eyes were fixed on the scene in front of him, the mother reading nursery rhymes to her child.

"Look at the pretty picture, Jobie. Look!"

As Winifred Kraus held the book up, Pendergast got a glimpse of the illustration. It was an old book, and the page was torn and stained, but the picture was still discernible.

He recognized the image instantly. The revelation hit Pendergast so suddenly that it was like a physical blow, staggering him. He backed away from the glass.

Job beamed and went *oooooooooo,* his head rolling back and forth.

Winifred Kraus smiled, face serene, and turned another page. The unnatural, electronically amplified voice of the mother continued to crackle through the loudspeaker.

> *What are little boys made of, made of?*
> *What are little boys made of?*
> *Snakes and snails and puppy dogs' tails,*
> *That's what little boys are made of . . .*

But Pendergast had not remained to hear any more. The cluster of psychiatrists and students at the glass did not even notice the dark, slender presence slip away, they were so busy discussing just where the diagnosis would be found in the *DSM-IV* manual—or if, indeed, it would ever be found there at all.

About the Authors

DOUGLAS PRESTON and LINCOLN CHILD are co-authors of the bestselling novels *Relic, Mount Dragon, Reliquary, Riptide, Thunderhead, The Ice Limit, The Cabinet of Curiosities,* and *Still Life with Crows.* Douglas Preston, a regular contributor to *The New Yorker,* worked for the American Museum of Natural History. He is an expert horseman who has ridden thousands of miles across the West. Lincoln Child is a former book editor and systems analyst who has published numerous anthologies of ghost stories and supernatural tales. The authors are working on their new novel, *Dance of Death.* They encourage readers to visit their Web site, www.prestonchild.com.

1

Agnes Torres parked her white Ford Escort in the little parking area outside the hedge and stepped into the
cool dawn air. The hedges were twelve feet high and as
impenetrable as a brick wall; only the shingled peak of
the big house could be seen from the street. But she
could hear the surf thundering and smell the salt air of
the invisible ocean beyond.

Agnes carefully locked the car—it paid to be cautious, even in this neighborhood—and, fumbling with
the massive set of keys, found the right one and stuck
it into the lock. The heavy sheet-metal gate swung inward, exposing a broad expanse of green lawn that
swept three hundred yards down to the beach, flanked
by two dunes. A red light on a keypad just inside the
gate began blinking and she entered the code with nervous fingers. She had thirty seconds before the sirens
went off. Once, she had dropped her keys and couldn't
punch in the code in time, and the thing had awakened
practically the whole town and brought three police

cars. Mr. Jeremy had been so angry she thought he would breathe fire. It was awful.

Agnes punched the last button and the light turned green. She breathed a sigh of relief, locked the gate, and paused to cross herself. Then she drew out her rosary, held the first bead reverently between her fingers. Fully armed now, she turned and began waddling across the lawn on short, thick legs, walking slowly to allow herself time to intone the *Our Fathers,* the *Hail Marys,* and the *Glory Bes* in quiet Spanish. She always said a decade on her rosary when entering the Grove Estate.

The vast gray house loomed in front of her, a single window in the roof peak frowning like the eye of a Cyclops, yellow against the steel gray of the house and sky. Seagulls circled above, crying restlessly.

Agnes was surprised. She never remembered that light on before. What was Mr. Jeremy doing in the attic at seven o'clock in the morning? Normally he didn't get out of bed until noon.

Finishing her prayers, she replaced the rosary and crossed herself again; a swift, automatic gesture, made with a rough hand that had seen decades of domestic work. She hoped Mr. Jeremy wasn't still awake. She liked to work in an empty house and when he was up everything was so unpleasant; the cigarette ashes he dropped just behind her mop, the dishes he heaped in the sink just after she had washed, the comments and harsh laughter and the endless swearing to himself, into the phone or at the newspaper, always followed by a cruel cackle. His voice was like a rusty knife—it cut and slashed the air. He was thin and mean and stank of cigarettes and drank brandy at lunch and entertained sodomites at all hours of the day and night. Once he had tried to speak Spanish with her but she had quickly put an end to that. Nobody spoke Spanish to her except family and friends, and Agnes Torres spoke English perfectly well enough.

On the other hand, Agnes had worked for many people in her life and Mr. Jeremy was very correct with her employment. He paid her well, always on time, he never asked her to stay late, never changed her schedule, and never accused her of stealing. Once, early on, he had blasphemed against the Lord in her presence and she had spoken to him about it, and he had apologized quite civilly and had never done it again.

She came up the curving flagstone path to the backdoor, inserted a second key, and once again fumbled nervously with the keypad, turning off the internal alarm.

The house was gloomy and gray, the mullioned windows in front looking out on a long seaweed-strewn beach and an angry ocean. The sound of the surf was muffled here and the house was hot. Unusually hot.

She sniffed. There was a strange smell in the air, like a greasy roast left too long in the oven. She waddled into the kitchen but it was empty—the dishes were heaped up and the place was a mess as usual, stale food everywhere—and yet the smell wasn't coming from here. It looked like Mr. Jeremy had cooked fish last night. Labor Day had come and gone a month before, but Mr. Jeremy's weekend parties wouldn't end until late October.

She went into the living room and sniffed the air again. Something was definitely cooking somewhere. And there was another smell on top of it, as if somebody had been playing with matches.

Agnes Torres felt a vague sense of alarm. Everything was more or less as she had left it when she went away yesterday afternoon, except the ashtrays were overflowing with butts, empty wine bottles stood on the sideboard, dirty dishes were piled in the sink, and someone had dropped soft cheese on the rug and stepped in it.

She raised her plump face and sniffed again. The smell came from above.

She mounted the sweep of stairs, treading softly, and paused to sniff at the landing. She tiptoed past Mr. Jeremy's study, past his bedroom door, continued down the hall, turned the dogleg, and came to the door to the third floor. The smell was stronger here, and the air was heavier, warmer. She tried to open the door but found it locked.

She took out her bunch of keys, clinked through them, and unlocked the door. *Madre de Dios*—the smell was much worse. She mounted the steep unfinished stairs, one, two, three, resting her arthritic legs for a moment on each riser. She rested again at the top, breathing heavily.

The attic was vast, with one long hall off which were half a dozen children's bedrooms, a playroom, several bathrooms, and an unfinished attic space jammed with furniture and boxes and horrible modern paintings.

At the far end of the hall, in the last bedroom, she saw the bar of yellow light under the door.

She took a few tentative steps forward, paused, crossed herself again. Her heart was hammering in her chest but with her hand clutching the rosary she knew she was safe. As she approached the door, the smell grew steadily worse.

She tapped lightly on it, just in case some guest of Mr. Jeremy was sleeping in there, hungover or sick. But there was no response. She grasped the doorknob and was surprised to find it slightly warm to the touch. Was there a fire? Had somebody fallen asleep, cigarette in hand? There was definitely a faint smell of smoke, but it wasn't just smoke; it was something stronger. Something foul.

She tried the doorknob but found it locked. It reminded her of the time when she was a little girl at the convent school, and crazy old Sister Ana had died and they had to force open her door.

Somebody on the other side might need her assistance; might be sick or incapacitated. Once again she fumbled with the keys. She had no idea which one went to the door, so it wasn't until perhaps the tenth try that the key turned. Holding her breath, she opened the door, but it only opened an inch before it stopped, blocked by something. She pushed, pushed harder, heard a crash on the other side.

Santa Maria, it was going to wake up Mr. Jeremy. She waited but there was no sound of his tread, no slamming bathroom door or flushing toilet, none of the sounds that signaled his irascible rising.

She pushed the door open and was able to get her head inside, holding her breath against the smell. A thin screen of haze drifted in the room and it was as hot as an oven. The room had been shut up for years—Mr. Jeremy despised the children—and dirty spiderwebs hung from the peeling beadboard walls. The crash had been caused by the toppling of an old armoire that had been pushed up against the door. In fact, all the furniture in the room seemed to have been piled against the door, except for the bed. She could see the bed on the far side of the room. Mr. Jeremy was lying on it, fully clothed.

"Mr. Jeremy?"

But Agnes Torres knew there would be no answer. Mr. Jeremy wouldn't be sleeping, not with his charred eyes burned permanently open, the ashy cone of his mouth frozen in a scream, and his blackened tongue, swelled to the size of a chorizo sausage, sticking straight up from it like a flagpole. A sleeping man wouldn't be lying with his elbows raised above the bed, fists clenched so hard that blood had leaked between the fingers. A sleeping man wouldn't have his torso scorched and caved in upon itself like a burned log. She had seen many dead people during her childhood in Colombia, and Mr. Jeremy looked deader than any of them. He was as dead as they come.

She heard someone speaking and realized it was herself, murmuring *"En el nombre del Padre, y del Hijo, y del Espíritu Santo . . ."* She crossed herself yet again, fumbling out her rosary, unable to move her feet or take her eyes from the scene in the room. There was a scorched mark on the floor right at the foot of the bed: a mark that Agnes recognized.

In that moment, she understood exactly what had happened to Mr. Jeremy Grove.

A muffled cry escaped her throat and she suddenly had the energy to back out of the room and shut the door. She fumbled with the keys and relocked it, all the while murmuring *"Creo en Dios, Padre todopoderoso, creador del Cielo y de la Tierra."* She crossed herself again and again and again, clutching the rosary and holding it up to her chest as she backed down the hall, step by step, her sobs mingling with her mumbled prayers.

The cloven hoofprint burned into the floor told her everything she needed to know. The Devil had finally come for Mr. Jeremy Grove.